FROM HEAVEN TO EARTH THEY CAME

BOOK 3

DESTROYER FROM THE LOST PLANET

A Sci-Fi Adventure of Gods and Aliens

BY NEAL ROBERTS

CHAPTER 1

WHEN THE PROGENITOR roughly seized Catharine by the arm, David crept up behind him and blew his head off; simple as that. Though David had had no qualms about his actions at the time, he was troubled by them now.

He tossed and turned in his bed, unable to sleep, and it struck him as ironic that he was feeling low now mainly because he hadn't felt low *then*. He still didn't feel guilty for what he'd done, but rather for not having felt guilty at the time. He remarked to himself (not for the first time) that the mind is a tricky place.

It's always been difficult, Enki had said, for the power-mad to identify someone suitable to serve as a progenitor for a strain of drones. *Why?* David wondered. *What special qualities are necessary for a suitable progenitor?* David doubted that such qualities included a propensity for leadership or particularly high intelligence.

No, what a progenitor needed was the ability *telepathically* to receive imagery from his drones and *telepathically* to send them his commands. As the progenitor's neurophysiology would provide the basis for his drones', it stood to reason that the progenitor himself would require such psychic capabilities. And such activity was probably the *only* innate characteristic needed to become a progenitor. Everything else could probably be taught.

Unsurprisingly, the neurologists had recently confirmed that David's brain showed activity associated with psychic phenomena. Did that mean that David himself would be a suitable candidate for progenitor?

His mind wandered. He thought back on shooting the progenitor, and wondered who his victim had been earlier in life. A carpenter? A pawnbroker? A law professor? Had he received the gift of long life? If so, from Anzû? *How long would the progenitor have lived if I hadn't shot him?*

It troubled David that he'd become increasingly preoccupied by his own mortality, but what he found most troubling was that it had apparently been Anzû's principal intention, during their brief discussion, to instill that very preoccupation in his mind. And he resented the feeling that he was, in a sense, running a program implanted by Anzû.

Finding his room too warm, David folded Elijah's mantle, placed it on the nightstand, and kicked his other blankets to the floor.

Drifting off, once more he was confronted by his dream of the falling moon. But this time he was not alone … and neither was the moon.

David lies asleep in a large bed that rocks under him. A chilly salt breeze blows over his face. His eyes still closed, he caresses the hand of his sleeping bedmate. Inanna was so beautiful, so warm, so feminine all night that he feels nothing but gratitude for her persistent advances, and regret for his earlier rebuffs.

The bed's rocking grows more pronounced, and there's a tiny splash next to his head. He opens his eyes to find the bed floating on a moonlit ocean with no land in sight.

The cloudless night sky is lit by two celestial lights: the moon, and a planet enveloped in a smoky, maroon-tinged atmosphere. The two celestial bodies appear almost to touch each other, and seem so close to the Earth that David imagines he can feel their combined pull.

His breathing and his heartbeat accelerate. He sits up, preparing to rouse his bedmate but, looking upon her, he hesitates—so beautiful is she in the white moonlight and the maroon glow of its strange companion. Despite the immediate peril, he's loath to disturb her. Instead, he's tempted ... so tempted ... to touch her.

But reaching over to rouse her, he's horrified by the decrepitude of his own hand, mere bones partly covered by desiccated scraps of blackened skin, the segments of each digit strung to the others with ligaments no more substantial than worn rubber bands. His arm, similarly skeletal, is covered by wasted skin like the weathered hide of an abandoned carcass, covered with the brown and black splotches of age and death. To his horror, it occurs to him that, just as his limb is rotten, his face must be a veritable death's head.

Were he to rouse Inanna now, surely she would recoil from him in disgust. He thinks better of it and withdraws his hand.

How could he have gotten so old so quickly? For the first time, he wonders when *this dismaying scene is taking place. Searching for an answer, his gaze returns to the sky.*

The moon and the strange planet have each moved a few degrees of arc, but at different rates, the faster-moving planet now partially hidden behind the moon. As David watches the majestic movement of the spheres, suddenly the moon shivers, as from an impact with the planet behind it. A stress fracture appears on the moon's face near its northern pole, where a huge chasm forms and begins ripping its way toward the southern pole, so that the moon must soon crack in half. And he realizes that he's seeing events that will (or may) take place four hundred years hence.

The moon splits and begins to crumble. A large chunk breaks away from the main body and begins to rotate slowly, exposing a part of the moon's core to the sun's light for the first time in what must be billions of years. A haze of pulverized lunar soil develops around the main fissure.

David's heart aches to witness the end of all things.

Though until now his nautical bed has remained upright and afloat, the sea has begun to heave and roll in response to the moon's disintegration. The bed pitches and yaws, and David realizes that it cannot long remain atop the peaks of the mounting waves threatening to engulf it.

Searching desperately for some means to assure Inanna's safety, he overcomes his self-disgust just long enough to reach out with his necrotic arm and draw her further into the fragile safety of their little vessel.

But the sleeping Inanna rolls off and disappears soundlessly under the waves. Gone forever. Dead.

He's failed her.

His vision goes black and his mind is jarred by Anzû's sibilant, disembodied voice.

So ... you dwell upon this catastrophe? asks Anzû.

I wish to save Inanna, David replies.

Simply a pipedream, hisses Anzû. *The celestial collision you imagine won't happen for four hundred years, and you can't live more than another sixty of those. How can you hope to save her—or anyone else—from this event, when you will have been dead more than three hundred years?*

The voice fades, leaving a sickness in the pit of David's stomach.

———————⟶o⟨⟨⟩⟩o⟵———————

THE NEXT MORNING, David received a message from Houston that a Space Force colonel was on his way up to Inanna's pyramidion to debrief him.

At the appointed hour, there was a knock at the door and David opened it to find an efficient-looking colonel in uniform, sporting salt-and-pepper sideburns. David offered him an upholstered seat and took a cater-corner seat for himself.

"I'm Doctor Jensen Young," said the colonel as he sat down. "You look familiar."

"Do I?"

"Aren't you … the King of Connecticut?"

"No, I'm not," said David. "In fact, I don't think Connecticut is a kingdom. Unless you count the king from *A Connecticut Yankee in King Arthur's Court*. But, even if you do, I think Arthur was the King of *England*."

"Where are *you* from?"

"I'm just a kid from Canarsie, which is located in Brooklyn, New York."

Doctor Young snapped his fingers. "That's it, the Kid from Canarsie."

David was in no mood to be patronized. "Let's cut the baloney, colonel. You knew who I was before you came up here. How many ambassadors to the Anunnaki are there, after all? In fact, I'd bet you have a dossier about me in your briefcase and you were reading it until you came aboard."

The colonel gave him a confessional smile and posed a question no doubt prompted by David's bloodshot eyes and slightly slumped posture. "How have you been sleeping?"

"I thought you came here to do a military debriefing," said David skeptically.

"I did," said the colonel, eying David warily. "But I'm also a psychiatrist."

"Is that why you're asking about the quality of my sleep?"

The colonel shrugged.

David said sullenly, "Suppose I don't want a psychiatrist."

The colonel shrugged again. "Look, professor. You've been in an incident in which you shot and killed someone. It's part of my job to see if you need some time off and a little talk therapy. Sometimes, someone who's been through a violent incident needs to be removed from the situation for a while to ensure they're … stable and not overstressed."

"And that's why you're asking about my sleep?"

The colonel shot him a sympathetic smile. "Just making conversation," he said. He arched his eyebrows. "So?"

"So ... *what?*"

"So ... how have you been sleeping?"

David sighed. "I've slept better, I suppose."

"Something troubling you?"

David could feel his inner troll gaining strength. "Well, except for the Earth being invaded by two separate sets of aliens, at least one of which would like to see me and my lover dead ... nothing, really." He adjusted his seat. "How've *you* been sleeping?"

The colonel smiled patronizingly. "*I'll* ask the questions."

David shrugged and smiled pointedly. "Just making conversation," he echoed. David's insistence on controlling the interview had begun to irk his visitor, who opened his eyes wide and blew out a breath. This made it a perfect time for badgering. "So," David observed wryly, "*you're* not sleeping well either, I see."

"I'm sleeping *fine,*" said the colonel as he opened his briefcase and pulled out a file devoted to David.

"I see I was right about the dossier, too," David observed.

The colonel conceded the point with an exasperated nod. "Let's talk about how you feel about the ... incident the other day."

David let himself feel his dismay. "I feel kind of crappy about it."

"Crappy? In what sense?"

The question was a bit too open-ended for David to take it seriously. "In a *crappy* sense, I guess." The colonel waited for him to continue. "You know, that wasn't the first time I'd shot one of those *things.*"

The colonel cocked his head, obviously not following what David had said. "Do you feel like you might have done the wrong thing?"

David shook his head. "No. The choice was clear both times. To be honest, I think those freaks are less than human, anyway."

"Those *freaks?*" asked the colonel.

David cocked his head skeptically. "How much do you know about these ... incidents?"

"Not as much as I would like. Who are *those freaks?*"

"The squarebeards," said David, and waited for the colonel's reaction.

"*Squarebeards,*" echoed the colonel quietly. Clearly, he had no idea what David was talking about.

"*Whoa!*" said David. "What's your security clearance?"

"Top secret," said the colonel. "Why?"

"Then you're not cleared for this intelligence." When the colonel sat up with surprise, David added, "And why do you think I'd need 'time off and some talk therapy'?"

"Well," replied the colonel, "you're a *peacemaker*, not combat-trained, so we naturally expected that your own violent action might be particularly ... traumatic for you."

"Who's *we*?" asked David.

"Me ... and the person who sent me."

"Who sent you?"

The colonel checked the cover of the dossier. "Navy Admiral Simmons. Do you know him?"

David nodded. "I know him well. Would you mind if I call him before we begin?"

"Not at all. Perhaps his endorsement will put your mind at ease."

David called the admiral, who picked up on the second ring. "Good morning, admiral. Dave Schubert. You sent me a Space Force headshrinker?"

"What?" said the admiral. "Oh, yes. Since I neglected to have you debriefed after your ... trip with Catharine, I just wanted to make sure you didn't again escape the insufferable boredom of being debriefed."

As the colonel was within earshot, David tried to speak circumspectly. "The colonel doesn't seem familiar with what happened after the summit."

"Not surprised," said the admiral. "The agency has deliberately suppressed knowledge of the whole incident."

"Nothing's gotten out about it?"

"There have been a couple of rumors," said the admiral, "but they were quickly squelched."

"Does the colonel have a 'need to know'?"

"Ah," said the admiral. "I see where you're going with this. Hand him the phone."

David extended the phone to the colonel. "The admiral would like to speak with you."

The colonel gave David a skeptical glance and put the phone up to his ear. After a few turns of *yes, admiral, I see*, he handed the phone back to David.

"Listen, David," said the admiral. "He doesn't need to know what happened on the ground. This isn't a military debrief. We've already got everything on video. I sent him up there for medical purposes only. I told him you'd had to shoot someone. That's all he needs to know. So, just avoid the specifics, but do me a favor and make him feel like he didn't waste the trip."

"Okay, admiral," said David, "and thanks." He hung up.

The colonel reached into his briefcase for a blood-pressure cuff. "Roll up your sleeve, please," he said dispassionately. He applied the cuff to David's upper arm and pumped it up. "Hmm," he said, "your blood pressure's quite good. That's a good sign. Are you on medication?"

David shook his head. "Whole-food, plant-based diet," he said.

The colonel's eyebrows shot up. "That explains it. Tell me, where do you get your protein?"

"It's really not an issue," said David, "but mostly from beans and other legumes."

"Take B-12?"

David nodded. "Every day."

"Good for you," said the colonel as he put the blood-pressure cuff away. "Now … have you had trouble sleeping?"

David pondered how to respond. He considered saying: *I've been having a repeating nightmare about the end of the world, which begins with a collision between the moon and a strange planet that comes around every few thousand years. In my dream, I feel like a failure because I'm unable to save the Queen of Heaven from drowning; I've been dead for four hundred years, you see. Also, I suspect that an evil alien planning to conquer the world with his army of plant-based monsters is trying to bribe me with an offer of immortality.* But that might start a whole conversation. So instead, he said, "Not really."

"No?" asked the colonel with eyebrows raised.

"Well," said David reluctantly, "sometimes it takes me a long time to drift off. I keep remembering what it felt like to pull the trigger."

The colonel nodded sagely. "That's to be expected. Pretty normal, really."

"That's reassuring," said David, pleased to have faked a normal-sounding reply on such short notice.

"You want me to give you something to help you drift off?" asked the colonel.

David equivocated.

The colonel said, "Totally non-addictive, I promise."

"Do you have it with you?"

"I expect so," said the colonel, reaching into his briefcase. "I was told not to expect this ship to have a normal pharmacy." He pulled out a translucent pill box. "Yes, I have some." He handed David the pill box. "Just don't take more than one a day, and only take them when you're sure you want to sleep." He snapped his briefcase shut and headed for the door. Before leaving, he turned and said, "The admiral told me that, if you were to tell me all that happened, I'd be unable to cure your nightmares, but you'd give me plenty of my own." He looked at his feet and shuffled a moment. "So … thanks for not giving me nightmares. But I really *do* know what I'm doing. If it gets to the point where you can't handle it alone any longer, promise you'll call me." He handed David an old-fashioned business card.

"I promise," said David, accepting the card and seeing the doctor out.

David realized he was *already* approaching the point where he couldn't handle things alone and needed to talk with someone. Since the problem was *not* all in his head, however, he realized that professional help wouldn't suffice. He needed someone who understood his predicament. But no one knew the substance of his telepathic conversation with Anzû. Not even Catharine.

He tossed the pillbox in the trash, grabbed the phone, and called the admiral, who answered on the first ring.

"Yes, David," said the admiral, "did you forget something?"

"I've had a couple of conversations you need to know about, but we can't talk about them on this line."

"From the tone of your voice, it sounds pressing," said the admiral. "I'm at my home for the next couple of days. Tell you what: I'll send up a shuttle for you tomorrow morning to bring you down here. And I'll try to get our mutual friend to come over, too."

"You and I will need to talk alone for a while."

"Okay, then I'll ask her to come a couple of hours later."

David breathed a sigh of relief. "Sounds great, admiral."

"See you then," said the admiral.

After a moment's silence, David said somberly, "Thank you, sir."

The admiral picked up the cue right away and, after a brief silence, replied, "It's what I'm here for."

Chapter 2

LATE THE NEXT morning near Chesapeake Bay, David sat across from the admiral in the upstairs salon where they'd first met. Each had a cup of coffee before him on the table.

David looked around and recalled how he'd first met Catharine right here in this very room. He was pleased to think she was scheduled to arrive in an hour or so.

"So," the admiral began, "what's on your mind?"

"You haven't asked me what happened after I shot the progenitor."

The admiral nodded. "I knew you'd get around to it when you were ready. Care to tell me now?"

"Well," said David, "first I'll tell you what was said, then how it's affected my thinking."

The admiral nodded. "You have the floor."

"I saw that the pilot light on the progenitor's earpiece was still on, so I took it in hand. I wanted Anzû to see my face, to show him I wasn't afraid of him. When I looked into the camera, I heard his voice, but not through the earpiece."

"Telepathically?" asked the admiral gravely.

David nodded.

"What did he say to you?" asked the admiral.

David sipped some of the hot coffee. "First, he berated me for trusting Enki."

"For him to *start* with that subject must have seemed a little off the point," said the admiral, "as you'd just destroyed one of his progenitors and a whole strain of drones."

"As soon as I heard his voice," said David, "I knew he had an agenda ready for me."

The admiral nodded. "Anzû said that Enki was untrustworthy … on what grounds?"

David said, "Based on something Enki supposedly did thousands of years ago to one of my early forbears, named Adapa. Now that I think of it, I suppose Adapa was also one of *your* forbears—indeed, a forbear of every human alive today."

David recounted the Sumerian tale told by Anzû. "King Anu, who was father to Enki and his half-brother Enlil, had heard that Adapa was an extraordinary human being, rivaling the Anunnaki in learning and intelligence. Anu urged Enki to send Adapa to Planet Nibiru, so Anu could meet him. Before sending Adapa, however, Enki instructed Adapa to refrain from consuming any food or drink that might be offered to him, as it would poison him to death. When Adapa went to Nibiru, he was brought before King Anu, who (naturally) offered him food and drink. As the tale goes, Adapa declined, and so survived the encounter." David took another sip of coffee.

The admiral said, "So far so good."

David shook his head. "Except that Anzû told me the food offered by Anu would have conferred *not* death, but immortality, and that Enki had known it all along."

"Why would Enki want to deny Adapa immortality?" asked the admiral.

"According to Anzû, the immortality conferred upon Adapa would have been *heritable*—and therefore universal to all of Adapa's descendants. Enki feared that, with the gift of immortality, humans would surpass the Anunnaki in learning and intelligence."

"And become a threat to the Anunnaki themselves?" asked the admiral.

"Yes. In fact, Anzû pointed out that, in the few thousand years that have passed since the Anunnaki left Earth, humans have closed much of the knowledge gap with the Anunnaki even *without* the gift of immortality."

The admiral looked skeptical. "It sounds like Anzû's selling Enki short. I've been in Enki's presence and found him … impressive, to say the least. I, for one, haven't mastered that little trick of sending a message—through no known medium—thousands of miles with a wave of my hand."

David snickered. "I'm kind of behind on that skill, too."

"How did you respond to Anzû?" asked the admiral with concern.

David was a little abashed. "I shifted the subject to *my* agenda. I told him that, if he didn't leave Catharine alone, I'd kill him."

"How did he respond?"

"To my surprise," said David, "he seemed to take my bravado rather seriously."

The admiral scoffed. "Well … you *had* just blown one of his men's brains out."

"I'm not the only one he needs to take seriously."

"He needs to be concerned about someone else, too?" asked the admiral.

David nodded. "If you already know what I'm about to say, admiral, I apologize for repeating it: In ancient times, when Anzû committed the grievous crime of stealing the Tablets of Destinies, he fought like mad to hold onto them—with success—until there ensued a furious air battle in which Anzû was defeated by Enlil's firstborn, Ninurta."

"Is Ninurta still around?" asked the admiral.

"Evidently, no one knows." David shrugged. "At least, no one will *admit* to knowing."

"If Ninurta bested Anzû, why is Anzû still at large?"

David sipped his coffee. "The Anunnaki publicly reported that Anzû had been tried and executed. Well … he'd been tried alright, but *not* executed. Enki had commuted his death sentence to permanent exile. The commutation was kept secret. I told Anzû in our telepathic conversation that, had the decision been left to me, I would *not* have commuted his death sentence as Enki did. His response was … surprising."

"How so?"

"Anzû said he had no doubt that I would have been merciless. He added that we humans are regarded as bloodthirsty by both the Anunnaki and the Dagon, and that the Dagon's current presence on Earth was designed to keep an eye *not* on the Anunnaki, but on … us."

The admiral seemed surprised. "Well, that casts a new light on things, doesn't it?"

David equivocated. "*If* you believe Anzû. I, for one, don't trust him worth a damn."

"Nor do I," said the admiral, "but there could be something to what he said. What do you think he was trying to accomplish by telling you all this?"

"It's pretty obvious that one of his principal objects was to sow distrust of Enki. But I think his agenda may have included something more troublesome … for me, personally."

"What was that?"

David shrugged. "He seemed to be trying to sell me on the benefits of immortality."

"Why, do you suppose?"

"I'm not sure, but I think he may be trying *to enlist* me."

"That's what *I* was thinking," said the admiral.

"You were?"

The admiral nodded emphatically. "I expect that whole conversation was a personal test from beginning to end. First off, his attempt to communicate with you telepathically was a test. If Enki's surmises are correct, a progenitor's telepathic skills are limited to communicating downstream; that is, with drones of the progenitor's own strain. Ordinarily, a progenitor *can't* telepathically communicate upstream with Anzû. You, on the other hand, seemed to do so without effort."

David's eyes opened wide. "I hadn't even thought of that."

The admiral smirked. "Well, Anzû had. If he'd found that he needed to rely on the earpiece to communicate with you, it would have meant your telepathic skills were no greater than those of the progenitors he already has. Since you *could* hear him without the earpiece and talk to him without a microphone, he'd confirmed that his communications with you would be uninterruptible and that your telepathic abilities are unlimited. So, it would help him enormously if you were to serve."

"Serve?" asked David, though he was pretty sure what the admiral meant. "As one of his progenitors?"

"Well, as *that*, I suppose," said the admiral and shook his head, "but not *just* that. Anzû may also have suspected that you could communicate telepathically with other progenitors—a skill Anzû himself lacks. If his suspicion was correct, you could conceivably serve as telepathic intermediary between him and his progenitors, effectively acting as his first officer."

"As his … vizier," mused David, "as my ancestor Joseph served Pharaoh."

The admiral shrugged. "And Anzû seems to have been implying—without saying as much—that he'd give you immortality, if only you'd sign up."

"He *was* pushing the immortality angle pretty hard," said David. "The last thing he said was that I should consider what I could accomplish if I were immortal. The thing is, before then I'd never given it any thought."

"No?" said the admiral. "I thought that was the kind of thing that goes through *everyone's* mind at some point."

"Perhaps fleetingly," replied David. "But that was before I met intelligent creatures who'd actually lived for thousands of years, who've shown me that immortality isn't all it's cracked up to be. Look at Doctor Zia. He lost his wife—I don't know *how* many years ago—and he still mourns her passing. In speaking with me, he minimized his loss by assuring me that she'd passed many years before, but I could see in his eyes that he's still in mourning. She'd probably lived with him for millennia. Then she died, and now he'll mourn her—*forever*, or at least until he's crushed by a meteor or meets some other unavoidable fate. Or take Inanna. She's gone through lots of men. (Indeed, she seems to have a preference for mortals.) There's one husband she still mourns especially. His name was Dumuzi and, although he was theoretically immortal, he was murdered. Do you know how long ago he died?"

"No idea," asked the admiral.

"So long ago that one whole month in the Sumerian and Hebrew calendar—Tammuz—commemorates his passing. As Catharine pointed out, that calendar is nearly *six thousand years* old. Who would envy someone who's mourned a loved one for so long, with no end in sight?"

The admiral smiled. "So then, you see no upside to immortality?"

"I *didn't*," said David, "but I've begun to dwell on the question. We know that Nibiru's nearest approach is still about four hundred years away, right?"

"We *think* that," the admiral corrected.

"Well," said David, "I've had a recurring nightmare about Inanna. We're together in a bed afloat on the ocean. She's sleeping, while I stare up at the night sky. Suddenly there's a collision between Nibiru and Earth's moon. The moon starts to break up, the waves surge around us, and I reach over to stop her from falling into the ocean. Except my arm and my hand, and everything about me, is rotten. I'm a corpse."

The admiral's eyebrows shot up. "*Why?*"

David shrugged. "Because I've been dead more than three hundred years, I suppose."

"No," said the admiral suspiciously. "I mean, *why are you in bed with Inanna?* Are you in love with her?"

"No, of course not," said David, flustered. "It was a *dream*, for heaven's sake! I love Catharine." He threw his hands up. "*That's* your takeaway from my dream? Not that a planet smashed into the moon and will destroy all life on Earth? Not that I've been dead for three hundred years? But that *Inanna's in my bed*?"

"Well, where's Catharine at that time?"

David was exasperated. "*In four hundred years?* I don't know. Maybe she's dead, too. Why? Do you think *she'll* live another four hundred years?"

The admiral scoffed. "Well, *you* sure won't if she hears about this dream."

"And just *how* would she hear about it?" demanded David indignantly. "From you?"

The admiral waved his hands defensively. "Of course not."

"Then she *won't* hear about it at all," said David. "Besides, it's not *about* her. I think I've told you that I feel the need to protect Inanna because we're ... related."

"Which only makes it creepier that you're sleeping with her," said the admiral, sitting up straight. "You're not sleeping with her *now*, are you?"

"Of *course* not!" said David, exasperated.

"But the thought has occurred to you from time to time," suggested the admiral, "hasn't it?"

"Well, she *is* gorgeous," said David. "I'll bet it's occurred to *you* from time to time, too, and you're a lot older than I am."

"Don't drag *me* into this," said the admiral indignantly. "And what about Catharine?"

David threw his hands up and shouted. "Catharine's the most drop-dead gorgeous woman I've ever seen!"

Catharine's unexpected voice floated down the hallway, announcing, "I like the sound of that—" David's eyes popped and his heart nearly stopped. Evidently, Catharine had arrived. Her footsteps approached the parlor door. She knocked, and David abashedly let her in "—though I don't quite understand your stridency," she added, completing her thought.

Catharine was dressed for midwinter, sporting a white-on-red snowflake sweater over a white satin collared blouse, and a Royal Stewart pleated tunic.

"Catharine," said the admiral, "it's great to see you. Thank you for coming. David was just holding forth on how important it is to ensure your safety."

At first she nodded, but then turned to David quizzically. "Just because I'm pretty?"

David shook his head mournfully, amazed that declaring a woman beautiful could be construed as something other than high praise. "There are so many reasons you're irreplaceable to me," he assured her. "I—I just *started* with that one. It was the first thing that came to mind."

"David," said the admiral, full of bonhomie, "what do you say we put our conversation on hold until we've spent some time with these lovely ladies?"

David glowered at the admiral a moment, then softened. "That sounds like a wonderful idea."

Catharine shook her head. "Not yet. I've been summoned by Missus Simmons—alone. Dinner will be served in a half-hour. See you then." She closed the door on her way out.

"Where were we?" asked the admiral.

David became momentarily surly and crouched down in his chair. "I was telling you a dream—the involuntary product of my unconscious mind, by the way—and you'd just hijacked the occasion to judge me on my choice of bedmate."

The admiral nodded. "I'm sorry if I'm overprotective of my adjutant. I think of her as a kind of niece."

"See?" said David. "When a man becomes fond of a woman, he needs to shoehorn her into some familiar relation. It starts with the way he feels about her. Then he asks himself which *other* women in his life make him feel the same way."

"That's true," said the admiral. "When we have trouble fitting a woman into a given mold, it can pose a problem. I suppose it helps us keep forbidden thoughts tucked away."

"Thanks for the concession," said David.

The admiral looked at David skeptically and spoke in hushed tones. "Are you telling me *that's* why you dreamed you were sharing a bed with Inanna?"

David smirked. "Well, maybe *you* can tell me what type of familial relationship I'm supposed to have with the Queen of Heaven, because so far it's proven a bit much for me to figure out."

The admiral shrugged. "I guess even Marilyn Monroe was *somebody's* sister."

David waved off the present discussion. "All this is off the point," he said. "I was explaining the dream to you only because it seems designed to make me think that if I were immortal, I'd be there to save Inanna."

"Designed?" asked the admiral. "So, you think your dream was generated by Anzû?"

David tried to remember whether he'd had the dream while wearing Elijah's mantle. Until now, his working hypothesis had been that the mantle would protect his dreams from invasion by anyone hostile, such as Anzû. "I'm not sure," he admitted.

The admiral looked out the window. "If the dream was *designed* at all, it seems to have been cleverly fashioned to persuade you that voluntarily remaining mortal would be selfish on your part. Maybe that's why your bedmate was Inanna, not Catharine. Four hundred years from now, there'll be nothing you can do for Catharine—even if you were immortal."

David shrugged. "I guess I should be worried about Catharine, not Inanna."

"Now you're talkin'," said the admiral. "Inanna's survived this long without your help. She's pretty resilient. It's Catharine who needs you. Believe me, you'll have your hands full caring for a woman—even a mortal one." He shrugged philosophically. "At least that's been my experience." He sat up as though arriving at a conclusion. "Do what you can to help the gods who help *us*. But, for the most part, let 'em worry about themselves."

CATHARINE ENTERED THE library that the admiral's wife used as her informal headquarters. Two young maids dressed in traditional black and white took Catharine's entrance as their cue to leave.

Missus Simmons smiled and pointed Catharine to an adjacent chair. "Sit down, dear," she said.

Catharine took the designated seat.

"That's a lovely outfit," said Missus Simmons admiringly, "but mightn't it prove a bit warm? You know how the admiral loves his fire on the hearth when there's a cold snap."

"Fortunately, Missus Simmons, I'm wearing a blouse underneath, so I can shed the pullover at need."

The older woman waved dismissively. "Oh, enough of that. Call me Betty."

To Catharine, addressing the boss's wife by her first name seemed more than a bit presumptuous.

Evidently, Missus Simmons had read her thoughts. "What's the matter?" asked the older woman. "Is it the difference in our ages?"

Catharine chuckled. "Not exactly. It's more that even the *admiral* doesn't refer to you as Betty. He refers to you as 'Missus Simmons.'"

"Well," said Betty, "that may be the way he *refers* to me, but in *addressing* me, he calls me Betty." She searched her memory. "And I can recall once or twice when he's muttered a few less flattering names under his breath."

Catharine smiled. "Okay. Betty it is."

Betty smiled back in a motherly way. "So, what are your plans with the professor?"

"I suppose I *should* have some plans with him," said Catharine, "shouldn't I?"

Betty blushed. "Well, it's hardly my place to—"

"No, that's quite alright," said Catharine. "We ... well, we haven't discussed long-term plans."

Betty looked at her forbearingly. "I suppose things are a bit different nowadays. The truth is, there's never been a regular schedule for discussing long-term plans—at least, not during my lifetime." She sighed. "Quite haphazard, really. I suppose when you're flying all over the world doing intelligence work, and the professor's on Inanna's ... spaceship, or whatever they call it—there's even less of a timetable—or even an *opportunity*—for romance." She rubbed her hands together and regarded Catharine sympathetically. "You *do* love him, don't you?"

Catharine was truly touched by the fond interest taken by this kind woman. "It's obvious. Isn't it?"

Betty smiled devilishly. "Yes," she barked and then leaned in confidentially. "But it's equally obvious that he's nuts about you."

"Well, you know," said Catharine with a sigh, "he's a widower."

"How long has it been since she passed?"

"Two ... three years."

Betty waved dismissively. "It's not the *deceased* one I'd be concerned about; it's that *tramp* up there in orbit. Have you at least staked your claim?"

Catharine came up empty. "Just how would one do that in a situation like this?"

"You need to get him alone," replied Betty. "Will you two be traveling together soon?"

"Um ... yes, I think so," replied Catharine, anticipating a joint trip to the virtual-reality facility, wherever that was. "Pretty soon."

Betty sighed. "You must consider what you'll say to the professor. These men," she said, shaking her head in exasperation, "if we left it to them, nothing important would ever happen."

CHAPTER 3

Lord Enki had summoned David to appear at his chambers at a prescribed hour.

Learning of the appointment, Doctor Zia told David that Enki was known to speak loudly enough to be heard in the hallway, and so cautioned him to avoid taking the elevator to Enki's floor more than five minutes prior to the scheduled appointment.

David forced himself to heed Zia's advice, despite his wish to avoid keeping Enki waiting.

Precisely four and one-half minutes before his appointment, David pressed the button to summon the elevator and waited impatiently for the car to arrive. Fortunately, the wait was not long.

He got in and pressed the button for Enki's floor. Before the car moved, the elevator performed a retinal scan and said, "Good morning, Excellency," which was the appropriate form of address for an ambassador. David surmised by the tone of the disembodied voice that its greeting was intended to elicit a vocal response, no doubt so David's voice could be matched to a voiceprint. David wondered what would happen if he declined to speak, so he stood in silence.

What happened was … nothing. The elevator didn't move. So much for taciturnity as a tactic of resistance. "Good morning, computer," he said at last.

Without another word, the elevator swooshed up to Enki's floor. As soon as David got out, the doors closed and the car went on its way. Evidently, no further conversation was required.

David walked down the hall and gazed up at the bejeweled greeting above the double doors to Enki's chambers. As he was about to reply with the required assurance that he harbors no malice, Enki's voice boomed angrily in his chamber, penetrating into the hallway.

"Do you have any idea how dangerous it was to have my urgent summons go unanswered by our fighters?" demanded Enki.

Several baritone voices responded at once with different phrases all meaning one thing: *Extremely dangerous.*

Enki's voice boomed out, "Do you know how *humiliating* it was to have my own pilots fail to respond to my emergency call?"

Quite humiliating, said the men, each in his own idiom.

For some reason, Enki had chosen this moment to rebuke his generals. As their failure to respond to his distress signal had occurred several days earlier, David assumed that some sort of investigation (or at least an important milestone) had just reached its conclusion. Whatever the reason for Enki's timing of the rebuke, David felt certain he was not supposed to be overhearing it. He'd decided to return to the elevator when a door down the hall opened and Doctor Zia emerged, looking pale and a bit sweaty.

"David," called Zia in a hoarse whisper, gesturing for him to wait.

Smiling wanly, Zia approached, placed his hand on David's back, and escorted him to the elevator, where he pressed the button. "Let's go to the commissary," he whispered. "Lord Enki knows you're here. He'll call me when he's finished with … present business, and we can return then"—Zia glanced over his shoulder and sighed anxiously—"whenever that might be."

The elevator arrived. Instead of pressing the button for the commissary floor, Zia said, "Elevator, take us to the commissary."

"Yes, doctor," said the elevator. "It's good to see you." After a pause, the elevator added: "And you, too, Excellency."

David ignored the mechanical voice and cleared his throat. "I take it that the fighters' response was delayed by some sort of breakdown in communications." To his consternation, the chatty elevator replied, "I'm sure I wouldn't know, Excellency."

David let his irritation show, and Doctor Zia took the point immediately. "Elevator, *silence*!" said Zia. Turning to David, he said, "It's not clear just yet what caused the failure to respond to Lord Enki's distress signal. As you can imagine, the generals are all pointing their fingers at each other, which only infuriates Lord Enki all the more."

"As well it should," muttered David. "Fortunately there were American fighters in the vicinity, although I understand their first contact with the enemy was touch and go."

Zia kneaded his brow. "I've heard that the American fighters who first responded were fresh recruits. Is that true?"

Before David could respond, the elevator stopped and the doors sprang open. A cheerful electronic voice said, "Good morning, Your Excellency. Good morning, Doctor Zia. Enjoy your meal."

They stepped off, and the door shut behind them. David shook his head. "That's obtrusive."

"What is?" asked Zia, obviously long-accustomed to talking to machines.

"Being spoken to by inanimate objects," said David. "On Earth, people would suspect that the machines are keeping track of their movements."

"Oh, they're most *certainly* doing that," said Zia with a shrug, "but what can one do about it?"

"I noticed the elevator obeyed when you told it to stop talking," added David. "Can you tell it to stop listening, as well?"

Zia smirked. "I expect you can tell it that."

David asked. "But it won't stop listening, will it?"

Zia shook his head with an expression that said *of course not.*

A pretty escort appeared, bowed, and awaited instructions. It occurred to David that even *she* might be a machine. But then she winked at him, which put him at ease—until he realized that a machine that can be taught to seat customers can also be taught to wink at them.

"A private room for two, please," said Zia. "Bring us coffee. After that, see that we're not disturbed. If we need anything more, we'll use the intercom."

The escort bowed. "Certainly, sir," she said and scurried off.

Zia shut the door behind them and took a seat at the table, which appeared to be made of Nibirune stonewood. With some trepidation, David took a seat across from Zia's, imagining that the table might somehow grow a square beard and spring on him.

Zia must have read his mind. "Relax, David," he said. "It's just a slab of dead wood. You were about to tell me about the heroic American fighters who first responded to the call."

"They were a Space Force practice squadron," said David. "Although it might add romantic flair to the story if the pilots really *had* been fresh recruits, in fact each of them had clocked many hours on fix-winged aircraft. On the other hand, only the two squadron leaders had *any* combat experience. And *neither* of them had combat experience in the saucer craft they were flying that day, which had just been put into service. Ironically, their laser cannon had been disabled at Lord Enki's request."

Zia sighed and nodded wistfully. "I shudder to think that such a simple precaution might have cost us the day," he said.

"It *might* have cost us both Lord Enki and the President," David corrected him. "Incidentally, you've already met one of the squadron leaders."

Zia's eyebrows shot up. "You don't say. Which one?"

"One of them was Buck Buchanan—"

"I remember him well!" exclaimed Zia. "He addressed the Council with … Weldon and that other chap."

"He did," said David with a smile, "and just after that meeting, on the way back to Earth his shuttle was attacked by one of Anzû's fighters."

Zia frowned. "Well, we all know how *that* turned out, don't we? Well done. This Buchanan must be some pilot."

"Indeed, he is," said David. "As you'll recall, he was Weldon's pilot in escaping that nuclear blast near the North Pole." David quietly laughed at himself for referring to Catharine as *Weldon*, but everyone else seemed to be calling her that.

Zia sighed long. "I expect that, someday, Lord Enki will award Buchanan a medal for bravery and excellence." He sighed again. "For today, we'll be lucky if his lordship doesn't flush his own generals out into space on grounds of incompetence."

"Incompetence?" asked David. "Is it not possible that their failure resulted from …"

"*Misfeasance?*" said Zia. "Lord Enki is deeply suspicious that there's a traitor aboard, and I know from past experience that he'll be badly out of sorts until he puts it right."

"Does his lordship harbor any doubt that an emergency call was sent by the American radio operator?"

Zia shook his head. "No doubt. We've heard the recording."

"The call came from Lorraine, right?"

"Yes, that was her name."

"Was the signal sent on the correct frequency?"

Zia nodded. "There's also no doubt about *that*," he replied. "The real mystery arises in respect of a 'message received' confirmation in response to her call."

"So, no confirmation signal was sent?"

"To the contrary," said Zia, "the signal—just a short blip, really— *was* sent by someone and *received* by Lorraine. It's audible on the American recording of Lorraine's communications. But our onboard equipment shows no record of either our receipt of her emergency message or our transmission of a 'message received' confirmation."

David thought for a moment. "That's anomalous."

"To say the least," confirmed Zia.

"Are your radio communications routinely recorded?"

"Absolutely."

David asked, "Was there an interruption in your recording after Lorraine sent her warning?"

"None we can readily identify," said Zia, "although that's a fairly technical matter, and I'm not sure our best engineers have yet taken a look at the recording."

"Is your transmission of a 'message received' confirmation automated?" asked David.

"How do you mean?"

"I mean to ask: Must such a confirmation be initiated by a living person, or can it be sent by an unattended computer?"

"I don't know," said Zia. "What I've been wondering is: Wouldn't someone receiving such a confirmation, such as Lorraine, expect such a beep to be followed by voice contact?"

"Ah, I see," said David. He shook his head. "Not necessarily. I suppose it would depend upon what she'd been told to expect. Besides, once she saw that the American fighters had engaged the enemy squadron with success, and that an additional American squadron was about to arrive on the scene, she'd be less concerned with a response from the Anunnaki fighters, except to help avoid friendly fire incidents."

Zia's phone beeped and he glanced at the screen. "Our turn," he said nervously. "Let's go."

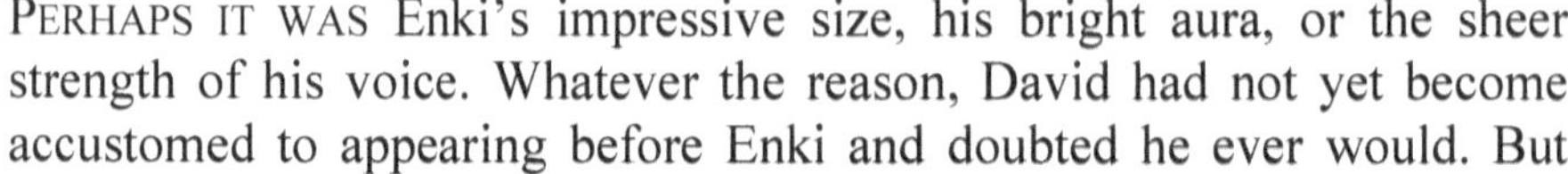

PERHAPS IT WAS Enki's impressive size, his bright aura, or the sheer strength of his voice. Whatever the reason, David had not yet become accustomed to appearing before Enki and doubted he ever would. But that's where he was now—and he would have been at wit's end but for Doctor Zia's reassuring presence by his side.

"I'm sorry, ambassador," said Enki, "that you had to hear my dressing down of my generals. That was not meant for your ears, and my timing was poor."

David wasn't sure whether a verbal response was required, so he bowed silently.

Enki continued. "Although I have already thanked your President and the admiral for the American response to Anzû's dastardly attack, I wish to thank you personally for disabling a whole strain of Anzû's drones. I know that your immediate objective was to aid Weldon, but your courageous act allowed the American forces to put down Anzû's ground attack. For that, I will forever remain in your debt."

David was pretty sure this called for a verbal reply. "It was my privilege to be in the right place at the right time, my lord. And, as for any indebtedness you feel to me, please apply it against a tiny portion of mankind's tremendous indebtedness to your lordship."

"Well spoken, ambassador," said Enki. "As a demonstration of my favor, I have arranged for you and Weldon the privilege of taking a virtual-reality overflight of Nibiru. You have asked several times about our planet and its population, and I expect you might learn much from such an overflight."

David smiled and bowed again. "Thank you so much for your favor in this matter, my lord. Words fail me."

Enki smirked, emitting a sound that reminded David of a snorting bull. "Words never fail you, David. It's your gift. Besides, don't be too grateful. I'm informed that we lack the necessary virtual-reality equipment on this pyramidion, so you two will need to … travel."

"If I may ask, Lord Enki," said David, "where must we go?"

"To King Enlil's flagship, which is a large pyramidion."

David asked, "Even larger than this one?"

"*Much* larger," said Enki. "A king requires considerably more room."

"Where is His Majesty's pyramidion?"

"It's guarded by his fleet, which is presently located within the sphere of the sixth planet."

"Lahmu?" asked David. "The planet that the Romans called Mars?"

Enki smiled. "The same."

"It would truly be an honor to appear before King Enlil," said David, "but our own scientists tell us that it would take as long as eight months to reach Mars, and the same amount of time to return."

"While we have not yet learned how to exceed the speed of light," said Enki, "we can transport you much faster than that. The trip will occupy fourteen days each way, if you're willing to go. To keep the arithmetic simple: If you were to travel there by a craft capable of the speed of light, you'd get there about seven thousand times faster than we can send you."

David's jaw dropped. "But even the speed you're capable of is … mind-boggling, my lord. What if we were to run into some … obstruction at such speeds?"

"We've developed techniques for collision avoidance," said Enki with an incandescent twinkle in his eye. "You may recall a near-collision between this pyramidion and a certain … American submarine?"

David smiled and bowed again.

Enki continued. "I have no idea if King Enlil will be of a mind to entertain you, but I must caution you to expect him to look different from anyone you've met. For one thing, he's larger than I. For some reason known only to the ultimate Creator, dominant males of the Anunnaki species grow physically in accordance with their rank. And there's no greater rank amongst us than King of Nibiru."

David nodded nervously. "Thank you for the admonition, my lord."

"Also, King Enlil is of a military bent, far less indulgent than I," said Enki.

"I will discuss with Weldon this favor you have granted, my lord."

"Do so," said Enki. "Meanwhile, I wish to mention a few other things. You need not take notes now, as a fuller report will be sent to your computer in a few minutes and you'll be free to forward it on to the President and the admiral."

"Is it about the journey to Mars, my lord?" asked David.

"No," said Enki shaking his head gravely. "Rather, we believe we've located Anzû's forces on Earth."

David nodded and waited.

"We're not certain how long he's been on Earth," Enki began. "It's our belief that he was still obeying the terms of his exile (or at least had no active forces on Earth) at the time the remaining Anunnaki left the Earth, around the advent of the latest Age of Pisces."

Doctor Zia stepped forward as he was wont to do when Enki said something unlikely to be understood by the listener. "My lord, if I may," said Zia.

Enki nodded assent, and Zia addressed his comment to David. "The Age of Pisces began very near the birth of Jesus, so that the ambassador may conceive the Age of Pisces as having begun in the Year One, there having been no Year Zero."

"Thank you, Ziusudra," said Enki, and turned to David. "At this moment, Anzû's people are concentrated in two locations. First is their Arctic location around (or rather mostly beneath) the Beaufort Sea, with various installations spread around the Arctic Ocean, extending down into the Northwest Territories and as far south as Northern Alberta and Saskatchewan. Anzû's other main installation, which appears to be somewhat older, is located on land located under the permanent ice of

Antarctica.

"It appears that Anzû's two locations are connected by frequent flights of aircraft. We have observed straight condensation trails over the Pacific Ocean running the full length of the Earth between the north and south poles. Such long contrails can be left only by extremely high-speed craft. We expect that their speed is roughly equivalent to that with which we propose to send you and Weldon to the Mars system. Anzû's technology in this respect may therefore be comparable to ours."

THREE DAYS BEFORE Catharine was scheduled to join David for their upcoming journey to the Mars system, Shiduri appeared at the door to David's room rubbing her hands apprehensively.

"Ambassador," she said in quiet distress, "the Queen of Heaven, Beloved of Anu, requests your attendance for a private luncheon at her Throne Room."

David took Shiduri's hand and led her into his room. She entered hesitantly and bowed. He closed the door so they would not be overheard.

"What has happened, Shiduri?" asked David sympathetically.

She began to weep, and he handed her a tissue. "Her Majesty has received an unexpected message from an old friend. It has reminded her of some sad times long ago. She wishes to discuss these with you and seek your advice. I hope you will comfort her." She wiped her eyes. "Will you not come?"

David quickly assented. "I will certainly try to comfort Her Majesty, Shiduri, but it would help if you could tell me who sent the message and what it was about."

Shiduri shook her head. "She won't tell me."

"I'll be there," said David, "as soon as I bathe and robe myself properly."

A FEW MINUTES later, David knocked at the door to Inanna's throne room. Shiduri appeared instantly, and bowed.

"Welcome, Mister Ambassador," she said. Though her face still showed signs of apprehension, she seemed less distressed than earlier. Perhaps she was just relieved that he'd arrived.

Though the pyramidion remained in orbit, conditions in the throne room had been altered to evoke a rare rainy day in the desert: dimly lit, warm and slightly moist, redolent of date palms, and complete with the sounds of rain on a tent roof and the occasional roll of distant thunder. Though cinematic, the somber effect was quite captivating.

Shiduri escorted him around the turn into the throne room to a banquet-sized tent newly erected in a corner. One flap was open, revealing a table set for an intimate luncheon for two. At the table sat Inanna, her face the picture of sadness.

David stepped forward, bowed low, and waited to be addressed.

"Rise, David," said Inanna. "Thank you for responding to my call." Her voice was even, but subdued.

"Thank you for bearing our friendship in mind, Your Majesty," he replied.

Inanna turned to Shiduri. "You may begin serving," she said.

Shiduri bowed and scurried off to the galley. Inanna indicated a seat for David at right angles to her own. "I assume you are still faithfully observing the dietary strictures laid out for you?"

David replied. "I am, Majesty."

"Good," she said with a wan smile. "It is best for you. I apologize for my own meal, as the Anunnaki are true omnivores, and we cannot survive without some meat and dairy."

"As you wish, madam." As they were seated so close to one another, he had a perfect view of her face. It was awe-inspiring in its flawlessness.

She cocked her head. "I see more admiration in your eyes than I'm accustomed to."

He blushed. "Your Majesty looks ever the same to me." He smiled. "Always perfect."

She bowed her head listlessly.

"I cannot help but notice," said David, "that the mood in this room is … downcast. Is something troubling Your Majesty?"

She heaved a great sigh, and removed a folded sheet of parchment from her robe. Instead of showing it to him, she placed it on the table near her eating utensils. "I've received a message from someone I haven't heard from in a long, long time. For you to understand its meaning, you will need to hear an ancient narrative. Have you such time to spend with me?"

David nodded respectfully. "I'm flattered that Your Majesty deems my understanding important enough to warrant so much of your time. I cannot imagine a more productive or pleasurable use of *my* time."

Shiduri served the soup and withdrew discreetly.

Inanna sighed as she began. "You know that, for many years after the Anunnaki arrived on Earth, there was … contention between the clans of King Anu's two sons, Enki and Enlil. In Anunnaki tradition—even on Nibiru—the favored method of uniting contending clans of the royal family has been intermarriage."

She sighed. "As you probably know, I am descended from Enlil. Many years ago, I fell in love with a beautiful shepherd named Dumuzi, who was Enki's youngest son. From the moment I brought Dumuzi to the attention of my followers, he was hailed as a strong, kind, and beautiful man. My sister had already married another of Enki's sons, namely, Nergal, who later became a staunch ally of mine.

"But now the tale darkens. Enki's *eldest* son was Marduk, and Marduk strove to ensure that Enki's clan would predominate throughout the world, which led to fighting between the clans. He also strongly believed that the clans of Enki and Enlil should remain separate, precluding any rapprochement-by-marriage. Marduk let it be known that he regarded the existing marriage between his brother Nergal and my sister as an affront. More to the point, he also vehemently opposed my plan to marry his youngest brother Dumuzi. So … what did Marduk do?"

At this point, Inanna bitterly muttered something in her native tongue, and tears formed in her eyes. She poked her soup bowl with a spoon and pushed it away before continuing. "Marduk had Dumuzi *murdered.* Dumuzi bravely fought Marduk's assailants. But they were too many. They followed him for many miles and attacked him repeatedly like hounds after a deer. Eventually, badly wounded, my sweet Dumuzi found himself exhausted, and he drowned while attempting to swim across a swift river." She placed her face in her hands and took a few moments to compose herself before continuing.

"The women in all the lands about, who had learned to love Dumuzi and anticipated our nuptials, bewailed the loss for a full month. That month was eventually named Tammuz, as I expect you are aware, since you 'Hebrews' still use the Sumerian calendar to this day.

"To revenge the heartless murder of Dumuzi, my people made war on Marduk. With the help of my sister's husband (Marduk's younger brother Nergal) we trapped Marduk inside the Great Pyramid. We demanded that he permit us to enter, but he refused, and remained hidden like a coward. Ultimately, the Council ordered Marduk to emerge from the pyramid and gave him a trial at which he was convicted of Dumuzi's murder and exiled for violating the Council's laws. Marduk served his full sentence, but even thereafter continued to wander alone in the wilderness."

"Why would Marduk exile *himself*?" asked David.

She scoffed. "As I told you, he was mad. But never *so* mad as to let his mad claims of primacy fade from the public mind. To keep his claim alive, Marduk had his son Nabu appear in numerous contested cities, always preaching the need for the locals to renounce all other gods in favor of Marduk. It galls me to remember his persistent arrogance."

"So," said David, "I assume that the message you wish to discuss with me is not from Marduk."

"Hardly," said Inanna. "Marduk has been dead for thousands of years. He died in Babylonia."

"What did he die of?"

"No one is sure. He refused to be examined for many years before he passed. It is my belief that he caught a disease from philandering with so many human females. They'd carried diseases long before the Anunnaki came."

"That might explain Marduk's madness," said David. "Some sexually transmitted diseases can have that effect."

Inanna shrugged. "This brings me to a later tale of Marduk, which brings us closer to our discussion of this message," she said, tapping her perfectly manicured fingers on the folded parchment.

"For the next part of the tale," continued Inanna, "you must understand Marduk's reason for believing he was entitled to hegemony over the whole Earth. And for that, you must understand the Anunnaki methods of governance and timekeeping on Earth.

"Though Enki had long resided on Earth, as soon as King Anu's lawful heir Enlil arrived, Anu granted Enlil dominion over the whole Earth, which was quite a large area to govern. Enlil and Enki, half-brothers who knew each other well, reached their own accord concerning day-to-day governance. They divided the occupied Earth into two regions, with Sumeria and the Middle East being principally governed by Enlil's clan, and Africa (including Egypt) by Enki's. The system worked reasonably well for a long time. Although Enlil had royally been afforded primacy over the whole Earth, he respected Enki's rule over his assigned region.

"Earth lacked a method of keeping time. Enki (ever the engineer) divided Earth's sky into twelve constellations of approximately equal size. Together those twelve became known as the zodiac; they occupied twelve roughly equal sectors, each having approximately thirty degrees of arc. Enki divided time into a cycle of 'ages' based on the zodiac. The 'age' of the Earth in any year would be determined by the zodiacal sign in which the sun rose on the first day of spring of that year. This method of reckoning is called 'zodiacal time,' and it was established long before Marduk was born.

"In the fullness of time, Enlil and Enki fathered later generations of their respective clans. With the advent of subsequent generations, descendants of the two clans became estranged from one another, which resulted in numerous bloody wars. Eventually, it became obvious that a more even-handed method needed to be established to govern which clan would rule Earth at any given time. So, King Anu, Enlil, and Enki agreed that the two clans would *take turns* having ultimate authority on Earth. As Earth was then in the Age of the Bull, and the bull was Enlil's celestial sign, it was determined that Enlil's clan would have worldwide primacy until the arrival of the next age, which would be the Age of Aries, at which time Enki's clan would ascend the worldwide throne. And so on. This grand bargain was intended to lead to a permanent peace. But, alas, it contained a fatal omission."

Shiduri reappeared, accompanied by two female servants carrying jugs. Inanna and David remained silent while the wine was poured. David remarked to himself how clearly Inanna had explained the grand bargain. While he would have considered this a question of politics (and therefore outside Inanna's realm of interest) he realized that, because the concept of *family* was so central to it, she'd taken a deep interest.

When the servants left, David asked, "What was the fatal flaw in the grand bargain?"

"Well," said Inanna, "as you know, the zodiacal constellations are just imaginary pictures in the night sky. Although they were a valiant attempt to divide the sky into twelve equal parts, the zodiacal 'pictures' are *not* precisely equal in size. Although, in terrestrial time, each age would last approximately 2,160 Earth years, the grand bargain failed to express whether the duration of a clan's dominion would be measured by terrestrial time (that is, 2,160 Earth years) or by zodiacal time (that is, according to the actual size of the zodiacal constellations).

"As with humans, over time Anunnaki males tend to lose interest in dominance contests and delegate much of their power to their eldest sons. Enki's eldest son Marduk wished to assert his clan's primacy at the earliest possible moment. Directly opposed to Marduk's view was Enlil's eldest son, Ninurta, who wished his own clan to continue to rule for as long as possible. Ninurta found a strong ally in *my* ancient ally, Nergal, who'd married my sister. As I hated Marduk with all my soul because of his murder of Dumuzi, I longed for his defeat—and Ninurta's success.

"As the zodiacal bull occupies substantially more than thirty degrees of arc (and therefore its zodiacal age lasts substantially more than 2,160 years), according to *zodiacal* time Enki's (and Marduk's) clan would have to wait several more centuries before assuming global power. So, needless to say, Marduk insisted that the accord be governed by *terrestrial* time (2,160 Earth years), according to which he would ascend the worldwide throne immediately.

"The dispute was placed before the Council, and both sides were heard. The Council held that the agreement would be governed by zodiacal time, and so ruled against Marduk. Marduk went into another long period of voluntary exile.

"As no one knew where Marduk could be found, and Ninurta wished to remind him (wherever he might be) that the Age of Aries had not yet arrived. Ninurta ordered that stone observatories be built in various strategic locations on Earth so that Marduk could not avoid visible proof that the Age of the Bull had not yet passed. One of these observatories was built on the island of Britain, on the Salisbury Plain."

"Stonehenge," David proposed.

"Yes," said Inanna, "but there are several more, some in the Middle East, others at scattered locations all around the globe."

The main course was served, and they ate in silence. Now that Inanna had eaten something and (more importantly) moved on from the tale of Dumuzi's murder, she perked up as she resumed. "During Marduk's exile, he began to act as though his age of power had already begun."

"How so?" asked David.

"As I mentioned, Enki's family held sway over Africa, but *not* the Middle East. Nevertheless, during his exile Marduk issued edicts (through his son Nabu) requiring those throughout the Middle East to worship him only."

"Marduk unlawfully expanded his influence eastward into Sumeria?" asked David.

"With a vengeance," replied Inanna. "He turned Sodom and Gomorrah into vassal states; they now lie dead at the bottom of the Dead Sea. Marduk also expanded his influence into Sumeria, renaming it Babylonia, and forbade the worship of any other gods." Inanna grew angry as she recounted. "It was a deliberate insult to all other Anunnaki. He conjured up a false goddess of beauty and dubbed her 'Marduk-beauty.'

There was no room for me in his sick mind, you see. In Marduk's imaginary pantheon, Ningishzidda was supplanted by an imaginary god named 'Marduk-iron,' and so on. He even went so far as to require his acolytes to refer to Planet Nibiru as *Marduk!* The other gods were outraged—even Anu himself, who had always been slow to anger. Followers of the other gods fought to contain Marduk within his rightful bounds, but they never invested the time and treasure needed to defeat him."

David chimed in. "I assume Ninurta had his victory over Marduk?"

Inanna nodded equivocally. "It was a Pyrrhic victory. A sad tale."

"So," asked David, "what was it that persuaded the senior members of the Council to stop Marduk at last?"

Inanna cut some meat on her plate while assembling her thoughts. "It was Marduk's attempts to capture the two remaining spaceports that—*at last*—stirred the Council to take action against him. The attempt on each spaceport is touched upon in your Bible, in fact. The spaceport that Marduk first attempted to take over was the one at Baalbek, in what was then Babylon, where you and I first met face-to-face a few months ago. That was the larger spaceport, and it was located in a zone long assigned to me, Queen Inanna, Beloved of Anu, as a member of Enlil's clan. The enormous landing tower that Marduk tried to build there is referred to in your Bible as the 'Tower of Babel,' a tower designed so that one reaching its top could ascend to the heavens, literally. The construction was to be performed by earthlings. What defeated Marduk's foul intentions at Baalbek were the enormous differences in the languages spoken by the humans enlisted in his project. At that time, you understand, every city was a separate nation with its own king and its own unique language."

"Which spaceport was the object of Marduk's second attempt?" asked David.

"That was located on the Sinai Peninsula," said Inanna. "By that time, the Great Ones' tolerance of Marduk had been exhausted. Enlil's eldest son Ninurta, together with Nergal, insisted that the Sinai spaceport and the cities of Sodom and Gomorrah be denied to Marduk at all costs, even at the cost of destroying them all with the Seven Great Weapons."

David asked a question that had occurred to him earlier. "Was Nergal's wife the sister into whose service you ordered my deceased wife Sharon?"

Inanna dropped her fork onto her plate, blushed, and openly wept. "Oh, David," she said, "please forgive me for that. That never happened.

I played it out during your dream to try and persuade you that your Sharon had been banished to the underworld, where my sister reigned." She hid her face in her hands. "I would never send anyone to Ereshkigal, who had tried to kill me and would have done so were it not for Enki, who sent his androids to save me." She sobbed. "Oh, I am truly worthless."

David rose and knelt by her side. "No, my Queen. You are more valuable than rubies. Granted that you are sometimes ... impetuous, but that partly makes you who you are."

She stroked his hair. "Your Sharon is, and always was, beyond my reach, beyond the reach of any of the Anunnaki. I am so sorry for my deception."

"I forgive you, Inanna," said David. "As you say, Sharon was not there. So you did her no harm."

"But I harmed *you* in making you believe it," she sobbed.

He shook his head. "But I did *not* believe it."

"No?" asked Inanna with relief.

"No. I knew Sharon too well to believe she would have obeyed your command to abandon me. She would have attacked you ... physically, even without hope of success."

Inanna's sobs turned to nervous laughter. As she wiped her eyes, she said, "Good for her! I wish I had known her while she lived."

David grew misty-eyed. "I wish she had lived to meet you."

If the mood in the little tent had not been entirely morose earlier, it certainly was now. David resumed his seat. Inanna possessed herself again and pushed away her food as though her appetite had now left her entirely.

David brought her back to the main topic (or what seemed to be the main topic, as in truth she hadn't yet identified it). "You mentioned the destruction of Sodom and Gomorrah," he said. "The Bible tells us that the Lord and two angels appeared before the tent of Avram and confided that they would destroy Sodom and Gomorrah—"

Inanna interrupted. "Those 'angels' would certainly have been Ninurta and Nergal."

Inanna seemed once again to be attributing to the Anunnaki acts that the Bible attributes to God. David pressed her on the question. "But the Third One," said David, "was referred to (and addressed) as the Lord."

Inanna merely shrugged. "Is the *third* the one who predicted that the agèd Sarai would bear Avram a child?" (Here, she used the Sumerian names for Abraham and Sarah.)

"Yes."

"I'm forbidden to discuss Him with you, David."

David suspected that Inanna believed the one referred to as 'the Lord' to be either Enlil, Enki, or even Anu. But he shied away from further inquiry. "In the Bible, the Lord never specifies the great sin rampant in Sodom and Gomorrah that brought on His wrath, though it's long been believed the sin was engaging in deviant sexual practices."

Inanna shook her head. "No. It was much more serious. The sin was worshiping the god Marduk who, along with his son, had transgressed by converting those Enlilite cities to his own worship. The Seven Deadly Weapons had never before been used on Earth, so Ninurta and Nergal had no experience using them. When the Council granted its consent to use of the weapons, Ninurta and Nergal had no idea that detonating them would result in a huge poisonous cloud that would drift over Sumeria and kill everyone there. But that's what happened. Even Ninurta's wife Bau was killed—and he has mourned her death and kept to himself ever since that day."

David shook his head. "Is that the same Ninurta who'd defeated Anzû in aerial combat?"

She smiled wanly. "The same."

David sighed. "Eternity is a long time to mourn," he said. "*Too much* time, perhaps. Ninurta is much to be pitied, as is everyone who loves him."

"Indeed," said Inanna, "I myself miss him greatly. As I look back on my long life, I realize Ninurta is one of the very few who fulfilled his promises to me, who helped me in my hour of need. It is far too long. In fact, none of us has heard from him for four thousand Earth years."

She tapped the folded message on the table, and said:

"Until today."

Chapter 4

As Inanna unfolded the message, the room brightened.

At first David thought the change was solely in his own imagination but, looking around, he realized that the light was indeed growing brighter and more like sunshine, the thunder had ceased entirely, as had the sound of rain on the tent roof, and the room was becoming noticeably warmer and less humid by the second.

Realizing that the change wasn't merely imaginary, he wondered whether Inanna had thrown some unseen switch to change the mood in the room. But then he realized the truth of it.

The room itself had detected the change in Inanna's mood and begun the process of conforming to it. David didn't know whether the process was technological (which he strongly suspected) or some form of divine magic (perhaps akin to Enki's transmission of his warning message to Catharine), but it amazed him that the gods had brought to life in their personal quarters a phenomenon that writers of fiction had long called the *pathetic fallacy*.

"This message came as a rare addendum to a lengthy message from the royal pyramidion," said Inanna.

"Is that unusual?" asked David.

"Quite," Inanna assured him. "The royal pyramidion is reserved as a place of quiet pilgrimage. Communications to and from that point are restricted to essential royal business. Only a few great personages may avail themselves of the privilege of sending a private message from that place or receiving one there."

"And the message you've received is from such a personage?"

"It is from Ninurta himself," she said with a note of awe in her voice, "authenticated by a signature consisting of a combination of characters known only to him and me. Even the transcriber doesn't know from whom it came. Only I know." She smiled wanly. "And now *you* know, too, but you can't tell anyone."

David bowed and tried to speak, but found himself too humbled to utter a word.

"It is written in intimate Nibirune," continued Inanna, "the mutual language of our birth. I will translate it for you. 'To my dearest Queen of Heaven, Beloved of Anu, and beloved of all who know that only such beauty as hers can confer meaning upon the vastness of time and space ...'" She paused, obviously overcome by Ninurta's opening words.

David could barely believe what he was hearing. Unless he was sorely mistaken, these were words of *love*, penned by a god who'd lost his beloved wife four thousand years before. David asked gingerly, "Is this a *formulaic* form of address to Your Majesty?"

She shook her head pensively.

"Then it's encouraging indeed," said David.

Inanna shrugged. "Perhaps," she said, having (no doubt) had every possible variation on such sentiment poured into her ear since time immemorial. She continued translating Ninurta's message. "'Of late, I have found myself fretting for your welfare, sensing that your personal well-being is threatened by an approaching cataclysm. I have also sensed in your midst a son of Joseph of Egypt, upon whom you have conferred Elijah's mantle.

"'So portentous are these signs that I find myself impelled to end the long atonement for my past sins, so that I may avoid compounding such sins by failing to avert tragedies yet to come. If you can find it in your heart, my sweet Inanna, please confirm that you will suffer my assistance, freely given with no expectation of recompense. And, if this new Joseph is with you, I bid you dispatch him to me as soon as possible, so that I may consult with him face to face.'"

Inanna refolded the message, placed it in a ceramic plate and set it aflame with a candle. She looked at David as it burned to ash.

"What do you say to this message, Mister Ambassador?" she asked. "Would you travel to Ninurta at my request?"

"In truth, Your Majesty, I can think of nowhere I would not travel at your request. I understood you to say that Ninurta is with His Majesty. As it happens, I am already scheduled to leave for King Enlil's pyramidion in the Martian system in three days' time."

Inanna's eyebrows shot up in surprise. "Surely, there is some Providence in this coincidence."

David shrugged. "Though I find it difficult to believe that Providence is unable to identify a more promising vessel than I to fulfill its purpose, if Your Majesty will give me your blessing, I will meet with Ninurta there. I'm told that the journey to the King's pyramidion will take a fortnight."

"Kneel before me, Mister Ambassador, and I shall bless you on your journey."

David rose and knelt before the Queen of Heaven, who placed her hand on his forehead and recited a blessing in a vaguely familiar language he couldn't understand.

⟶∘⧜∘⟵

DAVID WAS IN his temporary chamber on Enki's pyramidion, reading about virtual reality, when he received a call from Doctor Zia.

"You asked to be notified when your antimatter craft docked," said Zia. "It's here. Come up to my chambers, if you like. My window looks out on the docking bay."

As David entered Zia's chamber, he was awestruck by the sheer size of Zia's picture window, which commanded a full portside view of an antimatter craft docked at one of the pyramidion's external ports. He surmised that the craft was too large to fit into any of the internal bays.

The perimeter of the craft was outlined by blinking operating lights, its sleek white airframe brightly lit by floodlight beaming from the pyramidion. Though the craft was larger and more cylindrical than David would have expected, in truth he had no right to any expectation about its shape, since neither he nor any other earthling had ever seen such a craft before (unless one were to count Zia).

Regardless that the craft was designed primarily for interplanetary travel through airless space, the designers had masterfully avoided any non-essential protuberances that might have interrupted its aerodynamic contours. From this, David surmised that there were circumstances under which the craft would operate in-atmosphere.

Hugging the airframe immediately behind the rearmost of three portside windows was a sweptback wing with two reverse thrusters. (Slowing the craft down from its cruising speed must be quite a feat in itself, he realized.) To David's eye, the wing at first appeared entirely fixed, but a momentary squint revealed a few joints near its rear that could signify the presence of aileron-like flaps.

Through the craft's windows, David could see that its interior was brightly illuminated by cheery lights, much like a modern airliner, so the cozy-looking cabin contrasted starkly with the blackness of space surrounding it. He could also see several interior exit signs, making him wonder how one might gracefully exit a craft traveling at nearly 100,000 miles per hour. The exit signs had been conveniently translated into English (presumably for the upcoming Martian journey). There were a few instructional signs, as well. While David hoped that these had likewise been translated into English, he couldn't make out the language from this distance.

Estimating the size of the craft was difficult in the absence of some familiar object to provide scale. Assuming that the interior exit signs were approximately the size of those seen in auditoriums, however, David estimated that the craft would be approximately two hundred feet long, plus a segmented rear appendage containing the positron-powered antimatter engine and its physically small fuel supply.

Behind the nose of the craft, where one would expect to see its name painted, was a word in an alphabet unfamiliar to David.

David smiled at Zia. "What's the craft's name?"

"Vessels of any importance are named (or, as in the case of this craft, *renamed*) at the whim of Queen Inanna."

"I would have expected that prerogative to be reserved either to the king or Lord Enki," said David.

"The king leaves such administrative matters to Lord Enki, and it's always been Enki's choice to leave ship-naming to Inanna."

"Why?" asked David.

Zia shrugged. "Enki finds Inanna's thinking impossible to fathom, but—despite his public insistence to the contrary—he has a good deal of faith in her choices when it comes to matters of the heart. Her Majesty has said she was moved by a recent dream to rename this craft *Yi-ud*."

"*Yi-ud*," echoed David. "How would that be translated into English?"

Zia smiled with chagrin, as he often did when asked to translate from the old tongue. "You might say it means *destiny*."

"As in His Majesty's Ship *Destiny*?"

Zia nodded equivocally.

"Sounds ominous," remarked David apprehensively.

"I was sure you'd interpret my translation that way, given the imprecision inherent in all translation. But *yi-ud* does not at all mean what you would call *fate*. It's rather more optimistic."

David arched an eyebrow. "Perhaps it could mean *the way forward*? As in His Majesty's Ship *The Way Forward*?"

Zia seemed satisfied. "Let's call it that. Though the translation is less literal, the tone is more accurate. Perhaps you should have been an interpreter."

David scoffed. "I think that would require me to speak more languages than I do."

Zia shrugged and looked out at the craft. "This will be quite a journey for someone accustomed to the subway trains of New York."

David nodded. "It certainly will. I'll bet some U.S. pilots would give their eyeteeth just to tour this craft."

"His lordship just approved the admiral's request to send up a U.S. pilot on the shuttle with Weldon," said Zia.

David turned to Zia. "Oh? Is it the pilot you once met?"

"No, this one's named Gary Sullivan."

"But surely they don't expect him to pilot a craft he's only *toured*," said David skeptically.

"No," Zia chuckled, "for this turn, he and his assistant will just be tourists on this pyramidion—although they'll be permitted onto the antimatter craft during preparatory maintenance. Then they'll remain here on the pyramidion until you and Weldon return."

"Gary's bringing an assistant?" asked David, wondering if perhaps that meant Buck Buchanan.

"He's been given a choice whether to bring one or not," said Zia. "As for *whom* he might bring, we'll have to wait and see whom he turns up with. His lordship's only requirement was that any assistant has been vetted by the U.S. Government."

"By the way," asked David, "who *will* be piloting the craft?"

Zia smiled. "Your favorite Trans-African driver."

David had to ponder that for a moment. "*Enkidu?*"

"None other," said Zia. "Besides Enkidu's being an excellent companion, his feature set and databases are state of the art and include the most current Tablets of Destinies. He'll be assisting in maintenance of the craft, as well, so your Lieutenant Sullivan will have an opportunity to meet him. I trust you'll find Enkidu a good conversationalist on your voyage."

"But he'll be piloting the craft," protested David. "How many things can he do at once?"

Zia searched his memory, as though the question was serious. "As many as 640,000, depending upon complexity."

"So ... he can chew gum and walk at the same time?" asked David.

Zia responded archly. "Depends on the flavor."

David regarded Zia skeptically. "But it's such an imposition to take your man's man away from you for a whole month. Wouldn't you rather send someone else to serve as our pilot?"

Zia folded his arms as though considering how much to say. He shook his head. "These artificial beings may look alike to you, but they've each had different teachers and different life experiences. There's no substitute for ethics and experience, and Enkidu has an abundance of both. Do you remember once asking me about Gilgamesh?"

David nodded.

"Well," said Zia, "the original Enkidu's experiences are contained in *this* Enkidu's databanks."

David scowled incredulously. "Do you mean to say that this is the *same* Enkidu who fought beside Gilgamesh?"

Zia shook his head. "No. As the Sumerians recorded, the *original* Enkidu was put down like an old horse at the end of his useful life—ostensibly as punishment for Gilgamesh's transgressions in destroying the Guardian of the Cedars and slaying the Bull of Heaven. But Lord Enki saved his databanks, and they form a part of *this* Enkidu's mind, if you will."

"They were transferred?"

Zia nodded sagely. "What is an android, after all, but a bucket of bolts with a memory? In fact, the same thing could be said of an Anunnaki body ... or a human one. What each individual has that's worth saving and imparting to others comes from his or her unique experiences. This Enkidu can literally recall what it felt like to grapple with Gilgamesh, to defeat the Guardian of the Cedars in Lebanon, and destroy the Bull of Heaven. In a reflective moment, he can remember the anguish on Inanna's face when Gilgamesh boorishly denounced her love." He leaned into David confidentially. "I wouldn't entrust your care—or Weldon's—to anyone else. Don't worry about me. I'll be just fine."

TWELVE HOURS LATER, Zia and Enkidu met at David's chambers, and the three sauntered together to the elevator bank where Catharine and Gary would come aboard the pyramidion. From the banter *en route*, David could see that Enkidu had learned both Zia's ethical sense and his understated sense of humor.

As the three were not equipped for airless conditions (though David expected air was purely optional for Enkidu), they waited by the elevator while the shuttle docked at an internal port. In a few minutes, the swoosh of the elevator car became audible and, in another few seconds, the doors opened and Catharine, in uniform, literally ran out of the elevator car and embraced David.

God, he loved her.

"A vacation at last!" she said with a laugh, taking his hands and dancing about him as though he were a maypole. Her shiny blonde locks bounced about her shoulders.

"Whoa, lieutenant commander!" said David. "Aren't you required to wear a ponytail?"

She stood stiffly at attention while everyone looked on. "Mister Ambassador," she said formally, "my commanding officer has expressly authorized me to wear my hair below the lower edge of the collar of my blouse, jacket, or coat." She added in less formal tones, "He also authorized me to dress out of uniform until such time as I return to Earth."

"Quite an understanding fellow," said David, smiling at Catharine along with everyone looking on.

David had barely noticed the two men who'd stepped off the elevator behind Catharine. Each was carrying some baggage and both looked familiar.

David extended his hand to Gary. "Hey, y'old air pirate," said David with a smile and a little nod.

"Good to see ya, chief," Gary replied, "or should I say Mister Ambassador?"

David couldn't help but smile. "*Chief* is fine under the circumstances, Gary. Or should I say lieutenant?" Without awaiting an answer, David extended his hand to the quiet African fellow at Gary's side. "Have you and I met before?"

"Yes, sir," replied the fellow, "but only once—in Namibia," letting on that David should not mention their later meeting at the White House.

"Oh, that's *right*," said David. "As I recall, you were aiming an AK-47 at me and the lieutenant commander."

Hendrick bowed apologetically. "Sorry. I had no idea who the two of you were."

David motioned toward Doctor Zia and Enkidu, and introduced them to Gary and Hendrick. "When Catharine and I visited the *El Paso* in Omitara, these are the gentlemen who dropped us off. This is Doctor Zia and his assistant and driver, Enkidu."

Hands were shaken all around.

A young-looking Anunnaki officer walked up to Gary and Hendrick. Only slightly taller than the humans, he wore a *shendyt*, and looked vaguely familiar to David.

"Aren't you Kassam?" asked David.

The young man looked pleasantly surprised to be recognized. "*I am* Kassam, sir—aide-de-camp to General Shulgi. I'm surprised you recognized me, as I believe we met only once."

David nodded. "It was that day I came aboard Her Majesty's pyramidion for the first time."

"Just so," said Kassam. "With your permission, Mister Ambassador, I thought I'd show our new friends to their rooms."

"Good idea," David replied. "Let's all meet in two hours at the bay where the craft is docked. If you have any trouble finding it, just call Kassam here. Other than Doctor Zia, he's the only one who seems to know his way around."

Enkidu pointedly cleared his throat, and David accepted the implied correction. "Except also for Enkidu," said David, "who not only knows his way around the pyramidion, but the Mars system."

⟶◦⟨⟨⟨⟩◦⟸

AN HOUR LATER in Catharine's room, a very content David lay under the covers next to her.

His mobile phone rang.

"Who's it from?" asked Catharine.

David picked his head up off the pillow, took the phone from the nightstand, and read the screen. "It's Zia," he replied.

"Better take it," she said, and kissed him. "We've got two weeks to do this as much as we like." She tossed the blankets off and headed to the shower.

David took the call. "Yes, Doctor Zia?"

"I just received notice that a five-person maintenance crew will arrive at the shuttle bay in forty minutes. I'm planning to meet them at the elevator with Enkidu. Any interest?"

David gave it a moment's thought. "Yeah, I guess my guys should be there, too."

"I was hoping you'd say that," said Zia. "Will you notify them, or should I?"

"I'd much appreciate *your* doing it," David replied.

"How about Weldon?" asked Zia with thinly veiled amusement. "Is it necessary for me to call her?"

"No," said David, taking the point, "I'll tell her myself."

"I expect you will," said Zia, and hung up.

"Dirty ol' man," muttered David good-naturedly.

<hr>

FOR THE SECOND time in as many hours, David found himself with friends, waiting for an elevator full of people whose business it was to ensure the success of his upcoming journey to King Enlil's pyramidion.

Enkidu carried a few items of equipment, including a small tool case stained with splotches of long-dried black ink, and a pack of a half-dozen aerosol cans of compressed air.

"What's the ink for?" asked Hendrick.

Enkidu looked down at the tool case as though he'd forgotten he was carrying it. "Checking for leaks in the engine seals."

Hendrick seemed confused by the answer at first, but then snapped his fingers. "Of course. Like when you fix a flat tire, you find the leak by immersing the tire in water and seeing where the bubbles come from."

"Just so," said Enkidu, "But there are good reasons not to use water near this type of engine, so we use … *I* use black ink."

"Did you ever get any on you?" asked Hendrick.

"I'm as careful as can be," said Enkidu.

Hendrick shrugged. "Well, I suppose it's no great effort to get it off your skin."

Enkidu smiled forlornly. "For *you* it would be no great effort, but for me it's not so. *You* have flexible skin and constantly circulating blood. On me, it can take a long while to disappear."

As the elevator car swooshed toward them down the shaft, everyone seemed at ease—except Hendrick, whose edginess David found interesting. It seemed there were *two* Hendricks, and, at least temperamentally, they had little in common. There was Hendrick the Geologist, and there was Hendrick the Bodyguard. Hendrick the Geologist was voluble, generous with his learning and analysis, and open to the contributions of others. On the other hand, Hendrick the Bodyguard (who snapped to his post whenever Gary was present) was close-mouthed—all darting eyes and taut muscles, conveying the distinct impression that anyone making a hostile or ambivalent move was liable to have his face slammed into the wall and his arm twisted to near-breaking behind his back.

Hendrick caught David surveying his face for a moment, and winked, no doubt as assurance that he recognized he was among friends—at least nominally.

The elevator doors opened wide, and its occupants began stepping out. Two smallish Anunnaki mechanics emerged first, each carrying his own tool case. Another mechanic, a diminutive female earthling, wore a U.S. Navy blue flame-resistant coverall and matching watch cap bearing no ship insignia.

The last person remaining in the elevator was artificial—an unnervingly precise duplicate of Enkidu. The resemblance took David's breath away. It wasn't merely remarkable. It was total. For two androids to look so identical, they would need to have been cast from the same mold, using the same materials, pigments, and textures. Indeed, they looked more alike than identical twins, whose different life experiences leave them with different scars and facial lines, and different resting expressions.

As soon as Enkidu spotted his unexpected twin, he snorted loudly and stepped athwart the twin's path, trapping him in the elevator. For a good ten seconds, the two looked each other in the eye with the same deadpan expression.

"Is this some sort of *joke*?" said Enkidu at last, through clenched teeth.

Zia said, "Enkidu, please let this fellow off, so the elevator can move on."

Enkidu glanced at Zia skeptically, but did as he was bidden—though barely. He let his doppelganger off the elevator, but only a *half-step* off. As it turned out, it was not quite far enough to allow the automated door to close behind him on the first try; the electric eye must have regarded the billowing of the doppelganger's jacket as an obstruction, so the doors sprang open again. Enkidu took another half-step back, the double stepped forward a like amount, and this time the doors closed and the elevator moved off.

"Who *are* you?" Enkidu demanded of the duplicate.

"Enkidu Improved Class, Unit 142," said the duplicate. "I'm a journeyman mechanic." Even his voice and his accent were undistinguishable from Enkidu's.

Enkidu arched an eyebrow. "Do you have a name?"

"Not really," said the android, "though I suppose one could say I'm known as Hammy."

"Hammy?" asked Enkidu derisively.

"Yes, you know," replied the double. "It's what everyone shouts at me all day. Hammy the wrench. Hammy the pliers." He smiled hesitantly.

Though several people laughed (save Hendrick), Enkidu was having none of it. "What maintenance are you conducting on the antimatter craft?"

The double shrugged. "Whatever I'm asked to do." He pointed to Enkidu's ink-stained toolbox. "What will *you* be doing? Calligraphy?"

While the remark was evidently intended humorously, Enkidu openly took offense and shot a glance at the unsmiling Hendrick. "I will be checking all seals in the engine compartment. Stay out of my way. And for your information, *idiot*, the surest way to check a seal is with air pressure and ink."

"Calm down, fellow," said the chief Anunnaki mechanic, patting Enkidu kindly on the shoulder. "We'll keep Hammy clear of the engine room. He's not certified for engine work, anyway." He took a long look at Enkidu's tense posture. "But ... just out of curiosity, why so much concern about the seals?"

Enkidu didn't answer, just shook his head and stormed off alone toward the maintenance bay.

Doctor Zia extended his hand to the chief mechanic. "I'm Doctor Zia," he said.

"Yes, sir," said the mechanic, "we know of you. I'm Sibzianu, chief mechanic, at your service."

Zia shook his hand. "You'll have to forgive our Enkidu. Many years ago before Enkidu received any mechanical training, one of his companions was severely injured in an antimatter malfunction. An engine seal failed and released excessive gamma rays into the passenger compartment. The victim was an Anunnaki, so he didn't succumb right away." He shook his head sadly. "As you'd imagine, it's not the kind of death you'd wish on anyone. Enkidu resolved to earn certification as a mechanic to make sure that sort of thing would never happen again."

Sibzianu nodded sadly. "Well, sir, that must have been an engine of the original design. As I expect you know, the current models powered by positron fuel are far less hazardous—not that we'd allow a leak like that to happen even now." He pointed with his chin toward the place where Enkidu formerly stood. "Is he certified for this work?"

Zia nodded emphatically. "I have his certificate right here." He drew an official-looking paper from his breast pocket and handed it over.

Sibzianu examined it, whistled softly, and turned toward his fellow mechanics. "This Enkidu fellow's got twice as much experience as all of us put together."

"Maybe he'd want to do *our* jobs," jibed one of the others.

Sibzianu handed the certificate back to Zia and said, "Lead on, doctor, if you would."

Gary turned to Zia and said, "Would you mind if Hendrick and I went ahead to find Enkidu?"

"Not at all," replied Zia.

⟶◦⟝⟞◦⟵

THE WAY FORWARD'S interior was fully pressurized, so people could walk about it unencumbered by breathing apparatus. The craft's door was connected to the maintenance bay by a brightly lit flexible corridor projecting out from the passenger compartment and affixed to a purpose-built port in the bay's outer hatch. The corridor provided a pressurized, heated passageway where two Anunnaki could comfortably walk abreast (or in opposite directions), allowing for a constant workflow.

The console controlling conditions in both the bay and the corridor was manned by Kassam, General Shulgi's adjutant. When David and Catharine arrived in company with Zia and the newly assigned mechanics, Kassam was already typing something on a keyboard and watching for the results on a flat video screen. David observed that the virtual screens so ubiquitous on Inanna's pyramidion were evidently—on *Enki's* pyramidion—reserved for the bridge.

"Good day, Kassam," said Zia. "Is Enkidu already aboard the craft?"

With both eyes on the console, Kassam replied, "He *is*, Doctor Zia, but in an unusually foul mood. The mechanics also boarded just now." He looked up at the group in front of him. Spotting Hammy, Kassam's eyebrows immediately shot up. "At least, I *thought* Enkidu was aboard. Let me check the live schematic." He poked a few keys on the keyboard. "Yes, he's in the engine compartment." Perplexed, he looked again at Hammy. "Who are *you*?"

Hammy replied, "Enkidu Improved Class, Unit 142, sir."

Kassam muttered, "The resemblance is striking."

The mechanics handed their identification papers to Kassam, who reviewed them cursorily. He typed information from the papers into the console for a couple of minutes. "I've added you all to the universal database. If you find yourself being spoken to by a locked door, an elevator, or the like, you'll need to respond aloud but, once you do, you'll be admitted to any place you're permitted to go. If your entry is declined after speaking, you have no business being there, so turn around." He scanned the visitors' ID papers and handed them back. "You may enter," he said. They hoisted their tool cases and climbed the ramp into the corridor.

Only Zia, David, and Catharine remained. To them Kassam said, "I take it you're all here for tourism purposes?"

Zia smiled. "You seem very fluent on the computer, Kassam."

Kassam bowed his head at the compliment. "Thank you, doctor."

"What's your specialty?"

"My certified field of study is robotics," said Kassam, "with a concentration in artificial intelligence."

"Interesting," said Doctor Zia, then returned to the matter at hand. "I'd like to give Ambassador Schubert and Lieutenant Commander Weldon a feel for what they'll be experiencing in the craft. I guess there's no place better to do that than in the craft itself."

"Sounds like a good idea," said Kassam. "But you're not planning on entering the engine compartment, are you?"

David shook his head. "I'm afraid that, if we get a flat tire or run out of gas *en route*, we'll have to call Triple-A. I wouldn't know the first thing to do in the engine compartment."

Kassam looked confused. "Triple-A?"

David and Catharine laughed together. David replied, "Something we'd do at home in the event an automobile breaks down. Triple-A provides roadside repair service."

Kassam smiled. "Ah. I'll keep that in mind if ever I'm driving in the United States. Welcome to *The Way Forward*."

David was surprised to see that his tentative English translation had already made its way into official parlance. Catharine looked at him askance. David explained, "It's my rough translation of the craft's name."

She nodded approvingly. "*The Way Forward*," she said. "That's encouraging."

David chuckled.

Though David continually reminded himself that he and Catharine wouldn't be leaving for another full day, just climbing into the craft gave him a thousand butterflies in his stomach. Catharine obviously shared no such apprehension.

The corridor was only about forty feet long, but each step they took seemed spongier than the last. Reaching the halfway mark, David asked Zia, "What's happening to the gravity?"

"*The Way Forward* is zero-gravity," said Zia. "The device that provides the pyramidion with its gravitational pull is far too massive to be used on an antimatter craft of this size." He glanced at David and explained. "The antimatter engine is designed to bring the craft's mass to an almost unbelievable velocity, so mass must be kept to a minimum."

David nodded, wondering silently how they were supposed to perform ordinary bodily functions in weightless conditions. But it had been done before and, he supposed, if one man can do it, so can another.

"Antimatter travel has its drawbacks," said Zia, "another of which is that you'll have no reliable radio contact while at cruising speed."

Catharine turned to Zia. "Doesn't the positioning system need to refresh itself continually in order to stay on course?"

Zia smiled at her astuteness. "Actually, your location and related computations will automatically be confirmed while you're at low speed."

Catharine regarded Zia skeptically. "You mean, once we reach cruising speed we're operating on ... *dead reckoning*?"

Zia nodded. "Only for so long as you remain at cruising speed. Don't be concerned. Once during each day of the flight—or more often, if the pilot so chooses—the craft drops to low speed, confirms its coordinates and those of all massive bodies within range, sends and receives whatever radio traffic there is, then resumes cruising speed. As for the big massive bodies, such as Earth's moon, Mars and its moons, and all known comets and asteroids, their orbits have been mapped since Lord Enki drafted the original Tablets of Destinies, and their orbits won't change while you're out there. As for collision avoidance, I believe Lord Enki has mentioned to you that we have technology to avoid destruction even in the event of unavoidable collision, so long as the target's not too massive." Zia pointed through the starboard-side windows into the blackness of space. "Ironically, at cruising speed, you'll be able to visualize your progress through the windows, but your craft won't be able to use its radar or other reckoning instruments."

"Like a submarine in full stealth mode," muttered Catharine. "Except subs have no windows and they check their position more often, whenever possible."

"As I said," said Zia, "the pilot can do it as often as he likes. Ah, here we are. This is the passenger cabin. There's some slight gravity here at the moment, but it's from the gravitational unit in the pyramidion. Once you're away tomorrow, you'll be weightless."

There was not a sharp or unbuffered edge in sight. Virtually every surface in the cabin was firmly cushioned, even the floor, which was carpeted over several layers of springy underlayment. At strategic points all over the walls and ceilings, straps and tufted grab-handles were affixed to the airframe.

They moved slowly to the cockpit, which conspicuously lacked a canopy, windshield, or forward-facing plexiglass of any kind. Instead, outward-looking views (taken by cameras situated at various points outside the craft) appeared on no fewer than five videoscreens mounted around the pilot's seat, which was currently occupied by Enkidu.

"Good morning, Enkidu," said Catharine. "Have you completed your maintenance work?"

Enkidu, who'd been preoccupied, seemed surprised to be spoken to. "Good morning, lieutenant commander," he replied. "I *have* completed it. Aren't you all a day early?" He turned to Zia. "And you, sir. Your name is not on my passenger manifest."

"That's because I'm not going," said Zia. "I'll expect you to take good care of my friends, though."

"I shall," said Enkidu. "You might care to show your friends how to use the galley. That seems to confuse many people."

"I'll make sure they're well advised, Enkidu," said Zia, patting the android on the shoulder, and pointed out two side-by-side cushioned chairs well behind the pilot's seat. Zia said, "These are suitable for sleeping."

"Why would anyone want to sleep *here*?" asked Catharine incredulously.

Zia said, "The vastness of space is such that traveling through it can be quite dull, even at a couple of million miles per day. Besides, if you sit here, Enkidu can happily regale you with stories of Earth's past."

"Oh, boy, Bible stories," muttered Catharine sarcastically.

David snickered. "As long as Enkidu doesn't fall asleep."

Zia shook his head reassuringly. "Enkidu doesn't sleep, nor does he grow bored. He's on duty all day every day. He doesn't even need food or bathroom breaks."

Catharine quipped, "Like the perfect daddy. If we bicker, will he threaten to turn this craft *right around*?"

Zia shook his head and smiled benevolently at Catharine. "Wicked girl. Would you want him to?"

Zia led them to the dorm. There were two separate chambers, each with three bunks. Catharine plopped onto one and admired the mattress. "These are the best bunks I've ever seen onboard … *any* means of conveyance."

Zia pointed to a webbed restraint mechanism on each mattress. "Don't forget to buckle yourself in before you drift off." He glowered at Catharine. "And I'm quite serious about that. Otherwise, if you run into an emergency, you could find yourself unable to get your bearings or even end up splattered on the ceiling."

"Speaking of emergencies," said David, peering up at an instructional poster, "I see the posters *are* in English."

"Would you prefer a different alphabet?" asked Zia.

"Like cuneiform?" said David.

Zia laughed. "Be careful what you wish for. That can be arranged." He escorted them through a little gym where all the equipment was bolted to the airframe, to a latrine with showers and a small row of lockers.

David glanced around. "You know, we haven't seen the maintenance crew?"

Zia shrugged. "As for Enkidu, we know where he is. As for the others, they're probably running diagnostics, testing moving parts, and so on. Let's return to the pyramidion and get a meal ... one you won't need to eat in zero gravity."

CHAPTER 5

AFTER TOSSING AND turning all night, David rose, put on his formal ambassador's suit and went to the commissary, where Catharine awaited him in a skirted dress-blue uniform. For the moment, the place was pleasantly quiet. They each grabbed a cup of coffee and a roll. While on their second cup, their solitude was interrupted by Doctor Zia, Gary, and Hendrick.

"There they are," said Gary. "Well, lieutenant commander, you look fresh as a daisy. David, you look like you've been wrestlin' with angels all night."

"That bad?" asked David.

Hendrick was amused. "Don't worry about missing sleep. Doctor Zia tells us that a half hour after you jump to operating speed, you'll be dozing the whole way there."

Zia added, "The vessel's entertainment center is jammed with Earth's movies and television shows, every novel ever written, and headphones for privacy and quiet. I expect, like most Anunnaki, you'll fall asleep before you get far into any of them."

Although their small group was alone in the commissary at this hour, David softly said to Zia, "Our spacecraft easily sleeps six—"

"Eight," Zia corrected, "if you count the visitors' chairs in the cockpit."

David continued. "Should we allow anyone else aboard?"

Zia searched his memory. "Standard operating procedure would dictate that no one else comes aboard, except for necessary repairs or refueling."

"What about bringing someone back here?" asked David.

Zia smiled. "Like a hitchhiker?" He patted David comfortingly on the shoulder. "No one is to be brought back here, except with prior leave of His Majesty the King given in-person. And good luck getting that."

"Where is Enkidu?" asked David.

"Well, let's see. Standard operating procedure would put him in the pilot's station no later than two hours before departure," replied Zia. "We haven't seen him since yesterday, but I expect he's already been in the pilot's seat more than an hour. Remember, however, he doesn't mind waiting."

Together, they cleared the cups and plates from their tables and walked to the dock. David was having trouble believing that, in two weeks' time, he'd be visiting the king's fleet in the Mars system. It still felt somehow as though all such notions were simply daydreams, and that in fact he'd be taking the next shuttle down to Houston.

As Zia opened the door to the bay, a fresh floral scent wafted out. Even from where David was standing, he could see that the light emanating from the bay was unusually bright.

Zia, evidently surprised at what he saw inside, turned to the rest of them and said quietly, "Her Majesty is present, accompanied by Shiduri and two flower girls. Stay behind me. Be sure to avert your eyes from the Queen's. I'll stop twenty feet from Her Majesty. I believe she's about to pass out this way. Bow *low*. *Don't* speak and *don't* approach unless spoken to or beckoned." Duly warned, they entered the maintenance bay.

David stole a quick glance before casting his eyes down. Inanna was arrayed in ancient Egyptian fashion with the addition of a few modern accessories, such as white gloves, and silver leaf woven into her hair. Her black hair and dark eyes appeared to have been accentuated for the occasion, perhaps to contrast them with Catharine's gold and green. Inanna stood in front of Shiduri, but behind two young girls languidly strewing fragrant petals before her.

Zia led his company to Inanna, but she snubbed him, addressing David instead. "Good morning, Mister Ambassador," she said.

"Good morning, Your Majesty," said David, bowing low.

Inanna seemed displeased by the conduct of someone standing behind David. The only person behind him was Catharine, who stood at attention with her eyes averted and face turned down. It took David a moment to realize the grounds for Inanna's displeasure. Catharine was bowing like a *man*. He turned slightly toward Catharine and made an understated curtsying motion, which must have looked ridiculous to anyone watching. And, of course, *everyone* was watching, but they refrained from any perceptible reaction.

Catharine's face turned red and she curtsied low (if a bit awkwardly) in her fitted skirt. David tried to persuade himself that Catharine was embarrassed, but he knew quite well she was smoldering.

"Mister Ambassador," said the Queen, evidently mollified by Catharine's compliance, "please approach."

David had no choice but to pass Zia on his way to Her Majesty, but he made sure to nod to Zia as he passed.

Inanna extended her open hand to Shiduri, who placed in it a sealed envelope of royal stationery. Inanna handed it to David in turn.

The envelope was addressed simply: *To His Lordship.* The Queen whispered to David, "This is for our long-unseen friend. Should you happen to encounter him face to face, please hand him this without comment, except to inform him that I wish him to keep the contents secret."

"It would be my privilege, madam," whispered David, placing the envelope in the pocket of his jacket. While she beamed at him, he silently repeated a sort of mantra. *Please don't kiss me. Please don't kiss me. Please don't kiss me.* That would be all that was needed to ensure Catharine's lasting doubt. David bowed low.

Inanna said, "May the Creator of all watch over you both on your journey and bring you back safe."

He replied. "And may the Creator watch over Your Majesty and keep Your Majesty safe always."

Inanna directed the flower girls to proceed past the rest of the company on the way to the door. But as she was about to pass Catharine, who was still frozen in mid-curtsy with her eyes downcast, Inanna halted the little procession to look at her.

David's silent mantra quickly became, *Please don't speak to her. Please don't speak to her. Please don't speak to her.* He winced as Inanna spoke to her.

"Weldon, rise," said the Queen.

With eyes still averted, Catharine rose to her full height and raised her chin.

The Queen, considerably taller than Catharine, bent to study her face closely. In no apparent haste, she glanced at David and smiled approvingly. She then passed judgment with a single word, warmly spoken:

"Enchanting."

After the little royal company had passed through the door, Shiduri turned and smiled at David as she closed it behind her.

"Well, *that* was unexpected," said Zia. "Evidently, David, she expects you may bump into someone in particular. I wonder who that could be."

David shrugged. "I'm not at liberty to say," he replied abashedly.

"It's probably no one," said Catharine resentfully. "It was just her excuse to have a *little secret* with His Excellency, the Ambassador."

Gary, who was standing a few feet off, said, "Lieutenant commander, may I speak with you privately a moment?"

Catharine accompanied Gary a short distance away.

"What'd I do now?" she asked quietly.

"Well," said Gary, "where should I start? Your temper is showin' and it's makin' you look small. The Queen of ... the Universe, or whatever ... just gave you her seal of approval."

"She did?"

"Yep," he assured her. "When she was lookin' at your face, she smiled approvingly at David. I think she's moved on from him, or at least she's tryin' to."

She shook her head. "Why do guys always think it's about *them*? What makes *you* think this is about David?"

Gary looked at her in confusion. "What else would it be about?"

"This is between Inanna and me."

He scoffed. "Well, whatever the contest ... *you won*. Don't grasp defeat from the jaws of victory. And, if I may, I'd advise the lieutenant commander to show some empathy for a guy who's tryin' to keep the solar system from blowin' itself apart. The USA has some real enemies. The Queen is *not* one of 'em. And David is *definitely* not one of 'em, so cut him some slack."

Catharine took it all pretty well, musing that navy flyers seemed to have a special ability to deliver constructive criticism to superior officers. Or maybe it's just that they're all navy. She nodded and muttered, "Point taken. Thanks, Gary."

He winked at her discreetly. *"Death from above."*

She smiled despite herself and responded in kind. *"Death from below."*

⸺⸻⊷◦◦⊶⸻⸺

CATHARINE AND DAVID'S luggage had already been brought aboard. They said their goodbyes and received boarding clearance from Kassam, who blessed them and their travels in the Anunnaki language.

They walked up the brightly lit flexible corridor side by side. About halfway to the craft, they clasped hands firmly and walked on together, and David could feel from Catharine's grip that they were very much in this together and that the bond between them was as solid as could be.

As soon as they entered the passenger compartment, they turned left to pay their respects to their pilot.

"How does the space traffic look?" asked David.

Seated at the pilot's station, Enkidu turned and impassively watched them enter. "Fortunately," he said, "there's no traffic between *The Way Forward* and the king's fleet. The only known massive body near our path is Earth's moon, which we'll pass in a few hours. You'll have a good view of it from the starboard side as we pass by. After that, there'll be not much to see for ten Earth days or so."

David nodded. "I suppose it's time to brush up on *long* Russian literature. Dostoyevsky, perhaps."

Instead of making an erudite retort as David expected, Enkidu merely smiled distractedly. "I'm signaling the maintenance bay that we're all aboard. The corridor will be retracting and the vehicular seal emplaced. You might wish to take a seat." He pointed to the two chairs behind him. "Right there, if you'd like."

David and Catharine took the proffered seats. David noticed that, at his right hand, a bottle of champagne was chilling in a bucket of ice. The bottleneck protruded through a central opening in what appeared to be a small nylon web designed to stop the bottle (once weightless) from floating out of the bucket. He turned the bottle to read the label.

"It's a 1990 Veuve Clicquot, Cave Privée Rose," he said with a laugh.

She turned to him with a quizzical look. "Isn't that—?"

He nodded. "It's the champagne I ordered the night we met Miriam and Doctor Iskender. There's a note attached."

"What does it say?" asked Catharine.

"It's signed by Miriam Azeri, Gary Sullivan, and Hendrick."

"How nice of them!" she said.

"At the bottom, there's a handwritten note from Zia. 'To the sincerest earthlings I've met: Get ready for the best view of the moon that two lovers have ever had. Incidentally this bottle was contraband on the pyramidion, which means it was smuggled by a true professional, one of whom has signed above.'"

Catharine laughed. "Gary, of course."

"Who else?" said David. "Can you imagine Miriam smuggling?"

"If she were caught," said Catharine, "she'd apologize contritely."

"And then send a polite, handwritten follow-up note," he added.

She nodded. "No more than two weeks later."

Enkidu interjected, "As you haven't uncorked the bottle yet, if I were you I'd wait to open it until we've fully accelerated." He turned. "Forty minutes or so. Buckle up. We're about to be shoved off."

There was a sudden change in cabin pressure that made their ears pop, and a blue light flashed silently on the pilot's panel.

"We're cleared for departure," said Enkidu. "Get ready for a lateral jolt, and keep your head back on the headrest for a few minutes."

What felt like a gigantic hand shoved them sideways, away from the pyramidion. Because there was nothing to hinder their motion, they continued drifting away at a good clip. A few seconds later, Enkidu pushed two buttons simultaneously and they felt a gentle thrust forward, such as one might feel in an airliner beginning acceleration down the runway.

Another button was pressed and the acceleration became more aggressive. They felt themselves being pressed insistently against their cushioned seats.

Enkidu visually checked their condition, then returned his attention to the panel. "Beginning acceleration to cruising velocity."

Now the acceleration became eye-popping. It felt as though they were being pressed against their chairs by leaden blankets—enough to interfere with normal breathing but, fortunately, not enough to trigger the impulse to fight for air, which was just as well, as the feeling went on for a good half hour without letup. Then suddenly, all sense of pressure— indeed, of *motion*—simply stopped.

Enkidu turned to them and said, "It's happy hour."

David looked at him incredulously. "We're still moving?" he asked.

Enkidu smiled. "Very quickly."

David removed the bottle of chilled champagne from the bucket. It was more slippery than he expected and nearly floated out of his hand.

"As soon as you pop the cork, cover the top with your thumb," said Enkidu. "No glasses, I'm afraid. Pouring is a bit tricky and unreliable. You'll have to sip from the bottle, but I doubt the two of you will mind sharing."

As Enkidu didn't drink—anything—David and Catharine toasted his health, and the health of Doctor Zia, Queen Inanna, and Lord Enki. Then they added His Majesty King Enlil. Since there was still champagne left and nothing else to do, they added toasts to the health of every living person they could think of having anything to do with their present circumstances, beginning with those who'd procured the champagne, the admiral, the admiral's wife, the President, and the lamented Ibrahim. By the time they finished the bottle, they were both well and truly sloshed.

David looked up at the videoscreens, in which the moon appeared noticeably larger than it had when they began toasting.

Enkidu, as though reading David's thoughts, said, "This might be an appropriate time for you two to retire to the starboard dormitory. The view will be best from there. Before you get up, however, remember that there's no gravity and you're a bit tipsy, so take care. Also, if you feel as though you may … regurgitate your beverage, make sure you make it to the latrine first and that you close the door. Otherwise, conditions in the cabin will become very … unpleasant, and remain that way until such time as we can clean up."

Enkidu accepted the empty bottle from David and shoved it into an opening in the wall that sucked it in with a clamor. Then he did the same with the bucket of ice.

David and Catharine got up and made their way carefully to the dorm, laughing at their own clumsy missteps along the way. They reached the dorm a bit winded, and plopped side by side onto a cushioned sofa, belting themselves in. In this posture, with few words, they gazed out the starboard-side window until the moon occupied their whole field of vision and was too bright to stare at.

Coming down from the champagne high, David silently remarked (mostly to himself) on his incredulity that the craft was not a motion picture theater or a couch in a living room. It was a spaceship. And that huge, bright object out there was neither a photograph nor a motion picture. It was *the moon*, the same that had enchanted lovers on Earth for millions of years. The moon that made the tides, which were essential to life.

Catharine drifted off and David gazed at her lovingly. The bright whiteness of the moonlight showed every little detail of her face. Although it was as beautiful to him as any he could imagine, he realized it wasn't her looks he loved, but what the poet once called the "pilgrim soul" in her.

Pace, *Anzû. What would be the point of my surviving her?*

The moon began to slip behind them. Not for the last time, David wondered idly if it would still be there in five hundred years.

⇒∘◁≪▰≫▷∘⇐

THOUGH DAVID EXPECTED that he and Catharine would spend most of their traveling time making love, that's far from how things turned out. Weightlessness made their first bout absurdly awkward although, as David optimistically observed, *any* sex is better than none. But *none* was what it soon turned out to be, or very little at any rate.

In fact, weightlessness quickly made it hard to feel exultant about any aspect of the human body—whether one's own or another's. Eating out of individual trays with plastic utensils was hardly the most romantic form of dining. And, though the rigorous application of a travel wipe at a picnic may be fine for a few hours, it proved a poor substitute for soap and hot water on a long voyage. By Day Two, the entire cabin was redolent of the wipes' cloying perfume, and the air-cycling system, however efficient at removing offensive odors, proved incapable of wafting away the odor of a scent that pervades one's own skin.

For the better part of several days, Catharine and David conversed quietly, comparing their upbringings, then sharing a meal and dozing. Once the novelty of those activities wore off, they spent a few hours each day staring out the window together at the blackness of space with its generous spattering of stars. But from one hour to the next, there was no perceptible change in the stars, and it felt as though *The Way Forward* was making no way at all. And there was no reliable way of detecting the passage of days, except by glancing at the wall-mounted clock-calendar.

They decided to raid the entertainment system's seemingly endless array of motion pictures, starting with films that had been released in the motion picture theaters that had chugged along reasonably well until the advent of COVID-19 and its successor strains. After suffering through a few deadly years of infection, theater audiences, which had been dropping off for years, rapidly dwindled to nothing, relegating viewers to an endless choice of streaming services that could be tapped from one's living room without exposure to deadly diseases.

The two made liberal use of the limited exercise equipment, if for no other reason than to help them sleep.

Once or twice each day, one or both of them would go and check on Enkidu, who did no more than politely acknowledge their presence and answer their questions rather tersely. In fact, they were more than a little disappointed with Enkidu who, despite Zia's earlier assurances, seemed unwilling to share stories of the distant past.

Fortunately, both David and Catharine were avid readers. At first, they took turns reading aloud from C.S. Lewis's *Out of the Silent Planet*, and marveled at Lewis's quaint conception of space travel which, though interesting, differed completely from their actual experience.

After they reached the halfway point, David and Catharine needed a change of pace and decided to descend upon Enkidu together. After all, they were halfway to Mars with nothing of consequence standing between them and their destination, so Enkidu could have little else to preoccupy him.

When they entered the cockpit, Enkidu smiled at them. "I take it you've succumbed to the boredom of travel in near space."

As they belted themselves into the passenger's seats, Catharine said, "You call this *near* space?"

Enkidu turned back to the console. "Oh, yes," he assured her. "Travel to an adjacent planet in the same solar system? A mere jaunt across the pond. You can measure the distance in millions of miles. This craft is equipped for travel to destinations *billions* of miles away."

Catharine laughed. "Now *that* would be boring."

Enkidu kept his eyes fixed on the monitors. "For that, you'd be placed in hibernation. You wouldn't be bored at all. Unless you're of that rare breed bored by its own dreams."

Catharine was intrigued. "How long does the trip have to be for the passengers to be ... hibernated, or whatever it's called?"

"Well," said Enkidu, "it depends upon whether the passenger needs to engage in strategic planning *en route*. If not, hibernation is usually used for a trip longer than an Earth-month or so."

"Is hibernation used to slow the aging process?"

Enkidu shook his head. "No—well, there *is* a deep-sleep state that has that effect, but that's not why the Anunnaki use it. They're immortal, so they needn't worry about ... aging."

David detected a note of disgust in the way Enkidu pronounced that last word ... *aging*, as though the very notion was beneath him. For an artificial person such as he, immortality was evidently assumed— perhaps regarded as well-deserved.

Catharine was evidently thinking the same thing. "Then why do the Anunnaki subject themselves to a deep-sleep state?"

Enkidu sighed, as though the conversation was a bit wearisome. "Experience shows that the Anunnaki grow restless and depressed after more than a few weeks of continuous confinement. Evidently, for them it's quite unpleasant."

"I can understand that," conceded Catharine.

David said, "I'm enjoying reading Dostoyevsky, whom I've escaped until now."

This drew neither comments nor questions from Enkidu, which struck David as inconsistent with his reputation; Enkidu was known as a first-class conversationalist. And, as everyone knows, a good conversation is one in which each participant shows interest in what the others have to say. As yet, Enkidu hadn't posed a single question, which perversely made David want to extend the conversation.

"Tell me, Enkidu," said David, "do you like Queen Inanna?"

Enkidu seemed in no hurry to reply. In his own good time, he sighed and said, "I rather find Her Majesty beyond my likes and dislikes. For someone, such as myself"—by this David took him to mean an android—"Her Majesty is a 'great person'; one to be served rather than judged."

Catharine smiled privately at David, as though to say: *How's that for diplomatic evasion?*

"Fair enough," said David, though he was experienced enough to know when a question had been evaded. "Perhaps you can tell us how you felt when Gilgamesh denounced Her Majesty's affections?"

"How *I* felt, sir?"

"Yes."

"Well … I wasn't there, was I?"

"Do you recall how the *original* Enkidu felt when Gilgamesh reviled Her Majesty's affections?"

Enkidu took a moment, perhaps to make a minor adjustment to their course … or perhaps to delay answering. "If memory serves, at that point in the story, Enkidu should have been dismayed by Gilgamesh's lack of gallantry, especially as it would soon put Enkidu's life at risk, fighting to the death with the Bull of Heaven."

After a bit more one-sided banter, David and Catharine returned to the starboard dormitory.

Catharine asked, "Why do you suppose Enkidu's so reticent?"

David leaned into her ear and spoke at a low whisper. "Let's talk about that later. I'm beginning to suspect that the walls have ears."

As had become their habit, they each returned to their own reading, but eventually David began making use of two handheld readers, rather than one. Catharine's curiosity was piqued, and she watched David turn back and forth between the readers for a while until he looked up. He smiled at her.

"You're a two-fisted reader," she observed. "What are you reading?"

"As we may soon meet the King of Nibiru somewhere extraterrestrial," he said, "I thought it prudent to compare the few extant records of men who did so in the past."

"Other humans met the king and recorded the experience?" she asked.

"Yes," he said, "as you might imagine, that's kind of a big deal—

something that someone would think most worthy of being recorded, don't you think?"

"I suppose so," she granted. "What do the records say?"

David focused on one of the readers and put the other aside. "Well, there's the tale of Adapa, the wisest man alive, which was recorded on cuneiform tablets." He repeated the tale of Adapa's visit to King Anu, which he'd earlier discussed telepathically with Anzû and related to the admiral.

"So, *that's* why we're not immortal?" she mused.

"That's the upshot of the story, but I was focusing on what it looks like visually to be brought into the presence of a god." He put his finger on the reader and swiped backward several pages. "The story's pretty vague on that. It says that Enki 'made Adapa take the way to heaven, and to heaven he ascended.' When he approached the gate of King Anu he was halted by two gods, Dumuzi and Gizzida, just as Enki had earlier predicted."

"I wonder if we'll be halted by the same two gods," said Catharine.

David shook his head. "Not likely. Dumuzi is dead, murdered on orders of Enki's eldest son, Marduk, who's also dead. I heard the whole tale from Queen Inanna. She still mourns the loss of Dumuzi. Now, Gizzida"—he flipped back a few more pages—"he might still be there. Never heard of him before, but"—he put the reader aside and took up the other one—"Enoch says a lot more about how it looked to appear before God." He regarded her gravely.

"Scary?" she asked.

"Well, I'll tell you what the Book of Enoch says and you can decide for yourself how scary it is. Let me point out first that the Book of Enoch has been excluded from both the Old and the New Testament, although the writers of those texts (at least subsequent to the Five Books of Moses) clearly knew of the Book of Enoch."

"So, Enoch is apocryphal?" she asked.

He nodded equivocally. "The word 'apocrypha' means books that are hidden away, that is, not included in the canonical Bible. Only one sect includes Enoch in the canon, that's the Ethiopic sect. Western scholars refer to the Book of Enoch as 'pseudepigraphic,' meaning 'misattributed,' the suspicion being that it was written much later than the time of the historical Enoch, and there seems little doubt about that. The historical Enoch was born before the Flood. He was the seventh generation after Adam, and was a great-grandfather to Noah."

"You mean, to Zia?" she asked.

Again, he nodded equivocally. "So it would appear. Also, Enoch did not die on Earth, if he died at all; he was taken up to heaven bodily at the age of 365 years."

"Is he at the place we're headed to right now?" she asked.

"I suppose he could be. But it's not clear where in 'heaven' Enoch was taken, and remember that we're not currently headed for Nibiru, but rather for the king's fleet. With our current technology, Nibiru will still be out of reach for centuries.

"So," said Catharine, "how did Enoch see heaven in his vision?"

"I'll read it to you from a translation," said David, smiling fatalistically. "Hold onto your hat."

Behold, in the vision clouds invited me and a mist summoned me, and the course of the stars and the lightnings sped and hastened me, and the winds in the vision caused me to fly and lifted me upward, and bore me into heaven.

And I went in till I drew nigh to a wall which is built of crystals and surrounded by tongues of fire: and it began to affright me. And I went into the tongues of fire and drew nigh to a large house which was built of crystals: and the walls of the house were like a tessellated floor made of crystals, and its groundwork was of crystal.

Its ceiling was like the path of the stars and the lightnings, and between them were fiery cherubim, and their heaven was clear as water. A flaming fire surrounded the walls, and its portals blazed with fire. And I entered into that house, and it was hot as fire and cold as ice: there were no delights of life therein: fear covered me, and trembling got hold upon me. And as I quaked and trembled, I fell upon my face. And I beheld a vision, And lo! there was a second house, greater than the former, and the entire portal stood open before me, and it was built of flames of fire. And in every respect it so excelled in splendor and magnificence and extent that I cannot describe to you its splendor and its extent. And its floor was of fire, and above it were lightnings and the path of the stars, and its ceiling also was flaming fire.

And I looked and saw therein a lofty throne: its appearance was as crystal, and the wheels thereof as the shining sun, and there was the vision of cherubim. And from underneath the throne came streams of flaming fire so that I could not look thereon. And the Great Glory sat thereon, and His raiment shone more brightly than the sun and was whiter than any snow. None of the angels could enter and behold His face by reason of the magnificence and glory, and no flesh could behold

Him. The flaming fire was round about Him, and a great fire stood before Him, and none around could draw nigh Him: ten thousand times ten thousand (stood) before Him, yet He needed no counselor. And the most holy ones who were nigh to Him did not leave by night nor depart from Him. And until then I had been prostrate on my face, trembling: and the Lord called me with His own mouth, and said to me: 'Come hither, Enoch, and hear my word.' And one of the holy ones came to me and awoke me, and He made me rise up and approach the door: and I bowed my face downwards."

Catharine gazed out at the unmoving stars. "I hope that's not where we're going."

David shrugged. "I expect that, to the extent the vision is accurate, it's not a vision of Nibiru, but of the king's pyramidion—although I could be wrong. Besides, Enoch's description is probably not the way things would appear to people of the twenty-first century, such as you and I."

"How do you mean?" asked Catharine.

"Well, he describes just about every architectural element of the place as being crystalline. That could mean—"

"Glass!" said Catharine.

"Or, not to put too fine a point on it, plexiglass."

"Even the tiles in the tessellated floors could be made of glass crystals," she said.

"And glass is transparent," said David, "which means that the image of the universe on the ceiling in the first house might not have been painted *onto* the ceiling at all, but rather a direct view of the stars *through* the ceiling."

"What about the flames everywhere?" asked Catharine.

"To someone living before the Great Flood, any artificial light would appear to be fire," said David, "and, while one would expect a well-lit room to be warm, with present technology it might be cold, or at least colder than expected. And lightning shooting everywhere could be the sight of spacecraft firing their rockets."

"They had no electric lights," she said with a nod, "only fire. What about a first house being followed by a second house?"

David said, "That tends to indicate that Enoch's description *is* of the place where we're going. Separate enclosures within a ship, located perhaps at the pinnacle of the king's pyramidion."

There was a long silence between them. They were like two children stunned by contemplation of an approaching terror. David broke the silence.

"And there's something else," he said.

"Dragons? Demons?" she asked. "*What?*"

"Nothing like that. I was just going to tell you that Azeri pointed out that Adapa, in the Sumerian tale, and Enoch in the Hebrew retelling, might have been the same historical person."

It all seemed too much for Catharine to take in, and she soon drifted off, leaving David to contemplate their situation alone. Judging by a glance through the window, their craft appeared to be motionless. The moon had long disappeared from view and the stars were unmoving. What if, in fact, the craft *wasn't* moving?

That led him to ponder just how absolutely dependent they were upon Enkidu's skills and ... good intentions. Slumber beckoned, if only as a means of escape from such unwelcome thoughts.

His eyes closed, and suddenly his mind was overcome by a single thought:

What if the android in the pilot's seat is not Enkidu?

He felt clammy about the collar. His palms began to sweat and the room seemed to become uncomfortably warm. Involuntarily, his eyes opened again.

Zia's Enkidu was known as a conversationalist. But the pilot had seemed rather to discourage conversation. Could it be because he had nothing much to say? Or because he's unaccustomed to literary conversation? The pilot had shown no recognition of Dostoyevsky's name. The real Enkidu would have known Dostoyevsky by heart (given his huge memory banks), and would have been only too happy to converse about *not only* Dostoyevsky, but Tolstoy and Orwell, to boot.

David forced his eyes to close once again.

As a child, when he was in bed, he imagined that any hand or foot allowed to project over the edge of the mattress might be devoured by one or more monsters lurking on the floor, so he was careful always to retract his arms and legs. Somehow, he knew intuitively that such monsters were unable to climb up the bed, and he knew from experience that they were always gone by morning. Nevertheless, the puzzle had presented itself: *How could he be sure to continue retracting his limbs once he'd fallen asleep?* That puzzle seemed insoluble, and he quickly came to the practical conclusion that there was nothing he could do about it. He simply had to sleep. And so he did. In any event, he managed to escape infancy with all his limbs intact; whether that was because his limbs had never once protruded during sleep or because there'd never been any monsters on the floor in the first place he could never be absolutely certain. But, over time, he grew increasingly confident that the monsters had been figments of his imagination—which, of course, he'd suspected all along.

What's more, he'd never heard of a spate of children losing their hands or feet by sleeping with their limbs flung wide. While it's true that he might have been shielded from such knowledge by his parents, they'd always seemed pretty careful to tell him how to avoid household hazards, a category that any reasonable parent would recognize as including not only electrical outlets and unattended flames, but also floor-dwelling monsters.

So, he'd solved that problem by ignoring it.

When he was sixteen, he felt a painful swelling in his armpit. It wasn't alarmingly swollen or alarmingly painful, so he ignored it, and a couple of days later it was gone without a trace. He never learned what it was.

He'd nearly decided to adopt the same solution to his present doubt about whether the pilot was really Enkidu, when he turned toward Catharine and opened one eye. It lighted on Catharine, sleeping the sleep of the innocent. While he'd be tempted to ignore the question if it were only his own welfare at stake, he'd sworn in his soul to protect her from harm.

Still, if the pilot were a wicked Enkidu, he could have killed David any number of times before now, and there an end.

Catharine must have heard David shift because she opened her eyes and looked into his. Seeing his concern, she whispered, "It's probably him. He just doesn't know us well enough, so he's not comfortable opening up to us." She turned away and, just before she fell back to sleep, added, "Take care of it in the morning."

So surprised was he that her thoughts coincided with his, he wondered if, as a child, she'd also slept with her limbs retracted. In any event, she was obviously aware of the long-standing tradition that, come morning, self-respecting monsters are customarily gone. Maybe these would be, too.

But he didn't think so.

CHAPTER 6

DAVID DID NOTHING to verify that the pilot was Zia's Enkidu. Not only did everything seem to be running smoothly on the craft and at home (based upon the few messages Catharine had received from the admiral), but any radio message they might have cared to send would have had to go through the pilot, which would have rendered the effort self-defeating. While David could have tried to bypass the pilot's prying eyes by using some sort of code, no such code had been supplied to him prior to their departure, and it was implausible to think that he could (on the fly, no less) create one that the pilot couldn't readily crack. He decided they were pretty much stuck with their pilot, at least until reaching the royal fleet.

Through their long voyage, David and Catharine retained only the vaguest sense of the passage of time, but they clung to enough to know that *The Way Forward* had been *en route* for nearly two weeks. Like children trapped in the back seat of a car on an interminable trip, they were eager to be done with it and began climbing into the front seat.

⸺⟫∘⟅⟫∘⟨⸺

DAVID AND CATHARINE monitored Enkidu's videoscreens in vain for some sign of change. Eventually, they dozed off, confident in their pilot's automated attentiveness.

Suddenly (though, in such a torpid environment, *any* change would have seemed sudden), Enkidu emitted a short, quiet grunt, like a doctor finding something unexpected on an X-ray. Then came a short burst of typing, after which he pressed SEND. A short while later, a green light flashed silently on the console, indicating an incoming message.

Enkidu pressed another button, and a brief message in the Anunnaki language appeared on one of his screens. The screen directly in front of him then automatically cycled through the different views supplied by the craft's external cameras, and came to rest on its default view, looking straight ahead. Enkidu turned toward his human companions, as if suddenly realizing he had learned something they might find interesting. Catharine, who'd been keeping one eye open, pointed to the screen and nudged David, who sat up bleary-eyed.

Recognizing the familiar view on Enkidu's screen, David blinked twice to clear his vision, but also to feign interest. "Ah," he muttered approvingly, "more nothingness."

"Not exactly," said Enkidu, pointing to a dull reddish dot at the center of the screen. "You see that dot?"

"Yeah," said David.

"That's Mars."

Catharine scanned the screen. "Where's the royal fleet?"

"It's in hiding," said Enkidu.

Catharine looked at him skeptically. "In … another dimension?"

"No," said Enkidu, "same dimension. The fleet's behind Mars."

"So, they can't see us?" she asked.

Enkidu winced and shook his head, which was evidently as close as an android could come to rolling his eyes. "They *can* see us."

"How?"

"Space probes aimed at us," replied Enkidu.

"So, they know we're here?" she asked.

Enkidu was openly patronizing. "They just acknowledged receipt of our message, which specified our space coordinates, so … yes … that seems likely."

"So, they're tracking us?"

"Certainly."

"How long till we reach them?" she asked.

Enkidu performed a mental calculation which, to a human, seemed instantaneous. "Thirty-six hours, give or take. To avoid collision, we'll have to resume low speed before we're flung around the planet."

<hr>

"WHAT DO WE do with the laundry?" David asked Catharine.

Catharine, who'd been neatly repacking her things, stopped and looked at him as though he were a simpleton. "Well, evidently you haven't realized that there are plastic bags atop the high shelf in each closet. If I were you, I'd start by putting your laundry in them. And try to separate the darks from the lights—although I have no idea if we'll ever see anything resembling laundry service out here." She glanced around the dormitory area and placed her hands on her hips. "We may end up on the return trip doing laundry manually and hanging the wash on makeshift clotheslines."

He smirked. "That *would* be remarkable, since this craft has no freely running water."

"Well," Catharine shrugged, "we'll just have to pick up some sweat clothes from the gift shop to wear until we get home." David turned to her, showing mild irritation.

Before he could open his mouth to speak, Catharine apologized. "I'm sorry, David. That was completely inappropriate. I'm trying to remain calm, but I'm jumping out of my skin." Her eyes welled up. "We're about to come as close to meeting God as any living mortal ever has, and I feel entirely unworthy."

He put down his bag and hugged her close. "If there's ever been anyone *worthy*, it's you, Catharine. Heaven knows, you've got more business being here than I do."

She was still distraught. "But I've killed people, or … whatever those drones are."

He shook his head. "So have I, and I'd do it again. But, more importantly, remember that the king himself is no saint. He's a lifelong soldier—and that life has been *quite* long."

She shrugged. "Maybe a woman won't be admitted to the king's presence."

"Oh, I don't know," he said jocularly. "Inanna was admitted to Anu's presence when he was king, and to Enlil's presence before *he* became king. And she was admitted to Enki's presence—"

"And took half his stuff," Catharine interjected.

"Yes," he said, "see? You're *better* than Inanna. You won't take his stuff!"

"Well," she joked, "less than *half* of it, anyway."

"I'll remember that," said David archly. "Look, you're a daughter of Israel. Your pedigree may not be quite as old as theirs, but you hail from the oldest civilized nation on Earth. Hold your head high. As for this 'no girls allowed' business? Forget it. Remember: No women, no Anunnaki."

She smiled.

David began stuffing his laundry into bags. "And they're going to learn this, too: No Catharine, no *David*."

She grimaced. "No. You can't refuse to do your diplomatic job because they won't admit your girlfriend."

"Watch me ... lieutenant commander." He winked.

THOUGH *THE WAY Forward* was running at low speed, when it swung around the Red Planet the centripetal force whipped up its velocity so high that Enkidu needed to deploy reverse thrusters three separate times to maintain control.

As they cleared Mars, the royal fleet appeared in stark relief against the planet in orbit on a single plane, each ship lit by not only its perimeter lights, but floodlights mounted on its exterior. The fleet appeared to be moving in a racetrack pattern that enabled it to remain on the side of the planet invisible from Earth.

"My God," said Catharine. "There must be more than forty spaceships out there."

Enkidu nodded. "Fifty-two, to be exact, assuming none of them is off on separate duty." He pointed to the foremost ships. "The little saucers up front are fighters in vanguard formation. You'll also see rogue fighters sprinkled throughout the plane of the fleet, as well as above and below."

Catharine nodded. "They're performing the same function as jets and submarines in an ocean fleet. Eyes above and below."

Enkidu acknowledged the accuracy of her remark and continued. "You would call those large arrowhead-shaped battleships 'cruisers'; they're for projecting power beyond the fleet. They carry large crews and massive firepower. The dark-colored, cigar-shaped craft nearer the center of the fleet are what you might call destroyers. Their principal function is to protect the flagship."

"The flagship is the one with the admiral aboard?" asked David.

"Ordinarily that would be the case," said Enkidu, "but this is the *royal* fleet, so its flagship boasts the King of Nibiru."

"Is this the only Anunnaki fleet in the vicinity?" asked Catharine.

Enkidu nodded. "Yes, but only because the Anunnaki were not expecting any hostile engagements. The only power in this sector capable of opposing an Anunnaki battle fleet is the Dagon, and we have every confidence in their peaceful intentions. If we'd been expecting a hostile engagement, there would have been several fleets here, but *not* the royal fleet. In the rare instances when the royal fleet closely approaches a hostile engagement, great effort is expended to ensure that no one knows where it is."

"Where are we docking first?" asked David.

Enkidu shrugged. "No orders yet received. I'll move us further from the planet so you can get a better view of the king's pyramidion. I'm told it's truly magnificent." As he took the craft up, several fighters ignited their thruster rockets and broke ranks with the fleet. They seemed to be converging on *The Way Forward.*

"Does the fleet use fossil fuels?" asked Catharine.

"To a limited extent," said Enkidu. "The Anunnaki have developed highly stable forms of fossil fuels for use in short-burst guidance and retro rockets."

"*Stable* fossil fuels?" asked Catharine.

Enkidu nodded. "They've been synthesized to have flash points well above those of any equivalents currently used on Earth, and they're required to meet stringent safety standards."

A voice came on the radio. "We're speaking English as a courtesy to *The Way Forward* pilot. Please identify yourself and closely adhere to the approaching fighter escort. Acknowledge. Over."

David was astonished to learn that his emendation to the craft's name had already been adopted not only locally, but as far away as Mars.

Enkidu looked a bit disappointed as he replied. "This is the pilot of *The Way Forward* speaking. My name is Enkidu. Receipt acknowledged. Before following escort, I request permission to assume a higher elevation in order to show the royal pyramidion to my diplomatic passengers. Over."

There was a momentary delay and the voice came back on the radio. "Request denied, Enkidu," it said, "but the fighters will be escorting *The Way Forward* directly to the royal pyramidion, so your passengers will be seeing it up close quite soon. Please acknowledge acquiescence. Over."

Catharine discreetly squeezed David's hand, and David patted her hand comfortingly.

"Acquiescence acknowledged," replied Enkidu. "Fighter escort, we're in your hands. Over."

The Way Forward followed the leader of the fighter escort as it swung down below the fleet and slowly moved up toward the flagship. Enkidu's console lit up all over.

"Why's that happening?" asked David.

"We're being scanned by every craft we pass," replied Enkidu. "No one approaches the king without passing universal scrutiny. If any one of those vessels sees anything it doesn't like, we stop … or they destroy us."

David said, "Well, that's comforting."

"Doesn't matter," said Enkidu. "We're not carrying anything of importance"—he nodded respectfully—"except for our passengers, of course."

The king's pyramidion came into view. Both David and Catharine gasped. Even with no familiar object to provide scale, it was obviously the largest pyramid they'd ever seen—many times larger than the Great Pyramid of Giza. And its outer structure might have been fashioned of glass, but to David it appeared to be comprised of … diamond. Only its base was opaque, which David assumed was because the base housed the heavy machinery needed for a sizable gravitational platform. Well, at least they wouldn't be weightless while inside.

Immediately above the gravitational device was a level consisting of dazzling white lights that shone up into the pyramidion's core.

Atop the lights sat the brilliant, tessellated floor of the pyramidion's lowest habitable level, composed of individual crystals, each of which acted as a prism, breaking the whiteness into every imaginable color. *The Way Forward* rose slowly until it was eye to eye with this level.

As they approached the flagship, David and Catharine did their best to peer in, but they could make out only a few definite shapes amidst the riot of light and spectral color. Of the opaque shapes in the pyramidion's upper interior, they could see vague suggestions of a few large enclosures of various shapes, some cubicle, others more elongated. Some were opaque, others translucent, but no sharp details could be made out.

David spotted a small vehicle moving vertically inside the pyramidion. An elevator, no doubt. While it wasn't precisely opaque, it seemed to be sliding up a dark vertical track.

The Way Forward began moving laterally around the pyramidion.

"Where are we going?" asked Catharine.

Enkidu assured her, "We're moving to a facet that's fitted with a port suitable to admit this craft."

David remarked to himself that the English word *facet* that the Anunnaki used to denominate one side of the pyramidion would have been as well suited for the side of a diamond.

"This craft is small enough to dock inside that one?" asked Catharine.

"Yes," said Enkidu. "The royal pyramidion can readily accommodate a craft the size of *The Way Forward*. As you can see, it's far larger than Her Majesty's pyramidion—or even Lord Enki's."

"*I'll* say," said Catharine.

Enkidu shrugged. "Even a less majestic vessel, such as one of those arrowheads—pardon me, *cruisers*—could swallow this one whole."

The craft slowly rounded the edge of the pyramidion and took up a stationary position about fifty feet from what appeared to be a huge glass wall split vertically down the center—evidently a portal for craft such as theirs. Beyond the portal were shapes suggesting a spacecraft maintenance bay, but there was no one moving about inside.

Exterior lights aimed at the portal flooded it with a cold light. David quietly recited from memory: "*I drew nigh to a wall built of crystals and surrounded by tongues of fire.*"

Catharine looked at him sidelong. "So, Enoch was here," she whispered.

David nodded. "So it appears."

Catharine said, "You don't suppose he's here *now*, do you?"

"I doubt it," mused David, "but how can we be sure?"

The vertical seam between the glass doors split open and the doors opened wide. At the same moment, the videoscreen on Enkidu's console went momentarily black, and flashing white letters appeared:

CONTROL: EXTERNAL

Enkidu drew his hands away from the console as though to avoid an electric shock and turned to Catharine and David. Seeing concern on their faces, he reassured them. "Nothing to worry about. We're in."

The pyramidion doors finished retracting, and *The Way Forward* was remotely guided in. The first thing David and Catharine noticed was the feeling of being insistently tugged down toward the floor. At first, David felt he would collapse onto the deck of his own weight, until he realized what had happened. He'd been returned to normal gravity (or at least normal on Nibiru, which was likely a bit more massive than Earth).

As soon as the craft had passed all the way into the bay, the exterior doors shut firmly behind and the bay began to repressurize. The craft floated to a far corner and was gently lowered onto the floor of a well-lit maintenance bay full of various items of equipment, some seemingly familiar enough to be found in an automotive repair shop on Earth, and others of unrecognizable shape and unknown function. The translucent floor was sparkling clean and the lights below beamed up through it.

The Way Forward needed to wait no longer than a minute for the surrounding bay to be fully repressurized. Its passengers watched the onboard monitors as a door to an adjacent chamber opened. Two sword-bearing Anunnaki soldiers attired in traditional battle dress, complete with shendyt, marched smartly in, and together took up a position precisely where the craft's staircase would touch down when lowered.

One soldier wore a light headset. When he spoke, his voice came through the small craft's public address system.

"Enkidu," he said blithely, "this bay is now fully pressurized and suitable for breathing. Please open your doors, lower your staircase, and prepare to disembark. Leave the passenger's bags on board. We'll have them brought up."

Enkidu pressed a few buttons on the console. As the craft's airtight seal was broken, its internal air pressure equalized with that of the repair bay, leaving Catharine and David with an unpleasant pressure in their ears. They swallowed, as they'd been trained to do, and the pressure dissipated.

Enkidu escorted them to the hatch leading to the staircase and bowed as they passed, Catharine holding tight to David's hand.

As David and Catharine descended, the soldiers came to attention and patiently waited for them to gain their footing and acclimate to the unaccustomed gravity.

David stepped off the staircase and the soldier wearing the headset said, "Good day, Mister Ambassador." He turned to Catharine. "And to you, lieutenant commander. Please pardon our failure to introduce ourselves by our full names, but we expect you would have difficulty pronouncing them. Please address me as Aleph, and my companion here as Bet."

"A pleasure to make your acquaintance," said David, noticing that Enkidu did not descend behind them. "Will you be seeing to … quarters for our pilot?"

Aleph smiled patronizingly. "We will see to your Enkidu unit's maintenance, Mister Ambassador. They *are* lifelike, are they not?"

"Indeed," said David. "Before meeting others aboard, we'd greatly appreciate an opportunity to wash up."

"We'll escort you to your room, sir," said Aleph, "where we hope you'll enjoy the accommodations all the more, having contended with rather Spartan conditions *en route*. I propose we pass through the main observation lobby. Many visitors enjoy the view from there." He walked to a nearby door, opened it, and bowed as David and Catharine stepped through.

As one, David and Catharine looked up in awe. The huge atrium window was filled with an unobstructed view that snatched their breath away. It was the planet Mars, with its scarred rust-colored surface seeming close enough to touch. Indeed, the pyramidion was simply too close to allow the window to take in the whole planet at once. Centered in their view was the planet's lower half, marred by a hideous gash that continued east-west for three thousand miles.

So this is what the universe looks like to its masters, thought David. *A picture window looking out on whatever heavenly body happens to be nearby. No real fear of falling or illness. A mind clear enough to enjoy the music of the spheres without the constant preoccupation of mortality.*

On Earth, he'd occasionally been called *privileged*, but he'd never felt that way. Here and now, however, he *was* truly privileged and with it came an exultancy beyond imagination. *Mine to enjoy, fully and forever.*

Forever? His unmitigated joy proved fleeting, for it took only a moment for the nagging truth to intrude. He was *not* immortal and, unsurprisingly, that dampened his spirits. But it was really the memory of Anzû's thinly veiled offer of *immortality* that spoiled the view.

The elevator car was crystalline, too. The door, the floor, the walls— even the ceiling was crystal. Try though David might to look impassive, he felt giddy. Only one thing was keeping his feet firmly planted: Catharine's hand grasping his own, nearly (but not quite) to the point of pain. Even so, the preponderant impression was that they were being *flung* up to their room, rather than carefully carried. The only visible reminders that they were in fact being carried were a shiny elevator cable (visible through the ceiling) made of some composite he'd never seen before, and the vertical track to which their car was firmly anchored.

The car slowed and stopped, and the door opened onto a wooden floor with throw rugs. "This is as far up as you go for the moment," said Aleph, extending his hand through the open door. He and Bet, still armed with their swords, escorted David and Catharine to their room.

David turned to them. "Are we in danger?" he asked, "Or are the swords purely ceremonial?"

Aleph and Bet exchanged a brief smile. Aleph replied, "As an ancient Anunnaki warrior once said, they're ceremonial … until they're not."

"Sounds like a wise man," said Catharine. "I would have loved to meet him." The guards again exchanged an amused glance.

"Ah, but you *will*, shortly," said Aleph. "In the meantime, your clothes are being laundered and will be brought up later. Please take this hour to cleanse yourselves thoroughly and put on nothing but the traditional Anunnaki garments and sandals in your closets. You will be meeting one who may be approached only in proper clothing and a respectful frame of mind. While neither of you needs to be reminded, please remember your place, and that you will soon be admitted to the presence of the One True King."

While ordinarily David might have offered a friendly quip, instead the blood drained from his face. "You speak true, Aleph. We are ... well aware. Thank you, gentlemen."

The soldiers silently saluted, turned on their heels, and headed back to the elevator.

Standing before their assigned room, Catharine reached for the door-knob, but as soon as her hand approached it, the door opened and allowed them in. Once inside, it closed firmly behind them. "Something tells me security is not an issue here," she said nervously.

David smirked. "I'd imagine security on this ship is the tightest in the solar system."

David finished washing and dressing ten minutes early, while Catharine was still primping before a mirror. The robes they'd been given were made of muslin, and fitted the body's shape closely.

"I think the thread count of this fabric is in the thousands. Kind of gives new meaning to the term *king's muslin*." She turned sideways and examined the reflection of her shape. "The undergarment they gave me is just like a one-piece bathing suit."

David looked up at her. "Whatever it is, it's quite flattering."

She regarded him skeptically. "I couldn't find any makeup. That's unfair to blondes. I look washed out."

David looked at her face. There *was* a certain lack of definition around her eyes, but he'd seen blondes without makeup before, and this one didn't have a bad angle. "You look wonderful. And remember what Zia said. With your coloring, you could be Lord Enki's own daughter. Use it to your advantage."

She turned to him. "Have you noticed how the Anunnaki seem to be mostly either Norse or Semitic?"

"I have."

Suddenly, they were jarred by Aleph's voice emanating from a public address system they didn't know was in the room.

"Bet and I are on our way to your room," said Aleph's disembodied voice.

Catharine was alarmed and mouthed, "Can they hear us?"

"And don't be concerned," said Aleph, "this is a one-way communications system. We can't hear you."

Catharine raised a skeptical eyebrow.

There was a knock at the door. Catharine reached for the knob and once again the door sensed her motion and opened automatically.

Aleph stood outside. Catharine was about to ask him in when she realized that his sword was too bulky to allow him to enter in any event.

"Shall we proceed to the gatehouse?" asked Aleph.

"We're at your service," replied David. "By any chance, will we be awaited by two guards?"

"I expect so," said Aleph. Bet, who'd maintained silence and a stoic expression until now, nodded in agreement.

They proceeded to the elevator, sandals slapping against the hard floors and padding across the rugs. Aleph pressed a button for the top floor, and the door closed.

"Straight to the top," remarked David.

Aleph shook his head. "There are higher floors, but they can't be reached by this elevator bank. You'll need a special escort to get up there."

The door opened, and the brightness was so overwhelming that David and Catharine had to be urged to get off.

"Why's it kept so bright?" asked Catharine.

"You might ask those to whom we'll hand you off," said Aleph, and pointed ahead. "When you get to the gatehouse, please give our best regards." He and Bet snapped to attention and saluted. "God save the king," they pronounced.

Catharine looked to David, who nodded. "God save the king," they echoed as one.

Aleph and Bet reentered the elevator, and the doors closed behind them.

David and Catharine followed a narrow, curving path outlined in blue. At its other end they found a flood-lit structure bearing no resemblance to anything they might have conceived of as a gatehouse. It was an austere, steel-and-glass (or steel-and-crystal), single-storey structure brightly lit both outside and in.

"Why would someone erect a building inside a spacefaring vessel?" asked Catharine. There appeared to be nothing special about it, except that it was a separate structure inside the much larger superstructure of the king's pyramidion.

David shrugged. "If I had to guess, in broad terms, it's a replica of a guardhouse that protected the King of Nibiru long ago, one important enough to warrant its duplication for use in interplanetary travel."

"It's awfully austere," said Catharine. "If the original looked the same, it would have been hard to get sentimental about it. That would be like getting choked up over a bank building on Eighty-Sixth Street."

David shrugged. "The Anunnaki have probably had structures like this for thousands of years."

As they approached the guardhouse, the door spontaneously sprang open, and two big, muscular Anunnaki emerged one at a time, attired in muslin tunics. Their physiques rather resembled those of imaginary superheroes, with massive chests, shoulders, and arms, and staunch thighs and calves. As though to bear out Catharine's earlier observation, one was blond and the other swarthy and Semitic.

"I am David Schubert, United States Ambassador to the Court of King Enlil," David pronounced formally, "and my companion is Lieutenant Commander Catharine Weldon of the United States Navy."

"We've heard a great deal about you both," said the dark one and turned to David with a bemused expression. "Do you know who we are?"

David scratched his head and smiled at the friendly challenge. "I know of only a single Sumerian text naming the Anunnaki king's two guards and that was written long, long ago."

The dark one cocked his head as though failing to recall which text David meant. "And who were the guards?" he asked.

"The king was King Anu, may his name be forever revered."

The two guards muttered a blessing for the dead king in their native tongue.

"That narrows it down," said the dark one, "but not quite enough."

"One of the guards was betrothed to Her Majesty Queen Inanna," said David, "but he is long past."

The dark guard winced. "You refer to Dumuzi, of course," he said, "and that means you are referring to the Book of Adapa."

David bowed respectfully.

The guard continued. "And that also means that the other guard was one of two possible Anunnaki. I would guess it was Ningishzidda."

"Right again," said David with another bow, "although the name has been transcribed as *Gizzida*."

"That's the familiar form of the same name," said the dark one, admiring David's learning.

"It was my pleasure," said David, "to meet Ningishzidda aboard the pyramidion of Lord Enki. Even before that meeting, he'd saved the lives of Queen Inanna, myself, and all the others aboard her pyramidion."

"So, you were aboard when the missile was fired at her?" asked the dark one.

David added, "I boarded Her Majesty's pyramidion shortly after the missile was launched, but before it approached the ship. I was on the bridge with General Shulgi—"

"That *ass*," muttered the dark one.

David struggled not to smile. "Well, the matter was resolved favorably by General Ningishzidda's intervention, whatever General Shulgi's deficiencies."

"*Whatever deficiencies?*" exclaimed the guard. "Wasn't it you who humiliated him and an entire detachment of Anunnaki soldiers using nothing but a small handgun—which you never even *fired* on anyone, Joseph? Do you call that 'whatever deficiencies'?"

Joseph? *Now* David smiled, not because of anything Shulgi had done, but rather because the guard had given away his identity before he intended.

"I am *David*, my lord," David corrected him, which was his way of telling the guard that he now knew his identity.

The dark guard smiled, acknowledging that he'd lost a round he hadn't known he was playing.

David ventured, "I take it you are Lord Ninurta."

The dark one nodded.

It seemed premature to David to mention Queen Inanna's letter to Ninurta, both because there were others present and because he couldn't deliver it presently; he'd been required to leave his bags in *The Way Forward*, one of which contained Inanna's letter. If he were to mention it now, word might get around, and the letter might … disappear.

"May I know the identity of this other gentleman?" asked David.

"This is my cousin Nergal. Welcome aboard."

David bowed briefly and his eyebrows shot up. "So, you are the husband of Queen Inanna's sister Ereshkigal?"

"Ah," said Nergal with a nod, "I see that my fame has preceded me."

David bowed. "We are truly exalted," he said, "to have come face to face with two such great historical figures. Her Majesty spoke most favorably of you both."

What he didn't say was that he was unnerved to be in the presence of the two men who destroyed Sodom and Gomorrah and started the first nuclear war on Earth in their attempt to stop Marduk from seizing the spaceport in the Sinai Desert.

"Well," said Ninurta, "please come in."

As David and Catharine crossed the threshold into the guard house, they barely noticed that its walls and floors were comprised of the same brightly illuminated crystal as the rest of the pyramidion. What struck them was the ceiling, which seemed entirely absent. It was transparent, providing an unobstructed view of the vastness of space, in which one could also see various ships of the fleet maneuvering from place to place, a few firing guidance rockets to make fine adjustments.

Enoch's words echoed in David's mind. *Its ceiling was like the path of the stars and the lightnings, and between them were fiery cherubim, and their heaven was clear as water. A flaming fire surrounded the walls, and its portals blazed with fire.*

CHAPTER 7

BACK IN EARTH orbit on Enki's pyramidion, Gary and Hendrick stood in the chief engineer's booth overlooking the repair station while the pilot of a damaged Anunnaki saucer attempted to guide his craft in.

Though the engineer's booth was comfortable, the repair station on the other side of the glass was airless, as the outer portal had already been opened to admit the craft. In accordance with standing orders, the damaged saucer was making a very low-speed approach from about a thousand feet away.

The engineer's console displayed a detailed moving image of the damaged craft, with hash marks showing all material distances.

Tension in the booth was palpable.

The chief engineer turned to Gary. "I don't like the way that craft is wobbling. If the pilot's unlucky, he could damage the repair bay doors." He adjusted the view on his screen. "And then we'd really have a problem."

Gary asked, "What happens if the doors are damaged?"

"Well," said the engineer, "there's another repair station on the opposite side of the pyramidion, but it has only three bays and they lack the most advanced equipment, most of which is bolted to the floor right here. We'd prefer not to be without our most advanced equipment, especially with potential hostiles on the planet." He turned to Gary and Hendrick and nodded apologetically. "I meant to say *on Earth*. Sorry."

"It's okay," said Gary. "We know Earth's a planet."

"As you can imagine, our crews have come to rely on the most advanced equipment, and they'd have to be retrained to do things the old-fashioned way."

"I know that tune by heart," said Gary.

The engineer turned to him. "Figure of speech?"

Gary smirked. "Yeah, sorry. What kind of clearance does the pilot have coming through the portal?"

The engineer fussed with his dials. "An incoming saucer has only ten feet of lateral clearance on each side of his craft, and the vertical clearance is even smaller." He looked at Gary dismally. "About six feet."

Gary whistled softly. "That portal is designed too small."

"We've been saying that for thousands of your years," said the engineer, "but nobody listens, and we've had only one potentially catastrophic entry in all that time."

The image of the saucer on the screen slowly drifted off its vertical orientation and then violently shook with a sudden back and forth, as its wobble was violently corrected by onboard computers that seemed to overcorrect, then overcorrect in the opposite direction. This back-and-forth struggle continued several times until the craft at last restabilized.

Gary shook his head. "This pilot's brains are gonna be a milkshake if you leave him out there much longer. What are his options if you abort entry into the repair station?"

"Well," said the engineer, "none of the other craft in our detachment—"

"Detachment?" asked Gary.

"Yes, Lord Enki's group is just a detachment from the king's fleet. As I was about to say, the risk to the other craft of allowing a damaged saucer to board would be exponentially greater. They wouldn't end up with just a damaged door (serious as that is); their whole craft could be threatened."

"So where does the pilot go if he can't get in here?" asked Gary.

"He'd have to *try* to land safely on Earth." The engineer shook his head gravely.

"You don't like his prospects," said Gary.

The engineer pointed at the image. "That kind of wobble is barely manageable in space, with no air resistance. In-atmosphere, it's a death sentence. The internal correction mechanism is inevitably overwhelmed by capricious air currents." He glanced up at Gary. "You know of the crash at Roswell, New Mexico?"

Gary's eyebrows shot up. "That was one of yours?"

"No, but our saucers suffer from the same infirmity as theirs." A red light on the console began to flash. "Oh, damn. The pilot is losing consciousness."

"Can you take control of the craft from this booth?" asked Gary.

The engineer nodded. "Androids don't care, of course," said the engineer, "but you wouldn't believe how live pilots hate it when we do that."

"I'd believe it," said Gary, "and can well understand it. A craft is an extension of its pilot. At least, that's how the pilot feels. Havin' your craft flown to safety by somebody on the outside is like bein' a sportsman carried off the field. Much better to go under your own steam."

The mechanic nodded sagely, but then looked at Gary with a confused expression. "Humans play sports with steam?"

Hendrick turned away to hide his smile.

Gary smirked. "Just an expression. It means it's better to leave on your own two feet than be carried off the field."

The mechanic nodded. "Yes, this seems to be very much the same."

"Do it," said Gary, rather preemptively. "Take control."

The engineer pressed a button on the console and the panel lit up with outsized letters. CONTROL: EXTERNAL.

The videoscreen now showed the view from the pilot's seat. Almost on cue, it began to jitter violently again.

Gary said, "Geez, I can't imagine the pilot's disorientation during one of these jitter sessions. Scrambled brains."

"It's alright," said the engineer, pointing to the pilot's vital signs. "He's unconscious."

"You gonna bring 'er in?" asked Gary, noticing a certain reticence on the engineer's part.

"I have no choice," he said. "But I'm an engineer," he said with a crooked smile, "not much of a pilot."

The engineer flipped on power to a joystick built right into the console and awkwardly placed his hand on it. The pilot's-eye view on the videoscreen showed the saucer slowly approaching the repair station's open portal. Gary could see himself, a dot in the engineer's booth ahead. It was a strange out-of-body experience.

When the craft had reached the halfway mark, the jitter began again.

"Oh, shit," muttered Gary. "Better stop and wait for the correction."

The engineer stopped the craft and took his hand off the joystick. Gary glanced over at him and saw that he was sweating profusely.

Gary said, "That jitter goes *way* beyond your portal's clearance. You're gonna have to try again when it dies down. If it jitters on the way in or, worse, after it enters the repair station, there's gonna be a world-class shitstorm." He glanced at the walls of the little booth. "Needless to say, we'll be the first casualties."

The engineer was near tears. "I can't let that happen."

Gary looked at him grimly. "So, what're you gonna do? Send him to crash in the desert?"

The engineer shook his head. "I can't do that, either. He's unconscious; he could kill others. He can't land at all."

"So—" Gary stopped himself. He thought he knew where this was going, and didn't care for it one bit. He put his hands on his hips. "So, what are you gonna do?"

The engineer pointed to a flashing red button that showed a simple line-drawing of a saucer behind the universal red slash symbol, such as one would see on a traffic sign on Earth.

Gary regarded him with horror. "You're gonna kill a sleeping pilot?"

"It's protocol," said the engineer, his eyes red with horror. "I have no choice." He put his hands over his face. "And this pilot's one of my closest friends."

Hendrick saw Gary's face and body tense up as though he was about to deliver a roundhouse right to the engineer's face. He placed a restraining hand firmly on Gary's shoulder. "Can *you* bring it in, boss?" he asked.

Gary calmed down enough to begin thinking clearly again. He would ordinarily have said *or die trying*, but rejected that phrase as unhelpful under the circumstances. "I think so. Engineer, can you tell from your computer there how often one of these jitter episodes happens and how long it takes to self-correct?"

The engineer snapped to attention and began typing into his console, having been assigned a purpose only he could fulfill. "The past three episodes—uniformly—took twelve seconds to begin and conclude. Between the end of each jitter session and the commencement of the next has been—fairly uniformly—ninety seconds, although there's some variability."

"So," said Gary, now sweating, "if we move the saucer to a point just outside the portal, wait twelve seconds for an event to commence and subside, and we bring him in immediately, we'll have about ninety seconds to land him in a repair bay and shut him down. Is that enough time?"

The engineer used his arm to wipe the sweat from his brow. "An average landing takes one-hundred-twenty seconds from entry to touchdown. Oh, but that's under pilot control—and without duress."

"What about under external control?" asked Gary.

"We don't keep statistics for that. There are no standard times for landing a dangerously incapacitated craft in a repair bay—since we never admit them."

"Well," said Gary, "this one's not dangerously incapacitated as long as its episodes are predictable." He looked at the engineer with a deliberately innocuous expression. "Would you like me to bring him in?"

The engineer hopped out of his seat like it was hot, and said, "Please."

Gary sat down and put his hand on the joystick. "Can I take it once around outside, just to get a feel for it?"

"I suggest you do," said the engineer. "Just keep the speed down, just in case we lose control."

Gary grunted his assent. "This is weird," he said. "I'm in the pilot seat, but I can see myself in this booth." He scratched his head. "Well, that should help, actually."

He turned the craft about and proceeded some distance away from the pyramidion. He gently turned it a few times, accelerating and decelerating.

The engineer interrupted his train of thought. "Don't wander too far. Traffic lanes begin only a few thousand feet out from the pyramidion."

"Got it," mumbled Gary as he turned the craft slowly back toward the pyramidion. The craft moved gracefully toward the portal until Hendrick could see its running lights right outside the portal, where it came to rest.

The saucer sat quietly for a minute or so, then began to list almost imperceptibly to starboard. Instantly, its onboard computer righted it, but overcompensated and it listed to port. Back and forth it went several times before coming to rest just outside the portal.

But then, for the first time, it listed to starboard *again* and underwent another jitter episode of the same duration. Gary wiped his brow. "Well now, *that's* new." Without hesitation, he added. "Which numbered bay, Eng?"

"Two," said the engineer. "Watch the scaffolding."

"Time me on this, Eng. As soon as the jitter calms down, I'm bringin' her in."

Under Gary's control, the saucer slowly entered and began creeping toward the bay with a large numeral 2.

"Counting up. Fifteen seconds. Thirty seconds."

The saucer made a controlled turn.

"Forty-five seconds."

Now Hendrick found himself sweating and wanting to cheer Gary on like this was a horse-race.

The saucer moved over a few large items of equipment in Bay 3.

"Sixty seconds," said the engineer. "Better pick up the pace, lieutenant. It takes fifteen seconds just to lower the craft into position."

While it wasn't visible through the videoscreen, Gary could see through the glass that the craft's wheels were not quite high enough to pass safely over a few beakers sitting atop some sort of console.

"What's in the beakers, Eng?" he said with that amazingly calm pilot voice. "I'd rather not push the craft up if I can avoid it."

"Nothing of consequence," came the reply. "Crash them."

One of the craft's tires bumped the beakers off the console, which crashed noiselessly to the floor in the airless lock.

But the craft moved steadily.

Having maneuvered the craft over the vacant bay, Gary said, "Lowering now."

The craft came down to about five feet off the floor and began slowly listing to starboard.

"Shit!" said Gary and pulled the lever all the way down. The craft dropped the last few feet with no visible damage—and corrected to port. "Kill the power, Eng!" he shouted.

Before he even got the words out, the engineer slammed his palm down on the power switch. The craft wobbled slightly and stopped cold.

That was it. The craft was safely at rest.

"Afraid your buddy's gonna have a bad headache after that bounce," observed Gary.

The engineer jumped for joy and grabbed Gary by the hand.

"Thank you, lieutenant!" he said warmly. "Thank you for saving my friend's life."

Gary smiled smugly. "Least I could do for a fellow pilot," he said. He wagged his finger in the engineer's face. "You gotta enlarge these frickin' portals, y'hear?"

"I'll tell my superiors," said the engineer, who then proceeded to give Hendrick a big hug.

⤐∘⟃⟄∘⬳

IN A HALF hour, the portals had been closed and air returned to the repair station. The pilot was removed immediately through the craft's emergency hatch. Though he was unconscious, his vitals were strong, and Gary and the chief engineer got a robust thumbs-up from the emergency technician.

While collapsible scaffolding was wheeled up to the malfunctioning craft, Gary said to the chief engineer, "I'm surprised this doesn't happen more often, with all the junk orbiting around Earth."

The engineer regarded him curiously. "What makes you think it *doesn't* happen all the time?"

"You mean, it does?"

The mechanic nodded. "We've had to do fourteen repairs on saucers colliding with orbital junk since we arrived here."

"Really?"

"Yes," replied the engineer. "In fact, some of our mechanics have developed a specialty in this type of repair. A dedicated repair crew will be arriving in a minute."

As Gary and Hendrick looked on, two mechanics appeared and raised the collapsible scaffolding to the level of the engine repair hatch.

"Come on out to the repair floor," said the engineer, opening the door and descending the small staircase.

While Gary and the engineer conversed, Hendrick (in full bodyguard mode) saw a door open across the repair bay. Through it emerged a group of three familiar faces. Though it took Hendrick a few moments to recall precisely where he'd seen them before, he knew immediately that someone was missing—someone who'd been with them last time. A woman.

Gary recognized them, too, and broke off his conversation with the engineer. He hailed the leader of the group.

"Hello, Sibzianu!" he shouted. "Where have you been these past two weeks?"

"Vacation!" shouted Sibzianu across the bay. Sibzianu nudged one of his companions and pointed toward Gary and Hendrick. Sibzianu and his companion both waved.

Gary and Hendrick waved back, all smiles.

Sibzianu walked toward Gary and Hendrick with his friends in tow.

As the newcomers approached, Gary said, "You mean, you and your lazy crew haven't done a lick o' maintenance since certifyin' our friends' antimatter vehicle?"

"Haven't lifted a finger," announced Sibzianu proudly, as his two khaki-clad companions, who evidently had no interest in small talk, climbed up the scaffolding to commence repairs.

Hendrick paid no attention to the remaining banter between Gary and Sibzianu, preoccupied as he was watching the other two team members climb the scaffold, especially the android, who so resembled Doctor Zia's Enkidu.

The android wore a khaki shirt with quarter-length sleeves, precisely what he'd worn the last (and only) time Hendrick saw him. For all

Hendrick knew, the android might not even have changed clothes since working on the antimatter craft (what was it dubbed later? *The Way Forward?*), as his synthetic body probably didn't secrete anything unpleasant. For androids, as everyone knew, clothes were just props.

That's when Hendrick caught sight of the streak of black ink and immediately sensed disaster. Four inches high and one wide, the streak ran from the android's right elbow up to his shirt cuff. There might even have been some ink on the bottom edge of the cuff itself, though Hendrick couldn't be sure from this distance.

He strained to recall everything about the first appearance of Sibzianu and his crew as they prepared to perform a preflight check on the vehicle that was, even now, transporting David and Catharine to the royal fleet. There'd been Sibzianu, another male mechanic, the android, and a female mechanic. *Where is* she *now?* he wondered.

Hendrick gently nudged Gary to get his attention.

Sibzianu, evidently realizing that Gary was being called away, ended the conversation affably. "Let's have a drink after this job."

"Good deal," said Gary and shook Sibzianu's hand, a human custom that lower-level Anunnaki had readily adopted. Sibzianu followed his crewmembers up the scaffolding.

Gary turned to Hendrick. "'Sup, boss?" he said.

"You remember the last time we saw this crew?" asked Hendrick.

Gary nodded. "There was a woman, too, wasn't there?"

Hendrick nodded. "Yeah. Where is she?"

Gary shrugged. "I suppose she might have been called to another job."

"True," admitted Hendrick, "but *that's* not my worry."

Gary's forehead furrowed. "You've got a worry? Tell me."

Hendrick proceeded. "You remember how Doctor Zia's Enkidu droid got all angry when he saw that the mechanics had brought an 'improved' version of the same android line?"

"Called himself 'Hammy,'" said Gary humorously. "Dead ringer."

"You remember that Hammy made fun of Enkidu because he was going to check for engine leaks using black ink?"

Gary nodded again, warily this time. "Yeah," he said. "As I recall, Enkidu stormed off and boarded the vehicle first."

"Right," said Hendrick. "That guy at the computer looked up Enkidu's location and told us Enkidu was alone in the engine room." He paused. "Do you suppose Enkidu would have let Hammy into the engine room?"

Gary shook his head emphatically. "No way. He was in no mood."

"Okay," said Hendrick. "Now, be careful not to show any reaction, boss. Just casually look up at the android on the scaffold when he turns away."

Although Gary regarded Hendrick skeptically, long experience told him to take Hendrick's intuition seriously. Gary casually knelt to re-tie one of his shoes, then slowly rose and glanced up at the android. Careful to avoid staring too long, he quickly shifted his glance to Hendrick. "Okay, what am I looking for?" he asked.

"You see the black streak on his right arm above the elbow?" asked Hendrick.

Without looking again, Gary nodded. "Saw it," he said matter-of-factly. Then its significance slowly dawned on him and he turned away from the repair crew. His eyes went wide. "What does it mean?" he asked warily.

Hendrick also turned away from the repair crew. "It could mean a few things. It could mean we're wrong, and Enkidu allowed Hammy into the engine room while he was checking seals. But we've already agreed that's unlikely."

"Or," said Gary, picking up the thought, "it could mean Hammy got a black streak on his arm at some other job." Gary shook his head and criticized his own observation. "But the team leader just said they haven't done any jobs since they were here." He turned to Hendrick. "What explanations does that leave us?"

Hendrick sighed. "The droid up on the platform is Zia's droid. Enkidu."

Now Gary was worried. "That would mean that the droid piloting David and Catharine's craft is Hammy." His consternation grew. "But what would be the *point* of switching the two?"

"Not sure," said Hendrick, "but I can't think of a reason that isn't *really* bad for the home team."

Gary was quiet for a minute. "But, if the one on the platform is Enkidu, why would he join a conspiracy? Why wouldn't he act like himself? I mean, he hasn't so much as *acknowledged* us."

Hendrick was quiet for a while. Finally, he shrugged and said uncertainly, "Could they've reprogrammed Enkidu ... and Hammy, too?" He snapped his fingers quietly. "The guy at the console—what was his name?"

"*Kassam*, I think," offered Gary.

"Yeah, that's it," replied Hendrick. "Didn't he say he was a robotics expert?"

Gary nodded apprehensively. "With a minor in artificial intelligence." He turned to Hendrick. "We've got to tell someone about this."

"Tell *whom*?" asked Hendrick.

"Well," said Gary, "we're duty-bound to tell the admiral first."

Hendrick frowned. "How do we do that without telling a lot of other people at the same time, such as someone who's in on the conspiracy? We'd have to send the admiral a message by encrypted radio. But we've been ordered to assume that the … locals have broken our encryption. We're also supposed to assume the walls have ears."

"Okay," said Gary, getting a bit frustrated. "Who do *you* think we should tell?"

"Zia?" proposed Hendrick with a shrug.

"What if *he's* in on it, Einstein?" snapped Gary. "Geez, we can't even tell one of the Anunnaki *generals*, like Shulgi, can we?"

"We *could* go straight to Lord Enki," observed Hendrick.

"Oh? And just how do we make an appointment directly with *him*?" asked Gary. "Somethin' tells me if we went up to his chambers, the best we could hope for is bein' dragged by the ear to the nearest exit, which *everybody* would learn about—and the bad guys would learn we're onto them." He moved his head from side to side equivocally. "On the bright side, the Anunnaki could just shoot us. *That* would solve the problem … but only for you and me. Besides … approaching Enki would be considered a *diplomatic* foray. Talk about somethin' I've got no authority or competence to do. Well, there's *another* bright spot," he said with a smile. "Uncle *Sam* could shoot us."

Hendrick smirked darkly and shrugged.

Gary said, "We need to tell *someone*. Gotta figure the odds on somethin' like this."

Hendrick perked up, because 'the odds' was something Gary usually seemed to have a handle on. "Perhaps a close family member?"

Gary chewed the inside of his cheek and reasoned aloud. "Ever read Shakespeare? Royal families are *teemin'* with traitors and usurpers. They're the ones with the biggest incentives to get rid of the top gun, so they can step right into his shoes." He relented. "Still, you've got a point." He looked up at Hendrick. "You thinkin' who *I'm* thinkin'?"

Hendrick whispered, "Ningishzidda?"

Gary nodded. "Yeah … but, geez, he's Enki's eldest surviving son. Heir to everything Enki's got."

"I can't come up with a better suggestion," Hendrick admitted.

Gary shook his head with a sigh of resignation. "Now, we just gotta figure out how to survive the humiliation if it turns out Hammy just got some shoe polish on his arm."

Hendrick smirked and tossed out one of Gary's favorite sayings. "As you've often said, 'Better safe than sorry.'"

⟶◦⟅⟆◦⟵

GARY AND HENDRICK found Ningishzidda on the bridge of Enki's pyramidion, alone except for his executive officer.

Approaching the bridge, they introduced themselves through the wall-mounted intercom and asked to speak with the general privately. Ningishzidda asked if it was urgent.

"We think so, general," said Gary, "but we can't be sure."

Ningishzidda turned the conn over to his executive officer and stepped out into the hallway.

Gary began. "General, we—"

Ningishzidda put up his hand and shook his head. "Not out here," he said, and escorted them to a private room with a small conference table. "Go ahead," he said, taking a seat.

Gary deferred to Hendrick to say what first aroused his suspicion. Gary then advised the general of their speculation.

Ningishzidda held his hand up once again. "What's the nature of the repairs the suspect mechanics are making?" he asked.

"They're fixing a saucer that was damaged when it collided with some orbiting debris," said Gary.

The general pressed a button on the table. "Repair bay, this is the captain," he said.

"Yes, captain," said a voice.

"Repair bay, I'm concerned about the number of collisions we've experienced with space debris. I'd like to get a first-hand view from a repair crew. Do you currently have a specialized crew in the repair bay?"

"Yes, we do, captain. They're working on the repair right now. Shall I have them stop work?"

"No, let them finish. Have they worked on more than one repair of this kind?"

"Yes, sir. They've worked on all of them. They're the most experienced we have on this type of repair."

"Perfect," said the general with a wink to his visitors. "Keep them on premises. It may take me some time to get down there, so, when the repair is complete, tell the commissary to deliver whatever food they want."

"Yes, captain. *Er*, including spirits?"

"*Except* spirits."

The general pushed another button that cut the connection, immediately removed his handheld communicator from his pocket, and pushed a few buttons. He held the communicator up to his ear so that his visitors could hear only his end of the call.

"It's Ningishzidda, my lord. I hope I do not disturb you." There was a pause. "You are completely alone?" *Pause.* "Yes, completely, my lord." *Pause.* "No, not even Zia, my lord, and I request that he be sent away and not be told that I'm coming." *Pause.* "I shall bring with me two earthlings." *Pause.* "Very well, my lord. We'll be there in five minutes."

Ningishzidda pressed the button that cut off the connection.

"You've come to the right place, gentlemen," he said. "You're quite sure you've told no one else?"

"No one else," said Gary while Hendrick nodded in agreement. "We came straight here."

"Excellent," said the general.

Gary and Hendrick were surprised to learn that Ningishzidda had a private elevator. When the door opened, Ningishzidda held up his hand and got on first.

"Elevator," he said, "stop recording. Make no report or record of this trip or personnel."

"Yes, general," said the ubiquitous alto voice.

The general beckoned his companions onto the elevator, which zipped off much more quickly than the public elevators. When they arrived on Enki's floor, the general got off first and gesticulated with his hand. "Okay," he said, "the cameras are off. You can come out."

Ningishzidda led them through a door under an ornately carved saying that neither human understood. The door closed behind them and the general led them to the darkened receiving room where Enki awaited them on his throne.

"Ningishzidda, my son and heir," said Enki in a subdued version of his famously booming voice, "let us hope that this is the beginning of the end for our disloyal subjects." He turned to Gary and Hendrick, who both bowed before him. "Thank you for coming, gentlemen. My son informs me that you have been most discreet in the way that you approached him. That is commendable."

Gary and Hendrick straightened and were a little unnerved to find themselves being observed by the luminous eyes of a giant.

"We wish to help, my lord," said Gary, a phrase that sounded absurdly formal in a West Texas accent. "We would have gone to our own people first, but we expected that our communications might be monitored by the very people we wish to expose." Gary explained Hendrick's discovery of the ink mark on the android and its likely meaning.

Enki leaned back and, after contemplating the situation, arrived at his conclusion. "I could send one of you back to Earth with this news on some pretext, but I'd prefer to wait for you to be called. How much longer are you planning to remain with us on the pyramidion?"

Gary replied, "We were planning to stay until our friends come home from Mars." It sounded so weird to hear himself say that, as though he'd found himself trapped in some sci-fi novel. "That's at least a couple of weeks."

Enki shook his head. "That's too long for this business to wait. Let's wait a day or two and see how things develop. If need be, we'll come up with some reason to send one of you down there sooner."

CHAPTER 8

THE MARINE DIMMED the lights in the Oval Office, and drew down a flexible videoscreen for use.

The President shook his head mournfully and took a sip of coffee. "Bob, I must be gettin' old," he told the admiral. "I can remember when the thing they'd be pullin' down was a blank screen, and they'd be wheeling in a projector. Now all the electronics have been shrunk down into this paper-thin widescreen image—with stereo sound, no less."

The admiral looked at his friend askance. "You've got to admit, Jim, this screen provides a much better view."

"Oh, I'll admit it," said the President reluctantly. "Still ... just doesn't feel right."

The marine snapped to attention. "Sir, would you like me to stick around ... or are you confident with that handheld control device?"

The President raised the device in his hand and shook it at the marine. "They used to call this a 'remote.'"

The marine smiled. "They still do, sir, but they're usually talkin' about a device that changes channels. There's only one channel on this screen, and it's a live, encrypted broadcast. That handheld you've got there is basically just a volume control for the audio. It's also got a *Pause* button, but I wouldn't use it if I were you; you'll lose simultaneity with the action. And good luck getting it back on track once that happens."

The President raised an eyebrow at the admiral, silently mouthed *simultaneity*, and arched an eyebrow at the marine. "You think you should stay? Just in case?"

The marine equivocated. "Well, sir—"

The admiral interceded. "Marine, what say you give your mobile number to Holly and hang around outside, so's we can drag you in here if we really bollocks things up?"

The marine waited for the President to chime in. When he didn't, the marine said, "I think that's a terrific idea, admiral." He saluted and left the two old friends alone. As yet, the screen was blank and quiet.

"What're we seeing here first, Bob?" asked the President.

"First shot should be from a few hours ago when the whack-a-mole popped up through the Antarctic ice."

"How'd we know when that would happen?" asked the President.

"Well, Jim," said the admiral, "the bad guys don't coordinate with us. But they've sent out a fighter at the same hour every day for the last nine days—which is as long as we've been surveilling their little hole in the ice. Besides, if the bogey hadn't appeared on schedule, this exercise would have been canceled, and you and I would be playing poker instead of watching this screen."

"And who did you send to intercept the bogey?"

"Buck Buchanan and … Muñoz—one of his trainees," said the admiral, "in one of those little SF-5s."

"Navy flyers are *really* gettin' used to that saucer contraption?" the President asked skeptically.

The admiral exuded confidence. "Like fish to water."

"Lousy metaphor for a machine that flies. Won't the bogey spot Buck?"

"Nah," the admiral assured him. "While the bogey's airborne, Buck's closest approach will be about thirty miles to its rear, so he'll be hidden from view by the curvature of the Earth."

"How's he gonna get a clear view of the bogey from so far back?" asked the President.

"We've got more than a dozen skeeters aloft, two of which will practically be flyin' up the bogey's ass."

"Skeeters?" echoed the President, evidently unfamiliar with the term.

"Technically, they're *photodrones*, but we call 'em *skeeters*."

"What happens if the bogey catches sight of a skeeter?"

The admiral smugly removed two cigars from his breast pocket and offered one to his friend.

"Not for me," said the President, waving it off. "But you can feel free."

The admiral put the declined cigar back in his pocket, peeled the cellophane and label off the other one, and cut off the tip with a device he kept attached to his keychain. Only since America's nuclear arsenal had begun to return to service did the admiral feel confident enough to bring a cigar into the Oval Office. "Never in a million years," he said with relish, "will a bogey catch sight of a skeeter."

"Why not?" asked the President, confident the admiral wanted him to ask just that.

"Because they're smaller than male mosquitoes," said the admiral, "and they transmit encrypted video signal."

"Why use so many?" asked the President.

"Well, they're not rockets, after all, so they wouldn't be able to keep up with a saucer going full tilt. So, we place skeeters at strategic locations in the sky—at points where we expect they'll provide us with important views."

The President asked, "Who's directing this *cinéma-vérité*?"

"Which camera's feed appears on this screen is determined by a computer program known as *Director-in-a-Can*. What you and I see will be based in part on which camera's detecting the most movement, but the software has brains enough to know which parts of the mission are most important to us." The admiral took another puff. "As for why we've got so many skeeters up there? Well … once in a long while, one of 'em will get snapped up by a predatory bird. When that happens, we still have a bunch of 'em on duty."

Without warning, the videoscreen lit up a beautiful bright blue. At first glance, there seemed to be no image at all. The whole frame seemed to consist of sky. But a moment's study revealed a whitish blur at the base of the screen.

"This was taken a few hours ago," said the admiral. "That's a skeeter's-eye-view of the enemy's Antarctic hidey-hole."

"Why was the camera aimed so high?" asked the President, but his question was quickly answered when a small dark object spurted up from the hole into the sky, then leveled off and flew past the camera in a split second. "Was that the bogey?"

The admiral nodded gravely, leaned in toward the screen, and took a puff from his cigar. "Since this footage was recorded, Buck's taken up a position on the bogey's usual route where he can lie in wait."

Now that the President had something to look at, he leaned in earnestly, too. "Is Buck gonna shoot him down?"

The admiral scowled and shook his head. "*No way.* The purpose of the mission is to capture the bogey's radio equipment … so we can figure out how to foul up his communications. Can't get working equipment from a total wreck."

The President seemed confused. "I thought you said the bogey's pilot would be killed."

"He will be," said the admiral, "but Buck's job is limited to hoodwinking the pilot, making him doubt the airworthiness of his craft so he'll land out of caution and get out to check his airframe. Once the pilot is … destroyed on the ground, Buck's orders are to land real quick, grab the radio, and run like hell." He blew a smoke ring. "If we've learned anything from Hendrick, it's that the only way to understand alien technology is to get our dirty little hands on the real thing and put our scientists to work on it."

"So," said the President, "if Buck's not going to take out the pilot, who's going to do that?"

"Cannon drone," replied the admiral. "It's been programmed to blow the pilot's head into tiny little pieces without damaging the craft."

"Sounds gratuitously violent," observed the President.

"Not at all," the admiral assured him. "Remember: Whatever the pilot sees, the *progenitor* sees. It would defeat our whole purpose if the bad guys were to learn we've got one of their radios. If the bogey pilot sees the radio being taken, the progenitor would see it immediately. Even if the pilot *doesn't* see the radio being taken but his *headset* still works, it can send a zombie radio signal, providing the bad guys with plenty of information that we don't want them to have. On the other hand, if both the pilot and his headset are dead, Buck can remove the radio unseen. As soon as he clears the area, the drones will obliterate what remains of the enemy saucer, so there'll be nothing left to tip off the bastards that we've got one of their boomboxes."

"Sneaky," muttered the President admiringly.

The feed changed to another skeeter. The bogey flew past it and once again receded into the distance. Yet another skeeter showed the bogey come into view and rocket past.

"Okay," said the admiral, "that's the end of the feed showing the bogey's takeoff early this morning. Everything from now on will be in real time."

The image cut away to a real-time skeeter view.

The admiral said, "The skeeter sending us this feed is waiting for the bogey to arrive at the Straits of Magellan at the tip of South America." Almost on cue, the bogey appeared as a dot on the screen and began rapidly growing in size. As it approached the camera, the admiral shouted, "That's it! See it wobble?"

"Yeah," said the President. "What's going on?"

"At this point, that's what the *pilot's* asking himself. He has no idea that Buck's jamming his stabilization system." A minute later, the admiral added, "About now, he's looking for a place to land."

"Where is he, again?" asked the President.

"Southern tip of Chile, where he'll find lots of promising landing spots."

The view was handed off to another skeeter that showed the bogey land on a remote mountainside. When the enemy pilot's hatch popped open, the skeeter-cam zoomed in on it. The square-bearded pilot climbed down an emergency ladder, dropped to the ground, and began toward the rear of the saucer. But he never got there. Instead, his head disappeared in a spray of red.

In another minute or so, Buck's saucer appeared in the frame and landed next to the downed bogey. Buck got out and visually confirmed that his adversary (and his headset) were out of commission. He climbed up the alien saucer's emergency ladder and into its cockpit, where he began tugging on a component in the control panel that didn't seem to want to budge.

The feed showing Buck contemplating how to remove the radio disappeared, replaced by blue sky, with a little white ice at the base of the screen. Apparently, the "director" was resuming the feed from the first skeeter, the one that—hours earlier—had spotted the bogey emerging from under the ice.

"What the hell?" said the President. "Why are we back at Square One?"

The admiral sat up slack-jawed, and the lit cigar dropped from his lips to the table. "This feed is in real time. This skeeter must be detecting motion. Oh, shit," he muttered, as two more bogeys spurted through the hole in the ice and rocketed past the skeeter in the same direction as the first. "The bastard must have gotten a signal off," said the admiral. "Probably a passive alarm." He stood up excitedly. "Buck," he shouted, pressing the palm of his hand to his forehead with a look of utter dismay, "grab it and get the hell outta there!"

The President's eyes opened wide. "Can he hear you?"

The admiral picked up the cigar from the table before it could start a fire and shook his head sadly. "No, he can't."

ON THE ROYAL pyramidion, Ninurta and Nergal escorted David and Catharine along several vacant passageways flooded by light that shone up at them through the floors below. After a few twists and turns, David realized that they were being guided through a highly complex labyrinth.

"I was wondering," ventured David, "how we could ever get back here without your guidance."

Ninurta exchanged a knowing glance with Nergal and they snickered.

"It's not for you to know," said Ninurta.

Catharine and David exchanged a glance of their own. Evidently, they both found Ninurta's phrase rather paternalistic, much like "don't worry your pretty little head about such matters." David stored the phrase away for future use.

Their long passage through the maze brought them to double wooden doors several times taller than those barring entrance to the throne room on Enki's pyramidion. The doors to the royal throne room, like those leading into Enki's, were topped by bejeweled words. Though these words differed from those at Enki's, they appeared to be written in the same Hebrew-like characters.

David tried in vain to sound out the letters in his mind, applying the limited skills he'd learned as an adolescent in Hebrew school, but several letters were either drawn differently from their equivalents in modern Hebrew—or were native to an entirely different (though similar-looking) alphabet.

As there seemed to be a hush over this part of the pyramidion, David whispered. "Is that a riddle, like the one over the entrance to Lord Enki's throne room?"

Ninurta leaned down and whispered. "It's not a riddle, but it's referred to in your Bible. I'll translate it for you sometime, but not now." Before Ninurta could knock, someone inside the throne room opened the door a crack.

A very tall, blonde Anunnaki emerged with her finger over her lips, leaving the door behind her ajar. Through the small gap between the doors, David and Catharine could see that the room was dark. (Evidently, His Majesty was not best pleased by being blinded by bright lights shining up through his floor at all hours.)

A breeze wafted out into the hallway, gently tousling the lady's long golden locks. It was unexpectedly strong, suggesting that the room from which she'd emerged was quite large. Its pleasant scent reminded David of well-curated parchment documents, as though he and Catharine were standing outside a museum's great hall after hours, awaiting admission by special invitation.

Nergal and Ninurta both silently dropped to one knee before the lady, and David and Catharine followed suit.

The lady pulled the giant door nearly shut behind her and whispered to Nergal. "His Majesty sleeps," she whispered.

Ninurta raised his face to avoid the need to raise his voice. "We would not disturb His Majesty, my mother Queen Ninlil, but that His Majesty ordered us to do so upon arrival of the two *adams* who now kneel before you." David recognized *adams* to mean *earthlings*.

Queen Ninlil pursed her lips. "Who are they?"

Though tempted to introduce himself, David recognized that it was not his place to interrupt speech among foreign royals or to address them until spoken to.

Ninurta pointed his chin at David. "This man is ambassador from the *adams* to His Majesty's Court. The woman is a famous warrior who has been victorious in a skirmish against Anzû, destroying one of his spacecraft and numerous subjects."

As David anticipated, the Queen ignored him completely and placed her palm under Catharine's chin, raising her face to view.

"So beautiful," said the Queen, "and so delicately small. Yet, so deadly. We know many species with females of this kind. Is that not correct, Ninurta my son?"

"Truly, madam," said Ninurta.

To David's surprise, the Queen left the door open and took a further step forward. "Far be it from me to countermand the King's command," she said quietly. "Try not to disturb His Majesty's slumber longer than necessary." And with that, she walked off toward the maze, evidently confident in her knowledge of the way through.

David's eye followed the Queen until she disappeared around a turn. When he turned back, all eyes were on him. Ninurta bowed to David and Catharine, and beckoned them with a wave of his hand to enter the throne room. Nergal followed them in.

Even in darkness, the room was most impressive. It appeared to be nearly square, roughly one hundred twenty feet on each side, lined with perhaps thirty fluted Doric columns. The ceiling was too high to see in such dim light. The floor was marble, or some Nibirune equivalent. A foot or two above eye-level (which *was* eye-level for the average Anunnaki) were wall hangings, presumably rugs and paintings, all too dark to make out, though many appeared to be framed in a shiny metal, presumably gold.

At the center of the room stood a massive pedestal on which sat a huge sculpture of a seated nobleman enrobed as an ancient Greek (perhaps a shrine to the late King Anu), calling to mind countless statues of Zeus and other ancient gods. The throne on which the figure rested was about the size and shape of the statuary chair at the Lincoln

Memorial in America's capital. David recalled hearing that, if the figure of Lincoln had been depicted in a standing position, his statue would have stood nearly thirty feet tall.

Ninurta and Nergal escorted David and Catharine to the far end of the dark room, turned them about to face the central statue, and stood sternly at attention with their partisans at their sides.

David turned and whispered to Ninurta, "Has someone been dispatched to rouse His Majesty?"

Ninurta regarded him skeptically and pointed his chin upward toward the head of the statue which had, until now, been too dark to see.

When David looked up this time, however, the statue's eyes were open, emitting golden beams of light that quickly swung down to spotlight him and Catharine.

So it became clear that this colossus was not an alabaster likeness of King Anu, as David expected, but rather his son King Enlil—in the flesh.

So shocked was David that he gasped aloud and would have fallen over backwards had each of Ninurta and Nergal not grabbed him by a shoulder and propped him up long enough to regain his footing. As he recovered, he glanced over at Catharine who seemed frozen in terror.

"Which of you is the warrior?" asked King Enlil in a voice that—though calm and measured—was a full octave deeper than that of his brother Enki, and twice as loud, bouncing off the surrounding architecture and resonating in David's chest.

Catharine looked to David as though to ask whether she was free to speak. He nodded curtly.

Catharine took a cautious step forward. "I am the warrior, Your Majesty," she said in as strong a voice as she could muster, though it still sounded small and flat.

"What is your name?" boomed the King.

"Your people call me Weldon, Majesty."

"My people call you? Is that not your name?"

"It is my family name, Majesty. My given name is Catharine."

"We would say *Ketura*," mused the King.

"Close enough, Your Majesty. It would honor me to be called Ketura by King Enlil."

"So shall you be, Ketura. What were the circumstances of your skirmish with Anzû's acolytes?"

"Anzû's acolytes," said Catharine, adopting the King's phrase, "had abducted several young scientists and planned to take them from Earth against their will."

"How did you stop them?" asked the King.

"We found them on a great lake by means of a small underwater boat. We took the hostages back by force, and destroyed the small spacecraft that Anzû had sent to carry them away."

"It is well that you stopped them, Ketura," said the King, "and no loss that you killed some. Do you know what Anzû wants on Earth?"

She hesitated. "Any opinion on my part would be purely speculative, Your Majesty."

"Would it surprise you," asked the King, "if Anzû's creed has its acolytes on Nibiru also?"

Catharine was clearly non-plussed by the question, and she thought for a moment before speaking. "Even with the little that I know of this matter, Your Majesty, I *would* be surprised."

The King barked a deep, rhythmic sound that, despite its frightening overtones, David took to be an innocuous chuckle.

The King spoke again. "You shall see Nibiru while you are on this pyramidion. Keep an open mind, Ketura, and you will learn much. Now pardon me as I converse with your companion."

Joseph!

David felt the name in the center of his brain, and the power behind it nearly knocked him over. It took a moment for him to realize that the King had not spoken it aloud.

David forced his face up to look at a point as close to the King's luminous eyes as his own eyes could bear, and sent a return telepathic message. *I hear you loudly, Your Majesty. There is no need to shout.*

The King chuckled and tried again in a much more restrained tone. *Pardon me, Joseph. There are few who can hear me communicate in this way, no matter how I shout. How about this? Is it more to your liking?*

Yes, thank you, Majesty.

Joseph, you are unique among earthlings in your ability to hear without ears and speak without a mouth. Know you this?

David nodded. *I know that the ability is rare, Your Majesty, but did not know it was as rare as you suggest. And my name is David, Majesty.*

The King chuckled yet again. *No,* he said, *you are not David, for I knew David and he was not you. I knew his son, as well.*

King Solomon, Majesty?

The King silently nodded his giant head. *Yes, he who built the Temple in Yerushalayim, bless his memory.*

David bowed. *I am honored to answer to any name by which Your Majesty chooses to call me.*

I shall call you David, if you wish.

David bowed gratefully.

The King changed the subject. *You heard me speak with Ketura about Anzû, did you not?*

I did, Your Majesty.

Do you know why he wants to enlist you?

David nodded. *I believe Anzû wishes me to help his army of drones conquer for him, because few others can hear him speak as Your Majesty and I are speaking now.*

Enlil shook his head. *There are no others, David. There is only you. And you appear to have been brought to us by the God of All Things to save us from this peril.*

It simply cannot be that I am the only one, Majesty. That is too much responsibility for one man to bear.

The King sighed. *Here I sit every day for near-eternity to interpret sights, messages, and thoughts from everywhere in the galaxy so that I may help my people. That is my responsibility, David, and my plight.*

Yes, Majesty.

Contending with Anzû ... that is yours. You know by what means he tries to ensnare you, David?

David nodded. *He tries to persuade me that I need to live as long as the Anunnaki and hints that he will grant me long life. He knows I feel the need to protect my woman from peril. Can he indeed grant me long life?*

I will leave this for you to learn from Ninurta. But do you need such long life to protect Ketura?

No, Majesty. I need to outlive her by only a moment to assure that she is protected for her whole life.

If you love only Ketura, you have no need of immortality. And Anzû knows this. So, he tries to persuade you that you love and need to protect a different woman ... one of long life. Is this not so?

David hadn't given much thought to the origins of his romantic crush on Inanna. He'd simply chalked it up to a man's natural penchant for falling in love with any beautiful woman who falls in love with him. Yet, King Enlil's suggestion had the ring of truth to it.

David needed to know more, and seated before him was probably the only living being who could tell him.

I'm not sure that my feelings for Inanna could be characterized as love, Your Majesty, but they are undeniably strong.

The King chortled deeply. *David, any man who does not fall in love with Inanna has no heart. Be on guard against your feelings for her. They're more durable than you might expect. Tell me, do you know the country of which she is queen?*

I confess I do not.

The King explained. *Inanna was granted control of several areas on Earth: in Babylon, the Indus Valley and a few others. But she is not the queen of any country. She is rather the Queen of Men's Hearts, a joy to us all. No man is immune to her charms, nor free of the desire to please her, to keep and preserve her. So pure of heart is she that she follows her affections blindly, lacking the guile to suspect that her feelings can be manipulated by those wishing her ill. Do you know who reported your existence to Inanna?*

Well, Zia told me—

Pah! Zia is a good man, but he was merely repeating something he'd heard. It was one of Anzû's agents at your university who informed Inanna of your existence, one who knew all too well that Inanna had loved your ancestor Joseph beyond reason—as much as she did the long-lost Dumuzi—and still longed to have Joseph by her side.

David marveled at the plot described by the King. *Does Your Majesty suggest that it was Anzû who brought me to Inanna's attention, so that she would fall in love with me? And I, being a mortal man, would have no choice but to fall in love with her, and eventually realize that I'd have need of the eternal life that Anzû could grant, so that I might care for her?*

David looked up at the King's face. He was nodding.

David felt doubly … *trebly* betrayed. *Anzû is a filthy deceiver.*

The King wholeheartedly agreed. *Anzû is indeed a filthy deceiver, a common and a grand thief, a usurper, and a murderer. He has tried to use what's best in you to harm you. But you must bear in mind that Inanna has never betrayed you. Nor do I think she is truly capable of betraying anyone.* He chuckled again. *Perhaps Enki feels otherwise, I don't know. But Enki was even more of a fool for Inanna than I was.* The King sighed long. *And I was a great fool indeed.*

David just stood there, still overwhelmed by the farsighted audacity of Anzû's plot.

The King began again. *Can you not see that Ketura was placed at your side to be your savior? She appeared at precisely the right moment to protect you—not from Inanna—but from Anzû.*

David looked up at the King. Is it possible—? Unable to hold in the question, he posed it foursquare: *Was it Your Majesty who sent Cath-*

arine to me? Were you playing the other side of Anzû's gambit?

No, David, the King assured him. *You give me both too much—and too little—credit. I know many things, but not everything. And I do not deceive the innocent. Ketura was sent to your side—if by anyone—by the God of All Things. Praise His Name.*

Praise His Name, David echoed.

I will say to you as I have said to Ketura. You will see the likeness of Nibiru while you are on this pyramidion. Keep your mind and your heart open, and you will learn much. The King hesitated before moving on to another thought. *I know, David, that, like my half-brother Enki, you expect there is a traitor among the Anunnaki.*

The possibility troubles me deeply, Your Majesty.

As well it should. Although I doubt that the traitor is on this pyramidion or within this fleet as it is presently constituted, I share your unease. I wish you to know only that you can trust Ninurta and Nergal completely. There is not a jot of guile in either of them.

David wished to turn about and look at Ninurta, but realized that would be a mistake, for what he wished to know *concerned* Ninurta. *Can Lord Ninurta hear this conversation?*

He cannot, replied the King, *although he can hear me when I speak in this way ... to him. I know what you wish to ask and shall answer you before hearing your question. You may give Inanna's letter to Ninurta without hesitation.*

At first, David couldn't fathom how King Enlil knew of the brief correspondence that had sprung up between Ninurta and Inanna. But then, he realized, this is the King's ship. If an encrypted message is sent or received by his communications room, surely he would know of the message and its contents.

But how would the King know that Inanna had replied by means of a written note entrusted to David?

The King's thoughts intruded on David's. *I knew how she would respond to Ninurta's message, David, simply because I know her. As you truly wish to see her well cared for, resolve yourself to protect and help Ninurta. Grapple him to your soul with hoops of steel. Pay no mind to his jests or his affected arrogance. He is probably the best friend you will ever have, having learned humility through the catastrophic failure of his own actions long, long ago. When the time is right, you may choose to ask him about immortality.*

David understood the King's reference to Ninurta and Nergal's use of the Forbidden Weapons in the Sinai that resulted in the end of

Sumeria and the death of Ninurta's wife.

Go in peace, said the King.

And then David felt a forcible decoupling from the King's mind, which left him feeling deflated—somehow lesser—than when he was locked in an exchange of telepathic thoughts with the King of Nibiru. But who wouldn't feel that way?

The King then spoke aloud to Ninurta, directing him to escort David and Catharine to the Virtual Reality chamber. This David overheard through his ears, which now somehow seemed a dull and vulgar way of hearing.

CHAPTER 9

ON AN ANDEAN mountainside, Buck had no idea there were enemy spacecraft on their way to the spot where the downed bogey lost contact with the enemy.

Buck was dripping with sweat by the time he located the clips holding the bogey's radio in place. There was a beep in his headset, followed by a young woman's voice.

"How we comin' there, boss?" asked Lieutenant Muñoz.

Buck snorted. "You're only a few feet away from me, Sofia, and you've got the scopes. Why don't *you* tell *me* how I'm doin'?"

"Can't see your progress from the cockpit, boss."

"Actually," said Buck, "I've been stalled here for a while, but I finally figured out that the bogey's radio is a rackmount job."

"What does that mean?"

Buck guessed that his co-pilot hadn't been as nerdy growing up as she was now. Anybody who's ever crawled around on a floor setting up (or fixing) electronic components knows what *rackmount* means.

"It means the radio sits on a pair of rails. I've been feeling for the clips or set-screws that keep it from slidin' out, and I think I just found 'em. Cross your fingers. I'm gonna give 'em a tug." He placed a thumb and forefinger on the clip to the left of the radio and did the same with the clip on the right. When he pulled the clips away from the radio, it came loose.

"Lemme know how that works," said Muñoz with the slightest hint of urgency.

"It's worked already. I can feel the whole assembly slide," said Buck with a grunt, "but I'm still encountering some resistance. Something's holding onto the back end. Probably just a cable conducting signal in and out of the radio."

"Is the plug secured with screws or anything? Or can you just pull it off?"

"Don't know yet," said Buck, his patience with the conversation waning. "Um, is there some reason you're pestering me, or you just gotta pee? 'Cause, you know, you got a whole mountainside to yourself and I promise not to peek. Couldn't see with all this sweat in my eyes anyhow."

"Pee's already taken care of boss," said Muñoz humorously. "I'm only pesterin' ya 'cause we got a call from base."

"Oh?" said Buck as he blindly groped for the plug at the back of the radio. Finding it, he rocked it back and forth with his fingers. "How are things on the ground? They want us to bring 'em takeout on the way home?"

"No," said Muñoz. "Seems a coupla the bogey's friends just popped outta their icy hole about five minutes ago. Same type craft as the one you're sittin' in."

Buck sat up and frowned. "Talk to me, lieutenant."

"The good news is the hidey-hole's about three thousand miles away from here, and any craft will take some time to chew up that distance—if they're even headed here."

Buck wiped his brow on his sleeve. "Safe bet is they're on their way here. And the bad news?"

"Well, they have hypersonic capability, so they can move like a bat out o' hell. HQ says they could get here in less than an hour. Worse is that they have orbital capability, so they can go way up, greatly extending their line of sight. We don't know much about their optical capabilities, so we have no idea when they'll get us in their scopes. But HQ guesstimates they'll have a line of sight to us about twenty minutes from now."

"Think we should call in the Anunnaki cavalry?" asked Buck. "They've got orbital supremacy right now."

"Got no clearance to do that, boss," Muñoz replied. "Meanwhile, they don't have a great record of comin' to the rescue, do they?"

"Got that right," said Buck, shaking his head. "They almost got our whole damn squadron chewed up while they were asleep at the switch."

"Did we ever learn how they managed to crap out that day?"

"Nope," said Buck. "*Damn.* We don't even know how the enemy found out this bogey went down. This craft I'm sittin' in could be sendin' out a continuous signal. Hey, Muñoz, are your sensors pickin' up any emissions from this craft?"

"Lemme check," she said. "Meanwhile, let's take the music out of their party. Pull the radio out, and let's take it home." She came back on in a moment. "I'm gettin' no signal from the downed craft, sir."

Buck had to work the plug back and forth a dozen times before it yielded at last, and came loose from the radio. "Here goes nothin'," he said and pulled the radio toward him. A second later, it was sitting in his lap, fully intact. He breathed a sigh of relief. "Got it!" he shouted. "Warm up my seat, Muñoz. I'll be there in a sec!"

Soon they were airborne, heading north with the bogey's radio strapped to the airframe and Buck in the pilot's seat. To render their craft more difficult for the enemy to identify, they matched their airspeed to the commercial airliners flying in the area, though their saucer could have flown much faster.

"Co-pilot," said Buck, "you got a camera trained on the grounded bogey?"

"Sure do," said Muñoz. "Whoa!"

"What is it?" demanded Buck.

"Looks like the site just got nuked."

Buck knew that the wreck was supposed to be destroyed by a conventional cannon drone. If it really had been *nuked* instead, that could only have been done by the enemy, and would have been done to ensure nothing could be taken from the downed bogey.

"Not *really* nuked, right?" asked Buck apprehensively.

"I'll have an answer to that in a sec. Waiting for the scopes to refresh." Muñoz took another moment to reply. "No, the wreckage is still recognizable as having been some kind of aircraft. That was some bright light, but there's no sign of nuclear destruction and no mushroom cloud."

Buck snorted and shook his head with mild irritation. "I'm gonna have to ask you to choose your words more carefully, copilot, given the tension in our current situation." In other words, *You just needlessly scared the crap out of me.*

"Yes, lieutenant," replied Muñoz, sounding a little crestfallen. "Sorry."

He glanced over at her. "Hey, Sofia," he said jovially, "call me Buck, okay?"

That did the trick; she straightened up and smiled. "Yes, sir—I mean Buck."

A brief radar pulse showed up on the scopes. Buck said, "Narrow down the source of that pulse, wouldja?"

"Source was in orbit. It was a circular sweep."

"Are we lit up?"

"No. The pulse was momentary, wide-area wattage, with no sign of a lock-on. It's a good thing we've got lots of stealth features. He was just takin' a wild-ass stab. My advice would be to maintain course and altitude."

"Copy that," said Buck, admiring her self-discipline at a time when every instinct must have been telling her to run like hell. "But I'd just as soon park this baby and hide out till the coast is clear."

"Where could we hide the craft?"

"I dunno," said Buck. "What're we approaching?"

"Comin' up on my part of Chile; it's called *Zona Central*."

"Do you speak … *Chilean?*" asked Buck hesitantly.

"No," she replied incredulously, "but fortunately Chileans don't speak Chilean, either. They speak *Spanish*, like I do."

"Gimme a break," said Buck. "You mean to tell me that a Castilian would understand the locals?"

"Well, not everything," she admitted. "Some people call the local language Chilean Spanish, but it's not really a separate language." She turned to him. "Why? You're really thinking of landing there?"

"Yep."

Hesitantly, she said, "My family operates a winery there."

Buck did a double take to see if she was serious. "No kiddin'?"

"No kiddin'."

"Geez, what are the odds? Do they have a building with a garage door and a tin roof big enough to hide this crate?"

Sofia gave it some thought. "I don't know if the roofs are really tin, but they're *some* kind of metal, I think. The winery has a couple of metal-roof sheds big enough to hold this craft, depending on what else is in there right now. And they have garage doors."

"How far from the Pacific is the winery?" he asked.

"In Chile, nothin' is very far from the Pacific. The country basically consists of three thousand miles of Pacific shoreline west of the Andes Mountains. You're not seriously considering landing us there, are you?"

"Never more serious in my life," said Buck. "I don't want to fight those bogeys. They have too many speed and loadout advantages over us, to say nothin' of there bein' *two* of them and only *one* of us. Can you get us to the winery by eyeball?"

"Oh, I can spot it alright," said Sofia. "I learned to fly when I lived here. I used to overfly the winery and wave to the family. Not that hard to spot. You're serious?" On second thought, she added, "There's no runway, y'know."

"As you well know," he said, "with this baby, we don't need one. Can you call ahead and make sure nobody shoots at us or calls the

Federales?"

"*Federales?*" she exclaimed as though truly offended. "*Qué gringo!* Chile is not Mexico. And even Mexico hasn't had *Federales* in, like, a hundred years."

"No?"

"No. And Chile has the *Carabineros.* Well," she said, still unsure whether he was joking, "I don't have a mobile phone that would work here."

"No," he agreed, "but you do have an encrypted *radio*. Call the base and tell them to place a phone call to your family and tell 'em to get the hangar ready. While you're at it, tell the base to notify the admiral that we'll be lyin' low for a day or two."

She hesitated before touching the radio. "Buck, we're talkin' about my *family*. If you're jokin', this is the time to come clean."

"Call!" he demanded. "And have them tell your folks to turn off all their phones and not to raise a fuss."

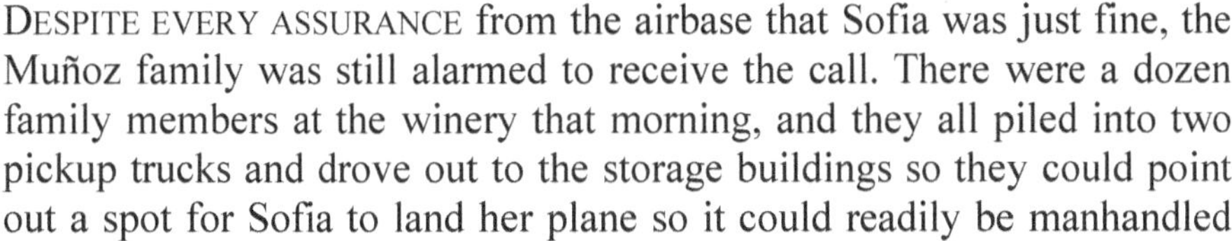

DESPITE EVERY ASSURANCE from the airbase that Sofia was just fine, the Muñoz family was still alarmed to receive the call. There were a dozen family members at the winery that morning, and they all piled into two pickup trucks and drove out to the storage buildings so they could point out a spot for Sofia to land her plane so it could readily be manhandled into one of the buildings.

Just outside the buildings, the younger generation set up a lawn chair for the family's undisputed matriarch, a wizened centenarian who couldn't stand for long. The family gathered around her, many placing their fingertips on her shoulder or back, as though for good luck, but really for a sense of security.

A quarter hour later, instead of the expected jet airplane, a dark saucer appeared in the sky and performed a beautifully controlled vertical landing a few feet in front of the gaping family.

THE DISPLAY INSIDE the saucer showed a nicely framed tableau of the Muñoz family frozen in shock at the realization that a flying saucer was landing at their winery.

Buck laughed. "Do their mouths always hang open like that?"

Sofia smacked him on the shoulder. "I'd like to see what *you* looked like when you first saw one of these things."

He pointed to the display. "Pretty much like that, I'd imagine." Scanning the tableau, his eyes lighted on a beautiful young woman. "Just not as good-lookin'."

She snorted. "That's my younger sister you're lookin' at. *Cuidado.* She's taken."

The saucer landed and Buck lowered the staircase to let Sofia out so she could enlist her young cousins to clear a path to the hangar and open the garage doors. As soon as she stepped onto solid ground, he retracted the staircase so he could drive the landed craft into its appointed shelter.

Buck watched from the display as the whole family descended on Sofia as though she were a victorious hero returning from war. Thanks to her strenuous insistence, in a few minutes a path had been cleared, with the matriarch and her folding chair having been respectfully carried away and safely relocated.

Buck eased the craft into the shed. Though there was ample clearance on either side of the craft, there was only about three feet on top, so he steered cautiously, as though guiding a wheelchair with an elderly person aboard. That operation done, he heaved a deep sigh of relief and wiped his sweaty hands on the thighs of his trousers, all the while wondering how he'd be greeted.

He turned the craft's controls to the Off position and deployed the staircase again, this time for his own descent. He wasn't much worried that the staircase might come down on someone, as it contained numerous electric eyes and pressure-sensitive retraction relays to guard against any such catastrophe.

Rising from his seat, Buck could detect a tuneful tumult outside. The family, having evidently gathered at the foot of the staircase, had begun singing, though he didn't immediately recognize the tune.

As the staircase began its automatic descent, and sound entered the cockpit from outside, Buck recognized the song, though even then it took him a moment. It was *America the Beautiful* with the lyrics being sung in outlandishly broken English; still, considering the nationality of the singers, he had to admit he'd heard worse. In fact, he'd never heard a group of native-born American singers (other than a navy choir) who could even remember the opening lyrics.

He was especially amazed to hear such an outpouring from citizens of a country that had reputedly suffered for many years from interference by American intelligence. America was largely blamed for the coup that upended the socialist Allende regime and resulted in Pinochet's brutal dictatorship. Buck had spoken with some CIA guys about that whole mess, and they'd insisted that America's involvement was much less than commonly believed.

Though Buck began his descent fully intending to trot down to meet the family, he was shocked to realize that their heartfelt rendition of the venerable old song had brought tears to his eyes. He stopped on the first landing, came to attention, and somberly saluted for the duration of the song. Glancing down at the little crowd of beaming Chileans, he was overwhelmed to see Sofia (probably the only American citizen among them) come to attention and return his salute with tears in her eyes.

Truth was, the family couldn't have done anything to make Buck feel more at home, and even *they* seemed emotionally jarred by the effect their serenade had on their new visitor.

The song came to a close after a single verse. Buck relaxed and tramped down the steel steps to the concrete floor with his hand extended to the nearest adult male, a silver-haired mustachioed gentleman with a dignified air.

Sofia stepped up to the gentleman as Buck shook his hand.

"*Papi*," said Sofia, "this is Lieutenant Buchanan. It was his idea to come here today." She then translated her own words for her father.

"Welcome," said Papi.

Buck nodded respectfully. "Thank you for your hospitality, sir. And for making room for our little aircraft."

Sofia translated.

Papi smiled and placed his left hand on Buck's right shoulder, convivially turning him toward one of the pickup trucks.

As they were leaving the hangar, Papi pulled the garage door closed. The construction of the shed's frame was so snug that the roof rattled. Buck noticed something unexpected about the sound it made but, anticipating a hot meal, he got into the pickup and rode over to the house.

When they reached the family's home and Buck had begun to recognize each family member as an individual, he was introduced to Sofia's beautiful younger sister Antonella, her straight, shiny black hair falling freely to her shoulders. She wore a simple cotton dress and a few pieces of craft jewelry, but no makeup.

Though there was substantial facial similarity between the sisters, their resemblance seemed to end there. Antonella was friendly, expressive, and appealing, appearing even more so by comparison to Sofia, who still wore her baggy pilot's uniform and her hair tautly pulled back in a knot.

Later, while Buck was sitting silently outdoors with Papi watching the sun descend from high noon, Antonella drew Sofia away, and the two disappeared, giggling.

Each time Papi and Buck finished a split of white wine, Papi would instruct one of the young people to bring him a split of another varietal. Buck told Papi, in a combination of broken Spanish and simplistic English that, although the wine was excellent and the hospitality unparalleled, no more wine should be poured for him, at least until suppertime.

While Buck basked in the pleasant sunshine that was both dimmed and cooled by the mist that wafted in constantly off the Pacific, his eyes closed of their own accord, and he dozed.

In what seemed like an instant (but was probably close to an hour), he was awakened by the pleasant tittering of young women. Opening his eyes a crack, Buck found himself looking into the beaming face of a woman so beautiful that she rivaled Inanna, the goddess of love, whom he'd been privileged to see close up.

At first, Buck thought the woman who awakened him was Antonella, as she was adorned much as Antonella had been earlier: a simple cotton dress, black shoulder-length hair, and a little craft jewelry. But the face that greeted him now wore some minimal makeup, including shiny red lipstick.

The face belonged to neither Inanna nor Antonella. Buck closed his eyes again, and would have been satisfied simply to take her image back with him to dreamland, but she wasn't having any.

"Buck?" said the woman insistently.

Buck opened his eyes again and blinked to clear his vision. The woman was speaking to him with *Sofia's* voice. He sat up with a start, realizing the incongruity of being unable to take his eyes off his copilot. He wanted to kiss this woman, and that was a feeling he hadn't had in a very long time, and one he'd *never* had for a copilot.

He squinted to clear his vision. "Sofia?" he inquired. "Is that you?"

"Who else?" she said, and twirled so the skirts of her dress blossomed out and came to rest.

Buck's self-consciousness about his feelings made him increasingly uncomfortable. He glanced about, and was relieved to see that the other family members had left him alone with Sofia. He checked twice to make sure Papi wasn't around.

"I had no idea you could look like that," muttered Buck. Before even finishing the sentence, he realized it had been badly phrased and could be construed as derogatory, implying that she didn't always look terrific.

But Sofia seemed to know how it was intended. "I'm not allowed to dress like this while I'm on duty, obviously." She twirled again and asked, quite innocently, "What do you think?"

"I'd tell you," he said, "but you'd think it inappropriate."

"Why would it be inappropriate?" she demanded to know.

"Because I've gotta be fifteen years older than you," he said with dismay, "and, while you might like to hear somethin' like that from a man your own age, I've learned it's unwelcome comin' from a guy ... like me."

She pursed her lips at his priggishness. "I give you permission to speak freely. What do you think?" she insisted.

"You remind me that I'm a man," said Buck, "and that I've never had any luck making a connection with a woman as desirable as you. You're gorgeous."

She seemed impressed by his honesty and dubious of his flattery. "You look at me differently outside the cockpit."

He nodded shyly. "Well, kissing you never once crossed my mind until now." He looked deeply into her eyes. "And now it's all I can think about."

She smiled coyly. "So, why aren't you trying to kiss me?"

"Because we're not safely *alone*—not with your whole family right there in the house," he said. "I'm sure your *abuelita* is looking through a window at us right now."

"Probably," she admitted, "but are you afraid of offending an old woman?" She settled next to him on the chaise. "If you think she'd be offended, then you know nothing of her life until now."

Buck raised an eyebrow. "I'm afraid Papi might be offended, too. There's an unwritten rule among men—"

She rolled her eyes. "Oh, here it goes."

He sighed and completed his thought, "—an unwritten rule that you don't start up with your host's daughter, especially if you're much older than she is."

"Papi wouldn't care about your age. Neither would *mi abuelita*," she said. "The only age they worry about is *mine*. My kid sister has found someone, while I have no one. And around here, no husband means a pathetic future."

"Well, you don't live here any more, do you? There are a million guys back home who'd give their eyeteeth for a woman as beautiful as you. And half of them are nearer your age."

She sighed with exasperation. "There you go with the age difference again. I think this is a gringo thing."

"You mean, you wouldn't mind if I kiss you?" he asked.

She smiled crookedly. "You'll never know if you don't try."

He sat up straight. Feeling like he was leading with his chin, and expecting that old familiar stiff-arm, he kissed her on the mouth. When she reciprocated, he felt he'd ascended into heaven. At last, he drew away from her, half-expecting Papi (or, worse, a few of the younger men) to emerge from the house to confront him. *Well*, he thought, *that kiss was worth a thrashing*.

But it didn't happen.

At last he knew the answer to the question the lieutenant commander had posed to him when they first met: *Why do you drink?* It was because he'd felt in his bones that he would never feel … like this. Sofia was what he'd always lacked. He resolved that, if that's what it took to have her, he'd even retire from the navy to avoid the regs prohibiting fraternization among officers.

As though reading his mind, Sofia rose, took him by the hand, and led him in to supper, where the rest of the family had already begun handing around serving plates. Though he didn't know the names of the dishes (and there were one or two that resembled nothing he'd ever eaten), he sat down and felt immediately at home.

And, just for a moment, he daydreamed of living and growing old right here in the soft breeze off the Pacific, with this beautiful woman. Of having children and becoming part of a family. And it just seemed so right.

NEXT MORNING, BUCK woke up alone on a Government-Issued air mattress on the floor of the saucer's dimly lit bridge. He vaguely remembered that, last night, he'd dimmed the light to its minimum setting.

Though his head was still swimming a little from the white wine of the previous evening, it was nothing compared to the tequila hangovers he'd awakened to recently. He put his hands together behind his head on the mattress and rested there, thinking of the previous day.

Kissing Sofia was unforgettable, and he recalled dinner surprisingly well, too, considering that he hadn't understood a word that wasn't translated for him. He smiled recalling one memory in particular. After dinner, Hector, one of Sofia's brothers (who looked twenty, but might have been younger) asked to drive one of the pickup trucks into town. Papi said *no*, on grounds that both pickups would be needed early next morning. The kid whined a little and asked a few more times. Sofia told Buck what the disagreement was about, and Buck, posing as peacemaker, dangled his personal keys in front of the kid, as though offering the saucer as an alternative way into town.

Hector and Papi found the thought of flying a saucer into town so outlandish that they laughed about it for several minutes. After that, Hector settled down and seemed to warm up to Buck considerably.

To top off the evening, Buck, Sofia, Antonella, and Hector took a walk along a local dock.

Antonella and Hector went down to the beach and had a contest skimming stones on the Pacific while Buck and Sofia watched from the dock, sharing tales of their pasts.

Strong as Antonella was, her throwing arm was no match for Hector's, and after a while she gave up and they all walked back to the house. By that time, the older folks were already in bed (evidently, Papi wasn't joking about the need to start work early).

Rather than create an appearance of impropriety, Buck had declined the opportunity to sleep on a couch and instead walked alone to the shed housing the saucer, where he'd climbed the metal staircase to the craft, let himself in, and fell asleep where he now lay.

Just as he was about to rise, the radio came on with a bit of static and a familiar female voice.

"Buck, you there?" asked Lorraine. "Over."

Buck popped to his feet, plopped in a chair in front of the console, and pressed the Send button.

"Whozis?" he said. "Over."

"Who do you think it is? Geez, you take a twelve-hour vacation and forget who your friends are? It's Lorraine. Over."

"I thought so," said Buck, "but last I checked you weren't operating out of Nellis AFB. You there now? Over."

"No, still in Dakota. You alone? Over."

"Yeah," said Buck. "Why are you calling directly? Shouldn't you be goin' through my base? Over."

"Got a call from one of your friends in orbit. Over."

"Yeah? He wants us to pick up some takeout? Over."

Lorraine laughed. "You need a new routine, Buck. I've heard that one a zillion times. I'm calling direct because this is a need-to-know. Your friend saw some bogey activity early this morning in southern Chile. Over."

Buck scratched his head and yawned. "Yah? How far south? Over."

"Well," said Lorraine, "they started out way south, like the Straits of Magellan, and they've steadily moved north ever since. They're up to Puerto Montt in the lake district. Over."

That caught Buck's attention. He was no expert in Chilean geography, but he vaguely recalled that Puerto Montt was just a few hundred miles south of the winery. "What are the bogeys doin'? Over."

"They're sending out some kinda ray at every small enclosure they can find, like barns and such. Your friend thought they might be looking for you, and he wasn't sure whether they could be a problem for you, since nobody knows where you're parked. Over."

"What else are the bogeys doin'?" asked Buck. "Over."

"So far, nothin'," said Lorraine, "but they're being mighty thorough."

Buck's foot started bobbing up and down, which happened when he got nervous. "Do we know what their X-rays can see through?"

"Nope," said Lorraine. "We think they *can't* see through metal, but we can't be sure. You under a metal roof?"

Geez! Buck kicked himself. He'd never confirmed it. He didn't know *what* the damned roof was made of. Then he remembered hearing the roof rattle when Papi closed the door yesterday, and gritted his teeth as he recalled that it sounded like plastic on wood. Why didn't he check it out right away?

"Hold, please," he said, grabbing a flashlight and yanking open the saucer door.

The shed was dark and smelled of clean sawdust. Buck stepped out onto the staircase and pointed the flashlight straight up. On second thought he turned it off, and what he saw made his stomach churn and his bowels beg to be purged. There was an even light coming straight through the corrugated roof shingles—as it would through polycarbonate, but not through tin or another metal.

He ran back into the saucer and pressed the Send button. "Lorraine, I'm not gonna tell you where we are, but we gotta get movin' pronto. I'll contact you aloft. Copy that?"

"Copy, Buck. Good luck! Over."

"Thanks, out!" shouted Buck. He released the button and scrambled to get his boots on.

Running full-tilt toward the house in the early morning light, he noticed that the sprinklers at the far-end of the vineyard had begun spraying the vines while a few family members watched. It was a bucolic scene. *Someday*, he promised himself. *Someday, I'll live a normal, idyllic life like this.*

But not today. Sure as hell, not today.

CHAPTER 10

As David and Catharine were guided out through the maze, David tugged Ninurta's elbow and drew him aside. Nergal stood a few feet off with Catharine.

"Yes, David?" said Ninurta a bit peevishly.

Especially in light of what he'd had been told by the king, David was baffled by Ninurta's attitude. "How have I offended, my lord?" asked David somberly.

Ninurta turned his head away in contemplation, then back to David. "In my whole life I have never been able to converse with my father telepathically."

David was confused. "But His Majesty said—"

Ninurta interrupted. "His Majesty is able to address *me* telepathically. I can hear his thoughts, but, alas, I'm unable to reply in kind."

"But what has that to do with me, my lord?"

"I'm His Majesty's son, and heir apparent to the Nibirune throne. It just seems … presumptuous (perhaps that's not the right word) that someone such as yourself, half of whom is an alien species that only learned to write a few Sars ago, can converse with him in silence." Ninurta sighed and softened. "But you're right; it has nothing to do with you. Please forgive my petulance. What did you wish to discuss with me?"

David glanced around. "Before going to the Virtual Reality chamber, there are a few things I need to discuss with you privately. Perhaps you might visit briefly in my room?"

Ninurta nodded. "Very well," he said and turned to Nergal and Catharine, who had begun conversing pleasantly. "Nergal, I'll be accompanying David to his room for a moment. We'll meet you at the VR chamber."

Nergal nodded respectfully and walked off with Catharine, who seemed a little forlorn to be left alone with one of her guards.

As David admitted Ninurta to his room, he was pleased to see that his bags had been sent up. He removed a small key from his pocket and used it to unlock an official-looking bag. Once inside, he zipped open the side pocket where he'd stowed Inanna's letter.

"What type of bag is that?" asked Ninurta.

Surprised at the question, David regarded the bag with new eyes. Viewed from any angle, it displayed two icons adapted from the reverse side of the American dollar bill.

"It's called a diplomatic pouch, my lord," replied David. "Its inviolability is respected by all civilized nations. A diplomatic pouch need not look like this, of course. *Any* area designated as a diplomatic pouch *is* a diplomatic pouch. Even an entire aircraft hold can be so designated."

"And those peculiar images that seem to have been copied from engravings?"

"This device," said David, pointing, "is the Great Seal of the United States. The other, a thirteen-step pyramid topped by a radiant eye and thirteen stars, represents the thirteen original states that formed the United States."

"What's the significance of the eye?" asked Ninurta.

"It's the 'Eye of Providence,' the eye of the Hebrew God," replied David. "I suppose in this context it's there to ward away any thief who fears for his immortal soul."

"There are few such thieves," said Ninurta.

David took out Inanna's letter and handed it over. "Her Majesty Queen Inanna asked me to present this to you, together with her request that you keep its contents to yourself, my lord, and I hereby discharge my duty."

"Have you read it?" asked Ninurta.

"No, my lord," replied David, incredulous at the question, "and I made no attempt to do so."

"Before I read it," said Ninurta, "will you tell me how the Queen feels about me?"

David could see that Ninurta's mind, if not precisely lovesick, had been lighting upon Inanna for some time, so there were innumerable ways in which any answer could redound to David's own detriment. "Her Majesty spoke fondly of you, my lord," he ventured. "First, she openly admired your defeat of Anzû who, as you know, is plaguing Earth once again. Then she pointed out the numerous grounds for her resentment of Marduk—"

"For the despicable murder of his own younger brother," muttered Ninurta with disgust, "who was my cousin Dumuzi and Inanna's betrothed."

David added, "—and also for your lordship's valiant resistance against Marduk's running roughshod over the Council's rulings."

"Is that all she said?" asked Ninurta, looking a bit disappointed.

"I hesitate to conjecture further, my lord, as I'm not one of Her Majesty's most intimate confidants—nor even, as your lordship has pointed out, wholly of the same species."

Ninurta scowled. "Oh, please don't carry that thought away with you. It was said in a fit of pique."

"Very well, my lord," said David, "but no human can live long enough to share much experience with an Anunnaki—*any* Anunnaki, let alone the Queen of Heaven. While I'm gratified that Her Majesty places some confidence in me, I doubt she'd be inclined to share with me her most intimate feelings for another of her race."

For a moment, Ninurta's expression turned faraway, but then he turned back to David and laughed heartily. "David, David. If you continue speaking the language of diplomacy, you'll forget who you are: Little David from Canarsie."

David laughed. "Surrounded as I am by members of the elder race, it would be difficult for me to lose all humility. Besides, I brought with me a woman who's only too happy to remind me of my humble origins."

Ninurta nodded. "They *all* do that, don't they?"

David smiled. "So it seems."

"What else did you wish to discuss with me?"

"Well, this is a delicate matter. You see, our pilot is an android—"

"Which model?"

David was chagrined. "I have no idea. In any event, we were told that we were being entrusted to the care of Doctor Zia's companion, Enkidu—"

"It seems androids are all (or almost all) named Enkidu," Ninurta interjected.

"But I suspect we may have gotten the *wrong* android."

"What makes you think that?"

David said, "Doctor Zia told us his android had been supplied with first-hand memories of numerous ancient affairs, specifically including those of the original Enkidu from his time with Gilgamesh—"

"First-hand memories?" mused Ninurta. "That would make him a very old model indeed. Those first-person experiences have not been implanted in new models for thousands of Earth years."

"Why haven't they?" asked David.

"Well," said Ninurta, "because they're essentially delusional. If I were to implant memories in you that you observed the initial landing of Anunnaki on Earth, you would be deluded on that point, wouldn't you?"

"I suppose," said David. "That's an interesting take on delusionality. In any event, our pilot has only *second-hand* knowledge of those Gilgamesh events, as though he'd only been *taught* the story. I know that's a thin reed to rest my doubts upon, but I've begun to think he's— he's not—he's not—"

"He's not the right Enkidu?"

Somewhat abashed, David nodded.

Ninurta regarded him skeptically. "Have you any other reason to suspect you've got the wrong Enkidu?"

"Well," replied David, "he has no sense of irony, or humor. In fact, he's far from being the conversationalist that Zia's Enkidu is known to be. This one is—rather dull. Of course, I have no intention of wasting your lordship's time complaining about an android's tediousness—"

"Of course not. But you're entirely *dependent* upon him. If some-one's switched androids on you, you could have much bigger problems than a bout of tedium."

"There's one other thing," said David. "As our vessel was undergo-ing final preparations for our voyage here, a late-model Enkidu appeared on the maintenance team, visually indistinguishable from *Zia's* Enkidu."

Ninurta was now intrigued indeed. "Well, that's not all that uncom-mon, but ..." He seemed lost in thought for a moment. "Leave it to me. I don't want you to be distracted during your 'overflight' of Nibiru. Let's go to VR now. It's rude to keep a lady waiting."

⸺⸺⸺ ◦◦◦ ⸺⸺⸺

MOUNTED ON THE wall outside the Virtual Reality facility was a vertical rack meant to hold the pointed weapons carried by many on the royal pyramidion. It reminded David of a place to stand one's cue stick between rounds of pool. One slot in the rack was already occupied by a partisan, which David took to be Nergal's, as he expected that Nergal and Catharine had already entered the facility.

Ninurta placed his partisan in the slot next to Nergal's and raised his hand to the door, which slid aside to admit him and David onto a ledge extending about eight feet into the facility, running the room's full length to right and left.

Nergal and Catharine awaited Ninurta and David on the ledge together with a dark-haired young woman, who was (for an Anunnaki) slight of frame. Though if she were human she might have been overlooked, she was considerably taller than Catharine and had a smile that positively lit up her face.

"Good day, Shagshag," said Ninurta to the woman, who was evidently in charge of the facility.

David was in awe of the brightly lit VR facility. Its "playing" area was as capacious as a world-class rock-climbing gymnasium. Hanging from the ceiling, which soared forty feet above the ledge, were a half-dozen VR suits suspended from brightly colored synthetic ropes not unlike those used in mountain climbing. The floor of the playing area (which excluded the ledge) was a giant pit, its bottom covered with an apparently spongy layer of countless wads of gray material cut into various shapes and sizes. Between the gray material at the base of the pit and the ceiling above was a span of about sixty feet.

Catharine looked down over the ledge nervously. "How deep and how *soft* is that layer at the bottom?" she asked Shagshag.

Shagshag took Catharine by the hand and held it sympathetically. "Are you concerned with the possibility of falling, Ketura?" she asked.

"Well," said Catharine, "frankly, yes."

Shagshag seemed accustomed to concerns such as Catharine's. In what appeared to be a well-rehearsed motion, she removed something small from the pocket of her gown and showed it to Catharine. "Do you know what this is?" asked Shagshag, handing her the object.

Catharine examined it, appearing a bit confused. "It appears to be a common emery board ... for filing one's fingernails." She handed it back.

"Indeed, that's what it is," said Shagshag, as she fastened her hair back in a bun. "Now don't be concerned about my well-being. I find this kind of demonstration harmless and very persuasive with those apprehensive about using this perfectly safe VR installation." She filed her fingernails as she backed up closer and closer to the precipice.

Reaching the edge, Shagshag serenely hopped backward and dropped out of sight.

Catharine gasped and stepped forward (too late to prevent Shagshag from falling), and Nergal grasped her firmly by the arm to keep her away from the precipice.

Suddenly, numerous places in the facility roared with the sound of huge electric fans, though none could be seen.

A moment later, Shagshag, still blithely filing her nails, popped up at precisely the location from which she'd dropped into the abyss moments earlier. She took a step forward onto the platform and stood face to face with an astonished Catharine.

Shagshag stopped filing her nails long enough to remove the band from her bun and release her tresses, which fell loose about her shoulders.

David laughed nervously. "Neat trick," he muttered. "You certainly made your point."

Still non-plussed, Catharine hesitantly confessed, "I don't have an emery board."

Shagshag smiled indulgently. "You won't need one," she said, "because you're not going to fall." Evidently unsure whether it was understood that her unharmed reappearance had nothing to do with the emery board, she hesitantly offered it to Catharine. "You can borrow mine, if you like."

⟶○◖▱◗○⟵

IT TOOK ONLY ten minutes to get both David and Catharine into their VR suits, and another ten to explain how to control their movements in the virtual world.

As Shagshag explained matters to them, in the virtual world they would see themselves and each other as wearing no special gear, free-flying over the super-high resolution virtual copy of Planet Nibiru. Because of practical computer-storage limitations, they would be overflying a three-dimensional two-hour VR video of Nibiru taken on a day when the planet was approximately a billion miles from the sun.

As for the travelers' control over their movement, they could soar or swoop down simply by pointing in the desired direction. As they chose to travel hand in hand, Shagshag assigned David's right hand as his control hand, and Catharine's left as hers. If they were to thrust their control hands in a particular direction, they'd move rapidly in that direction. Pointing more gently in the desired direction would result in a similarly gentle motion. As David and Catharine wished to remain together, in the event David's control hand were to point in a different direction than Catharine's, the computer would prescribe an intermediate path based on best-fitting-curve calculations.

The travelers could, of course, speak with one another at will and agree on changes of course, should they so choose. They could also speak with Shagshag at will through their headsets, but Shagshag told them she'd prefer to step aside once they'd become accustomed to the system.

David and Catharine's lowest practical altitude would be approximately fifty feet, although at such low altitude the resolution of anything on the ground would suffer, leaving details a bit smudged. Their highest practical altitude would be low orbit, roughly the altitude of Lord Enki's orbit around Earth.

In the real world, they would be moving minimally—just enough to provide a sensation of movement consonant with the visual images they'd be seeing, and their experience would be enhanced by the facility's fans, as moving air would enhance their sense of movement.

When asked their preferred opening altitude, David and Catharine chose to begin two hundred feet above the planet's surface, roughly the altitude of a low flying hot-air balloon on a fair day.

If either of them were to say the assigned word "panic" aloud, or if their vital signs (which would be constantly monitored) were to fail to meet safe values, Shagshag would stop both their virtual and real-world movement and appear in their screens for a calm interlude. If worse came to worst, they would be brought back to the ledge until such time as they were prepared to try again—or give up.

"Are you ready?" Shagshag asked through the headsets.

"Yes," they each replied.

David and Catharine's view of the VR facility slowly dissolved to black and they felt themselves being gently hoisted up, up, up until their hearts pounded.

"Easy now," said Shagshag, who was monitoring their vital signs. "No reason to get excited. Look down, but remember, it's just a video. No one can see or hear you. Even if a bird were to fly into you, there would be no collision, because you're not really there."

From the blackness slowly emerged a breathtakingly realistic view of a grassy green field area as viewed from two hundred feet above the surface. Dotting the grass were small herds of ruminants of various kinds, including cattle and sheep, grazing at whim, apparently untroubled by predators.

"What God hath wrought!" muttered David, as though to himself. He turned his head toward Catharine, who'd obviously heard his remark. He could see her face next to him, as though she were without helmet or VR suit. The luminescent maroon sky behind her, full of wispy clouds, caught his eye.

Catharine turned to see what David was seeing behind her. "What energy source," she wondered aloud, "could ionize an atmosphere to the point where it glows?"

David shrugged. "I don't know, but I'd bet it involves gold," he said, referring to Enki's arrival on Earth in ancient times to gather the gold needed to repair Nibiru's atmosphere.

Despite the apparent daylight, a nighttime sky could readily be discerned in the gaps between the clouds, with only the brightest stars visible through the atmospheric glow. David and Catharine both found the effect otherworldly, which should have been unsurprising as, after all, they were on another world.

"Where's the sun?" David wondered aloud.

Shagshag's clear voice returned. "I'll answer that question," she said, "but then I'll try to leave you two alone. If you look straight ahead, the sun is about fifteen degrees above the horizon. Once Nibiru reaches this point in its orbit, the sun at last becomes one of the brightest bodies in the sky. It's visible, but barely. Obviously, the sun is not what's providing the light in the atmosphere. During the course of your overflight, you'll probably also notice several constellations that, although they would be quite prominent from Earth, will look a bit distorted from your current vantage point nearly a billion miles from Earth. If the VR video were longer, the constellations would appear to you at different hours and locations than they would when viewed from Earth, and they would be moving in a different direction across the sky, as Nibiru revolves around the sun in a direction opposite that of Earth. Other constellations readily seen from Earth would be completely unrecognizable to you from Nibiru, though you'll unwittingly be seeing many of the individual stars of which they're composed." Shagshag paused. "I leave you to your own thoughts."

Catharine said, "So this whole panorama is a snapshot of two hours on a single day?"

When Shagshag didn't immediately reply, David ventured, "I don't know how long it took to photograph the whole planet, but that seems to be what we've been told."

A quarter mile in front of them, the head of a giant male Anunnaki bobbed up above the tallest trees, moving toward the grazing animals immediately below them. Beside the giant, several male figures a fraction of his size scurried along the lawn to stay even with him.

Like King Enlil, the figure was dressed much as an ancient Greek.

"Look!" said David. "Could that be King Enlil with a few of his subjects?"

"He really is a colossus, isn't he?" remarked Catharine. "He seems even larger than he appeared when we were in his presence."

"Well, we don't really know much about the biological effects of Anunnaki dominance—"

Shagshag couldn't resist. "You are both right and wrong. On the day chosen for this recording, our King Enlil had not yet assumed the throne. Whom you see here is our beloved Majesty King *Anu*, may his name be forever revered. If you had lived in Mesopotamia as recently as six thousand years ago, of course, you might have seen him in the flesh."

Catharine shook her head as though to clear it. "David," she said tongue-in-cheek, "it looks like we just missed him."

"Well," said David, "let's go and see him now."

He thrust his right index finger in the direction of King Anu and they floated to within a hundred feet of the King's head, looking down on his face. By the time the VR video was recorded, King Anu was a stern old fellow, but his visage was still pleasant to view. They could hear the twig-crunching sound of his majestic footsteps and the clamor of those trying to keep up with him.

"Impressive," said Catharine. "The Anunnaki accompanying him aren't even tall enough to be clearly displayed."

"Yeah," said David, "they do seem a bit fuzzy."

David's eye was drawn a few miles ahead to a sizable city laid out in front of a large mountain. There was something … incomplete about the buildings, most of which appeared to be made of steel and glass and were pressed right up against the mountain. In any event, while the city seemed sleek, it seemed purely functional. No joyous Emerald City this.

"I suppose that's the planet's capital city," said David.

"Stands to reason, since this is where the king lives," said Catharine, "but what's wrong with the buildings?" She gently pointed her left hand at the city, and they began moving in that direction at a gentle pace. Catharine laughed.

"What's so funny?" asked David.

She shrugged. "I don't know. I feel like Supergirl or something."

"It's amazing, isn't it?" said David. He glanced again at the buildings. "Oh, I think I know what's strange about the buildings' designs."

"Oh?"

"I think they're built right *into* that mountain," he mused.

"So, the Anunnaki are like … hobbits?" she said.

"I suppose they are, on their home planet," said David. "I expect that the mountain houses numerous large caverns. This way, the denizens can occupy the buildings when conditions on the surface are hospitable, and retreat into the caverns when the surface gets too hot for comfort. In fact, I'd imagine, that mountain may well be their reason for placing the capital city here."

"Do you suppose the goats and cows we first saw are what feed this city?" she asked.

He shook his head. "Too few in number, I think. That was probably a royal park, so those herds are probably dedicated to supplying meat to the king's household." Pointing his chin at the city, he said, "Just judging from the size of those buildings up ahead, they're occupied by tens of thousands of Anunnaki. Queen Inanna told me that all Anunnaki need to eat meat to survive, so the city probably has much larger herds and slaughterhouses of its own, some of which are probably underground."

"Don't we humans need to eat meat, too?" asked Catharine.

"Nope," said David. "The prophet Daniel proved as much, limiting his diet to those items God intended man to eat: fruits, vegetables, whole grains, beans, nuts, and seeds. No animal products and no processed foods. *I* haven't eaten meat for the better part of a year, and I feel better than ever. Queen Inanna confirmed that we got our custom of eating meat from the Anunnaki."

As they approached the city, they could see several uniformly gray monorail trains speeding soundlessly along their tracks. Some tracks led away from the city into the lands 'round about, and other seemed dedicated to local transit.

When David and Catharine came close enough to see a few Anunnaki standing on the train platforms, something seemed amiss.

"Notice anything unexpected?" asked David.

"You first," said Catharine.

"Okay," said David. "First, I don't hear a sound. The trains are silent. They must be levitated; otherwise, they'd be clattering along the rails. In fact, we know from the Sumerians that Enlil likes things quiet. The noise made by humans was one of the reasons he allowed us to nearly perish in the Flood."

"And we didn't have trains then. Notice anything else?" asked Catharine.

"There are comparatively few people around," said David. "Indeed, from what I see, it's hard to imagine how so few passengers could support a railway system of that size. Another thing I notice is that there doesn't seem to be any smoke coming from the city." He turned to her. "What do *you* see?"

"It's what I *don't* see," she said with a shiver. "I see no children."

"They have far fewer children than we do," said David. "They'd *have* to; they don't die of old age. A high birth rate would quickly lead to over-population. We humans are a case in point. The Anunnaki gave us the power of procreation only a few thousand years ago, and in that short time our population has burgeoned to almost nine billion."

"Still," said Catharine, "a life without the clamor of children would be fairly morose, wouldn't it?"

He nodded. "I suppose so. Our experience of the Anunnaki to date has not shown them to be particularly … lighthearted. Has it?"

"And no wonder," said Catharine.

David caught sight of smoke rising from a distant mountain. "I wonder if that's a volcano," he said.

"Why don't we get a bird's eye view of the planet?" suggested Catharine. "Maybe there are more volcanoes."

"You mean—?" began David, apprehensively pointing straight up. "Aren't you afraid of going so high?"

Catharine laughed. "Once Buck Buchanan's flown you in a fighter aircraft, the sky holds no further terror. If he didn't kill you, you're gold."

She thrust her left index finger straight up, and David's stomach turned to butterflies as they rocketed skyward.

⁓◦◦⁓

DAVID AND CATHARINE'S android was taken for examination to the android maintenance facility on the third level of the royal pyramidion. Ninurta, before going to examine the android, called ahead to add two specifications to standing orders; he ordered that the android be presented for examination in a soundproofed Faraday cage to ensure that neither sound nor radio waves could escape, and that an audiovisual recording be made of the examination.

Ninurta had stationed outside the facility a female radio technician of undoubted loyalty. Just before entering the examination room, he asked her, "Is the android transmitting anything now?"

"He's been pinging a single frequency once every two minutes since he got here—and probably before," said the tech. "There's no detectable data embedded in the signal. It seems to be just an all's-well beacon."

Ninurta nodded gravely. "Copy the ping into your computer and begin transmitting it at precisely the same frequency and duration as soon as I close the door to the exam room. Also, paste a copy into a handheld transmitter for me, so I can carry it around, and start and stop it at will."

"Yes, my lord," said the tech.

⟶⟶⟶∘⟨⟨⟩⟩∘⟨⟶⟶⟶

THE ANDROID WAS sitting alertly on a swivel chair in the middle of the room when Ninurta entered.

"So," said Ninurta with a smile as he shut the door behind him, "you piloted our friends all the way here from Earth?"

The android nodded. "Well … from Earth *orbit*, yes."

"What duty were you assigned to before that?"

"I was valet and companion to Doctor Zia."

"I see. For how long?"

"Pardon?" asked the android.

"How long were you with Doctor Zia?"

"Oh," said the android, as though searching his memory, "many, many years. Too many to count."

"Can't you answer that just by checking your internal service log?"

"As I'm running a self-diagnostic program," said the android, "the log is currently unavailable."

"I see. What's your name?"

"I'm called Enkidu."

"Have you no personal name?"

The android looked a bit confused, and shrugged. "Enkidu," he said.

"Is that what Doctor Zia calls you?"

"Yes."

"Did you personally perform any maintenance on the antimatter craft before leaving Earth orbit?" asked Ninurta.

"Yes."

"What was the maintenance that you personally performed?"

The android appeared to search his memory. "I checked the engine seals using air pressure and India ink."

"And did you find any broken seals?"

"No," said the android dubiously. "If I had, we wouldn't have left Earth orbit until it was repaired."

"Android," said Ninurta equably, "power down neocortex. Enter sleep mode."

The android's face registered momentary surprise, then slackened involuntarily, and his hands flopped to his sides.

Ninurta had vocally triggered an override mode in the android's processing unit that almost no one knew existed—not even artificial-intelligence specialists. The existence of the override mode was known to only five Anunnaki, and only their voices could invoke it. With Anu dead, only four remained: Enki, Enlil, Ninurta, and Nergal.

The radio tech's voice suddenly piped in. "My lord," she said, "the android just began broadcasting like mad. Sounds like a distress signal."

"Are his transmissions fully contained?"

"His transmitter's surprisingly strong, my lord, but our baffling and our jammer are far stronger."

"Good. Make sure it stays that way. If he pumps up the signal strength, pump yours up that much more."

"Yes, my lord."

Ninurta turned back to business at hand.

"Android," he said, "state your series data."

While in limited-access mode, the android's voice was hardly the robust baritone it used in all other modes, but a rather small, nasal, computer-generated voice.

"Enkidu Improved Class, Unit 142," replied the android.

"In Earth reckoning, how long ago were you commissioned?"

"Twenty-two days, fourteen hours, thirty-six minutes."

Ninurta rolled his eyes. *You're barely three weeks old*, he thought, *but you worked for Zia for too many years to count?* Somebody'd been hard at work on this android's memory and given the android no clue that it had happened.

"Android, who is your current handler?"

Though the android appeared to be ready to answer, his face suddenly began to twitch.

"Answer me directly, android," said Ninurta, tensing up.

"I'm searching for a surname," said the computer voice.

"Never mind that. What's your handler's *given* name?" Ninurta demanded.

Though evidently suffering some internal distress, the android's nasal voice said, "Kassam."

"Android," said Ninurta, "power up neocortex. Enter waking mode."

The android sat up attentively, apparently unaware that any time had passed.

"I'm sorry," said the android. "Did you ask me something?"

Ninurta ignored the question. "Do you know who I am?" he asked.

The android studied his face. "No," he admitted.

"I am Ninurta."

The android then did something that no properly programmed android would *ever* do. He reached out his right hand to grab Ninurta's throat.

But Ninurta was ready. He seized the android's hand in his own (much larger) hand and squeezed hard.

When the android tried to wrench his hand free, he found it immovable in his adversary's iron grip. His strenuous efforts to free his hand succeeded only in turning himself upside down, in the process of which he inadvertently kicked some nearby testing equipment, making quite a racket.

The door to the exam room slid open and the tech raced in with an electrical sidearm drawn.

"Shall I fire, my lord?" she asked, amazed that the android had somehow managed to invert itself while balanced on one hand held firmly in Ninurta's grip.

"Don't shoot," said Ninurta calmly. "We may need him." He turned to the android and repeated his earlier command. "Android," he said, "power down neocortex. Enter sleep mode and remain in sleep mode until I tell you to awaken."

The inverted android fell asleep and collapsed to the floor. Ninurta dropped its hand with mild disgust and turned to the tech. "Don't try that little trick. It won't work for you."

"No, my lord," answered the tech.

"And don't ever tell anyone what was said or happened here."

The tech bowed low. "Never, my lord."

Ninurta looked down warily on the android's now-slack body. He entertained none of the fashionable sentimentality some seemed to harbor toward these machines nowadays just because they'd been painted with human-looking faces. "Tech, I need you to examine the code and data in this android. I need to know what changes have been made to its default code, especially any violative instructions it's been given, and also what standard-issue data it's been made to *forget*."

"Yes, my lord," said the tech, "but that could take some weeks. How long do I have?"

"Three days ... or less," said Ninurta, impassively wiping his hands on a damp rag. "And *discreetly* find out who the devil 'Kassam' is. Meanwhile, I have some arrangements to make."

CHAPTER 11

SINCE LEAVING THE winery, Buck and Sofia had flown several thousand miles hiding amongst northbound commercial airliners. As yet, there was no sign that they'd been spotted by the two bogeys sent to search for them in southern Chile that morning.

"We really owe Gary … and Lorraine," said Buck to his copilot. "I would never have guessed they were tryin' that hard to find us. Now at least we've got some mileage between us and the bogeys."

"Let's hope," said Sofia, searching her scope for any sign of a tail. "Think we should call into base and ask for a welcome-home escort by our practice squadron?"

Buck looked at Sofia before replying. They'd left the winery in such a rush that she hadn't had time to get back into uniform. Instead, she'd thrown her flight suit on over her civilian clothes which, at that moment, consisted of a simple cotton dress. And he could see that, under her helmet, her face was still made up and her hair pulled back in a barrette. It looked a little out of place, but she still looked great.

Ordinarily, Buck's preference would have been to keep Nellis AFB in the dark until the moment they slipped into air-traffic-controlled airspace, but he'd come down a bit hard on Sofia when they recovered the bogey's radio and figured this might be a good time to show some flexibility.

"Okay," said Buck. "Care to do the honors?"

"Sure thing," she said. She called in their estimated time of arrival over the Nevada desert and asked to have two saucers from their practice squadron meet them there to escort them to the base.

Now that they were no longer flying in commercial air lanes, they weren't going to fool anyone by continuing to fly at commercial speeds, so Buck opened the throttle a bit.

After a few minutes of comfortable silence, Buck said, "I noticed your folks don't seem to have much in the way of anti-American feelings."

"Why would they?" asked Sofia. "Their daughter is in the U.S. Navy. Oh, you mean, for overthrowing Allende and installing Pinochet?"

"Yah," he said, "I've heard that a lot of Chileans blame American intelligence."

"My folks … and *their* folks … hated both Allende and Pinochet. With Allende, they knew how other Communists had murdered small landowners like them in order to steal their land and eliminate any opposition. With Pinochet … well, my grandfather, *Dios lo tenga en su gloria*, used to say that Pinochet was both a monster and a pig, and that to keep the monster away, you had to feed the pig. So he did. He paid his dues and kept his kids out of trouble—and that was that."

Buck thought that made a lot of sense. "Are you sure your folks' winery couldn't produce a good red?" he asked.

Sofia chuckled. "Why? You thinkin' of settin' up shop next door?"

"I was thinkin' about it, yeah," he said flirtatiously.

She smiled and leaned into her scopes. "Hold that thought. Here comes our pair of escorts." At the same moment, there was a loud warning beep. "Shit!" she said. "We're gettin' painted from above." She clucked. "Who knows how long those bastards have had us in their scopes?"

"Look on the bright side," said Buck. "Our cavalry has arrived just in the nick of time."

A voice came on the radio. "This is Ransom. You got two bandits comin' down on you from near-orbit. We're lookin' right at 'em. Recommend you take evasive action. Over."

Buck considered the situation. Ransom was a good pilot, and he was pretty senior, but he hadn't identified his second banana. "Who's *we*, Ransom? Over."

"I brought Hutton with me, lieutenant, just for laughs. You took my first choice Muñoz with you. Over."

"Privilege of seniority," joked Buck. "Over."

"Well, there's no doubt you've got loads o' seniority, sir," said Ransom. "I mean, you're practically a senior citizen. Hey, those bandits are comin' down on you fast. Looks like they mean bidness. Mind if I give 'em a big hello from Nellis AFB? Over."

"Go ahead, Ransom. Just be careful, and watch out for those laser cannon. You think you two can take them by yourselves? Over."

"*I* can, sir," said Ransom. "Hutton's just gonna eat popcorn and watch from the cheap seats. Over."

"Very well. I'm takin' evasive action to give you a clear field of fire.

See you back at base. Over."

Buck dropped his altitude, then accelerated to maximum operating speed. But no more than five seconds had passed when they heard several bursts of cannon fire above and behind.

Sofia was watching the fight through her rear-oriented scopes. "Well, Ransom got one of 'em already; he's goin' down in flames. If the other one's got any brains, he'll turn and run—oh, *shit!*"

Buck heard a gut-wrenching explosion behind them that had a metallic crunch in it. He'd heard that sound before, but only once, and he hoped to heaven there was a different cause for it now. His heart was going like a nuclear reactor pump at flank speed, and Sofia was maddeningly quiet.

"Report, copilot," he ordered.

"It was a mid-air collision, Buck." She was quiet for a moment. "Looks about as bad as it gets."

Hutton's voice came on the radio, uncharacteristically solemn. "That was Ransom, sir. He nailed one bandit and was about to hit the other when the bastard turned around too quick. Must have been in a panic, because he sailed right into Ransom. The bandit got the worst of it, but Ransom—hold on—hold on—HE GOT OUT! I see a parachute with an ejection seat hanging down. Over."

Buck and Sofia exhaled for the first time in what seemed like an eternity. "Can you see if he's conscious, Hutton? Over."

"Doesn't look like it, sir. I mean, he's not wavin' or anything. 'Course, that doesn't mean much. Over."

Buck began to turn the saucer, but Sofia objected.

"We can't go back for 'im, Buck."

He scowled at her and snarled. "That's pretty cold, lieutenant."

Sofia shook her head. "No, it's not. Ransom's got an uninjured pilot in a vertical-landing craft ready to take 'im home. You know navy pecking order, Buck: Save the mission, save the craft, save the men, *in that order*. And that radio you salvaged from the downed bandit and strapped to our airframe … *That's* the mission."

Buck admired his co-pilot's cool head. He nodded reluctantly and spoke into the radio. "Follow 'im down, Hutton. Pick 'im up, do any necessary first aid, and get him back to base ASAP. *Oh!* If you can easily grab the ejection-seat kit, bring that, too; its contents are still classified. Over."

"Roger that, sir," said Hutton. "Out."

THAT NIGHT, BUCK sat alone at a small, dark corner table at the officers' club staring at an unopened bottle of tequila that he'd asked the waiter to bring. Though his mouth was dry, he resisted the temptation to enlist the tequila in escaping the phone call he now had to make.

He could remember only too well the long-term funk that Gary fell into when a couple of his pilots were killed over the Bering Strait. It was so severe that Gary ended up leaving the service. And now Buck would have to call Gary on Enki's pyramidion to share the news about Ransom. He wanted to be in control of both his words and the little nuances that, uncontrolled, might magnify Gary's worry.

Mainly, he wanted Gary not to leave the service, both for selfish reasons and because he didn't think the practice squadron would ever be the same again if Gary were to quit under these circumstances.

Clenching his jaw, Buck took out his mobile phone and dialed Gary's encrypted line.

Gary picked up right away. "Hey, Buck. I was just thinkin' about ya."

Buck couldn't resist. "I hope you weren't in the shower. You sober?"

"Yeah, you?"

"Well … Got some not-so-good news to share." He could hear Gary sit up and take notice. "My copilot and I were worried that we might have been shadowed by a couple o' bandits."

"The ones I called Lorraine about?" asked Gary.

"Yeah, or two just like 'em. Anyway, my copilot suggested we call ahead to the base and get a couple members of our practice squadron to meet us in the airspace above the Nevada desert and escort us back to base. Two fighters showed, Ransom and Hutton. Now that I think back, it was probably their arrival that prompted the bandits into action. While the bandits were descending on us from low orbit, Ransom went after them both. He knocked one out of the sky—"

"Good for him," said Gary tersely.

"The second bandit panicked and turned around a bit too fast—"

"Oh, no," said Gary, full of dread.

"There was a mid-air collision—"

"Aw, *shit.*"

"Yeah. Anyway, Ransom had apparently managed to hit the Eject button. Hutton saw his 'chute open, and he landed at a controlled clip. As far as we can tell, he was already unconscious. Hutton picked him up and brought him back to base. He's"—Buck sighed—"beat up pretty bad."

"Life-threatening?"

Buck swallowed hard. Gary would never forgive him if he were to sugar-coat it and Ransom were to die. "Yeah. He's got a list of fractures as long as your arm, startin' with two broken legs—"

"He got those on ejection, right?"

"*In all likelihood* is what the docs say. They can't tell yet which of his other internal injuries were suffered aloft, and which came from impact with the ground. The docs did say that he has surprisingly little in the way of spinal injuries."

"That's damned good," said Gary.

"Yeah, it is. They're guessin' that, by the moment of impact, he was already clear of his craft, so some of the injuries could be from impact with shrapnel and some just from the shock wave. God knows how he had the time and the presence of mind to hit the button."

"Ransom's sharp," said Gary. "A sharp pilot expects everything. Has he regained consciousness?"

Buck swallowed twice. "Not yet, no."

"What's the prognosis?"

"Wait-and-see. Base commander's sendin' a couple of officers to provide Ransom's parents with a naval escort to base hospital tomorrow evening."

"No," said Gary incredulously. "He's still at the *base* facility? Isn't there a full-service hospital nearby?"

"The docs don't want to take the chance of movin' 'im."

Gary paused a moment before speaking. Buck knew what he was thinking. *If the docs are afraid to move him, that's a bad sign.*

"I'll be there tomorrow," said Gary.

"Listen, Gary," said Buck. "We wouldn't have known to expect the bandits if you hadn't told us they were comin'. If you're needed up there—"

Gary interrupted him again. "I'm not gonna let that brave man's parents suffer in doubt that he may have done somethin' to bring this on. I don't want them to have *any* unanswered questions. You'll be there, right?"

"Yep, and I'll make sure Sofia's there."

"Who—?" asked Gary. "Oh, you mean Muñoz."

"Yeah, she was my copilot and saw the whole thing on the scopes."

"Don't worry about takin' me away from here, Buck," said Gary. "It turns out I have some important personal stuff to take care of, but I'll come to you first."

So far, Buck was satisfied that he hadn't said anything to bring about a recurrence of Gary's career-ending funk, so he decided to make a quick exit. "Sorry we couldn't save you one of the bandits, Gary, so you could go up and shoot 'im down."

"It's okay, Buck," said Gary. There was a moment's silence, and he added with finality, "I'll kill the rest of 'em."

⟶∘⟋⟍∘⟵

AS SOON AS Gary got off the phone with Buck, he called General Ningishzidda and sought an emergency interview, to which he brought Hendrick in tow.

Gary spoke first. "One of the pilots in my squadron has been badly injured in a dogfight with Anzû's fighters, my lord. It's customary for the squadron leader to meet with the pilot's family. So, it looks as though I'll be the one headin' to the States first. I'd appreciate your people requisitioning a shuttle for me to leave sometime in the next few hours, and I'd be most pleased if you would tell me what you'd like me to tell the admiral about the apparent switch of the two androids."

The general arched an eyebrow. "Have you already made an appointment with the admiral?"

"No, my lord," said Gary. "That could have defeated the whole point of waiting for an authentic reason for one of us to return to Earth. Once I've finished at the air force base, I'll discreetly make an appointment with the admiral and meet him without fanfare."

Ningishzidda smiled. "Well done. Prepare to leave in two hours … and thank you for your cooperation. I'll bring you a note from Lord Enki to the admiral."

⟶∘⟋⟍∘⟵

DAVID AND CATHARINE overflew much of Nibiru's northern hemisphere, viewing cities, large and small, as well as many quaint villages, all built into mountainsides.

At any given moment, at least one-fourth of Nibiru's surface was obscured by cloud cover, which made the planet even less cheery than it might otherwise have seemed. Despite the activity of millions of Anunnaki, in the absence of bright sunlight and the capering of children the planet seemed a bit sad.

As for the distribution of wealth, each city and town contained a few neighborhoods that were well maintained, and a few much less so, but David and Catharine could detect no outward sign of the extreme poverty, filth, and neglect that typified slums on Earth. Whatever the relative status of any individual Nibirune, at least in the northern hemisphere starvation and serious privation seemed to have been eradicated eons earlier. On the other hand, telltale signs of crime prevention, such as locked gates manned by guards and dogs, seemed ubiquitous—suggesting that not all of the planet's inhabitants were pure in heart and deed.

The couple also overflew massive mountain ranges dotted with various types of volcanic activity, running the gamut from smoldering old craters with enormous associated geysers to lively, glowing lava flows that hissed and steamed their way to cold water, where they hardened into new stone.

Nibiru boasted ample bodies of water, but no central oceanic system, such as that occupying more than two-thirds of Earth's surface. Sleek vessels crisscrossed the waters; roughly half appeared to be devoted to the movement of cargo, while the other half consisted of well-outfitted passenger vessels.

Northern Nibiru presently bore no signs of war or armed conflict, nor any obvious scars of the planet's violent past.

Catharine thrust her left index finger upward, and soon they were in near-orbit once again.

Suddenly aware that their two hours on Nibiru was a bit more than half over, David suggested they go south.

"Lead on," Catharine replied.

David thrust his finger toward the south and they crossed the Nibirune equator in less than a minute.

They were dismayed to find that the differences between north and south were stark. Instead of finding the large shiny buildings they encountered in the north, they found that construction south of the equator was sparse and rudimentary at best. The pair overflew cities where entire precincts appeared to have been burned out and abandoned centuries earlier.

In many places, whole sections of brick had tumbled off a wall into the street, with no apparent effort having since been made to clear away the fallen debris, let alone to rebuild the ruined walls. Indeed, many brick buildings had been destroyed so long ago that their original footprints were indiscernible from the air.

Ancient black scorch marks on some buildings had been nearly washed away by centuries of rain. Architectural brass and copper had turned verdigris, and holes had appeared wherever parts had rusted out completely. One or two buildings vaguely resembled the remains of the Orizuru Tower that had remained standing after the nuclear destruction of Hiroshima.

Descending toward one randomly selected island, they found cottages made of canvas and rope secured to stonewood trees. Toward the center of the island, a brightly colored design about the size of a roadside billboard had been painted onto a remaining section of the only brick structure in view. David frowned and thrust his right index finger at the fresco, so they moved closer until they were barely fifty feet above it. Although the resolution of the VR image was a bit fuzzy, the message was clear as day. David looked to Catharine, who was as astounded by it as he was.

The fresco was a painting of the design David had seen on the nosecone of the missile sent to destroy Inanna's pyramidion; the same design that Catharine had seen on the flying saucer that she destroyed on Great Slave Lake.

It was the symbol of Anzû. *But what the devil was it doing here?*

As they tried to descend for a better look, they both felt pressure on their chests and the VR image before them was replaced by blackness.

Shagshag spoke once again.

"You've both come to rest on the cushion at the floor of the pit," she chirped, "so you can't go any lower. It's just as well, though, since your time's up. Don't move. I'll bring you up to the ledge."

Chapter 12

THE ORBITAL SHUTTLE was no longer a modified navy jet fighter, but an SF-5 saucer. It quietly touched down at Nellis Air Force Base on a pad hastily built to handle VTOL (vertical-takeoff-and-landing) craft. Gary stepped out of the shuttle, the door automatically closed behind him, and the shuttle took off immediately.

On his way to the waiting car, Gary contemplated whether the hasty deployment of the SF-5 and the construction of new landing pads designed for it were preparations for war. He hoped he was wrong, but he had a nose for these things, and expected he was right.

Buck was waiting for him in the back seat of a Jeep driven by Thurston, the kid who'd driven Gary around when he first arrived on the base. Buck's hope was that Gary would see Thurston as a sign that he'd come *home*, and it seemed to work.

When Gary spotted Thurston, his eyes lit right up. He got in the back, nodded to Buck, and put his bag between them on the seat. When he saw that Buck was smiling, he was a little puzzled.

Buck pointed his chin at Thurston. "Do you remember this youngster?"

"I sure do," said Gary, reaching his open right hand over the front seat. Thurston shook it with a big smile.

Buck said, "This young man has been accepted into the massive SF-5 expansion program. Before you know it, he'll be readin' our manual and drivin' one of our buckets."

"Hot damn!" said Gary with enthusiasm, and turned to Thurston. "If you drive that bastard with as much skill as you do this Jeep, you'll be a fine pilot." *There it is again—the massive SF-5 expansion program.*

"Thank you, sir!" said Thurston. "I can't tell you how encouraging that is, coming from such an accomplished fighter jockey."

Gary further encouraged the kid with a firm smack on the shoulder.

Thurston's chest swelled with pride. "Buckle up, sir," he said, and began driving them toward the base hospital.

Gary observed that Buck was still smiling broadly and shook his head disapprovingly. "What the hell you smilin' at?" he demanded. "You forget where we're goin'?"

But his annoyance only made Buck smile all the more. Buck leaned toward Gary, and said, "Ransom wanted me to welcome you back to base."

Gary looked at him, perplexed. "*Ransom?*"

Buck smiled and nodded.

"He's conscious?" asked Gary, a smile dawning at the corners of his mouth.

"Not only is he conscious," Buck replied smugly, "he's coherent, and tests perfectly for motor and sensation on all extremities. His spine's unaffected."

"*Unaffected,*" Gary echoed with deep satisfaction, almost dazed at the good news. "Excellent! His folks arrive yet?"

Buck shook his head. "They're still an hour out of Nellis, but we radioed 'em *en route* and gave 'em the good news."

Gary hesitated a moment, then asked, "Any *bad* news?"

Buck sighed. "Well, he's in a lotta pain. Docs say that'll last as long as four months, or even more, but—*hey!*—he'll walk, run, and fly again."

"Why don't we stop and get a drink to celebrate?" asked Gary. "That pyramidion's a dry county—at least for humans."

Buck shook his head grimly. "I guess *that's* the bad news. When I mentioned to the admiral that you'd be comin', he ordered me—and *you*—not to drink until further notice. Sounded like he has somethin' specific in mind for us."

Gary found this a little surprising. He hadn't contacted the admiral yet, so the old man had no way of knowing what surprises were coming his way. He briefly considered bringing Buck in on the news, but thought better of it. Instead, he focused on resenting the old man's peremptory order.

"Hey, Thurston," said Gary, leaning over the front seat, "does this bus stop at the officer's club?"

Thurston shook his head with enough exaggeration to ensure that the gesture would be seen from the back seat. "Sorry, sir. To stop there today, you'd need a transfer slip. *Er*, you wouldn't happen to have one of those, wouldja?"

"Not … *yet*," said Gary hopefully. "Where would I get one?"

"They never printed 'em up, sir," said Thurston. "Besides, I'll be damned if I'll forfeit my ticket to the expansion program by testifying under compulsion against a superior officer."

Gary glanced over at Buck, who shrugged.

Rather than let it pass, Gary said, "You know, smartass, the perfect driver doesn't listen to passenger conversation."

Thurston replied, "I guess the perfect driver doesn't belong to the U.S. Space Force, sir."

Buck laughed.

Gary laughed, too, and sat back with a sense of relief. *No drink ... but no condolence call, either. I'll take that tradeoff any day.*

⟶◦◖▰▰▰◗◦⟵

THE VIRTUAL REALITY system lifted Catharine and David off the pit floor and brought them gently up to the ledge, where Shagshag undid the grips and clasps holding them in their VR suits.

David and Catharine removed their helmets. As soon as Catharine's face was free, she began chattering enthusiastically. "What a beautiful planet!" she said. "It's hard to believe that a place could be that bright and livable so far from the sun."

"Oh, yes," said Shagshag. "In fact, it's *more* livable when we're far from the sun. Once the sun begins to grow large in the sky, Nibiru swelters and we retreat into the caverns." She picked up a little bottle of disinfectant and began spraying each item they handed her, then folded each of the soft items to be stored away. "I suppose it's not that way on Earth," she ventured.

Catharine was surprised by the comment. "You've never been to Earth?"

Shagshag shook her head. "I've *seen* Earth in the Nibirune sky—very close, once or twice—but never set foot on the planet."

"That's a shame," said Catharine. "We positively *live* for the summertime, when it gets warm. It's difficult for us to face the cold of winter."

"You know," said Shagshag, "on Nibiru, we don't even have words for summer and winter, for Nibiru has neither."

As Catharine and David finished removing their equipment, they thanked their hostess, and Nergal entered the facility, ready to escort them out the door.

Before they could leave, Shagshag said to Catharine, "Aren't you forgetting something?"

Catharine looked at her blankly.

Shagshag extended her hand, palm up.

"Oh, of *course!*" said Catharine with a laugh, and handed back Shagshag's emery board. "Thank you. It worked *perfectly.*"

"It always does," replied Shagshag smugly.

Outside the facility, Nergal grabbed his partisan.

David saw that there were no other weapons in the rack, and wondered whether Ninurta had read Inanna's note or investigated their android pilot.

BY PRIOR AGREEMENT, David and Catharine had refrained from discussing their VR experience until they were in private.

They were silently escorted to their room by Nergal, who left with a friendly nod.

"Quite a day," observed David, as he lay his head on a pillow.

"I couldn't believe how tall the king was," Catharine said. "You know what silly thought didn't leave my mind the whole time? I kept trying to imagine how his queen could … service him."

At first, David considered the question seriously, and shrugged, saying, "He wasn't *always* that size." Then he regarded Catharine as though she were mad. "All that went on there … and *that's* what stays with you?"

"Well, think about it," she said. "He's just so … *big*. It's as though he were a different species."

"Dimorphic," mumbled David.

"What?"

"Dimorphic," he repeated. "When the sexes of a given species diverge to the point where they look like they could be of different species, it's called dimorphism."

"Even if it's just that their body size is different?"

"I don't know," replied David. "If that's the only difference, I'd think the difference would have to be pretty extreme."

"Even if the size difference were dominance-related?"

David felt far out of his field. "What *you* need is a biologist," he said. "But I've heard the term applied to bees, whose size difference seems to be hierarchically significant, too. Leave it to you to fixate on the sexual aspect of size differences. Cut it out."

"Well," she said saucily, "I'm of the sex that has to accommodate such differences." She plopped herself on the bed beside him and began kissing his chest. "You want me to cut this out, too?"

He pretended to consider her question. "No. You can *never* cut this out." He stroked her hair. "You know what has me puzzled?"

"Oh, I don't know," she said. "Could it be why Anzû's logo was painted on walls in Nibiru's southern hemisphere?"

He nodded contemplatively. "I know that the king alluded to the possibility, but I have no idea what to make of it."

"Maybe people in the south think they've gotten the shaft," she said. "Could it be we're on the wrong side of this dispute?"

"No," he said. "If the Anunnaki were dishonest, they could easily have obliterated that image to make sure we'd never see it. Besides, Anzû has sent out hitmen to murder us. The Anunnaki haven't. In fact, they've treated us with respect. Until something happens to change that, I'm pretty sure we're on the right side."

"Actually," she said, "at the outset, the Anunnaki were most interested in *you*. But Anzû wants to murder *me*. He doesn't seem all that interested in you. Why, do you suppose?"

David had learned from his brief conversation with the king that Anzû's motive for trying to be rid of Catharine was to eliminate a serious rival for David's affection. If David were devoted solely to *Inanna*, as Anzû wished, David would need immortality in order to protect her. To get that, he'd need Anzû's help. And to get *that*, he'd have to serve Anzû. But he raised none of that now.

"I wonder what's going on back home," he said evasively.

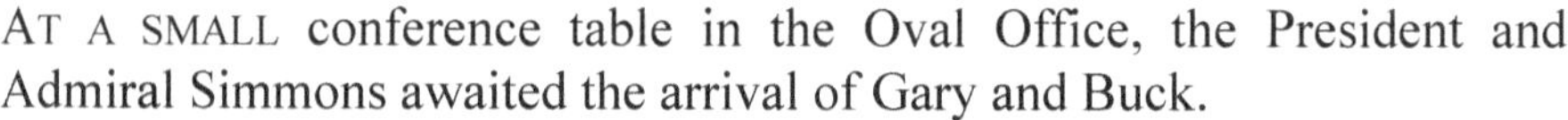

AT A SMALL conference table in the Oval Office, the President and Admiral Simmons awaited the arrival of Gary and Buck.

"How's the rapid Space Force development going?" asked the President.

"It's roaring," replied the admiral. "Both the air force academy and the naval academy have dedicated cram courses and new facilities to SF-5 engineering and training. Buck and Gary's manual is the most purchased book on either campus. Bet they never expected to write a bestseller."

The President scowled. "A bestseller? It's *classified*, isn't it?"

The admiral nodded reassuringly. "Of course. I was speaking of sales in the need-to-know community. It's going into a second edition already."

"Why?" asked the President. "Have they found errors in it?"

"A couple of typos, but that's all," replied the admiral. "I got con-gratulatory calls from a few instructors who couldn't believe it was completed in a few months." He laughed. "Amazing what those two cock-ups can accomplish when they're sober."

Holly's voice came over the intercom. "Mister President, Lieutenants Sullivan and Buchanan are here to see you."

"Send 'em in," said the President. "Speak of the devil."

Gary and Buck entered in service dress blues, and saluted with their covers in the crook of their left arms.

"At ease, boys," said the President. "Take a seat."

Gary and Buck sat down. "'Morning, Mister President," said Gary.

"First things first," said the President. "How's Ransom?"

"He's beat up pretty bad, sir," replied Gary, "but the docs say he'll be A-OK in a few months. Good thing, too. He's a shoo-in for squadron leader."

"How'd his folks take his injuries?" asked the President.

"They were upset to see their little boy in traction and a great deal o' pain," said Gary, "which is perfectly understandable, of course. But they were relieved to hear he'd fly again. Evidently, it's been his lifelong dream."

The admiral had a few questions.

"Who're you appointing as temporary squadron leader?" he asked.

Gary let Buck answer. "We were thinkin' of Muñoz, admiral."

"Good choice," said the admiral. "If she's as good as you expect, you can give her a squadron of her own when Ransom returns. Muñoz was your co-pilot on the mission to grab the bogey radio, right?"

"Correct, sir," said Buck.

"We watched part of your mission from here, y'know."

"Actually, I *didn't* know, sir. But, in that case, I'm glad it was suc-cessful. If you don't mind my askin', sir, has that radio been helpful?"

"To a point," said the admiral. "It proved that their radios have pretty much the same vulnerabilities as ours, but we're not sure if they're using frequency-hopping in their radio comms, which would have helped to know."

Buck was disappointed. "There was nothing in the radio to reflect frequency-hopping?"

"Not that our guys have found, as yet," said the admiral, "but that doesn't prove much of anything. Evidently, frequency-hopping can be programmed into an outboard unit and placed in a circuit prior to the radio itself."

"Damn," muttered Gary. "You mean we didn't get the whole radio?"

"You got the whole radio," said the admiral reassuringly. "Don't blame yourself for matters outside your mission parameters. The frequency-hopper, if there was one, could have been anywhere in the spacecraft. It could even have been concealed on the pilot's person."

"Damn!" said Buck. "He was *lyin'* there on the ground. I coulda—"

"Relax," said the President. "That wasn't your last mission, lieutenant. We'll have another try at it. In the meantime, however, we're going to have to assume we won't be safe jamming only a specific set of frequencies. That means we'd have to fry their radio comms completely, and that can only be accomplished—"

"With an EMP nuke," said Gary.

There was a moment of silence, as they contemplated that deploying an EMP meant a kind of nuclear war, which was expected to be difficult to contain.

"I gotta admit," said Buck, "I barely know the basics of that technology."

The admiral nodded indulgently. "That's because we withhold as much information about it as we can. We've known since the Second World War that even a relatively small nuclear explosion high up in the atmosphere sends out a series of electromagnetic pulses capable of destroying all electrical devices in a very wide area—except for specially shielded items."

"Such as?" said Buck.

"Well, it's no secret that much of our defense infrastructure is hardened against an EMP. However, much of the country's economy depends heavily on continuous electrical current and continuous computation. It's hard to imagine how medieval we'd become if most of our electronic infrastructure were knocked out by an EMP."

Buck nodded. "We know Anzû has nukes; one of his was detonated over the Arctic. What's stoppin' him from doin' a pre-emptive EMP strike against the USA?"

The admiral scowled. "Unfortunately, very little at the moment—at least, very little that Anzû knows about. He thinks our nuclear weapons have all been neutralized by the Anunnaki rays and that we can't mount a nuclear response."

"That's wrong?" asked Buck.

The admiral regarded Buck skeptically, then glanced over at Gary.

"*You* know whether that's wrong, Lieutenant Sullivan. Don't you?"

Gary shook his head. "To answer you frankly, admiral, I don't know *squat*. But I've done a truckload o' guessin'." He looked at the admiral awry. "Does it have somethin' to do with Hendrick?"

The admiral looked to the President for permission to disclose the information, and the President nodded.

"We've got most of our nukes up and running as we speak, thanks in large part to Hendrick," said the admiral. "But that's the most closely held secret in the solar system right now. It's possible Enki's guessed at it, but it doesn't leave this office. So, bear that in mind."

Buck whistled softly. "That changes things mightily, don't it?"

The admiral shrugged. "Some things it does. But some it doesn't. If Anzû knew we could obliterate him ten times over, he'd be real careful about provoking us—or giving us an excuse to whip his ass."

Gary added. "But since Anzû *doesn't* know, detonating an EMP has gotta be at the top of his bag of tricks."

"It's not that clear," said the admiral. "He'd still have to deal with an Anunnaki response."

Buck scoffed. "Unless they were to leave us in the lurch … again."

The admiral shook his head. "We still don't know what the Anunnaki have in mind, but if they're planning on moving in with us in a few hundred years, they can't have the planet poisoned indefinitely with radioactivity, or worse, occupied by Anzû's merry band of lunkheads." He looked at the pilots. "Believe me, I hate like hell allowing Anzû to think he's got a clear shot at us, but we just can't let him know we've got nukes; first thing he'll do is tell Enki."

Buck said, "If we want to keep open the option of being first to use an EMP, we've got to have conventional means from keeping every one of his aircraft out of U.S. airspace. Otherwise, he'll just retaliate and we'll be fighting with sharp sticks."

The President said, "What do you think the emergency ramp-up of the SF-5 is all about?"

Buck looked dubious. "How many are we gonna have, and how soon can they be deployed?"

"Seventeen squadrons," replied the President. "And whatever the Anunnaki can send us. Think it'll be enough?"

Buck shrugged. "How many squadrons does Anzû have?"

The admiral replied, "We have no idea. We know he has at least a few in the Arctic and at least one in the Antarctic. We expect a lot of those in the Arctic are kept submerged, so we can't get a count. As for the Antarctic, we know where the hidey-hole is that they fly out of. What they've got down that hole is unknown. They could have been building up down there for centuries."

Gary chimed in. "Any way we can get somebody down there to count? Skeeters, maybe?"

"No electromagnetic waves seem to escape their hole," said the admiral. "So, as far as we can tell, even if we get some skeeters down there, we're gonna have to get them *out* before they can transmit their intelligence to us."

"So, what's stoppin' us from sendin' in skeeters? They got a can o' Raid down there?"

The President scribbled on a pad in front of him. "We've hesitated to send them in. If we send them in numbers large enough to spread out and gather meaningful intelligence, they're likely to be spotted and draw some retaliation—such as an EMP." He looked up at the two pilots. "You think we're exercising excessive caution?"

Gary said, "It's a valid concern, but less so if we're ready with a one-two punch. If the skeeters get caught down there, we have to be ready with an EMP first-strike to pre-empt any retaliation."

The President resumed scribbling. "And then we're in a hot war, instead of the cold one we're in now."

The admiral changed the subject. "As for the Anunnaki leaving us in the lurch, we've analyzed both the recording of our request for Anunnaki assistance in Dakota and our receipt of a beep confirming receipt. Turns out neither our dispatch nor the confirmatory beep appear on Enki's recording."

Buck was puzzled, but Gary seemed to catch on. "It was all done down here, wasn't it?"

The admiral nodded admiringly. "Lorraine's transmission was jammed locally and the confirmatory beep was sent by a source no further than two miles from base."

"No more'n two miles?" Buck wondered aloud. "Geez, even our practice squadron was further away than that. The only ones closer were … the bandits."

"That's right," said the admiral. "Our engineers calculated the origination points of the jamming signal and the confirmatory beep. They both came from the same source, which was airborne and inbound toward the base. There's no doubt it was the bandits."

Buck's eyebrows went up. "That means that either Enki's in cahoots with Anzû or—"

Gary didn't even allow Buck to finish his sentence. "The Anunnaki have a traitor in their midst," he blurted out, and tossed a sealed envelope onto the table and slid it toward the admiral. "This is a note from Lord Enki confirming that, and adding another tidbit."

The admiral read the brief note silently, and his face blanched as he handed it to the President.

Buck was the only one who didn't know what was going on. "What happened?" he asked.

The admiral stared at Gary and pointed his chin at Buck. "Tell 'im."

Gary began. "David and Catharine have reached the royal pyramidion. Enki received an automated safe-arrival signal, followed up by a direct communication from the king, his brother. David and Catharine were supposed to be piloted there by a trusted android who's resided among the Anunnaki for thousands of years. But, just before they left for Mars ... *somebody* secretly substituted a different android, and we don't know how or why."

The President looked up from the note and said to Gary, "It was Hendrick who noticed this black mark on the android?"

"Yes, sir," said Gary.

"Geez," said the President, "he doesn't miss a trick, does he? Is he still on Enki's ship?"

"Yes, sir," said Gary. "Leastways, he was there when I left yesterday."

The admiral asked, "What steps has Enki taken to detain the android who was left behind?"

"Enki impounded him on the pretext that his battery was subject to a recall," replied Gary. "They're sure he's the one who was supposed to go with David and Catharine."

"How can they be sure?" demanded the President.

"You've read Enki's letter, sir," said Gary. "They won't tell us how they know, but they know the remaining android's date of origin is thousands of years ago, while their records show that the one piloting David and Catharine is practically brand new."

The admiral snarled. "We've got an ambassador and my adjutant up there in peril. If I were Enki, I'd be tearin' the place apart looking for the culprit."

"The problem with proceeding in that manner," said Gary calmly, "is that there are dozens of people in charge of their encrypted communications. If that unit's been infiltrated (as it probably has), the moment they sound the alarm, the traitors will know it instantly and start coverin' their tracks, escaping, or even implementing a planned rebellion. Hell, admiral, Enki wouldn't even send you notification by radio. He insisted the message be in pen and ink, and that it be carried by me. He even made me wait to bring it to you until I had an alternative reason to come down here."

Buck sat up. "You mean, Ransom's collision?"

Gary nodded.

The President chimed in. "How long have David and Catharine been on Enlil's pyramidion?"

Gary checked his watch. "About thirty-six hours, sir."

The admiral shifted uneasily. "There's something that makes no sense to me. If their pilot was a booby-trapped android, why did he successfully pilot them all those millions of miles to Mars? If he'd been programmed to do something sinister, why wait for the return trip?"

The President openly speculated. "It's possible he'd only do 'something sinister' depending upon the conditions he found on the royal pyramidion." He turned to Gary. "Is it possible the android isn't even conscious that he's programmed to do something wrong?"

Gary threw his hands up. "That's *way* above my pay grade, sir. Besides, it's a machine. Who knows if there's even a distinction between conscious and unconscious thought in a machine?"

The President acknowledged the flaw in his question. "Is there a back-channel for me to talk directly with the king? I mean, bypassing Enki's pyramidion?"

"None that I know of, sir," said Gary.

The President looked to the admiral. "What about Miriam's frog people?"

Gary and Buck regarded each other quizzically.

The admiral said, "I was just thinking of that, Mister President. But, no matter how heavily encrypted, the transmission is sure to be detected on Enki's ship. They won't know what it says, but they'll know we're communicating with Enlil's pyramidion."

No one at the meeting knew of the ancient cipher by which Ninurta had radioed Queen Inanna. And only one of them knew that David had a telepathic line to Anzû.

"I think we'd better get David and Catharine back here at once," said the admiral.

The firmness of the admiral's decision surprised even the President. "Bob, isn't David supposed to present his ambassadorial credentials to the king? And aren't the two of them supposed to do a virtual-reality overflight of Nibiru?"

"Once those are done," said the admiral, "I want them home as soon as possible. I'm profoundly uncomfortable having both our ambassador to the Anunnaki and the only officer who's successfully engaged with Anzû's forces *weeks* out of reach." He put on his bulldog face and shook his head gravely. "Talking to Gary and Buck today has made me more conscious that a lot can happen in the next few weeks, and I want David and Catharine where I can reach them as soon as I can get 'em. And we'll do whatever it takes to protect my adjutant."

Gary said, "But if they haven't replaced their pilot with a reliable one, sir … accelerating their return could also accelerate their … demise."

The President, who'd taken no pains to conceal his surprise at the admiral's sudden resolution, supported him. "We have to think about the interests of the United States, Gary. Each of us is in peril, and each of us is expendable."

ON THE ROYAL pyramidion, there was an urgent knock at David and Catharine's door.

Catharine was up like a shot and began searching her belongings for her weapon.

David smiled. "No weapons up here, young lady. Better go cover yourself. Hand me that robe, would you? I'll answer the door."

Catharine grabbed David's robe from a chair and tossed it to him before heading off to the bathroom.

David was shaking off his dreams as he adjusted his robe and grabbed the door handle.

It was Ninurta without his partisan, wearing a grave expression. "You've received orders from your President," he said, stepping inside and closing the door.

"What orders?" asked David.

"You're to return to Earth at once."

Strangely enough, David's first reaction was to dread facing two more weeks of weightlessness with its attendant discomforts.

"But … have you resolved the issue about our pilot?" he asked.

Ninurta shook his head.

Catharine stepped out of the bathroom with her body fully covered and her hair combed. "What's up?" she asked.

David said, "Evidently, we're going home."

"When?" asked Catharine.

"Now," replied David. "*At once*, on orders of the President."

"What about our pilot?" she asked, reasonably enough.

Ninurta said, "We haven't had time to resolve the issue thoroughly, but I did interview the android. What I found was that it was commissioned only three weeks ago, as measured in Earth time. It's definitely not Ziusudra's android and it's been programmed to not like *me*, that's certain."

"Have you had a chance to analyze his programming to determine why somebody switched him with the real Enkidu?" asked Catharine.

"As I was just explaining to David, we haven't had time," said Ninurta, "but we've made a complete copy of its programming and databases and will analyze them once you've left."

"But we'll already be at his mercy," Catharine protested.

"Not completely. I've had a transmitter installed in your craft so I can monitor your movement and other activity. The android has no knowledge of the transmitter. In addition, if I need to, I can shut him down and take direct control of the craft."

David's eyebrows shot up. "Why not just disable him, and guide us yourself from here?"

Ninurta shook his head. "The android's transmitting data about your progress, probably to Anzû. If we disable it, Anzû will know something's up. Besides, it's important for us to find out how the android's been tampered with, and what its altered instructions might be, as that could inform us of Anzû's intentions."

Catharine was quite skeptical. "And, to think, in order to gain that intelligence, you need only risk the lives of America's ambassador and a navy lieutenant commander."

"I assure you that I have no intention of losing either of you," said Ninurta earnestly.

"Of course not," said Catharine. "Think of the paperwork."

Ninurta found this puzzling. As he was about to speak, David put his hand on Ninurta's shoulder and said, "Best to let it go."

Catharine checked her watch. "We've been here less than two days."

Ninurta searched in one of his pockets, pulled out a slim headset with a built-in microphone and handed it to David. "This will ensure that you're not as isolated as you were on your voyage here. If you need to speak with me, press the blue button to talk. I'll hear you soon and respond through the headphones. Remember that the signal carrying your voice to me, and mine to you, cannot exceed the speed of light, so there will be a built-in delay. Also, remember that the pilot of your craft must not know of these, as he has the capability of disconnecting them electronically."

"So, you're giving this to David? How thoughtful!" said Catharine acerbically. "Is this a boys' club? There *are* two of us, you know."

Ninurta reached back into his pocket. "I have yours right here," he said, handing it to her. She seemed deflated by her own defensiveness.

David smiled so broadly he had to look away.

Ninurta's expression was one of incredulity. He said to Catharine, "What's a boys' club? Do you have clubs that admit only boys?"

Catharine's face turned bright red. "Only among children. Among adults, they're called men's clubs."

"They must be very dull," said Ninurta. "What do they do at a men's club?"

"I wouldn't know," said Catharine, "would I?"

Ninurta looked to David. "Do *you* belong to a men's club?"

David laughed before replying.

Catharine's expression clearly denoted her view that he was enjoying himself entirely too much.

"Too dull," said David. "Not only do I not belong to one, but I've never been invited to join one. In fact, I'm not sure they exist, except in the imagination of women who fear they're being excluded from them."

Ninurta seemed confused. "Why would they wish to join, if they're so dull?"

David abruptly shifted the topic, before he could get into more trouble. "Shouldn't the lieutenant commander and I at least pay our parting respects to His Majesty before going?"

Ninurta replied, "I've spoken to His Majesty, and he's assured me that he fully understands your need to depart immediately in compliance with orders. He's military both by training and disposition, as you well know."

David eyed Catharine, unsure whether to broach the next subject in her presence. He decided to risk it. "Has your lordship had occasion to review the missive from Her Majesty?"

"I have," said Ninurta with a wistful smile.

"I trust you are not disappointed in it?" said David.

"Not in the least," said Ninurta. "I expect you and I shall be meeting on that soon, and in the presence of Ketura. We don't wish to be dull."

As David and Catharine would presently be leaving on a two-week journey of many millions of miles, David had no idea how such a meeting might take place.

CHAPTER 13

THAT THEIR ARRIVAL had aroused no fanfare whatever made their departure ceremony all the more remarkable, befitting a head of state more than an ambassador and a naval officer. Though there were no children aboard the royal pyramidion to enliven their departure, instead there was an assembly of sixty uniformed troops at attention in full Etruscan dress regalia, with ceremonial swords and partisans. A band of six musicians, similarly clothed, played music that sounded as though it had originated halfway between Mesopotamia and the Indus Valley. The unmistakable drone of sitars underlay a somber melody following a non-Western scale.

Ninurta and Nergal escorted David and Catharine to the base of the ramp leading to the door-size boarding hatch of the antimatter vehicle, which appeared to have been washed down and spruced up for the occasion. At the top of the ramp, their android pilot stood at attention and bowed at their approach.

Ninurta left Nergal on the deck and escorted David and Catharine up the ramp. He spoke quietly to the android. "Please assume your pilot station, Enkidu, if you would."

The android acknowledged the order with a bow at the waist, and disappeared into the hatch.

Ninurta waited for him to disappear in the direction of the cockpit, and leaned in to address his two departing guests.

"I'm going in to check on a few things. I'm also setting a relay that, if triggered, will shut down the pilot's ability to see and hear through the onboard cameras and microphones mounted all over the craft. Your headsets"—he regarded them with sudden doubt—"you *do* have them, don't you?"

David and Catharine nodded confidently.

"Very well. The red button on your headsets will toggle the camera/mics on and off. Do *not* push that button unless I personally tell you to, for it's sure to arouse immediate suspicion and make our lives more difficult. For now, please turn and pleasantly face the assembled."

Ninurta disappeared into the antimatter vehicle behind them, and left them forcing a long smile for the assembled troops and musicians. In a couple of minutes, Ninurta reappeared, raised his hand (apparently the signal for the band to stop playing), stood at attention, and addressed the troops in English, no doubt for the benefit of the departing guests.

"On behalf of our beloved King Enlil—"

The assembled troops interrupted as required by protocol, reciting as one, "Long may he reign."

Ninurta resumed.

"—let us bid farewell to our visitors from the esteemed allied nation of America, and wish them and their nation long life and peace." He turned toward David and Catharine and took a step back from them.

"*Salom!*" Ninurta pronounced broadly.

"*Salom!*" the assembled echoed with equal vigor.

David turned to Catharine and whispered the count-off for their parting benediction. "One ... two ... three—*Shalom, and Long Live Good King Enlil!*"

The parting words had the desired effect; the well-disciplined troops dropped their salutes, laughed and applauded, chanting "Long Live Good King Enlil." David and Catharine shook Ninurta's hand, waved goodbye to Nergal, and passed into the cabin.

The hatch closed automatically behind them. Through the soles of their feet, they could feel the heavy ramp being rolled away from the craft and the troops being marched out of the bay in formation.

David plopped down in the first seat he came upon, which mystified Catharine. While she'd planned to take their bags directly to their sleeping quarters (second nature to the frequent traveler), instead she put down her bags and took the seat next to David, who'd become quite somber.

"What is it?" she whispered.

He laughed bitterly. "What is it?" he echoed in a whisper. "Our pilot is controlled by someone who'd rather see us *dead* than see us home. And, in a few seconds, we'll be completely dependent upon him once again, millions of miles from the nearest aid. And what do we have to protect ourselves? A couple of headsets." He shook his head hopelessly. "Like *they're* gonna save us."

"David," she said, "we're not in the android's hands. We're in *Ninurta's* hands."

He seemed to lighten up at that, but only slightly.

She continued. "He's the guy who kicked Anzû's ass all those years ago, remember?"

David nodded equivocally.

"Well, he's gonna do it again," she said.

"Then why isn't he aboard with us?" asked David.

She shrugged. "As my dad used to say, 'Never bet against the champ.' If we need Ninurta, he'll be here."

What David wanted to say was, *it would take him weeks to get to us.* Instead, he forced himself to brighten a little.

"Yeah," he said, "you're probably right."

The landing bay had evidently already been cleared and sealed off, as it was being rapidly depressurized. Once that process was complete, the big exterior door opened and an automated announcement came on the PA system, "Control: External."

The craft rose a few feet off the deck and slowly passed out into space. David and Catharine gazed forlornly at Mars. In a few minutes, even the cold comfort of having a dead planet nearby would be lost to memory in the indifferent void of space.

David felt all hope leave him, replaced by a ruthless determination that Catharine would survive this trip unscathed.

No matter who had to die to make that happen.

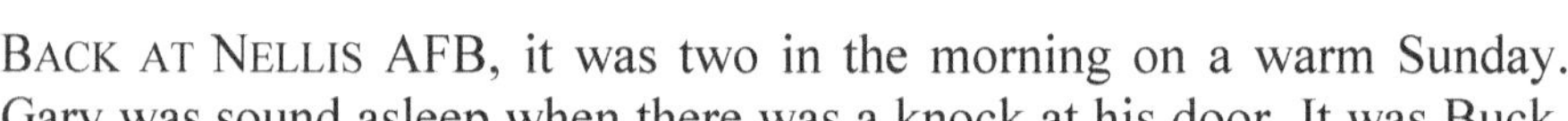

BACK AT NELLIS AFB, it was two in the morning on a warm Sunday. Gary was sound asleep when there was a knock at his door. It was Buck, in uniform.

Gary ran his hands over his face. "Hey, Buck," he mumbled in his West Texas drawl gazing at his friend's face through bleary eyes, "was I supposed to report or somethin'? I thought I had nothin' scheduled—"

Buck was distracted from whatever had caused him to visit in the middle of the night. He pointed at Gary incredulously. "You wear pajamas?"

Gary rolled his eyes. "Well, at least I don't sleep in uniform, like you apparently do. Gonna put me on report?"

Buck shook his head, as though he couldn't afford to get caught up in trivialities just now (much as he would have liked to). "No, it's just— Come with me to comms. There's no brass there, just somethin' I want you to see. Throw on a pair of jeans and a tee-shirt."

Gary put on the civilian clothes he'd been wearing before he changed into his PJs, consisting of a pair of black Levi's jeans, a brightly colored, billowy Hawaiian shirt, and leather sandals.

Buck silently shook his head disapprovingly. "Shoulda stayed in the pajamas," he muttered, and beckoned Gary to follow him to the Jeep.

An unexpected wave of jet-fuel vapor wafted over Gary's face, nearly making him choke. He glanced at the driver. "Thurston," he said, "is this guy makin' you drive around all night? That's against navy regs."

"Welcome to Space Force, sir," Thurston snickered. "It's okay. I was on duty anyway."

Before getting into the back seat, Gary glanced all around him. The hairs on the back of his head tingled. He'd seen preparations for conflict before, and the base was bustling with the telltale signs. Light shone out of widely separated windows in all the command-and-control buildings. There was more ground-crew activity on the tarmac than he'd ever seen on a Sunday night, and many more pedestrians on the street, virtually all in uniform and moving with evident purpose. An old quotation returned to him unsummoned: Something about preparations for war not "dividing the Sunday from the week."

He knew well that such hypervigilance could hang in the air for weeks (or even months), only to be instantly dispelled once the crisis was averted. But then there were the *other* times ... when events got out of hand.

The Jeep jerked to a halt in front of the radio shack. Gary and Buck got out and Thurston drove off without a word.

Every light in the radio shack was on, and a small group of techs had gathered around a large screen showing a radar sweep.

Gary was a little disoriented when Lorraine (of all people) popped out of the crowd to greet him. His puzzlement must have been evident, because she laughed and said, "I'm not in your imagination, Lieutenant Sullivan; I was just transferred here from Ellsworth." She regarded Buck skeptically. "I was the one who asked Lieutenant Buchanan to fetch you, though I assume he didn't mention that. Glad you're here; I need a reality check."

Lorraine turned to the screen showing the radar sweep. "Make a hole, please," she said, and several techs stepped aside, allowing her and Gary to approach the radar screen. She spoke to whoever was operating the screen. "Please cue up the first incursion, please."

Gary found the word *incursion* disturbing.

The screen momentarily cleared, only to be replaced by a clean radar sweep.

"Looks familiar," Gary said, in a lame attempt at humor.

Lorraine pointed to the northernmost periphery of the sweep. "Here it comes … five, four, three, two, one … *bingo*." She turned to Gary. "Did you see it?"

Gary nodded. "I saw *somethin'*," he said. "Play it again."

Lorraine counted down and, once again, an evanescent blip flashed at the north edge of the sweep looking suspiciously like something he'd seen on his fighter's scope on the last day of the summit meeting—just before his squadron descended on the enemy fighters.

"Could it be an electronic artifact?" asked Gary, turning toward Lorraine with an idea. "Y'know, on my SF-5, the computer has a module that makes a best-guess analysis of low-altitude objects."

Lorraine scoffed quietly. "The one on your craft's just a little mobile version of Big Sweeper right here." She pointed to a very ordinary-looking laptop.

"What does Big Sweeper say?" asked Gary.

"She says it's definitely not a radar artifact," she replied. "It's real … whatever it is."

Gary nodded cautiously. "Did she say it was a flock of migratory birds?"

"She said it looked like birds," said Lorraine, "but expressed low confidence."

"You know what else looks like birds on radar?" asked Gary.

Lorraine appeared stumped; she studied Gary's expression. "I'm gonna guess … a squadron of enemy flying saucers?"

Gary nodded somberly. "Or just about anything else with effective stealth measures. Has the incursion recurred?"

"Not yet," said Lorraine. "In fact, we woulda missed *this* one if it hadn't been for Big Sweeper's insistence."

Buck suddenly appeared at Gary's shoulder.

"Waddya think?" asked Buck. "Is it worth wakin' up the old man?" He smiled. "Or are you the oldest guy we gotta wake up tonight?"

Gary couldn't let that pass. He smiled broadly and said, "Screw you, Buck."

"Yes, sir," said Buck. "Thank you, sir."

"Let's wait and see if there's a repeat of this," said Gary. "If there is, we'll have to alert base commander."

There were a few raised voices in a group that had moved on to another screen.

"What is it?" shouted Lorraine. "Talk to me."

"Incursion happened again, ma'am," said a young radar tech wearing an old-style headset. "It looked exactly the same, likewise on the periphery, but this time it was about twenty degrees east of the original blip, moving toward Ellsworth."

"Don't tell me," said Buck. "That's right at the Canadian border."

"Correct, sir," said the tech.

Lorraine hit a few keystrokes on the laptop she'd dubbed Big Sweeper. "Same exact size and velocity as Blip Number 1." She typed another keystroke. "Big Sweeper says it's saucers—with high confidence this time." She turned to Gary. "Should we send up a fighter?"

"No," said Gary. "At the moment, they're just probing. Let 'em think we missed 'em." He turned to Lorraine. "They're not probing only our radar, y'know. They're probing our reaction. Wake up the base commander. Tell 'im it's my recommendation he contact Ellsworth with an encrypted message." He turned to Buck. "Do they have any SF-5s there?"

"They have a baby squadron," said Buck. "Should we tell 'em to send it up?"

"No way," said Gary. "Too likely to result in air combat, and they're not ready for that." He turned to Lorraine. "Anyway, our base commander should advise Ellsworth to send up an individual saucer as though it's on regular patrol. That'll make the bastards think we're patrolling, but they won't know they've been spotted."

Buck nodded. "Psych," said Buck. "Renders their whole probing mission a failure. Next thing for *us* to do is actually establish a regular patrol."

"Just what I was thinkin', Mr. Buchanan," replied Gary. "But the USA has ten thousand miles of border to patrol. How can we do that? And we can't let *one* of those bastards get in here."

Lorraine looked at Gary askance. "Why would just *one* intruder be a major threat? They got some kind of bomb that'll take out a whole continent?"

Gary and Buck exchanged a glance; as far as they knew, Lorraine wasn't cleared for this intelligence. Evidently, protecting against an EMP weapon wasn't even under discussion in the airborne services—except at the very top.

Gary said to Lorraine, "Buck and I are gonna get some coffee. You want anything?"

Lorraine made it obvious that she knew she was being shut out. "No," she replied resentfully.

When Gary and Buck got outside and began walking to the commissary across the street, Gary said, "I'm still not sure whether we should wake up the old man."

"How come?"

"As I see it," said Gary, "this can shake out in only a couple of ways. If the enemy is probing our defenses for a weakness, as I suspect they are, they would try to pierce them at the weakest point ... *eventually*."

"Makes sense."

"Yeah," said Gary, "but suppose *eventually* means *tonight*?"

Buck nodded thoughtfully. "If we don't wake him up, the USA'll be caught with its pants down, and it'll be *our* fault."

"On the other hand," said Gary, "if we *do* wake 'im up, at least he'll be runnin' the show, and he'll know all the alternatives."

"So, then, that would dictate that we wake 'im up, right?" replied Buck. "But if they're not gonna try to pierce our defenses *tonight*," he added, "why wake 'im up? Or should we wake 'im up every time they probe our defenses?"

They suspended the conversation to buy two takeout cups of coffee. On their way back to the radio shack, Gary said, "You asked the right question, Buck."

"I did?" asked Buck with surprise.

"Yes. The question is: *Under what circumstances should we wake up the admiral?* The only one who can prescribe those conditions is ..."

"The admiral?"

"Right," said Gary confidently.

"But we have to wake him up to ask him," said Buck, as though Gary hadn't thought of that.

"Exactly," replied Gary. "We're wakin' him up to ask him when we should wake him up."

"Makes sense to me," said Buck.

Gary nodded. "Which only goes to show we've both been in the service too long. It's rotted our brains."

When they returned to communications, Lorraine assigned them a room with conference-call capability so they could call the admiral privately. She personally walked them to the door. Before opening it, she leaned in toward Gary. "Are you guys worried about an EMP?"

Gary's eyebrows shot up. "Sorry, can't discuss it."

Lorraine pursed her lips impatiently. "I'm cleared for it. Ask the admiral. He's the one who cleared me."

"Okay," said Gary. "Go back to your job. If he says it's okay, we'll come gitcha."

That seemed to placate her.

Gary looked at Buck, who was sitting quietly. "Well, ya gonna call the admiral?" he demanded.

"Me?" objected Buck. "*You're* senior."

Gary shook his head disdainfully. "So, I'm too old for this job, *except* when it's convenient for you to hide behind your junior status?"

"Pretty much," said Buck.

Gary picked up the handset to the landline. "Nobody likes to wake up onto a conference call. I'll talk to him first."

The admiral picked up on the fourth ring, sounding groggy, and miffed at being disturbed. "Yeah, what's up, Gary? I have to get up early for church. What time is it? Aww, fer chrissakes, it's almost five in the morning anyway. What's up?"

"I'm calling from Nellis Air Force Base, admiral. I've got Buck here with me. Can I put you on the squawk box?"

"Yeah. What the hell? I'm up now anyway."

"Can we bring Lorraine in on the call?" asked Gary uneasily.

"Sher," grumped the admiral, "let's have a party."

Gary got up, stuck his head out the door and waved energetically for Lorraine to join them. As soon as she came in, he shut the door and began. "Admiral, Lorraine caught a blip on the radar, and the computer's pretty sure it's enemy saucers probing our defenses. As we have no clue whether and when they intend to follow up with an attack, we thought it best to clue you in at the earliest possible moment."

"Good morning, Lorraine," said the admiral. "Did it happen just once?"

"Twice, admiral," said Lorraine. "Second time was about … let's see … a quarter-hour ago."

"Whom have you notified?" asked the admiral.

"Just base commander, sir," replied Lorraine. "The bogey seemed to be moving eastward, so we advised the base commander to recommend Ellsworth send up an SF-5 and simulate routine patrol."

There was a moment of silence on the line while the old man assessed the advice. "That's good. Don't tell the bastards anything, and let 'em think we're up there all the time. Whose advice was that? Sullivan's?"

"Yes, sir," said Lorraine with a nod to Gary.

"Figures," said the admiral. "That was good advice. But there's one more thing we've got to consider."

Gary chimed in. "What's that, admiral?"

"We've got to become more aggressive probing *their* defenses. We've been too cautious until now. If they're gonna risk destabilizing the situation by sending out probes, they need to see us as just as aggressive." He sighed. "But I can't authorize that on my own."

The three at Nellis AFB knew that that could mean only one thing. The admiral had to call the President. Suddenly, their calling the admiral didn't seem like such a stupid idea.

They could hear the old man's bed creak, followed by a few muffled words from his wife.

The admiral spoke again. "Go and get some sleep, boys. If we're sending up a couple of fighters, you two are flying 'em. I'm gonna see if it makes more sense to go with skeeters, though. It's cheaper and less destabilizing. Meantime, Lorraine, I don't have to tell you not to wander far."

"I won't, sir," said Lorraine.

There was a click. The admiral had hung up without any cordialities, which meant he was intent … and nervous.

⸺⊰∘⊱⸺

HENDRICK HAD BEEN summoned to appear before Lord Enki.

"Where is your friend Sullivan?" asked Enki.

"He's still on Earth, my lord," said Hendrick.

"When will he return?"

"It's difficult to say, my lord," said Hendrick. "He has agreed to rejoin the navy for a time, so he serves at the pleasure of his commanding officer. It was my understanding, however, that he would return within a week of his departure." It unnerved Hendrick that every time Enki blinked his eyes, it felt as though the room lights had dimmed.

Enki nodded. "So, perhaps another few days. I wished to share with both of you what I have found about the android who remained here on the pyramidion."

"I listen with great interest," said Hendrick.

"The android's given name is Enkidu," said Enki. "He was made in accordance with my original specifications—nearly five thousand years ago."

"Is he indeed the very Enkidu who befriended Gilgamesh?"

Enki shook his head. "No. I know that parts of the Sumerian tablets have been ruined over the millennia, leaving details of the popular story in doubt. But I can assure you that the original android was destroyed on order of the Council, just as the story goes."

"*Why*, my lord—if I may ask?" said Hendrick.

"Because we realized—and I include myself in that group—that I had created a monster capable of bonding so strongly with Gilgamesh that it had turned its considerable powers against the Council. I preserved many of the android's sense impressions, however, and, once I'd designed appropriate safeguards, I conferred his impressions upon the next few generations of android."

"Under the circumstances, it would have been difficult to take issue with the Council's actions."

"The designated handler of the Enkidu left behind on this pyramidion has always been Ziusudra. I regret to say that some modification has been made to his memories, and some may be entirely lost. Whether his renowned personality is still intact remains to be seen. For now, the urgent matter is to ascertain *who* modified his programming. It would have taken a very skilled engineer. Very likely, that very engineer also modified the programming of the Enkidu piloting David and Ketura's craft as we speak. Do *you* have any idea who this engineer might be?"

Hendrick stood silent for a few moments. "I have my suspicions, my lord—but no evidence."

⟶∘⟪⟫∘⟵

THOUGH DAVID HAD been complacent much of the time *en route* to the royal pyramidion, for the first few days of the return trip he'd had no peace of mind at all. He'd planned on losing himself in Dostoyevsky or perhaps Orwell, but found that his fear of the android pilot had become an intrusive thought—not merely repetitive, as was often the case in obsessive-compulsive disorder, but rather *continuous*, which was even worse.

Unable to sleep for more than a couple of hours at a time, he'd taken advantage of what little physical room there was to move about the craft, floating here and there, plopping down on this or that seat—all aimlessly. Worst of all, at anxious moments, he'd begun fingering the headset Ninurta had given him, several times coming perilously close to touching the forbidden buttons that could tank their fortunes. All this while, Catharine (or *Ketura*, as everyone in the Anunnaki community now called her) slept the sleep of the innocent.

He awoke in the passenger section of the craft and found himself in the same seat he'd taken when they first came aboard on this miserable return trip. Navigating lazily into the dormitory, he gazed down lovingly at Catharine's sleeping form, his feelings for her untarnished. But he felt somehow estranged from her—indeed from anyone or anything that might provide any hope. He felt helpless. There wasn't a damned thing he could do to ensure her safety.

He resolved with substantial effort to do something he'd come to hate. He would visit the cockpit and watch what the android was doing. Not that he really expected to *understand* what the android was doing. To the contrary, he expected to understand no more than a five-year-old child given an opportunity to accompany a parent to work once a year. The child could see the parent pick up the phone and chat—pleasantly or unpleasantly—but with little or no understanding of the call's content.

He floated into the cockpit as nonchalantly as he could, and took a seat behind the pilot. As ever, the android took no apparent notice (Did they have to make him so *oblivious*?) but sat up a little more attentively just in case he'd need to field a question from his pesky guest.

"What's our status?" asked David.

The android turned his head a few degrees as though he'd originally intended to look his passenger in the face, but immediately returned to eyes front. "We're six days out from Mars, moving toward ... Earth's orbit."

Earth's orbit? There'd been a peculiar hesitation before the android spoke that ambiguous phrase. Why not just ... *moving toward Earth?* The phrases *Earth orbit* and *Earth's orbit* meant two completely different things. Earth orbit referred to the path circumscribed by a body revolving around Earth. *Earth's* orbit meant the circle described by the Earth as it revolved around the *sun*. He put the idea aside for the moment.

"And the craft?" he asked. "Is everything fully operational?"

Once again the android hesitated. "The craft is fully functional. Just the usual small glitches."

David's eyes darted around to detect anything suggesting a glitch. "Glitches? Like what?"

"Well—and you needn't be concerned about this—a few of our out-ward-facing scopes have become less than fully responsive to instructions from the cockpit. I hasten to add that we still have scopes providing a slightly diminished three-hundred-degree view of our *way ahead*—if you'll pardon my pun on the craft's name." The android must have been delighted with his lame pun, for he followed it with a nerdy snort.

"Any other glitches?" asked David impatiently.

"Well," said the android equivocally, "looking into my records of the way forward, I find"—he seemed to search for a suitable verbal formulation—"a diminished resolution."

"Diminished resolution?"

"Yes," replied the android, "no sentient being—a class in which I include myself—can perceive the objective world in *all* its attributes. (As I'm sure you've heard, at any given time, the unaided eye can see no more than four sides of an opaque cube.) The real world is a complex place, and there's simply too much data out there to be perceived and processed. Sentient beings, such as ourselves, see a phenomenon only at a certain level of detail."

Sensing David's bafflement, the android provided an example. "Say you're working at a task on your computer workstation. The images on your screen appear to you in high resolution; they're important to your task. Now assume that, before you logged on, someone had placed some flowers in a vase a few feet away. You know they're there. You can even see them from the corner of your eye. But the flowers don't appear to you at the highest resolution, as they promise neither assistance in—nor any impediment to—your task."

Though the concept was new to David, he nonetheless found its possible application to their present predicament a bit alarming. "So— you can't recall the way forward in the resolution to which you're accustomed?"

"That's correct," said the android.

"But, returning to your example," said David, "if I want to see the flowers at a higher resolution, I need only look in their direction. Can you also do that with the way forward?"

The android dismissed the suggestion. "I don't need much in the way of resolution to guide us through empty space, and I *won't* need it until we're so close to our destination that I need to calculate a safe ap- proach."

"So, our way home looks—a little fuzzy to you?"

The android nodded equivocally. "That's one way to put it."

"Has this ever happened to you before?"

"No," said the android, "but I don't have much experience guiding a craft through so much ... empty space."

Just heartwarming, David remarked to himself. *Limited knowledge, combined with zero experience. I wouldn't offer this droid a job tabulating student grades, let alone guiding a spacecraft over billions of miles.*

DAVID HAD A sinking feeling as he lay down next to Catharine, who snored lightly.

While an android would no doubt be capable of dissembling, he didn't think this one was. The android seemed to harbor no suspicion at all that, in all likelihood, someone had tampered with his memory of the way home. And David couldn't decide whether the android's guilelessness was a hopeful sign or not.

The android also seemed not to suspect that someone might have tampered with his scopes. David sincerely hoped that, if there *was* such a tamperer, it had been Ninurta. He placed his hands behind his head and closed his eyes, wondering how long it would be before *Anzû* made himself known.

He wouldn't have long to wait.

CHAPTER 14

"DAVID!" THE GRAVELLY voice was unmistakably Anzû's, and it wasn't coming to David telepathically. It was close. He was in the room.

David sat up in alarm and caught sight of Anzû standing right in front of the bed. Strangely, never before had he imagined what Anzû looked like—or whether he was human or Anunnaki. Even now there remained some doubt; he could have been either. Judging by size alone, he was Anunnaki—which only made sense, as his logo had been spotted on the Anunnaki home planet of Nibiru, painted on a wall in some sort of apparent protest. And his eyes emitted some light, though nothing resembling Enki's.

Anzû's face and scalp were an asymmetric, scarred, and bruised patchwork of hairless skin that had evidently been removed, stretched back over a damaged and misshapen musculature, and sewn back on. Anzû looked like nothing so much as a burn victim who'd been pieced back together by Earth's most inept or sadistic surgeon.

Strangely, although Anzû was ghastly to look upon, David's first feeling toward him was pity, rather than fear. *This poor bastard has had to present this face to the world since time immemorial.* It raised additional doubts in David's mind over the utility—or perhaps *futility*—of immortality. Would anyone looking like that choose to do so *forever*?

Sensing David's reaction, Anzû smiled a hideous grin, a rictus that bared a pair of unexpectedly long incisors. "You're shocked by my appearance," observed Anzû contemptuously. "Did you think that the loser of the greatest aerial battle of the ancient world would be left as beautiful as the winner? I take it you've seen a likeness of the lovely Ninurta?"

David nodded.

"Well," said Anzû, "take a good look at *my* face, David. This is how they leave you if you dare cross them—that is, if you're not *one* of them." He laughed bitterly.

David suddenly realized he was no longer in the dorm on *The Way*

Forward, but rather in the bedroom of his apartment in New York—the last place he'd expect to be confronted by this miscreant. And Catharine, who'd lain next to him while he slept on the interplanetary craft, was now nowhere to be seen.

"Have you yet come to love Inanna?" Anzû demanded. He snapped his fingers and, somehow, a slightly smaller version of Inanna appeared before David, the size of a human woman. His heart longed for her, and she smiled smugly, as though she knew it.

David looked past her to Anzû, and answered with the king's words. "Any man who doesn't fall in love with Inanna has no heart."

"And what of the shieldmaiden you've been sharing your bed with?" asked Anzû. "Are you prepared to serve *her* all your short life and forgo Inanna's eternal charms?"

"I haven't thought that through," said David—although, looking at Inanna now, the prospect of settling for someone else seemed less than enticing.

Anzû cocked his head skeptically. "Is that the truth, David? Or have you rather learned from the Anunnaki how to *lie*?"

"I haven't decided *what* I want, Anzû," said David, "and I still don't see why I owe it to you to do so."

"You've had plenty of time, David," snarled Anzû. "The time of choosing is upon you."

"Why must I choose at all?" demanded David. "And what business is it of yours?"

Anzû's face contorted in anger. "Perhaps I've allowed you to become too complacent. Well," he said with a cunning laugh, "I can change that." And he vanished.

But the human-sized Inanna remained. She sashayed appealingly to David, sat next to him on the bed, and kissed him on the mouth. He suddenly felt trapped in an unholy state between sleep and waking.

"Hey, sexy," said Inanna in a voice not her own, "wanna fool around?" Not only would those words never have been uttered by the Queen of Heaven, but they were spoken in *Catharine's* voice. The discordance between Inanna's dignified countenance and Catharine's colloquialism shook him to the core.

He opened his eyes to find himself back on *The Way Forward*, being kissed by Catharine. He recoiled. There was no way he could continue with that particular kiss; any way he thought of it, it was a lie.

Catharine sensed his internal dissonance and drew back skeptically. "Is *she* back again?" she whispered with uncanny accuracy.

David shook his head. "Not she," he whispered less than truthfully, "*he*."

"Anzû?"

He nodded.

"We have to dig out Elijah's mantle," she said. "Where did you pack it?"

"It's in one of my bags," he said, "but that's not what's important right now."

Catharine waited for an explanation.

"For Anzû to contact me," he said, "something major must have happened, something down on Earth, but I have no idea *what*."

"Why don't we call the admiral and find out?" she suggested.

He shook his head. "Same question, same answer. Anything we say will pass through that lump up front and will, presumably, be relayed to Anzû."

She leaned in and whispered to him, almost inaudibly. "What about … *you know*?" She winked knowingly, obliquely referring to the headsets given them by Ninurta.

He deliberately misinterpreted her suggestion and shook his head. "Is that all you can think of at a time like this?"

She smacked his shoulder. "Not *that*, you egotist."

"No, *I know* what you mean," he said with a wry smile, and rubbed his shoulder theatrically as he kissed her. "I'm going to see if I can learn anything from Lumpo."

David went off to the cockpit, where he found the android looking confused while leafing through a manual.

"Hello, Enkidu," said David. "How goes our progress?"

Enkidu turned away from him, as though lost in a particularly perplexing thought.

"Enkidu?"

At last, the android turned to him, abashed. "Um … I'm not sure," he muttered, and returned his attention to the manual.

"What do you mean, you're 'not sure'?" he asked.

"Well, things seemed to go swimmingly until a few hours ago." He pointed to his main monitor, which showed a lot of blackness and a few celestial pinpoints of light. "And now … nothing out there is where it's supposed to be."

David's heart sank. *Score one point for Anzû*, he thought. *I'm no longer complacent.* "Please explain," he said.

The android appeared genuinely frustrated. "When our points of reference are located where they are right now, I … I … have no idea … where we are."

"Can you check the *craft's* database?"

"That would be pointless," said the android. "My personal databases are much more detailed. This craft was designed to travel all over the solar system, and even outside it. It can't hold a detailed map of everything."

David began to simmer, but he managed to hold his temper. "Why don't you just radio ahead and ask for directions?" he asked.

"I tried that," the android admitted with chagrin. "But the radio has … ceased working."

"Which way were we headed when you … lost your bearings?"

"That's just it. I'm not sure. I thought we were heading toward the sun." He turned toward David to explain. "Obviously, as we're coming from the Mars system, Earth's orbit is in the same general direction as the sun. The sun's not so bright at this distance, but it's still the brightest object in the sky."

David searched the android's main screen for the brightest object in the sky. He pointed to it and said, "Is this the sun?"

The android shook his head humbly. "That's Alpha Centauri … I think."

I think? "How long would it take us to get there?" asked David.

"At the speed of light? About four and a half years."

"But we're not traveling at the speed of light."

"Indeed, we're not," the android confirmed. "And we don't have nearly enough provisions to survive that long in any case."

"Shouldn't we see Earth straight ahead of us?" asked David. "I mean, since we're supposed to be heading toward Earth?"

The android shook his head. "We're not supposed to be heading *straight* toward Earth."

"We're not?"

"No," said the android. "We should be heading toward the space that will be occupied by Earth when we get there." He added abashedly. "*If* we get there. Our task is less like firing a pistol than arranging a rendezvous." He became quite glum. "This is not supposed to happen to an android of my series."

"How long will our air, water, and food hold out?" asked David.

"That's a good-news/bad-news situation. We have enough of all of those to last for months. But, unless we recover our navigation and radio capability, no one will ever know where we are, so help will never arrive."

"So, we'd be goners?" said David.

"Well, *you* would be," replied the android with an apologetic half-smile. "As an artificial person, I don't need food, water, *or* air. And I can draw subsistence energy from the antimatter engine for millennia. But I have no intention of letting you perish out here. That would contravene my most basic programming."

"*Oh*," said David, "well, *that's* reassuring," his sarcasm evidently going to waste.

"Ahem," said Catharine at the cockpit door. David looked up and said, "To what do we owe this visitation, my dear?"

"Have we learned anything?" she asked.

David nodded dourly. "Seems we … have no navigation system, no radio, and … we don't know where we are."

"How are we going to get home?" she asked nervously.

"That's under discussion," said David. "Come back to our quarters, and I'll bring you up to speed." He took Catharine by the elbow.

Once in their room, he subtly began looking around for a camera. In other parts of the cabin, cameras were obvious, mounted a few feet above eye level, their tracking functions apparently activated by movement.

Catharine leaned into him and whispered, cupping her hand over her mouth. "There are no cameras in this room, but it's wired for sound. One mic is at the desk, and there's one in each of the two ceiling-mounted smoke detectors."

"When did you discover this?" he mumbled.

"As soon as we got here," she replied. "Checking for surveillance on arrival is part of basic intelligence training."

David whispered. "If we talk under the blankets, do you think we'll avoid being overheard?"

"I expect we will, as long as we keep our voices down," she said. "They might hear that we're talking, but probably not what we're saying."

He held his fingers to his lips and grabbed what he thought of as his gym bag. He threw a towel over the zipper to deaden the sound, opened the bag, removed Elijah's mantle and tossed it on the bed, then took the bag under the blankets on their bed. Never wont to be left out, Catharine joined him under there.

David reached into the bag and took out the headset Ninurta had given him. To his amazement, a tiny green light on it was flashing. He looked at Catharine. "Did anybody tell us to expect a flashing green light?"

She pursed her lips and shook her head. "No, but I'd expect it's either a message-waiting signal, or a signal for you to call in."

"Go and get *your* headset," he said. "We'll see if yours is flashing, too."

She got out from under the blanket and reappeared a few moments later with her headset in her hand. There was no flashing light.

She shook her head. "I suppose *this* is a boys' club, too."

He reexamined his headset and noticed that there was a tiny, barely visible arrow molded into the black frame right under the flashing green light. It wasn't painted or colored in any way that would have made it easily recognizable as an arrow. But now that he'd spotted it, he could see that it pointed to the Talk button.

"Hmm, you were right," he said. "It's a call-in signal." He put on his headset and moved his finger toward the Talk button, but then stopped and said, "Are we sure we're ready for this?"

"Ready when you are," she said nervously.

"On the off-chance that these headsets are conferenced, why don't you put yours on, too? Maybe we can all hear each other."

Catharine put on the headset and gave him a thumbs-up.

David pushed the Talk button. "Please stand by," said a female voice immediately. There's no way his call-in could have been received millions of miles away and answered so quickly, so the female voice must have been a recording stored in the headset.

After about thirty seconds, a familiar voice came on.

"I thought you'd *never* check your headset," said Ninurta, a note of exasperation in his voice. "Over."

"You never mentioned that *you* might try to contact *us*," replied David. "Were we supposed to intuit that? Over." He awaited the reply. Considering the pressure he was feeling, the delay seemed long, but in the back of his mind he knew it was much shorter than it should have been. *Ninurta must be closer than I expected.*

"Hear me out, David," said Ninurta. "Your pilot is steering you at right angles *away* from Earth on some pointless trajectory. In fact, he's got you headed out of the ecliptic plane occupied by all the normal planets as they orbit the sun. I'm sorry we needed to let the android continue to pilot your craft, but we had to see what his plan was. Now that we have, I need you to seize control of your craft as soon as possible, with a view to turning it over to me. You need to, *er* ... disable the android. Over."

David pointed to Catharine's headset. "Are you hearing this?" he asked.

She nodded.

David pressed Talk again. "Can't *you* disable him?" he asked. "He's just another machine, after all. I've seen that read-up on the monitor at least twice. It says: *Control: External.* Over."

"I *can* control it externally," said Ninurta, "but only with the pilot's consent. As long as he's in the cockpit, he can override me. Over."

David could feel the composure seeping out of his brain like a fluid, and its place being taken by quiet rage, like a holding tank being drained of water and filled with gasoline. He was furious at both the evil lurking everywhere, and the incompetence and disorganization of the forces opposing it.

Something's happened out there in the real world, he'd said. But something had also snapped inside *him.* The same ruthless abandon that impelled him to confront a detachment of Anunnaki soldiers at Westminster and to kill two of Anzû's henchmen threatening Catharine, once more welled up inside him like a separate personality. But this time, David was prepared to recognize him as an old friend, a permanent part of his own personality, who'd come in handy in the past and would undoubtedly be needed again quite soon.

There'd been a long silence on the line—evidently long enough for Ninurta to wonder whether they still had a connection. Some static had also begun seeping in.

"David, are you there?" he said. "Over."

David responded coldly. "Yeah. Over."

More static.

Ninurta sighed. "That static may be your android trying to jam this frequency. Are you up to this?"

"I don't know," replied David. "I only know I'm not happy about it, and you've gotta fix your software. Over."

"We will," said Ninurta, "as soon as this crisis has been averted. Over."

"Yeah, well, it's a problem for me *right now,* so it would be great if you could step on it. Over."

"You have to understand, David," explained Ninurta, "this safeguard stops people like Anzû from seizing control of a piloted craft. Over."

David laughed quietly. "Well, evidently it's not much help—*is it?*—once he's got control of the pilot. Then, evidently, he can lock *you* out."

He threw his hands up. "And suppose we manage to subdue him. Then we have no pilot at all."

The static became louder and more persistent.

"You won't need a pilot immediately," Ninurta assured him. "I've got both eyes on you. Believe me. And even with no pilot at all, your craft is equipped with the best collision-avoidance system in the solar system. Over."

"Even better than the one the Dagon have?" asked David skeptically. "Over."

"Well," said Ninurta, his certainty flagging, "all but theirs. The fact is, we don't know *what* they've got; they're quite advanced. But I do know what system *you* have. All you've got to do in order to survive this is remove the android from the cockpit and prevent him from breaching the hull. Over."

"So, what do you expect us to do to him? Should we blow him out of the airlock, like in the old movies? Over."

"No," said Ninurta, "you've got to keep him onboard, in case we need him later. Just remove him from the controls, subdue him, and prevent him from breaching the hull. Over."

"Is that what he's going to try to do?" demanded David. "To breach the hull? Over."

"As you may have guessed, we made a copy of his software while he was on the royal pyramidion. My robotics specialist says the android hasn't yet been given an imperative to breach the hull, but his software's open to remote adjustment by someone on Earth, and we're pretty sure that's Anzû."

There was another burst of static.

David ignored it. "Anzû contacted me a little while ago. Over."

"How?" asked Ninurta, but then he remembered David's telepathic skills. "Never mind. David, listen. You and I must remain a team. We'll have to work together in the coming days. We have to figure out a way I can defeat Anzû again without causing mass casualties and catastrophic collateral damage on Earth. Over."

David had already given that quite a bit of thought.

"You can't," he said despondently.

"I *can't*?" asked Ninurta.

"No," said David. "But *I* can."

Now the static dominated the line and drowned out their voices completely. David waited a full minute for it to subside, but it didn't. The connection was well and truly dead.

He looked at Catharine. "I think Lumpo's jamming the frequency, so he may have guessed we're talking with someone." He removed his headset and handed it to her. "Hide these," he said. "We're on our own for the time being."

David feigned patience, lying back and resting his head on the palms of his folded hands. "So, Navy," he whispered, "tell me how we're gonna kill this bastard."

"It's stifling under here," she said. "Maybe we'd be better off draping a blanket over a couple of chairs, like when we were kids."

"Where onboard do you suppose we might find something to help us subdue Lumpo?"

Catharine shrugged. "We might be able to use hammers, screwdrivers and other sharp items. And then we'll need something to tie him up with."

"Where would we find those?" asked David.

"Probably in the maintenance supply closet," she said.

He thought for a moment. "I passed it once or twice when we were a few days out from Earth … didn't seem to be locked."

"Are there closed-circuit cameras back there?" she asked.

"There's one, but you can easily reach it. You could just hang a garment over the lens."

"What if he sees me?" asked Catharine.

"He's completely engrossed in getting his bearings. But, if you want me to, I'll go and distract him … ask him stupid questions and such."

She furrowed her brow. "If he asks me later what I was looking for, what do I tell him?"

"I don't know," he said. "Disinfectant, maybe. For a mess in the latrine."

"Couldn't he see that there's no mess in the latrine? I mean, there's at least one camera in the latrine."

David shrugged. "Then make a mess there first. It'll test your acting skills. Spill a little pink soap on your shirt, and a little on the floor—just enough to present a slipping hazard. In case he's watching (which he won't be), make a fuss over your own clumsiness, march out to the closet, and hang your shirt over the camera lens."

As it got warmer under the blanket, she equivocated. "He'll see me without my shirt on."

David couldn't believe what he was hearing. "*He?*" He shook his head. "He's an *it*. He doesn't care about your body—or mine. Should I go and distract the android?"

"No," said Catharine. "He's already distracted." Without further discussion, she headed for the latrine to see what kind of pretext she could create for inspecting the maintenance closet.

Twenty minutes later, she returned a bit rumpled with a small splotch of pink soap on her shirt and a hastily scrawled list of useful items she'd found in the maintenance closet. She reconvened their under-the-blanket conference and read him the list in a whisper. "A fire axe, two ball-peen hammers, four screwdrivers with interchangeable tips, four eight-foot runs of yellow vinyl rope, and *this*," she said, exhibiting a pipe wrench about eighteen inches in length.

"Impressive," said David. "May I feel the weight of it?"

She handed it to him. Its heft suggested it was stainless steel. As far as he could tell, there was no aluminum or other lightweight metal in it. It was twenty pounds if it was an ounce—easily enough to knock a man into next Tuesday, and quite possibly kill him. But an android? Who knew? He handed it back to her.

"Also," she said, "there are two dozen rolls of silver duct tape."

"Why so much duct tape?"

"I don't know," she said. "Maybe the Anunnaki believe the old saying: *With enough duct tape and testosterone, one can accomplish anything.*"

He snickered. "I never heard that saying, but we'd better hope it's true."

"I couldn't help but notice," she said, "that several items suitable to serve as lethal weapons are located *outside* the maintenance closet."

"And those are?"

"The fire extinguishers," she said. "Ram somebody in the face with the butt end of one of those, and you've got his attention, if he's still conscious. There are eight spread around the craft."

He thought for a moment. "I'm surprised you didn't find a few extra extinguishers in the maintenance closet."

She smiled. "There were some replacements in there, but they'd been cannibalized for their parts. That's what made me think of them. Also, there's a pressurized tank—pretty big one—that I'd guess contains extinguisher fluid, just in case the ones out here get used up or lose pressure."

"Okay," said David. "Now we make a plan, and it'd better be good, 'cause our lives depend on it." He didn't like the look on Catharine's face, which seemed uncertain. "Problem?"

"There's no gravity on this craft," said Catharine. "That means that if we come down on him with something heavy like an extinguisher, the force that strikes him will be no greater than the force we put into it. We'll also need to have a wall at our backs; otherwise, our own force will push us backward. Even if we're pressed up against a wall, as soon as we hit him, he'll float away. One of us should attack the android frontally while the other remains behind to trap him in the *beaten zone*— which means just what it sounds like."

"But which of us should be in which position?" asked David. "Weightlessness gives the fighting edge to upper-body mass. Not gonna make any assumptions here, so I'll defer to your choice. I'm heavier on top, but you're in better shape overall."

She still looked uncomfortable, which made David feel that he was missing her concern entirely. He shrugged. "Talk to me."

"Lumpo doesn't seem to realize that he's been tampered with," she said. "I feel like he's just a schlemiel who's been thrown into this position. Do I really want to destroy him?"

David found her attitude difficult to understand. "First of all, he's a machine. He's not alive, so we're not gonna kill 'im. And he can't feel pain." In truth, he wasn't sure about that. "Second, do you have trouble getting mad at this thing? *I* sure don't. He's Anzû's puppet. Whether he knows it or not, he's gonna get us killed. Isn't that enough to get you riled up?"

"I don't know," she said equivocally, "how did you get mad enough to kill those squarebeards?"

He couldn't believe she didn't know. "*They were trying to kill you.* Anyone who tries to kill you is gonna die at my hand." He patted her shoulder. "Just remember that he's prepared to kill *me*. Won't that do it for you?"

She looked at him indecisively.

"*What?*" he said. 'I'm not *important* enough to you? You wouldn't kill him to save me?" He folded his arms. "Well, isn't *that* an eye-opener?"

"It's just that the situation's not the same. It's your *job* to protect me."

"Oh, and it's not *your* job to protect *me*?" he asked, exasperated. An idea dawned on him and he nodded smugly.

"What is it?" she asked.

"Say you're a mama grizzly bear," he posited. "And that man wants to steal your cub."

David was startled by the sudden change in her expression. Now, *that* was a war face, and no doubt.

She regarded David with resolve. "I'll take him head-on."

"Let's not be too hasty," said David. "As Churchill said, 'Jaw jaw is better than war war.'"

She looked at him as though he were mad. "I don't understand, you're going to try talking him into turning over the pilot's seat?"

He nodded. "As a first measure."

She examined his face to see if he was joking. Evidently, he wasn't. "Geez," she said, "you've got quite some confidence in your diplomatic skills."

"Before we take any drastic steps," said David, "I'd like to test his rational skills and see whether he has the courage of his convictions. Because, objectively speaking, he really *should* give up the pilot's seat. His database has obviously been deliberately tampered with, and he can't recover control over the craft until it's fixed."

"And if palaver doesn't work?" asked Catharine, still regarding him skeptically.

"Then we go to Plan *R*."

"*Plan R?*" she asked.

He nodded. "R for wrench."

She regarded him skeptically. "*Wrench* doesn't start with an *R*," she said.

He arched an eyebrow and nodded sagely. "That's why the name is so clever, don't you see?"

Still regarding him skeptically, she extended her hand, and they shook on it.

CHAPTER 15

WHEN DAVID ENTERED the cockpit again, the android had three books open at his workspace (presumably operating manuals), and the images on his screens were cycling rapidly in a sequence that made no apparent sense.

The android rubbed the side of his head as though in imitation of a human or an Anunnaki under similar circumstances. Perhaps he was more human than David thought. Perhaps he could even feel pain, and not as mere electronic impulses informing him of physical damage to his body, but actual *pain*. He forced the thought from his mind.

"Have you made any progress since we spoke earlier?" asked David.

The android sighed and shook his head in defeat. But that didn't stop him from leafing through the manuals' indices, which suggested he hadn't developed even a general approach to finding a solution.

David plopped down behind him in one of the passengers' seats. "Enkidu, it's time we had a talk."

Without looking up from the manuals, Enkidu shook his head and said, "If at all possible, I think it would be more helpful if you'd leave me alone and let me work through this problem."

"Enkidu," said David, "look at me."

The android turned his head, looked David up and down for a second, then returned to his manuals.

"Enkidu," said David, "stop what you're doing. Turn around and look at me while we talk."

Before turning around the android sat up straight, as it evidently dawned on him that this wasn't going to be just *a* talk, it was going to be *the* talk. Evidently considering what to do in this unanticipated situation, he swiveled around in his chair and faced David with dismay, as though he were being called on the carpet. "I don't understand what you're proposing, David," he said.

"That's because I haven't proposed anything. I'd like to reason this through with you before we jointly consider how best to proceed in everyone's interests."

"Everyone's?"

"Yes," David assured him, "in the interests of the passengers, the craft, our mission, and our valuable Enkidu. Now, what do *you* propose?"

"I think," said the android, "as I just said, that you should allow me to work my way through this problem."

"And how would you work your way through it?"

To David's amazement, the android blushed. *It's amazing how lifelike they make these things*, he thought.

"I ... I ... don't know."

"And yet you *did* know precisely what you were doing when you piloted us safely all the way from Earth to the royal pyramidion in orbit around Mars. Correct?"

The android seemed to equivocate before admitting the truth. "Yes, that's correct."

"Well," said David, "doesn't it stand to reason that all you'd have to do to return us to Earth is to reverse course, making some small adjustment to account for the continuous revolution of Earth and Mars around the sun?"

"Yes," said the android. "That's what I intended to do, but ..." His voice trailed off.

"Calculating such adjustments is well within the ability of an android of your class. Is that not so?"

"Yes, it should be," said the android, obviously mystified by his inability to do so.

"How much time would you generally expect it to take, to make such calculations?"

"Well," said the android, "because of the need to engage in an extraordinary number of brute-force recalculations, it would take approximately ... six seconds."

"And how much time have you spent working on this problem?" asked David.

"Approximately six hours," confessed the android.

"That's much longer than six seconds, right?"

"Three thousand six hundred times as long."

"And yet, you're no nearer to a solution than you were six hours ago. Correct?"

"Yes, I suppose so," replied the android.

"To what do you attribute your inability to begin solving the problem?" asked David.

The android shrugged. "A failure of my ability to calculate?"

"Didn't you just calculate the number of seconds in six hours, then divide by six seconds?" The android nodded. "So, you haven't lost your ability to calculate."

The android shook his head in agreement.

"To what else might you attribute your inability to begin solving the problem?"

The android shrugged, but seemed intrigued. "I suppose I may have forgotten the way."

David was pleased with their progress thus far. "Okay. As you sit here, I want you to imagine the way home. Can you do that?"

The android's face went through all manner of expressions as he tried to recall the path home. Ultimately, he gave up. "I can't."

"But you knew the path to the royal pyramidion, which is the reverse of the same path, with just a few small adjustments, correct?"

The android nodded.

"So that means you *forgot* the way, right?"

"That's right," said the android.

"What could possibly make you forget something so important that you knew so recently?"

"A failure of memory hardware, I suppose."

"Other than a hardware failure, Enkidu, what else might cause you to forget something you knew so recently?"

Enkidu shrugged. "I suppose someone might have deleted the information from my databases."

"Who would have a motive to make you forget your way to Earth?" asked David.

The android shrugged silently.

"Would your forgetting the way help either me or the lieutenant commander?" asked David.

"Not at all."

"So, we'd have no incentive to make you forget, correct?"

"That's correct."

"In fact, such forgetfulness, if it were to continue indefinitely, would result in our deaths, wouldn't it?"

"Most likely."

"By what name do the Anunnaki refer to the databases containing all known information about the location and movements of celestial bodies?"

"The Tablets of Destinies."

"Who stole the Tablets of Destinies from Enlil many years ago?"

"Anzû," replied the android confidently, as though he were an American eighth-grader who'd been asked which famous general betrayed the Continental Army in the American War of Independence.

"So, who might have stolen your copy of the Tablets of Destinies?"

The android's eyes opened wide. "Anzû?"

David nodded sympathetically.

"But Anzû is long dead," protested the android, seeming a bit confused.

David shook his head. "No, Anzû is *not* dead. Enki secretly spared him. He lives still."

There was no faking the android's surprise at this bit of news. "But, no matter who caused me to forget the Tablets of Destinies, if the tablets are gone and I have no radio enabling me to obtain another copy, I would *never* be able to find the way to Earth."

David nodded, as to an apt pupil. "That appears to be so. Under those circumstances, it doesn't make much sense for you to continue to pilot this craft, does it?"

The android's expression changed to one of horror. "But I can't leave my post. No one else aboard is certified to pilot this craft. And there remain untried solutions."

"What solutions might you try that would get us back to Earth?"

"Well, for one thing, I *must* fix the radio," said the android.

"What makes you think you can fix it?"

"I heard some static come over the radio a short while ago. It seemed to power up on its own, so it may be fixable."

David was reluctant to follow this line of questioning, as it might lead to discovery of their communication with Ninurta. "You heard static on the radio?" he asked incredulously.

"Yes."

"How is that even possible?"

"Someone not aboard this craft might have been trying to reach us. Of course, for the radio to spring to life, that would require them to have a very strong signal, and they'd have to be close by."

The accuracy of the android's conjecture sent a jolt up David's spine, which he hoped he'd been quick enough to conceal. "Did you hear any messages or voices?"

The android shook his head. "Just static."

"Is there a way for you to find out whether any words or images were contained in that static?" asked David.

"Probably," said the android. "It might be reflected in the radio's memory banks. I'd have to remove the radio from the control panel to examine them."

"Go ahead," said David.

"Now?" asked the android.

"No time like the present."

The android got down on all fours and began searching for the points where the radio was affixed to the control panel.

David said aloud, with as little emotion as he could manage, "Plan *R*."

While the android lowered his head to examine the radio, Catharine quietly tiptoed into the cockpit carrying the pipe wrench in both hands. She gripped it solidly, raised it above her head, and yanked it down with all her might, staving in the back of the android's head, the hardened resin of its skull proving no match for tempered steel.

The android collapsed face down on the deck. Although he was almost completely still and seemed incapable of initiating any volitional movements, his left shoulder cycled involuntarily a few times in a rotating motion, rising an inch or two from the deck, then dropping again. After cycling this way a few times, it whirred to a stop, and the only remaining sound was the faint snap of a sparking battery.

Catharine stepped outside the cockpit to grab the three rolls of duct tape she'd brought along. She tossed all three to David. "Go to town, Mister Ambassador," she said.

Before turning the android face-up, David triple-bound its hands together behind its back, and did the same to its ankles. Just as he was about to turn the android over, he realized that, if he did so, some of the contents of its head (which, to David's untrained eye, appeared to consist mainly of printed-circuit boards) would likely fall out. He turned to Catharine. "Would you get me a couple of big towels from the latrine?"

Catharine returned a minute later with the requested towels and several lengths of vinyl rope.

David draped a towel over the cavity that was formerly the back of the android's head, taped it on as best he could, turned him over, and sat him up against the console.

The android seemed to be neither asleep nor dead, nor in a state analogous to either. His body slumped forward and his head lolled, although that might have been from the weightlessness. He could have passed as a drunkard after a lost weekend, but for one thing: His right eyeball floated down to his cheek, suspended by a thin cable protruding out through his eye socket. Fortunately there was no blood or blood-like fluid seeping from the wound or spattered on the deck. Even the radio, which had been mere inches from his head when he was clobbered, was clean and dry.

David noticed that the android's left eye, still situated where its designer intended, was tracking his every movement.

"We're going to put you in one of the passengers' seats," David told him. "Are you in a great deal of pain?"

With great effort, the android shook his head.

"Good," said David. "I expect we'll get you fixed up as good as new once we get back to Earth orbit."

Even in weightlessness, the android seemed more massive than he looked. With Catharine's help, David dragged him to the first row of passengers' seats in the main compartment, and hoisted him into one. Once he was in place, Catharine had to use both hands to keep him from floating away. David taped him to the seat and also tied him there with vinyl rope. The ticking of an electrical short was quieter now, but still audible, and there was an acrid smell.

"Okay," David said to the android. "Sorry about that. We'll be back as soon as we can. Do we need to take care of anything for you before we go and speak privately?"

The android's head stopped lolling aimlessly and began purposefully nodding.

"Is that a *yes*?" asked David.

The android's head kept nodding, which seemed vaguely like a *yes*. Then he struggled to move his mouth. At first it just puckered and opened like a fish's mouth underwater, but with repeated attempts at vocalizing, the android managed to get out a soft grunt. Then he struggled to form a two-syllable word. It was either "ba-aa" or "ma-aa." About half the time it sounded like the former, the other half the latter. Either way, neither Catharine nor David could make sense of it.

"Are you asking for water?" asked David.

The android shook his head back and forth.

"We'll take that as a *no*," said David.

After another moment's observation, David and Catharine left him there, immobilized in his seat.

When David reconvened their under-the-cover meeting in the bedroom, Catharine asked why they still required such secrecy.

David replied, "Lumpo could be wired for sound. He could be passively broadcasting every word to Anzû. It's safer this way. Bring out the headsets."

She dug the headsets out of her bag, and handed David his.

"Hmm," said David with disappointment, "no flashing lights."

They put on the headsets. David pushed his Talk button and waited, but there was nothing. Catharine pressed her Talk button. Again, nothing. Neither headset gave any sign of being powered up.

On the off-chance that Ninurta might successfully contact them through the craft's (apparently inoperable) communications systems, they moved back to the passengers' seats in the cockpit.

Resigned that there was nothing they could do but hope to be found by Ninurta before dying of thirst or anoxia, they draped themselves in Elijah's mantle and fell asleep in each other's arms.

A SHORT TIME later, the blissful silence was shattered by an automated female voice blaring through the craft's public address system.

"FIRE, FIRE, FIRE!"

David awoke with alarm to the acrid smell of an electrical fire.

Next to him, Catharine shot to her feet and twirled about smartly to look out through the cockpit doorway toward the rear of the craft. "Fire in the hole!" she shouted instinctively.

"Do you see flames?" asked David.

"No. It looks like the fire just started," she said. "Smoke seems to be limited to the area just below the ceiling." She hurried out to investigate.

David couldn't help himself; before pitching in to the firefighting effort, he checked the pilot's console for any sign of activity.

But there was nothing. Neither the console nor the radio showed any sign of life. The monitors still cycled through the now-familiar views supplied by the exterior-mounted cameras. Nothing appeared to be happening outside the vehicle.

David rushed out of the cockpit door a few seconds after Catharine. He found her hovering over the slumping figure of the android, who remained affixed to the passenger seat just as they'd left him.

As David approached, it appeared that the source of the smoke was located somewhere on the android's abdomen. As bad luck would have it, the source seemed to lie underneath the yellow vinyl ropes they'd used to tie him down, which had now begun to brown and emit a cloying stink.

The android seemed to be trying to form the same word he'd been attempting when he was first bound up, but there was now an urgency to his attempts, and the word he struggled to say now sounded less like *ba-aa* and more like *baway*.

"Grab a fire extinguisher," shouted Catharine over the din of the smoke alarm.

David took an extinguisher off the wall and removed the plastic safety. He aimed the extinguisher at the android's abdomen, but hesitated to squeeze the trigger, as it suddenly occurred to him that he had no idea whether the suppressive in the extinguisher was vapor or liquid. If it were a liquid, spraying it on what smelled to him like an electrical fire might not be the smartest move.

"What are you waiting for?" demanded Catharine. "Spritz him!"

"You see any flames?" asked David. "We've got to establish the fire's source. If it's electrical, then spraying a liquid on it could spread the fire out of control."

Catharine frisked the android as though checking for firearms. "No flames," she said. "But there's a hot spot by his belly that I can't get close to because of the ropes."

"Cut 'em," shouted David over the *fire-fire-fire* mantra of the smoke alarm.

Catharine looked at David as though he'd taken leave of his senses. "What if he's waiting for me to cut the ropes so he can overpower me and breach the hull?" she demanded.

The android shook his head emphatically. "*Baway*," he said, "*BAWAY.*"

Still, neither of them understood what he was trying to say.

"Get a knife," said David. "*I'll* cut the ropes as necessary."

Catharine ran off to the maintenance closet.

While she was still away, David fixed the android's good eye in his stare. "Are you trying to destroy the hull?" he demanded menacingly.

The android shook his head and opened his mouth as if to speak.

"*Baway*," said David. "Yes, I know. If I loosen the ropes, do you agree not to try to escape?"

The android nodded his head emphatically.

Catharine returned and handed David a heavy steel scissor.

"Grab the extinguisher," David said. "If he makes a hostile move, knock his lights out." He turned to the android and said gravely, "If you make one false move, we'll put an end to you, and we *won't* be bringing you back."

The android nodded and didn't even say *baway*.

As David cut away the first few turns of rope, the smoke became more acrid and thick.

He suddenly realized what *baway* meant. "*Shit*," he muttered, as he cut the ropes even faster. "He's not trying to breach the hull. He's telling us how to *prevent* a breach."

"What?" said Catharine.

David ignored the question, pulled away the remaining ropes, and tore the android's clothing away from its torso, exposing the source of the smoke. It was a battery (or *baway*, as mispronounced by the android's mangled mouth), a bit *larger* than the one that nearly knocked Gary's plane out of the sky over Namibia. Judging from that limited (though unduly exciting) aviation experience, a mishap now would result in at least a one-kiloton explosion that would *surely* breach the hull and leave not the slightest trace of the craft or its final occupants.

Two metal terminals jutted up from the battery, one at each end. One terminal was covered by a red cap; the terminal at the other end was capless, though it was apparently designed to wear an identical cap, probably of a different color. An uninsulated copper wire protruded from the red terminal cover and ran nearly the length of the battery, ending only an inch short of the unprotected terminal at the other end. Every few seconds, at irregular intervals, an arc of electricity leapt sinuously from the wire to the unprotected pole.

Mounted front-and-center on the battery was an old-style meter with a needle indicator. It was unclear precisely what the meter was measuring, as the lettering on it was in a strange alphabet, probably Hebrew, or perhaps one of its precursor languages.

Whatever the meter was measuring, its needle was pinned to the top of the red zone—never a good sign. Obviously, the battery was experiencing too much of *something*, and that *something* had been causing smoke to billow from it so copiously that it now hid the craft's entire ceiling and extended down as far as the top of Catharine's head.

David concluded that the battery was likely about to blow itself apart. He took one small step backward and looked briefly at the android's face. Though David wanted to ask him if he'd been trying to say *battery* all along, time was of the essence, and taking time to pose the question might well render the answer superfluous.

He reached into his pants pocket and removed a handkerchief, wrapped it several times around his index finger, and used the shielded finger to shove the wire away from the uninsulated pole. The arcing ceased immediately. The smoke emitted by the battery also immediately diminished, but, to David's chagrin, for a while the needle remained pinned to the top of the red zone. Perhaps the meter had been measuring the battery's internal heat or pressure; whatever it measured, it was taking some time to recede. After a count of ten (while the smoke alarm continued blaring its warnings), at last the needle budged and began slowly dropping away through the danger zone and down to safe levels. David was surprised to see that the needle didn't stop there, but rather continued all the way to the bottom of the scale.

He looked to the android's face to see if the android was as relieved as himself. But the face was entirely impassive. The android was *off*; it must have depended upon the battery for its operation, and its failure had rendered the android likewise inoperative.

David looked up at Catharine.

"Is it over?" she asked.

He nodded. "So it appears."

"So, what was he trying to say?" asked Catharine, looking irritated.

"Evidently," said David, "he was saying *battery*."

"*Battery?*" she echoed incredulously, and shrugged. "Why didn't you realize that when we first tied him up? He was already saying it."

David couldn't believe what he was hearing. "Pardon me?" he said. "Why didn't *you* understand him?"

She shrugged. "Well … you have more experience with Nibirune batteries than I do."

That was plainly unfair. "You have precisely the same amount of experience with them that *I* do," he said in a reciprocally accusatory tone. "Perhaps I should ask why you hit him so damned *hard*! With half his head missing, it's a wonder he could say anything *at all*."

Catharine placed her hands on her hips. "Oh?" she said, "How hard would *you* have hit him? Besides," she said, indicating the android, "*you're* the one who killed him."

"I didn't kill him," he said. "He's not *dead*."

"How do *you* know?" she demanded.

He was about to say *because he was never alive* but, before he could form the retort, all at once the smoke alarm ceased its racket and there was a sudden swooshing in the air above their heads.

In half a minute, all the smoke had disappeared into the exhaust vents. It occurred to David and Catharine at the same moment that their bickering had arisen from nothing more than the stress of an impending disaster—a disaster that was averted through their cooperation; now that the danger had passed, they shared a clean, quiet, and reasonably safe environment that left them with neither need nor grounds for argument.

They collapsed into each other's arms and quaked as relief flowed over them. This time they returned together to the bedroom and made love, then fell into the sweet oblivion of a sound sleep.

Neither had dared to verbalize a dread that had passed through each of their minds independently—that, even if they were to survive their inevitable wait in the dead of space, they might awaken only to find that the one who reached them first was … Anzû.

CHAPTER 16

FIVE MILES FROM the center of Anzû's hole in the Antarctic ice, two SF-5s circled at high altitude, awaiting orders to release their payload. One saucer was piloted by Gary Sullivan, the other by Buck Buchanan.

"What if this plan don't work?" asked Buck. "Over."

"It'll work," Gary confirmed. "Over."

"We got a Plan B? Over."

"We do," said Gary. "That's the one that'll work. Over."

"What is it? Over."

"Can't discuss it unless it's implemented. Over."

"Can't discuss it with li'l ol' *me*?" wheedled Buck. "Over."

"Nope," said Gary. "Apparently, they're not real committed to it. Besides," he chortled, "you're kinda funny lookin'. Over."

"If *kinda funny lookin'* disqualified someone from gettin' information," said Buck, "they'd never have told you a damned thing. Over."

⇒∘⋙∘⇐

THE DHS REP had never been to the Oval Office before. Because of the importance of what she carried in her briefcase, she'd expected all eyes to be on her from the moment she walked in, and she was right about that.

Her eyes darted about nervously as she identified some major players: the President, Admiral Simmons, the Secretary of Defense. Her immediate bosses were there—the Secretary and Deputy Secretary of the Department of Homeland Security—as well as the Director and Deputy Director of the Central Intelligence Agency.

As she opened her briefcase, she gave the President a friendly smile.

To her surprise, he smiled back.

"What have you got for us this morning, Evelyn?" asked the President.

She blushed to think that the President already knew her name.

"What I have here, Mister President, is precisely what was requested last week. Needless to say, our best engineers have done nothing but work on these since receiving word that we'd be needing them."

From her briefcase, she withdrew two small drones, extended their compressed wings carefully, and placed them side by side in the middle of the table so everyone would have a good view.

"Special skeeters?" asked the President.

"Well, sir, these are a bit bigger than the skeeters we've all come to know and love—if one can ever really love an insect (real or mechanical), which I doubt."

"*We're* in love with your skeeters, Evelyn," corrected the admiral. "We're in love with anything that saves American lives."

"Yes, sir," said Evelyn, "but given that these are a bit bigger, we call 'em dragonflies. They *had* to be bigger. Our orders were that these need to safely record, store, and synchronously transmit audiovisual surveillance data on command."

The President turned to the admiral. "We got guys up there with these right now?"

The admiral nodded emphatically. "We've redoubled all our national coastal patrols: space force, air force, navy, and coast guard, just in case Plan A misfires and the bad guys decide to escalate immediately. As for the craft carrying the dragonflies, there are two up there now, and they're being flown by our best, sir. You've met 'em."

The President nodded thoughtfully. "Well, how do *they* feel about these ... dragonflies?"

The admiral took an unusually long time to answer. "Back when we were talking about the existing skeeters, you remember the pilots joking about the bad guys opening a can of bug spray on them?"

"I remember," said the President.

"Well," said the admiral, "they think these *dragonflies* are big enough to be spotted by radar, at least when they're swarming. They look a little weird on radar, but there's enough reflected signal there to reveal their presence. Our guys think that, one way or another, they'll encounter a can of bug spray."

The President frowned. "I don't want to get bogged down in metaphors here, but what kind of bug spray might work against these things?"

Instead of answering directly, the admiral turned to Evelyn. "Do you have an answer for the President, Evelyn?"

Her stomach churned. "Well, obviously, toxins won't work, Mister President, since these dragonflies aren't living things." She squirmed in her chair. "But the engineers said, kind of off-handedly, that a spray of sticky polymer might be effective against them."

The President frowned again. "You mean … glue?"

"Yes, sir. Glue spray."

The President turned darkly back to the admiral. "What's the plan if all these dragonflies get gummed up?"

The admiral cleared his throat nervously. "Our fallback plan is to send our fighters in with their automated cameras running."

The President's face reddened. "Well … how do they get out again?"

"Through the same hole in the ice, sir."

"Don't you think the enemy will anticipate that and cut off their escape?"

"We expect they'll try, sir," said the admiral gravely.

The CIA director leaned forward and said, "That could lead immediately to a hot war."

"And we have no idea how many wings they've got hidden from us," added his assistant. "Could be … rough."

The President nodded gravely. "Bob, what kind of contingency plans do we have if the enemy starts a massed attack?"

"Readiness is all, Mister President," said the admiral, and sat back in his chair as though the question had been fully answered.

The President shook his head and reluctantly gave the order everyone else seemed to be anticipating. "We're not ready. Tell our two pilots to return to base and stand by. Let's give it a few days, folks. I want a complete workup of contingencies, conventional and … unconventional." The room went deathly quiet at the President's use of *unconventional* in place of *nuclear*, which was what everyone knew he meant.

The CIA director said, "But, Mister President, we don't know what they've got—"

The President rounded on the director, eyes flashing and face flushed. *"They're not going to tell us that, are they?* Make whatever assumptions you deem reasonable and state them explicitly, so I'll know what the hell we should do based on what *they* do. You know how to write for contingencies. You went to college, *didn't* you?"

The director, who'd graduated Yale *magna cum laude*, looked down at the table and nodded, careful not to look the boss in the eye. "Yes, sir."

The President, deflated by his own outburst, rubbed his eyes with the heels of his hands. "Sorry for the fit of pique, Fred. Uncalled for … and that's on me."

"Completely understandable, sir," said the director sympathetically.

The President said, "Everyone leave me alone with the admiral, please."

The assemblage quickly gathered up its papers and filed out silently. As Evelyn needed to compress the wings of the specimen dragonflies and put them back in her briefcase, she was last to go. Her expression resembled that of someone who'd just been punched in the gut.

"Evvie—" said the President, "may I call you Evvie?"

She nodded emphatically.

"Evvie, your dragonflies will certainly be in the first foray. If they work and don't get gummed up, we may yet peacefully acquire the intelligence we need. But—" he glanced at the admiral "—if they fail, the odds of a hot war are quite high, so we need more time to get ready. But keep your powder dry and we'll see you soon."

"Yes, sir," said Evelyn. "Meanwhile, I'll ask the engineers what measures we might take to minimize the hazards of … bug spray."

"Good idea," said the President.

Evelyn looked slightly mollified as she turned and left, closing the door behind her.

"Well, *that* went well," said the President in a self-deprecating tone.

"*We* all let you down, Jim," said the admiral, shaking his head sadly. "We know *never* to offer the boss a 'best option' that's likely to start a standup fight. It's a failure of vision on our part. We're all thinkin' inside the box."

Having been reminded to think in less routine ways, the President realized he'd forgotten something that might be important. "What have we heard from our ambassador—and your adjutant?"

The admiral shook his head in frustration. "Radio silence. Evidently, there's a spy on Enki's ship. Until he can figure out who it is and take him out of circulation, he's avoiding all communication with David and Catharine."

"Why?" asked the President incredulously.

"Because, somehow, the android that was supposed to pilot David and Catharine got switched with a different one. Enki's worried that the one piloting David and Catharine's craft is under Anzû's control and could be relaying everything to him."

"How'd Enki find out that the androids were switched?"

"Remember Hendrick? The geologist?" asked the admiral.

"How could I forget him?"

"There were evidently some ink marks on the android who was left behind that could only have been on the intended pilot. Hendrick's the one who detected the switch."

The President nodded. "Guy's sharp as a knife. What do you hear from him?"

"He's on his way here from Enki's ship. I told the Space Force detail to bring him here as long as I'm still here."

"So, there's no contact between David and the outside world?" asked the President.

"Well—" the admiral began, but then dropped off.

"Well, *what*, Bob?" said the President. "We're grasping at *straws* here."

"Last time I spoke with David—when he was at my home—he told me he'd been … contacted by Anzû directly."

"You mentioned that," said the President, "but what does it have to do—"

"Not sure I mentioned that the contact was … telepathic."

The President regarded him askance. "I think you left out that little nugget."

"Well," said the admiral, "you asked whether there's any contact between David and the outside world. David's telepathic capability could mean that he's directly in touch with Anzû even now. Nobody knows how telepathic signals are carried or how fast they travel. There's *some* evidence that they're instantaneous, which is a little confusing, as it seems to violate Einstein's speed limit. David felt pretty sure that Anzû was trying to enlist him in his cause."

"Why *David* especially? Because he's privy to our intelligence?"

The admiral shook his head. "No, that's just the icing on the cake. You see, David seems to be the only person alive who can communicate telepathically with Anzû and also with Anzû's platoon leaders. Even Anzû can't communicate telepathically with his platoon leaders; those comms require a working radio."

"So, if Anzû's radio communications are interrupted by an EMP pulse," reasoned the President, "using David as his missing comm link, Anzû could still maintain command and control?"

The admiral nodded, letting that knowledge sink in.

"My God," said the President, "if Anzû's got David, then he can—and no doubt *will*—hit us with an EMP *with impunity*, because the possibility that we might retaliate in kind no longer serves as a deterrent. We'll be unable to knock out his comms."

"Anzû may *already* believe he can attack us with impunity," said the admiral, "as he has no inkling that we've restored our nuclear capability. Remember we haven't told Enki, so Anzû's spy couldn't have overheard it."

The President waved off that possibility. "Anzû may already know, but, even if he doesn't, he has no choice but to *assume* we've recovered at least some of our nuclear capabilities. Anzû's not stupid, and he can readily imagine what would happen if he were to attack us and it turned out we *did* have nukes."

The admiral nodded in agreement. "It's true. To the best of our knowledge, he's got forces in only two places, and they're distant from our population centers, so the occasion would be optimal for us to use nukes. But to return to the prospect that he could preserve his command and control while we lose ours: Yes, it would be destabilizing. With David in his corner, Anzû would have command and control, and we'd have none. *Game Over.* But I don't think Anzû's happy about the prospect, because that would really put *David* in the catbird seat. If David threatened to pull the plug, Anzû would have no choice but to give him anything he wanted—immortality—even Inanna, if he can swing it."

The President looked worried. "You think David might succumb to temptation of that kind?"

The admiral sighed. "The prospect of living forever with the most desired woman in the universe?" He shrugged. "Sure beats a sharp stick in the eye."

"Should we preemptively ... terminate David?" asked the President hesitantly. "He's the only thing that could assure our destruction."

The admiral just stared at him and waited for him to right his ship.

The President saw the disdain of his most trusted friend, blushed, and said aloud to himself, "We could never do that without clear evidence that David had turned coat, of course." He shivered as though death itself had momentarily lighted its icy hand on his head; he turned to the admiral. "Does Anzû have any information he can hold over David's head?"

"To blackmail him? Not that I know of," said the admiral.

The President slammed his fist down on his desk. "How the hell did *David* become central to all this? He's just an ambassador."

The admiral sipped his coffee and sighed. "There I can help you: The Anunnaki are (as a practical matter) immortal; to enjoy an Anunnaki woman forever, a man would have to become immortal himself. Now, somehow Anzû learned that the immortal Queen Inanna had been crazy in love with Joseph of the Bible thousands of years ago. Not only is David descended from Joseph, but he's Joseph's spit-and-image. One of Anzû's confederates evidently told Inanna about David and showed her his picture. After that, Inanna tried for months to seduce David, but to no avail, because David had recently met and fallen in love with *Catharine*."

"So," said the President with dismay, "now we're dependent on David's remaining in love with Catharine. This is mind-boggling. It's like a combination of three-dimensional chess and … high school."

The admiral agreed. "*The high school of the gods*—with the fate of two worlds in the balance. But, you know, that's nothing new. Earth's history is filled with wars over noblewomen. Look at Helen of Troy. She was supposed to be the daughter of Zeus." He furrowed his brow. "You don't suppose that Helen was … *Inanna*, do you?"

"What do you mean?"

"Well," said the admiral, "Zeus was the Greek name for King Anu. Inanna's name means *beloved of Anu*, and she's descended from him."

The President shook his head in exasperation. "I thought we were well past going to war to fetch the king a bride."

"We were. But *Helen* is back—and we seem to be back in the fight."

Holly's voice came over the intercom, bringing them gratefully back to Earth. "Mister President, there's a Mister Hendrick here to see you."

⟶∘C∕∕∕⟋∘⟵

HENDRICK'S OBVIOUS APPRECIATION of the hospitality at the Oval Office was having a calming effect on the President. As far as the admiral was concerned, that was all to the good.

"I've heard the story of how you discovered the switch of the two androids," said the admiral. "What has Enki done to detect and punish the turncoats?"

Hendrick replied, "He asked me whether I knew who the engineer was who tampered with the androids' memories, and I admitted that I didn't know. But I had my suspicions."

"Oh? Who topped your list?" asked the President.

"My Number One suspect was the engineer who oversaw the departure of *The Way Forward* from Enki's pyramidion. His name is Kassam, and he's General Shulgi's engineer. He's the only person who appears to have had time to effectuate the necessary changes to the androids' memories."

"Shulgi is Inanna's top commander, isn't he?" asked the President.

"He is," said Hendrick hesitantly, "but he's not well-regarded by the commanders of the other vessels of the fleet. And the humiliation he suffered at David's hands has further damaged his reputation. In fact, it's largely because of Queen Inanna's doubts about Shulgi that she bypassed him and asked *me* to pass along certain information to you instead."

"What information?" asked the President.

"The Queen instructed me to tell you first that you should act as though you do not have the information I'm about to give you."

The admiral shrugged. "Consider it done."

"Evidently, Queen Inanna's affections have shifted away from David toward Ninurta, who's historically been Anzû's nemesis. Ninurta's the Anunnaki who defeated Anzû in an epic air battle on Earth thousands of years ago. It was Ninurta who recovered the Tablets of the Destinies and returned them to Enki … or really to Enlil, to whom they belonged. Ninurta's wife Bau was killed in the fallout following a nuclear battle in the Sinai Desert, and he's been grieving her loss on the royal pyramidion for millennia. Initially, Ninurta served King Anu. When King Anu passed, perhaps a thousand years ago, Ninurta began serving King Enlil. A few weeks ago, Ninurta made a romantic overture toward Inanna. He sent her a message using a code known to only the two of them."

The President was amazed. "They both remember this code from thousands of years ago?"

"Yes," said Hendrick.

"That's amazing," said the admiral. "*I* can't remember where I left my glasses last night."

Unsure how to respond, Hendrick ignored the remark. "Ninurta contacted Inanna by radio, using their shared encryption method. Before David left for the royal pyramidion, Queen Inanna secretly told him of Ninurta's message. She then handed David a private note from her to Ninurta, to be delivered when David arrived on the royal pyramidion. She didn't tell me the personal part of the note, but she wanted me to tell you something that Ninurta wants only you two gentlemen to know initially."

"What's that?" asked the President.

"He wants you to know that the android that piloted *The Way Forward* to the royal pyramidion is an impostor commissioned less than two months ago, and that the android's official handler is Kassam."

"Wait," said the admiral. "Isn't Kassam the engineer you suspected of tampering with the androids' memory?"

"Yes," said Hendrick, "but as yet we're not sure whether Kassam knew the import of what he was doing and, more importantly, whether he was acting on instructions of General Shulgi."

The President asked, "Why didn't Ninurta just ask you to tell Enki?"

Hendrick said, "Because he wants one of you two gentlemen to tell Enki privately and in person—without using a radio—both to cement your relationship with Enki and to allow you and Lord Enki to coordinate your efforts in feeding the spy inaccurate information so that he will misinform his principal, and then in catching and punishing the spy. And there is one more thing Ninurta wanted you to know that Lord Enki doesn't know."

"Uh oh," said the admiral. "What's that?"

"Lord Ninurta is coming to Earth to challenge Anzû once again."

CATHARINE HAD COMPLETELY lost track of time and, as far as she knew, David had, too. Although her internal clock suggested that it had been perhaps three days since they implemented Plan R, there was nothing in space to distinguish between day and night.

Her internal estimate of the passage of time was subject to substantial doubt, as she guessed she'd probably just been counting the number of sleep periods and extrapolating from that. And, truth be told, she'd even lost count of sleep periods, as she and David no longer seemed to sleep for fixed periods. They just chatted, read aloud to each other at whim, and dozed off whenever they felt drowsy, which was often.

Any desire to adhere to eight-hour sleep periods had gone out the window as soon as they realized they were floating around aimlessly in uncharted space. She laughed at herself for ever having complained about being stuck in the *middle of nowhere*, because evidently there *was* a middle of nowhere, and she'd never been stuck there until now.

There was probably a clock in the cockpit, but there was no way she was going there, as she'd have to pass her mangled victim, whom David had dubbed Lumpo. Though she was finally coming around to the notion that Lumpo wasn't in pain or permanently disabled, she couldn't quite shed the eerie feeling that his good eye was tracking her whenever she went by—even though he'd been cut off from any power source.

She and David hadn't eaten in a while, so she went to the galley to find the ready-made reheatables they'd deemed palatable, and began, just as an aid to sanity, to prepare a romantic dinner for two, or as near as she could manage under the circumstances.

The moment it occurred to her that there might be a liquor cabinet, she noticed a smaller cabinet alongside the main refrigeration unit and wondered if that might be it. She put her hand on the handle but hesitated to open it. Ever since coming aboard, she'd had the haunting feeling that one of these days she'd open a door leading straight out into space or into some dangerous and forbidden part of the craft, and it would all be over in a second. *Oh, what the hell*, she thought, and swung it open.

It *was* a liquor cabinet and the moment she reached inside, she realized it had been keeping its contents at a uniform fifty degrees Fahrenheit. She silently thanked heaven when she saw that it contained only earthly beverages. The bottom shelf held good-label wines, evidently some red and others white, as well as a few bottles of champagne. While fifty degrees might be a bit warm for the whites, she reasoned, it was unlikely to be so cold as to ruin the reds. The next shelf up was populated by bottles of some truly excellent hard liquors, largely top-flight Scotch blends.

The topmost shelf held the most precious hard liquors of all, with two unopened bottles of *Bombay Sapphire* gin, and a selection of single-malt Scotches whose names were vaguely familiar to Catharine. She shuddered when she recalled the occasions on which she'd first heard their names spoken; it was Trevor (*ugh!*) who'd really enjoyed them, and that made them hateful to her.

But, at the very back of the top shelf was the most precious bounty of all: a light-blue teardrop-shaped bottle sealed with a distinctive copper-plated stopper in the shape of a miniature blue agave succulent. This was a rare bottle of *Zafiro Añejo*, known among tequila connoisseurs as the finest in the world.

Catharine took out the bottle and gave it pride of place, positioning it carefully in the hold-down receptacle at the center of the dining table affixed to the airframe. She set the table with the finest picnicware she could find, taking care to affix each setting to the table with blue tape, and placed some reheatables they both liked in the microwave, ready for action.

She alternately walked and floated into the dorm, awakening Prince Charming with a kiss. When he got frisky (and he *always* got frisky), she rebuffed his advance, took his hand gently, and led him to the commissary.

When he saw what she'd done, he smiled broadly and said, "This is the most appealing meal I've ever been offered—prepared by the most beautiful woman in the universe."

She smiled at him. "Well spoken, Mister Ambassador, but this is just the first of many uninterrupted romantic dinners, and—as you'll learn soon after we return to Earth—I can actually cook."

She escorted him to his seat and turned to the microwave.

As David was about to take his seat, there was a small but undeniable change in the direction of the craft.

Catharine turned to David to see whether he'd felt it, too. He had.

"Could be a number of things," said David reassuringly. "For one thing, it could be our collision-avoidance system getting us out of the way of some asteroid or something."

Catharine was only slightly mollified. And then it happened again, another small but noticeable course change. Catharine asked him, "What should we do?"

David got up and went to the main passenger compartment to confirm that Lumpo was still turned off. So far so good. Before moving on, he lay a blanket over the android's head to shake Catharine's feeling of being watched.

Then David popped his head into the cockpit, where conditions seemed unchanged. The same three manuals still sat open on the pilot's table, and the radio still jutted partway out of the console, as Lumpo had left it. There was still no sign of power in the console.

All that checking took a good two minutes and, as there'd been no further course corrections during that time, he returned to Catharine.

They ate. But the star of the meal was definitely the tequila, which tasted like none they'd ever had before.

"Y'know," said Catharine, "back home, this stuff's two thousand dollars a bottle."

"Yah?" said David. "Who pays that much for it?"

"Schlemiels like us," said Catharine.

"What does it cost the bar owner?" asked David.

"About four hundred, I think."

"Nice work if—"

David was interrupted by a hard rhythmic clanking on the outside of the craft. It seemed to be coming from the vicinity of the airlock at the rear of the passenger compartment, and sounded like someone was insistently knocking for admittance. Their smiles dropped away. They'd never seen the airlock used, as they'd always gotten on and off through the full-size doors while the whole craft was in a pressurized setting.

"Did you invite guests to dessert?" asked David with bravado.

Catharine shook her head nervously. "No. It's probably hitchhikers."

Together they maneuvered their way to the airlock's plexiglass enclosure. The banging had stopped, but now there was a rustling and scraping on the hull.

Suddenly a distorted, high-pitched voice rang out from everywhere at once. "*This is Ninurta. Who's in charge in there?*"

David was perplexed. "How's he throwing his voice into the cabin?" he wondered aloud.

Catharine dug through her memory and made a connection. "It sounds like he's on a *Gertrude*. It's a device for conducting underwater communications using sound waves. In this case, he's probably talking through a contact loudspeaker pressed up against the hull."

"But why does he sound like Alvin and the Chipmunks?" asked David.

"Heterodyning," she said. "A Gertrude changes the frequency to one that's most likely to be understood by the person listening. Let's chant. *We're in charge. We're in charge. We're in charge.*"

David joined in and Ninurta replied, "Okay, I hear you. Do you know how to depressurize the chamber so I can enter?"

"No," David and Catharine answered at once.

"Very well," said the squeaky voice. "First make sure you're *outside* the chamber and the door lock is engaged, or you'll suffocate. Press the *red* button once and shout when the *red* light goes off and the *blue* light comes on."

"Okay," shouted David and Catharine.

"Now, stand back," said the voice.

They'd practically had their noses up to the plexiglass, but took a step backward. The airlock's locking mechanism engaged with a *chunk*. There came the loud sound of air being sucked out.

In a minute the red light went out. For a tense moment, no other light came on, but (much to their relief) at last the blue light lit.

"*Blue light's on!*" they shouted in unison.

They watched as the hatch wheel on the hull unscrewed slowly and was pulled open from the outside, momentarily revealing only the blackness of space. Then Ninurta, clad in a formfitting white spacesuit making him look alien indeed, grabbed the top of the open porthole with both hands and pushed his way in, feet first. The last thing he did before closing the outer hatch was to release the mini-Gertrude from the hull.

Once Ninurta got everything safely aboard, he pulled the outer hatch shut behind him, turned the lock wheel, gave David and Catharine a thumbs-up, and took a seat on the only bench in the chamber.

"Very well," said Ninurta, touching his helmet to the plexiglass and speaking loud enough to be heard. "Hit the green button. Recompression will take a couple of minutes. When the green light comes on and stays on, press the gate-release button and I'll remove my spacesuit and come out to you."

The green light went on and stayed on, and they gave Ninurta the signal.

Ninurta slowly removed his helmet and breathed deeply. He removed his spacesuit and left it on the bench, donned an electronics toolbelt that he'd been carrying in a small bag, pulled open the plexiglass door, and emerged into the cabin.

"Smells like an electrical fire in here," he said curiously.

David explained. "Well, when we ... subdued the android, we inadvertently caused a short circuit."

Ninurta's eyes flashed. "A short? Where?"

"Well," said David comfortingly, "between the poles of the android's battery. An uninsulated wire affixed to one of the poles came within arcing range of the opposite pole."

Ninurta's eyes darted around the perimeter of the spacecraft as though to confirm that this near-calamity had caused no breach. "Wasn't the opposite pole capped?"

"No," said David, "though it may have been before we disabled the android."

"How long did the arcing last?" asked Ninurta.

David was a bit ashamed to reply. "The arcing was intermittent, but we think it lasted a few hours in all."

"*Hours?*" exclaimed Ninurta. "Is the android still aboard?"

David nodded. "Sure. You said we might need him."

"Yes," said Ninurta blithely, and muttered, "but we need this spacecraft, too."

David and Catharine brought him to see the disabled android, still taped to its seat with a blanket over its head. As David prepared to remove the blanket so Ninurta could inspect the damaged android, Ninurta held up his hand to pause the proceedings. He removed one of the items from his toolbelt—it looked like an ammeter—and swept it over the android's motionless form as though checking for electronic surveillance bugs. While David didn't know how to read the meter, it seemed to show no activity at all. Ninurta put it back on his belt and took out another meter.

"Keep the blanket over his head for the moment," said Ninurta quietly as though to avoid being overheard, making David wonder whether perhaps Catharine's fear of a zombie android was less crazy than he thought. "Just uncover the battery."

David lifted the blanket from its bottom edge and brought it up past the part of the abdomen where the battery stood exposed.

Ninurta took one look at the scorched battery and cast a frown that made David's blood run cold. He passed the meter over the battery. There was some minimal activity there, but nothing close to the red zone. Ninurta wet his index finger on his tongue, ran it over a scorch mark near the uncapped pole and examined the smudge on his finger.

"What is it, my lord?" asked David.

Ninurta shook his head. "You were about two minutes from kingdom come. It's a good thing you stopped the arcing when you did."

David felt a fool. Catharine rolled her eyes and exhaled loudly.

Ninurta used pliers to remove the battery from the android. He pocketed the battery, re-hooked the pliers to his belt, and ran the meter over the android again. This time it showed no electrical activity at all. "Very well. Please remove the blanket from its head."

David pulled the blanket off and began to fold it absentmindedly. Before he could finish, Catharine grabbed the blanket from him and, in two quick motions, folded it neatly enough for service at a five-star hotel, which made David feel even more incompetent.

Ninurta looked at the android's face and seemed perplexed by the eyeball hanging down to its chin. "*Gouged* him into submission, did you?"

"No," said David, "we gave him one solid whack with a wrench to the back of the head. The … ocular dislocation was an unintended result. But before that, my lord, the first thing I tried was to *persuade* the android to relinquish control of the craft."

"Interesting idea," said Ninurta. "How did that go?"

"Better than I expected," said David. "His console had lost power, so he was quite perplexed, although he still had a three-hundred-degree view forward." Ninurta grunted knowingly, but let David proceed with his tale. "The android seemed rational, which suggested to me that he had no idea that vital information had been deliberately deleted from his memory; he seemed as much a victim of tampering as we were. While I felt I was making substantial headway with my argument, however, he mentioned that he'd detected some electrical activity in his radio a few minutes earlier, and offered to examine the radio's memory banks to find out its origin. As I suspected that traces of our communications with your lordship had remained in the radio's memory, I abandoned rational argument and called for a change of plans."

Ninurta nodded approvingly. "Seems the appropriate time to go to a secondary plan."

Catharine interjected. "David called out 'Plan R'," she said derisively.

"What was Plan R?" asked Ninurta.

"I was to step forward with the wrench," said Catharine, "and smash the android in the back of the head."

Ninurta seemed confused. "*Wrench* doesn't begin with an *R*."

Catharine glanced darkly at David. But, to her chagrin, Ninurta looked at him also and, without a hint of irony, said, "*Clever.*"

Catharine rolled her eyes.

Ninurta pointed to the towels taped to the back of the android's head. "Remove these, please."

David removed each towel and, as he did so, Catharine grabbed it from his hands and snapped it into reusable shape.

Ninurta moved the android's head gently forward to examine the cavity at its rear. "By the Queen of Heaven," he said, "I've never seen an android's head reduced to this condition."

Catharine felt impelled to confess. "*I* was the one who struck him, my lord."

Ninurta was astonished. "*You* did this?" he asked, amazed. "Did you need to strike him so *hard*?"

Catharine blushed. "I had no idea how much force to use, my lord."

"It will be quite an effort to bring this android up to full function," said Ninurta, "but no matter." He pointed to the tape with which they'd held the android immobile. "A clever use of duct tape, I might observe."

Catharine suppressed a shriek at what she perceived as the universal collegiality among men, and could hold her tongue no longer. "When you two are done with your mutual-admiration boys' club, I'll be in the dormitory."

She stormed off.

Ninurta looked to David with utter confusion.

David, for his part, pretended to have no idea what was bothering Catharine, and escorted Ninurta to the cockpit.

CHAPTER 17

"*Ah*, THE SCENE of the crime," said Ninurta, pointing to weightless bits of shattered circuitry floating around the partly removed radio.

"I hope you'll acknowledge," said David, "that we hadn't received much instruction on how to subdue an android without destroying it."

"I suppose that's true," said Ninurta, removing one of the three open manuals from a hold-down clip on the pilot's desk. He examined the page the android had been studying. "Just as my assistant suspected, a great deal must have been removed from the android's stock memory. All three of these manuals were included in his original memory banks. There should have been no need for him to pick up *any* physical book and read from it—to say nothing of the slowness of that process under emergency conditions. And I see he was examining the *indices* of all three volumes. From this, I surmise he was still grasping at straws." He put the book back in its holder. "They deleted his knowledge of, not only the way back to Earth, but also the techniques he'd need to steer the spacecraft back on course."

Ninurta observed the videoscreens as they cycled through the views supplied by the craft's external cameras. "I'm the one who remotely killed the power on his flight control and radio. I also remotely blocked his access to the rear-facing cameras." He removed a small handheld computer from his toolbelt and plugged it into a port at the edge of the console.

"How did you manage that?" asked David.

While the handheld computer and the pilot's console underwent their coupling protocol, Ninurta turned to David and winked. "That's not for you to know."

"That's a bit paternalistic," said David, "don't you think?"

Ninurta shrugged as though it didn't matter in the scheme of things. "We *are* the senior species, are we not?"

"Might you at least tell me *why* you disabled the rear-facing cameras?" asked David.

"Simple," said Ninurta, pressing a few buttons on his handheld computer. "So he couldn't see what was behind him."

All the videoscreens suddenly displayed the feed from the rear-facing cameras. Evidently, *The Way Forward* was being closely followed by a gigantic, well-illuminated warship bristling with weaponry.

David shot upright in his chair. "Holy Mother o' God!" he exclaimed. "Is that a destroyer from the royal fleet?"

Ninurta beamed with pride. "She's much more advanced than any destroyer—mostly in her power drives and firepower. She's a battle cruiser; *my* battle cruiser, actually. She carries a long-range antimatter vessel much like this one, and she's large enough to carry several."

David bowed his head in appreciation. "A tip of the hat, my lord. She's a real beauty."

Ninurta sighed proudly. "Thank you, David."

"Might I interject a question here, my lord?" asked David. When Ninurta made no objection, he posed his question. "When Anzû was trying to enlist me to serve his side in the coming storm, he seemed to imply that he'd make me immortal. Does he have the ability to do that?"

Ninurta smoldered. "Although it would be an abuse on his part, I expect he can do it. Whether he would deliver on his promise is a different matter."

David said, "From the story of Enoch and Gilgamesh, it appears that the Anunnaki can confer immortality upon a human whenever they so choose."

Ninurta clearly pondered how much to reveal. "The prerogative belongs to the king alone," he said. "In doing so, the king usually relies upon the advice of the whole Council. It's a simple matter of preparing and consuming combinations of certain foods, but *which* foods, how to prepare them—and the proportions in which they must be mixed—is a sacred royal secret." A wave of disgust appeared on his face. "I don't doubt that Anzû put his filthy hands on that secret together with the Tablets of Destinies."

David could see that Ninurta found the whole notion distasteful, so he changed the subject. "Please pardon my interruption, my lord," he said gingerly. "You were extolling the virtues of your cruiser."

Ninurta's face brightened immediately as he fondly returned his gaze to the cruiser on the videoscreens. "She carries a fighter that I redesigned over a thousand years of contemplating what I'd need to battle someone like Anzû."

"Or Anzû himself?" asked David.

Ninurta considered how to reply. "You're asking when I learned that Anzû's death sentence had been commuted."

"I don't recall asking that, my lord," said David coyly. "Besides, I *know*."

"Oh?" said Ninurta. "What is it you know?"

"Perhaps it would be more accurate to say I *think* I know," said David, "since no one has ever told me. I *think* you knew even before Enki pronounced sentence on Anzû that his execution would be commuted. I think Enki consulted you in advance. In fact," said David, going out on a limb, "I think you *supported* Enki's decision to spare Anzû's life." David fixed a stone-faced poker stare on Ninurta.

Ninurta stared right back at him, controlling his evident irritation, and shook his head. "You earthlings can be truly infuriating. You live for what seems to us no more than a few months, but in that time you learn to intuit and conceal so bloody much." He leaned back in his chair and placed his feet on the pilot's table. "It's well-known throughout the solar system that earthlings excel at games of bluff and deceit."

David smiled slyly.

"We learned long ago to accommodate the human penchant for deceit," said Ninurta, "but that's not the trait that worries either us or the Dagon about you earthlings."

"It's not?" asked David.

Ninurta quietly studied David's non-committal expression. "No," he replied. "It's your bloody-mindedness, your predilection not merely to defeat your enemies, but to *obliterate* them. It's led your species down the road to all manner of warfare and genocide."

"To learn where we derive our tendency toward warfare, my lord," said David, "one need look no further than our Anunnaki heritage."

"*But*," said Ninurta, gently correcting his inquisitor, "annihilation has never been our way—at least not in recorded times. We've always known where *you* got that tendency, and it wasn't from us."

"Where did we derive it, my lord?"

"Well," said Ninurta, "your species has a common ancestor of two earthly primates differing markedly from one another. One, the chimpanzee, known as *pan troglodytes*, exhibits the same savagery as humans do, so it appears likely that your species inherited that trait from the same ancestor as chimps. Chimps are omnivorous. They'll eat anything, even other primates. A male chimp will occasionally eat a newborn chimp sired by another male. Also, males on border patrol will eat any animals they find trespassing on their troupe's territory ... and sometimes eat them *alive*."

"A gruesome practice," observed David.

"Indeed, it is," said Ninurta. "Although early humans didn't seem to follow the chimp's practice of cannibalism (unless they were facing certain starvation), we eventually discovered that your kind would kill others of your species—not to eat them, but to obliterate their genetic line."

David felt a bit shamefaced. "We humans have no direct memory of our distant ancestor."

"We Anunnaki have no direct knowledge of him either," replied Ninurta. "By the time one of your ancestors was first spotted, he already walked upright, lived separately from other primates, and bore little resemblance to any other primate."

"You said we had *two* living earthly relatives, my lord," said David hopefully.

"Yes," said Ninurta, "your other common ancestor was with the bonobo, also known as *pan paniscus*. Your descent from the bonobo may explain why humans were—and *are*—something of a duality, capable of both barbarism and genuine tenderness. The peaceful bonobo who, to the untrained eye, may be undistinguishable from the chimp, is actually quite different in temperament and behavior. For one thing, as Enki discovered, the bonobo is herbivorous. On further investigation, he ascertained that the bonobo belongs to a subset of herbivores known as frugivores, eating mostly fruits, nuts, and seeds. Like gorillas, they occasionally eat some arthropods—"

"Arthropods, my lord?" interjected David.

"Um ... bugs. You know, insects, spiders, lobsters and crabs, and so on. They'll also eat worms. Also occasionally a small fish."

"But what of our *third* nearest living relative: the Anunnaki?" asked David. "I wonder if the Anunnaki are really so different from chimps and humans in their aggressiveness," he said with open skepticism. "All those improvements you made to your fighter in case you needed to challenge Anzû again—How many of those improvements are designed to aid in his ... *capture*, I wonder? I'd venture that most of them are designed to kill. Your victory over Anzû occurred centuries before the Seven Deadly Weapons were used in the Sinai Desert, so I know that Anzû had nothing to do with the loss of your beloved wife—"

Ninurta's face dropped into sadness.

David continued. "But think of all the *other* Anunnaki and human men who will lose their wives or their *lives* if Anzû is allowed to bring his forces to bear. He's tried to kill Ketura several times." David sighed. "If I can avoid killing him, I suppose I will, but if he remains a threat to her, well, what would *you* propose, my lord?"

Ninurta remained lost in thought until his handheld computer beeped, and he sat up. "David," he said, "please bring Ketura into the cockpit, if you would."

With his question unanswered, David went off to find Catharine, returned with her, and offered her a choice of passengers' seats. She chose one, and he took the other.

Catharine's eyes were pinned to the screens showing Ninurta's battle cruiser. "Are we coming under attack?" she asked apprehensively.

Ninurta smiled at Catharine. "Hardly," said Ninurta. "That's my battle cruiser. We've been following you at a few days' distance since you left the royal pyramidion. That's the only way we could have reached you so quickly. Ketura, I asked David to bring you here because we're about to make a radical change of course and I didn't want you to be alarmed."

"Thank you, my lord," she said.

Ninurta pressed a button on his handheld. It beeped quietly. "I just sent the cruiser's temporary captain notice that we're about to change course." He pressed another button and for a brief moment they felt they were heading straight down. (Of course, as there's no *down* in space, they weren't falling.) The cruiser rapidly resumed its position behind *The Way Forward*.

Catharine asked, "Did you leave that cruiser in order to spacewalk to this craft, my lord?"

"That I did," Ninurta replied. "I expect we'll bring this craft aboard the cruiser before long."

Catharine seemed puzzled. "If this craft is going aboard your cruiser, then why did you trouble with a spacewalk to come here?"

Ninurta smiled. "I see that the female of the species is no less intuitive. I needed to make sure that this craft was not under enemy control and also that it hadn't been transformed into a potential hazard that could damage or destroy the cruiser once brought aboard."

Catharine felt foolish. "We *did* create such a hazard, didn't we?"

"Yes," said Ninurta indulgently, "but the emergency was resolved before I arrived."

"Then why doesn't the cruiser bring *The Way Forward* aboard now?" asked Catharine.

"I expect you know there are one or more spies in the Anunnakis' midst. As no one's yet been arrested on that count," he said, "I can't be certain we don't have one aboard our cruiser. As we need our conversations to remain private, I'd prefer not to bring this craft aboard quite yet. Don't worry; we'll board soon enough."

"How far are we from Earth orbit?" asked David.

"Just a couple of days," said Ninurta "If you would, I'd ask you two to take a few minutes to collect anything that might reveal there's been violence aboard, and prepare to jettison it."

AN HOUR LATER, Ninurta, David, and Catharine sat around the main table in the galley, passing around the artisanal bottle of tequila.

Ninurta took a sip and said, "This is from the blue agave of the western hemisphere, is it not?"

Catharine smiled. "It is."

"I thought it tasted familiar," said Ninurta. "You know who would really appreciate this?"

David and Catharine shrugged.

"Ningishzidda," said Ninurta. "He spent many years teaching and learning in the western hemisphere before it was discovered by the Europeans."

"You know much of our planet, my lord," said David. "May I ask you a few questions about your own?"

"Certainly," said Ninurta expansively. "As you've already had the grand tour, I can't imagine there'd be much that's off-limits to you."

David and Catharine exchanged a knowing glance.

David began. "When we overflew Nibiru's southern hemisphere, my lord, we saw a few instances of what appeared to be Anzû's emblematic symbol … painted on the walls."

"So," observed Ninurta, "we quickly approach our main purpose." He took another sip. "And I was so enjoying our little interlude."

Catharine frowned at David and began to apologize.

Ninurta held up his hand. "No apology necessary, Ketura, I assure you. This is an essential discussion—in light of where we're now heading—and you two have a right to give it unhurried consideration before being asked to do anything about … Anzû." A faraway look came over his customarily unflappable expression. "If anyone had told me when Anzû was sentenced that, so many years later, I would be on my way to deal with him again, I would have scoffed." He sighed. "But no longer."

Despite his best efforts, David found his heart going out to Ninurta, but wondered: *How could a mere mortal such as I feel sorry for a god who's already lived thousands of years?*

He was reminded of a poet who once wrote to his young friend Margaret as she mourned the fall of the autumn leaves: 'It is *Margaret* you mourn for,' wrote the poet.

Although David hadn't outlined his plan yet, if Ninurta were to go along with it, David—*not* Ninurta—would be in the crucible. Perhaps it was himself he was feeling sorry for.

OVER LOWER SIBERIA, one of Anzû's motherships released Earth's newest artificial satellite into a high east-west orbit.

After a few quiet hours aloft, the satellite began its overflight of the midwestern United States and began silently bombarding all known U.S. nuclear weapons sites with waves of three distinct types: The first was an electromagnetic wave having the same frequency as the principal harmonic of the Anunnaki disabling ray. Piggybacking on Anunnaki technology, this ray would detect whether there really were nuclear weapons at the expected sites.

The second wave consisted of mass rather than waveform, a neutron ray calibrated to force its target payload to release a few neutrons, but only from weapons-grade Uranium 235 or plutonium, and only enough to be measurable. This would confirm that, properly triggered, the weapon would present a thermonuclear threat.

The final ray also consisted of neutrons, but these would ascertain whether the weapon's nuclear trigger was functional. There was a calculated (but small) risk that this third ray—if it were to strike a functional nuke having a functional triggering mechanism—could cause a thermonuclear explosion. However, the damage to be caused by such an explosion would be restricted to a geographic area defined by a radius of a few miles around the underground explosion, rather than the widespread firestorm and atmospheric fallout that would result from an explosion at altitude.

Right on schedule, the satellite began emitting its rays at targets all over the United States and transmitting its results on a predesignated pattern of hopping frequencies.

The satellite's rays were detected by U.S. forces the moment emissions began. Within five minutes, a dozen U.S. anti-satellite missiles had been dispatched on a ten-minute ascent to their target, namely, Anzû's probe.

Alas, nine minutes after the missiles' liftoff, the enemy satellite completed its mission and finished transmitting its results. To add insult to injury, thirty seconds before the first missile would have made impact, the satellite self-destructed, leaving nothing large enough to present a target. All the incoming missiles were ordered to self-destruct to prevent the extensive damage they'd inflict if they were to fall back to Earth.

America's response had been a seventy-two-million-dollar exercise in futility.

For Anzû's part, he'd gained much by the exercise. He'd learned with virtual certainty that his enemies were armed to the teeth with functioning nuclear weapons. And he now had reason to believe that the Anunnaki had known that for some time, which just might help him to divide and conquer.

On the other hand, Anzû's satellite rays had inadvertently caused a one-kiloton fission explosion in an underground missile silo outside Mosquero, New Mexico. While no fallout had reached the surface, the seismic shift caused a stony hill to collapse, crushing two farmhands across the state line in Texas.

It didn't take long for the news to get around: Anzû had messed with Texas.

And Gary and Buck were both from Texas.

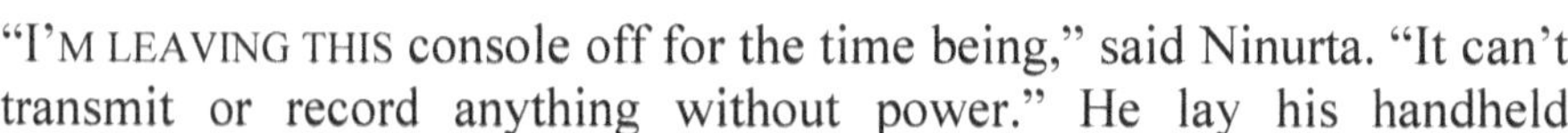

"I'M LEAVING THIS console off for the time being," said Ninurta. "It can't transmit or record anything without power." He lay his handheld computer on the pilot's table, still hooked up to the console.

Catharine led them back to the galley and they resumed their former places around the table.

"So," said David, resuming their earlier discussion, "why would someone like Anzû have a following of any size on Nibiru?"

"Excellent question," said Ninurta, "and not one that can be readily answered."

Catharine chimed in. "Is it simply a dynastic dispute? I've heard that King Anu usurped an earlier king."

"Before Anu ascended the throne of Nibiru," said Ninurta, "Alalu, who had been ruler of the southern hemisphere, claimed planetwide dominion and began a war to impose his will on the north. As Alalu himself was usurper of a king of the north, he never managed to achieve planetwide support for his kingship. When Alalu was deposed by Anu, Alalu felt his life was in danger, so he set out to prove his worth to the whole of Nibiru by finding a source of the gold that Nibiru needed to maintain its atmosphere, without which the people would all die.

"During a near approach to Earth, Alalu hijacked a spacecraft and flew to Earth—alone, mind you. His courage and dedication were not in doubt, but high esteem was never enough for him. By finding gold in the Red Sea, he hoped to be restored to kingship, whether by Anu's forcible removal or his stepping down without a fight."

"What role did Anzû play in this dynastic contest?" asked David.

"Anzû was reputed to be a southerner distantly related to Alalu," said Ninurta, "but he'd served Enlil as one of the Watchers (known as the Igigi) for so many Sars that his loyalty was deemed to be above suspicion. Indeed, he seemed to have no particular fondness for Alalu, as he made nary a mention of Alalu when he stole the Tablets of Destinies. To all appearances, Anzû was in it for himself."

"Why would his claim to the throne be taken seriously by anyone, whether in Nibiru's southern hemisphere or elsewhere?" asked David.

Ninurta nodded. "A logical question, but Anzû's dynastic pretensions were transparently vacuous."

Catharine was confused. "Well, *something* about him must have appealed to southerners. What do you suppose that was?"

Ninurta was chagrined. "I'll be damned if *I* know."

David waited for more, as Ninurta's remark had provided no information at all. "Well, what do southerners want that the offspring of Anu do not provide, besides a king from the south?"

Ninurta began such explanation as he could provide. "When Anzû's supporters are arrested on Nibiru, which they *are* from time to time—"

David interrupted. "Surely not just for supporting Anzû?"

"Certainly not," said Ninurta. "They're an unruly, nihilistic lot. When they're arrested, it's usually for petty crimes: vandalism, graffiti, trash fires, and so on. They're blatantly contemptuous of everything on Nibiru that's … good and decent, for lack of a better phrase."

"Is the south impoverished?" asked Catharine.

"Not under current rule. The south's standard of living *is* slightly lower than that of the north, but it's not for lack of food or public services. The government spends more money and manpower on the south than the north. The southerners *squander* what they're given while complaining that they're given *anything*. They profess to long for the return of some idyllic (but imaginary) past when people grew their own food and celebrated life in their own distinctive way.

"It's ridiculous, really. Before Anu ascended the throne, the south *was truly* impoverished. It was primarily agrarian—and highly inefficient even in that—and there was some starvation. They had no industry to speak of. If you go back a few Sars, they were still engaged in animal (and reputedly human) sacrifice to the Maker of All. It's been said they bridle under the yoke of sound policy and common decency."

"Are Anzû's followers organized?" asked Catharine.

Ninurta waggled his head equivocally. "My impression is that each of them is grievously unhappy within himself or herself, so organizing is not their strong suit. They militantly refuse to entertain the possibility that they themselves are largely accountable for their own misery, so they project blame onto the outward world instead. The irony is that most of them do not spring from objectively miserable circumstances. Many of them are creatures of great wealth and privilege, and so are relegated to bemoaning the misery of *others*, ostensibly providing an unsought 'voice to the voiceless,' which is so unpersuasive (and unappealing) that it's resented by those for whom they purport to speak. And their leaders—who are the most reprehensible—are quite wealthy and live in great comfort."

"Why most reprehensible?" asked Catharine.

"The advice they spew is invariably poisonous," said Ninurta. "They advise their followers to take measures that are sure to *compound* their personal misery, things like drug use, promiscuity, immodesty, intolerance of the opinions of others, obnoxious public conduct, and so on."

"Why does anyone choose to follow them?" asked Catharine. "Isn't their hypocrisy obvious?"

"It's obvious to all but the self-deluded," said Ninurta. "Unfortunately, self-delusion is what characterizes their followers."

David asked, "That emblem resembling one used in Earth's present-day Middle East and on Anzû's fighters ... does it symbolize this muddled philosophy?"

Ninurta nodded.

"And Anzû has settled remote precincts to colonize Earth with it?"

"Possibly," said Ninurta without embellishment.

"*Possibly?*" asked David incredulously.

Ninurta smiled. "Once again," he said, "that's not for you to know."

Catharine rolled her eyes, which got Ninurta to provide some explanation. "Well," he said, "we're not precisely sure how long they've had a presence on Earth. It was a condition to the commutation of Anzû's death sentence that Anzû would leave Earth and never return, yet he's obviously been back on Earth for some time. If he's been there for a thousand years—and I lack any knowledge about whether he has—it appears less likely that he intends to colonize Earth, as he's had plenty of time to do so. On the other hand, if he appeared on Earth only recently, he may have gone there primarily to oppose any attempt by the Anunnaki to colonize Earth, suggesting that he'd like to colonize it himself."

Catharine asked, "How can anyone colonize a planet that already has eight billion inhabitants?"

David ventured, "It's feared that one might start by eliminating a large number of Earth's current inhabitants."

"That's *our* greatest fear," said Ninurta, "although in truth I cannot state with any level of certainty that it's Anzû's present intention. On the other hand, I have no doubt that his fondest wish would be to eliminate the *Anunnaki* presence on Earth entirely."

"Would the Dagon allow that?" asked David.

Ninurta shrugged. "We never know what the Dagon have in mind. If you ask them, they'll tell you they're gathering data—in this case, to observe humankind and determine what you're capable of. But they explain *all* their activities as gathering data, and have done so for as long as records have been kept."

"So, *they're* paternalistic, as well," suggested David.

"Who knows?" said Ninurta. "Perhaps it's true."

David and Catharine exchanged a long stare.

"What do you think, Mister Ambassador?" asked Ninurta.

David said, "We can only compare King Enlil and Anzû based upon how they've treated us and how we've seen them treat others. So far, Anzû has stolen Catharine's laptop, fired on a peaceful group escorting Catharine and me to the U.S. embassy in Paris, destroyed that embassy, attempted to abduct American scientists from a fresh-water submarine, tracked Catharine and me across the oceans and across Africa—unless you *Anunnaki* wish to claim responsibility for any of those deeds, my lord?"

"None of those was an Anunnaki action, David. We *are* responsible for disarming Earth's nuclear weapons. Other than that, all we did was to move the mosque from the Temple Mount, establish a landing site at Baalbek, and remove a few feet of stone from the top of the Great Pyramid. I suppose we must also acknowledge responsibility for Shulgi's self-defeating confrontation with British forces at Westminster."

David resumed his earlier litany. "To add to Anzû's list of crimes, he has attempted to kill Queen Inanna and destroy her pyramidion, to kill or capture the President and Lord Enki at their summit, and to shoot down several American aircraft without provocation—to say nothing of his several unprovoked attempts to murder Ketura. I'd say Anzû has done the worst of it; so much so, that I don't much care to weigh the fine points of his atavistic ideology."

"What will you do?" asked Ninurta.

"Whatever's necessary," David replied curtly.

IN PREPARATION FOR an imminent visit by the President of the United States, security on Enki's pyramidion was tighter than it had ever been.

In a new SF-5 saucer (dubbed *Space Force One* for the occasion), the President and his closest adviser watched the videoscreens as their craft began to dock with the pyramidion.

The Vice President had remained in Washington in readiness for the possible commencement of hostilities with Anzû's forces, for Anzû had once again violated the territorial integrity of the United States. And, which was worse, in his latest foray he'd likely ascertained that America's nuclear arsenal was operational.

The President tensed up as he felt the thump of a secure docking. In sixty seconds, he'd emerge into the airlock where he and the other newcomers would be scanned for weapons. He'd then proceed to Lord Enki's chamber where, by agreement, the first half hour's conversation would be conducted with no one present but Enki and the President. The admiral would be admitted once the initial conversation was complete.

The President was met by Anunnaki guards armed with partisans, who bowed respectfully and escorted him to the ceremonial gate, where they escorted the admiral to a private room outside Enki's quarters and knocked on the great doors.

"Come," boomed Lord Enki's voice.

The doors swung open. The guards escorted the President into Lord Enki's darkened chamber and waited to be dismissed.

The President was once again impressed by the way in which the room was warmly illuminated by Enki's glow.

In light of his guest's importance, Enki rose from his throne.

Though the President nodded respectfully, he deliberately spoke first, as he'd been advised by his State Department befitted a visiting head of state.

"My lord," said the President, "it has been too long since last we met."

Enki smiled. "I was just about to say the same thing, Mister President. Welcome to my humble abode. May I offer you any food or drink?"

The President put both hands on his belly, which had begun to swell a bit in the past few months. "None, my lord. I've been advised by my physicians to limit my intake of food whenever possible."

Enki laughed sonorously. "Are all your physicians slim, Mister President?"

The President pictured his physicians. "Not in the least."

"We have an old saying: Advice should be heeded most closely when offered by those who *follow* it most closely."

"A good prescription against hypocrisy," said the President. "I must say, Lord Enki, that I'd like to proceed to the substance of our meeting immediately, if I may."

Enki cocked his head curiously and showed his upturned palm, as though offering the floor.

"I have three items of roughly equal importance," said the President. "As two concern your lordship's security closely, I'll address those first. As you know, we've received information that there's a spy (or more than one) aboard this pyramidion and that no one has been arrested on that score."

"True," said Enki.

"Our intelligence indicates that this spy, or his agent, has tampered with two of your Enkidu-model androids and has substituted a newly minted android having virtually no flight experience for the experienced android who was *supposed* to pilot our ambassador and his military accompaniment on their current expedition."

"Again, true," said Enki. "I expected you would know this, as it was your man Hendrick who discovered the switch."

"What we learned fairly recently is that Queen Inanna received an encrypted message from Ninurta, stating that the android piloting the ambassador's craft was commissioned less than two months ago and that its official handler is named *Kassam*. Hendrick said Kassam had always been his leading suspect, as Kassam was likely the only person who'd had enough time to make the necessary modifications to the two androids' memories. In Kassam's defense, I hasten to add that Hendrick had no evidence that, when Kassam made the alterations, he knew the import of what he was doing."

Lord Enki said, "Kassam was a natural suspect, so I've had him carefully watched since the android switch was first suspected."

"To my second order of business," said the President, "Lord Ninurta has informed Queen Inanna that he is coming to Earth to challenge Anzû once again."

This seemed a surprise to Enki. "Ninurta's leaving his pilgrimage to the royal pyramidion after all these millennia?"

"So he has told Inanna," said the President.

"I don't understand," said Enki. "Why wouldn't Inanna simply tell me herself?"

The President shrugged. "That's what happens when people lose confidence in the security of their communications. Messages move in unexpected channels. I expect the Queen surmised, in light of Shulgi's high office, that he would overhear any message passing through her radio room. Besides, Ninurta wanted me to deliver this news to you face to face, so that we could coordinate a technique to smoke out the spy, should we wish, whether by feeding him incorrect information or otherwise."

"I see," said Enki. "Before we try something as indirect as that, I propose to have Kassam interrogated without delay, with you as a witness, if you like."

The President was surprised and therefore cautious. "I assume that no torture or threats of torture will be applied?"

Enki nodded. "A fair assumption. Now, I believe you had a third item of information for me?"

Despite his best efforts, the President blushed. "Yes, my lord, but I expect you may not be as sanguine as with the first two."

Enki waited patiently.

"As your lordship will recall," said the President, "when the Anunnaki made their sudden reappearance a few months ago, your first action was to begin transmitting a complex ray that disabled my country's nuclear weapons—"

"Well," said Enki, "I hope you understand that that was a simple defensive measure."

The President nodded. "But, as a practical matter, it also upset the balance of power among the earthly nations, leaving my country open to nuclear blackmail by any country clever enough to overcome the effect of the Anunnaki ray. Although America had no intention of using any weapons, nuclear or conventional, against the Anunnaki, this was inimical to the interests of the United States."

"So … what did you do?" asked Enki.

"We developed a technique to neutralize the ray," said the President.

"I see," said Enki. "And when do you intend to implement this technique?"

The President swallowed hard. "It's already been implemented for several months."

"Your nuclear capabilities have returned in full force?"

"Yes, your lordship, but our intention never to use them or threaten to do so against the Anunnaki has remained unchanged." Unless Enki was a consummate actor, he was surprised and dismayed to hear this news, which only increased the President's confidence that he'd sprung the news on Enki at the appropriate time.

"We *could* modify our ray to render it effective once more," suggested Enki.

The President nodded broadly. "No doubt. But we ask that you refrain from doing so, my lord, as we will soon need our nuclear arsenal against Anzû, at the very least as a deterrent."

"And what guarantee have I that your nuclear arsenal will not be poised against us?"

"Well," said the President, "there is our conduct for the past five months, during which we never trained our restored weapons upon you. And, in terms of sheer self-interest … quite frankly, we need you as an ally. We don't know Anzû's capabilities, and we expect that our present inventory of orbital craft and trained pilots alone may be insufficient to defeat him."

Enki seemed to accommodate this new eventuality better than the President had expected.

"But why are you telling me this now?" asked Enki dubiously.

"We expect that hostilities are imminent, and we may be called upon to use these weapons—at least, as I've said, as a deterrent."

"And may I assume," said Enki, "that yesterday's underground nuclear accident signifies that Anzû has discovered your nuclear readiness?"

"We expect that he has learned of our restored nuclear capabilities, my lord."

Enki nodded thoughtfully and resumed his seat on the throne, pressing a button on one of its arms to initiate a voice communication with one of his retinue. "Has General Shulgi come aboard with the other generals?" he asked.

"Yes, my lord," came the disembodied reply.

"Very well," said Enki. "Bring the artificial intelligence specialist known as Kassam to the Tank. Tell him nothing of who is here or why anyone might wish to see him. Once Kassam is in the Tank, escort General Shulgi to Observation One. As with Kassam, tell him *nothing*."

CHAPTER 18

ON ENKI'S PYRAMIDION, there was a brightly lit interrogation room that had long been known as the Tank, because it resembled a fish tank.

The Tank was surrounded by four walls of one-way mirror. On the opposite side of each of the four walls was a darkened observational room whose occupants could see and hear everything taking place in the Tank. The subject in the Tank could neither see nor hear anything taking place in the observational rooms unless it was electronically routed to the Tank.

Today, the Tank contained not only the usual uncomfortable chair for the subject, but an elevated seat for General Ningishzidda, who would question the subject.

Lord Enki, the President, and the admiral were escorted into Observation Room Three in which Enki was placed behind a smoky glass to stop the light emitted by his person from overwhelming the one-way mirror and allowing him to be seen from the Tank.

Hendrick was ushered into Lord Enki's observation room. He humbly bowed to Lord Enki, nodded respectfully to the President and admiral, and took a seat apart from the others.

A minute later, the door to the Tank opened and a confused-looking Kassam was marched in and instructed to take his seat and wait quietly. He was left alone for a few minutes.

Hendrick shook his head. The President glanced at him.

"What is it?" asked the President.

"Either this man has balls of steel," said Hendrick softly, "or he has no idea what he did."

The admiral nodded.

There was a quiet knock on the door, and a guard stuck his head in. "Lord Enki," he said with a bow, "General Shulgi is under guard and seated in Observation Two. He was muttering about his 'right' to immortality on grounds that he's half Anunnaki."

Enki nodded and waved the guard out.

General Ningishzidda entered the Tank carrying some papers and notes. "Are you Kassam, the artificial intelligence specialist?" he asked the subject.

"I am, general."

"And have you just completed a shift?"

"No," replied Kassam, "I was just about to begin one when I was summoned."

"Were you expected to work with androids during your upcoming shift?"

Kassam smiled respectfully. "Not this shift, general. In fact, only a few shifts each week involve my specialty. During this shift, I was scheduled to command one of the airlocks. As no one is scheduled to arrive or depart the pyramidion during this shift, however, I expected to catch up on some technical reading. May I ask what the general wishes to ask me about in such a formal setting?" His eyes darted about nervously.

"We'll get to that shortly," said the general breezily. "I don't wish to keep you from your duties longer than necessary. Who's directly above you in the chain of command?"

"Well," said Kassam, "as I'm a technical specialist, I have no military chain of command. I answer directly to General Shulgi."

"Where are your quarters?"

"For the general's convenience, my quarters are located very near his. As General Shulgi is currently in charge of military matters for Queen Inanna, both our quarters are located on Her Majesty's pyramidion."

"So, you return there after you complete each shift?"

"Not immediately upon completion, but I return there to sleep."

"Has General Shulgi given you any orders in the past few weeks pertaining to the maintenance or repair of androids?" asked Ningishzidda.

At first Kassam began to shake his head, but then thought better of his answer. "Well ... once, yes."

Ningishzidda's open expression silently invited Kassam to continue.

"Just before the two Americans left this pyramidion on their journey to the Mars system," said Kassam, "General Shulgi instructed me to perform routine maintenance on the android who'd serve as pilot for the Americans. The android was Enkidu, the long-time companion to Doctor Ziusudra."

"Are you sure it was that very android?" asked Ningishzidda.

"There's no mistaking that," said Kassam with a hesitant smile. "He was one of the most interesting androids I've ever encountered."

"How so?"

"He was so steeped in literary and philosophical tradition, both Anunnaki and human," said Kassam, "that he was hard to keep up with. Though some might call him a cynic, I found him humorously skeptical. I suppose he may have learned much from the good doctor about both Anunnaki and humans. He was … pleasant company."

The general nodded indulgently. "What maintenance did you perform?"

Kassam shifted in his seat, as though straining to recall. "I upgraded his memory with current information about the journey to Mars and back."

"Was that all?"

Kassam tilted his head, as though trying to imagine what the general could be getting at. "As I recall, general, that was all. Pretty routine."

"Did you do any physical maintenance on the android at that time?"

Kassam shook his head without hesitation. "No, general. That's not something I would do. I wouldn't even know *how* to do it."

"Did you take handwritten notes of your maintenance?"

"No, sir. That's not the protocol."

"Did you have any writing ink at hand?"

"*Ink*, sir?"

"For writing," explained the general with a shrug.

"No, sir."

"Did you have ink for any other purpose?"

"No, sir."

"Did you apply any marks to the android's body?"

"No, sir."

"Did you make any changes to the android's series data?"

"No, sir. I wouldn't know how to do that."

"Why not? Doesn't series data form a part of the android's knowledge base?"

"Yes, sir," conceded Kassam, "but that information is imprinted at the time of manufacture for the limited purpose of ensuring that every android can be distinguished from every other. It doesn't affect the android's logic, or its long- or short-term memory, so I'd have no need to change it. Or even access it, generally."

"Did you change the android's other preset data, such as its name or commission date or its assigned handler?"

Kassam began to look worried. "No, sir. I'm not even sure an android's name or commission date are capable of change by someone having my level of security clearance ... at least, without a change of physical boards—and I certainly didn't do any such thing. Then or ever."

"Kassam, would you know if you were an android's assigned handler?"

Kassam nodded confidently. "Protocol requires that the handler be notified the moment the android is commissioned, sir."

"Did you ever receive notice that you were that android's handler?"

"Certainly not, sir."

"Have you ever served as an android's assigned handler?"

"Yes, sir. In fact, there was another, similar android at my station the same day for whom I *was* the assigned handler."

"And did you perform a memory update on him, as well?"

"I did."

"Do you remember anything about that other android—the one for which you served as handler?" asked the general.

Kassam exhaled deeply. "I recall very little about him." He searched his memory. "His appearance was identical to the other android. But he was a new issue, as I recall—no more than a few weeks old."

"Let's call him the new-issue android. Was the new-issue android good company, like the older android you'd worked on that day?"

Kassam frowned and shook his head. "No. The new-issue android was almost childlike. He appeared to know little or nothing about the world that hadn't been contained in his base module."

"How do you perform a memory update on an android?"

Kassam sighed. He could see he'd be here for a while. "Well, first I log on to the source computer—that's the computer that has the updated files."

"Do you have unique credentials permitting you to be identified to that particular task?"

Kassam hesitated. There could be no doubt that the general already knew all this quite well, having himself worked with the same computer system for many Sars. So the general could only be compiling a formal record—and that thought sent a chill up Kassam's spine. "Yes, sir. Everyone's credentials are unique."

"And after you log on, what then?"

"I proceed to the folder where the source files are located and prepare to upload them to the target android, overriding files of the same name already there in the android's memory," said Kassam.

"And how do you know which is the source folder for a given operation?"

"I'm informed by electronic message ahead of time."

"Who informed you of the source folders in respect of the two androids we're discussing?" asked the general.

"The messages came from General Shulgi."

"Are you certain?"

"Well, General Shulgi is normally the person who would send them to me. If anyone else had sent me such information, it would have been … *unusual*. So I'd remember that."

"And do the source files remain on the main computer indefinitely?"

"Yes," said Kassam, "consistently with a long-standing protocol that can only be superseded by express order of the Council in each instance."

"Did the Council supersede the protocol requiring *these* source files to be saved?" asked Ningishzidda.

"Not that I know of—and I'm *required* to be notified if that happens."

"Do you examine the contents of source files before uploading them to an android?"

Kassam shook his head emphatically. "No. My maintenance work is limited to ensuring a complete and accurate upload. In fact, for me to read the content of the files, I would first need to decompile the executable code back to source code."

"Would you be able to read the files once decompiled?"

"Yes."

"Have you ever written source code of that type?" asked the general.

"Oh, certainly. My specialty requires a high degree of facility in coding for androids and other artificial intelligence devices."

"So, why didn't you decompile the files and review them before you uploaded them to the androids?"

Kassam was beginning to feel beleaguered. "That could take *hours*, sir," said Kassam. "I was instructed to perform the upload and confirm that it had been properly completed. That's all."

"And you did that?"

"Yes, sir."

"To whom did you confirm the successful uploads?"

"To General Shulgi. And I made a record of the confirmations on the source computer, as required."

"So, from your viewpoint, in uploading the new files to the two androids, you were simply performing a clerical act on orders of General Shulgi?"

Though Kassam momentarily resisted the questioner's use of the term *clerical* in characterizing his actions on that day, he had to admit its accuracy. "Yes," he replied.

Ningishzidda relaxed visibly, having evidently reached a watershed in his questioning. "Kassam, our experts have retrieved and examined the source files you uploaded to the androids that day. Our experts tell us that some of the new memories were programmed to self-erase with the passage of time, and that, in the uploads, many memories had been switched between the two androids."

Kassam involuntarily shot to his feet in horror. "Switched? What? Why?"

"The files you uploaded to the old android made him forget not only who he was, but everything he'd learned since being commissioned. The files you uploaded to the new-issue android were programmed to forget"—he arched an eyebrow—"how to return from the Mars system."

"Oh, God of All Things!" shouted Kassam in horror. "What has become of the passengers?"

"Best we not discuss that now, Kassam. For the time being, you will be committed to confinement and your communication privileges rescinded. You may, of course, have private communications with a lawyer to be provided to you upon request."

Kassam's face turned white and his mouth fell open. Breathing heavily, he said, "I have no need of a lawyer. Is there nothing I can do to prove that I was duped?"

Ningishzidda, who'd been expecting Kassam's horror, asked, "Well, Kassam, are you accusing General Shulgi of sabotage?"

Kassam was exercised to the point of breathlessness. "Either General Shulgi was himself duped or he *is* guilty of sabotage!" he shouted.

"Can you offer me the name of someone who could have duped General Shulgi?"

"No, sir," said Kassam, nearly weeping. "If I had suspected someone of duping the general, I would have reported it long ago."

"Permit me to remind you," said Ningishzidda calmly, "that this suspension of your privileges is temporary only. I hope you can see that, with the fleet on heightened alert, we cannot afford to have anyone under suspicion in charge of anything of importance, especially communications."

"I quite understand, sir," said Kassam, "but it's horrifying—

especially at a time of such urgency—for me to find myself under suspension."

"There's one more thing you *might* help me with—" said Ningishzidda impassively.

"*Anything!*" cried Kassam.

Ningishzidda scratched his beard with the knuckles of one hand. "This requires you to refer to the time when Lord Enki and the President were under attack after the summit meeting. Do you remember that day?"

"It's indelibly etched on my brain, sir. I remember it with horror."

"Do you have any idea who confirmed to the Americans that Lord Enki's pyramidion had received their notification that the summit was under attack?"

Kassam desperately searched his memory.

After a few seconds, Ningishzidda said, "Well?"

"One moment, sir, if you please." Kassam's face reddened as he recalled a fact he would never have expected himself to recall. "I can recall something relevant to this matter, sir. When first I learned that aerial combat had taken place over the summit site, I strained to recall what I'd been doing at the moment when, unbeknownst to me, the Americans radioed for help."

Ningishzidda regarded him warily. "What had you been doing at the time?"

"Searching for General Shulgi … on a matter having nothing to do with the ongoing air battle, as I had no knowledge of that until after it concluded."

Ningishzidda sat up attentively. "Can you remember why you wished to speak with General Shulgi?"

"I cannot presently recall, sir, for which I'm truly sorry. I can check the ship's log to refresh my recollection on that score, if you wish. I do recall, however, that General Shulgi was nowhere to be found for about a half hour."

"Was that a long time for General Shulgi to be out of contact?"

"Very much so, sir. When I went to the general's quarters, I found the door ajar and gently pushed it open. I found the general hunched over a small radio I'd never seen before."

"I see," said Ningishzidda.

"The guards should search his quarters for the radio, sir."

"Oh, they *have* searched his quarters for it, Kassam," said Ningishzidda. "Unfortunately, there was no sign of it ever having been there.

But, of course, that's to be expected even if it *had* been there at one time. For your information, General Shulgi has denied ever possessing such a radio." He sat back in his chair. "Fortunately, however, it was seen by several others in addition to you."

"Heavens be praised," said Kassam, nearly collapsing with relief.

"Are you now ready to accuse General Shulgi of sabotage, Kassam?"

By this time Kassam's face glistened with sweat, but he shook his head mournfully. "I have insufficient information to make such a grave accusation, sir. But I can swear to you upon my soul: If you narrow the saboteur down to being either General Shulgi or me, it's *he*."

IN ENKI'S OBSERVATION room, the silence was broken by the restrained voice of his lordship himself. "Of course, Kassam would say *that* whether he were guilty or not," he said.

Unable to leave it at that, Hendrick spoke up. "True, your lordship, but General Shulgi's denial that he ever had such a radio is damning evidence that he was using the radio for purposes he knew to be illicit." He muttered under his breath. "He would have been better served by allowing the radio to be found where others had seen it, denying only that he'd used it for illicit purposes."

Enki smiled. "Why, Mister Hendrick, one would think your former job was to conceal contraband."

Hendrick replied uneasily. "That was not my job, Lord Enki."

Enki regarded him skeptically.

Hendrick blushed and admitted, "Concealing contraband would more accurately be described as a *subspecialty*."

The President and the admiral laughed quietly, and Enki came closer to laughing aloud than any of them could remember.

KASSAM WAS ESCORTED from the Tank, and his unenviable place in the hot seat was taken by a human male.

"Isn't that Shawn McCauley?" asked the President.

"It is, Mister President," said Enki. "He chose to come to this pyramidion last night at my invitation. I met with him upon his arrival and relieved him of the memorial suppression that's been plaguing him— much as you requested some time ago. It's your choice whether to allow him to give testimony today, of course. But I can assure you that no one else has spoken to him since his arrival and, since that meeting, he has not spoken a word to me or anyone else. So, he's had an uninterrupted period of twelve hours to recover and make sense of his recovered memories."

In the Tank, Shawn rose from the chair and protested. "I work for the Secretary of State of the United States. I refuse to be questioned without his written consent."

Ningishzidda was impressed with the stridency of the objection.

"Admirable," said Ningishzidda with an indulgent nod. "I would say the same."

Shawn was taken aback by the questioner's civilized, nay, *supportive* response, but he remained standing nonetheless.

"Well," said Ningishzidda, shuffling through his papers, "we seem to be all out of secretaries of state, but there may be *someone* here—"

His sentence was interrupted by a knock at the Tank door, which swung open to reveal the President of the United States. Shawn was speechless. He had met the President on a couple of occasions, and was struggling to find something—anything—about the person who just appeared that showed him to be an impostor. As yet, he'd found nothing.

"Hey, Shawn," said the President calmly.

"Sir," said Shawn, "are you here *alone*?"

"No, I brought a friend whom you've also met." There was another knock at the door. In walked the admiral.

"Hello, admiral," said Shawn sheepishly. He turned to the President. "Do I understand that you're waiving ambassadorial privilege, sir?"

The President nodded. "I am, Shawn. It's in the interests of the United States that you cooperate fully with this investigation. Um, you weren't doing anything illegal when you were struck by the memorial suppression, were you? I don't want this questioning to get you personally into hot water."

"Well, sir, as best I can recall," said Shawn with chagrin, "I *had* carried a paper cup full of non-kosher coffee into a kosher restaurant."

"How *could* you?" asked the admiral tongue-in-cheek.

The President shook his head reassuringly. "That's not the kind of thing I'm concerned with."

Shawn shook his head emphatically. "Nothing else, sir."

"Okay," said the President. "We'll watch your interview from off-premises. As far as proof of my waiver of privilege, I've requested Lord Enki to forward a full copy of this interview to the U.S. Archives, including our present visit."

"Thank you, sir," said Shawn.

The President and admiral removed themselves to Enki's observation room.

"Please sit down," said Ningishzidda. "Mister McCauley, you were burdened with memorial suppression until being relieved of it last night by Lord Enki, correct?"

"Correct, sir."

"Whether before or after Lord Enki relieved you of your burden, did Lord Enki or anyone else speculate on, or suggest, what you might remember?"

"No, sir."

"Has anybody suggested to you how to respond to my questions today?"

"No."

"Has anybody told you how to *frame* your answers?"

"No, sir."

"Well, then, have you applied such effort as you've deemed appropriate to recalling events that had been subjected to memorial suppression until last night?"

"I have, sir."

"Can you recall what you were doing when your memory was suppressed?"

"Yes, sir. I was speaking with my old friend David Schubert on the telephone from a restaurant overlooking the Temple Mount in Jerusalem."

"You were talking to the man who's presently serving as United States Ambassador to the Anunnaki?"

"Yes, sir," said Shawn proudly. "He was just a law professor then."

"If you can recall," asked Ningishzidda, "what was the last thing you saw before being stricken with memorial suppression?"

"I've thought about that a lot in the past several hours and I must say that what I saw seems … trivial. One thing that sticks out: I saw two men talking privately in the lobby of the hotel connected to the restaurant. One of their faces was badly scarred—and I mean *badly*. Most of it was concealed by a black cowl—like monks used to wear in ancient times. All I could think of when I saw him was, *Why doesn't some smart plastic surgeon help him?*"

Ningishzidda took a few notes. "If I have thirty or forty photographs flashed on this video screen behind me, could you tell me whether you see the face of the badly scarred man?"

"Certainly," said Shawn.

What followed was a series of sequentially numbered photographic facial portraits of men who appeared to be burn victims or wounded warriors with tragically scarred faces.

"That's him," said Shawn. "Number 23."

While Ningishzidda saw that Shawn had chosen a photograph of none other than Anzû, he assiduously avoided betraying that he recognized the person in the photo.

"Do you suppose you might be able to identify the face of the person who was speaking with the scarred man?" asked Ningishzidda.

"Well," said Shawn with a shrug, "his face was less memorable in that it wasn't badly scarred. However, he looked me square in the face, so I might recognize him."

What followed was a similar gallery of (unbeknownst to Shawn) Lord Enki's general officers wearing identical button-down shirts. To minimize any possible prejudice that might arise out of the sequence in which the portraits were displayed, Ningishzidda had made sure that Shulgi's portrait would be forty-ninth of fifty.

When the twelfth portrait appeared, Shawn said, "Wait."

Ningishzidda was alarmed, as it was too soon for Shulgi's portrait to have appeared. If McCauley were to give an inaccurate identification, it would throw the reliability of his memory into serious doubt.

McCauley looked at Ningishzidda curiously and said, "Isn't that *you*?"

Ningishzidda turned about and looked at the screen, which indeed displayed a picture of him taken at a time when he sported a thick black mustache and long sideburns. His face reddened with embarrassment, but he breathed a sigh of relief. "Yes, Mister McCauley, that's me. I should have removed that portrait from the gallery. Sorry I missed it."

The portraits resumed rolling by.

"Wait," said Shawn a few moments later. "That's him. That's the other man."

It was Number Forty-Nine. General Shulgi.

Suddenly, Shawn was startled by a loud commotion in one of the sound-proofed observation rooms. Someone was shouting like a madman, his voice rising and falling as though attempting to rouse to action a stadium full of primed fanatics. Then a fist pounded on the one-way mirror dividing the tumultuous observation room from the Tank.

Ningishzidda smiled smugly to hear Shulgi's vehement protest. He'd succeeded in getting under the bastard's skin, and it could be no more than a few minutes before Shulgi would hopelessly incriminate himself. *Mission accomplished.*

The tirade continued. *That bastard never could keep his mouth shut*, thought Ningishzidda, who smiled beneficently at Shawn. "Thank you very much, Mister McCauley," he said loudly enough to be heard over the tumult. "Please return to your quarters and await my contact."

⟶◦◖◢◤◗◦◅

LORD ENKI ASSURED the President, the admiral, and Hendrick that they should remain with him in the observation room. He summoned the guard from outside, who entered and bowed.

"Please escort General Shulgi here," said Enki. "If he acts up, subdue him by any means necessary." The guard had already turned to walk away when Enki added, "And you may disregard his rank."

The admiral's eyes went wide, signaling to the President just how serious that was.

In a moment, Shulgi's unabated shouting could be heard approaching from down the hall. At last, two guards wrested him into Enki's observation room and forced him to his knees. He glared up insolently at Enki, barely noticing the President, the admiral, and Hendrick.

Enki observed Shulgi quietly with the slightest expression of contempt, which was evidently sufficient to incite Shulgi to speech.

"What did you expect?" Shulgi shouted at Enki. "For millennia, you've selected me for positions of only the *least* importance."

Enki glowered at him but did not deign to answer.

Shulgi jutted out his jaw and said, "The final indignity was to put me in charge of protecting that … strumpet."

Enki addressed the guards who stood beside the kneeling general.

"Bring him to me," growled Enki.

The guards lifted Shulgi from the floor and placed him face to face with Enki.

"Are you referring to Queen Inanna as a strumpet?" asked Enki.

"*Strumpet* is too good a word for her," spat Shulgi.

With leonine quickness and strength, Enki slapped Shulgi's face so hard that he fell over on his side, momentarily stunned.

Certain that Shulgi must be unconscious or perhaps dead, the President gasped aloud, but was shocked to see Shulgi rise, only to be forced to his knees once again.

Shulgi rubbed his stricken cheek with his hand. "Oh, brave Enki—" he began, but he was interrupted.

"Stop it, you fool," said Enki. "You're beginning to sound like your idiot co-conspirator Anzû. Have you nothing to tell me before you're put on trial for your life? Nothing that might be useful to me, that might attenuate the circumstances of your crimes and therefore your sentence?"

"Such as?" asked Shulgi, who'd managed at last to contain his humiliation.

"The names of your co-conspirators," suggested Enki.

Shulgi shook his head bitterly. "There are Anunnaki in every part of the fleet who feel let down by the iron rule of Anu's heirs ... but none with the intestinal fortitude to join me in undermining their cause."

"So, you know of no one who's joined Anzû's army of malcontents?"

Shulgi shook his head. "No one," he said with as much resentment as he could muster.

"So," proposed Enki, "if we were to find your secret radio, and check its memory we would find that you have communicated with no one?"

"There was no radio," said Shulgi. "What do you offer if I help you now?"

Enki shook his head in disgust. "More than Anzû has offered you in exchange for your treachery, I'm sure."

"Oh?" said Shulgi. "More than immortality and North America?"

Enki laughed. "You fool," he said. "Anzû does not control North America and he never will. It's not his to give, so he might as well dangle it before you like a candy before the eyes of a baby. You've sold your soul for nothing."

"It's more than you and your royal brother would ever offer me," replied Shulgi bitterly.

"We don't offer what's not ours to give," replied Enki. "As we feel constrained to keep our promises, we can make only a few. And you've been promised no less than has the rest of our general staff. What promises have your brethren officers received?"

"None," spat Shulgi. "You Anunnaki pretend to *have* nothing only so you can demand service while *giving* nothing." He glanced at the President and the admiral as though noticing them for the first time, and turned back to Enki. "What have you told these dupes of your intentions, my lord? Have you told them why you've come to Earth?"

"Keep a civil tongue in your head, Shulgi," said Lord Enki. "These men are so far superior to you that you have no place insulting them.

They know more than you think."

"What have *you* led them to think, I wonder?"

Enki shook his head with disdain. "They know we've come to see what to expect if Nibiru's next approach results in a catastrophic collision."

Shulgi snarled. "A horror tale for fools. You have come to see if you can steal their planet if Nibiru collides with their moon."

"Rubbish," said Enki. "It's you and your master, that filth Anzû, who wish to steal their planet, and you feel no need to justify your doing so by reference to an upcoming catastrophe. You would conquer for conquest's sake."

Shulgi noticed Hendrick and said, "And why do you traffic with this African, who resembles the firstborn Adam?"

Hendrick rose from his chair and bowed to Enki. "If I may defend my honor, my lord?"

Enki gave it a moment's thought and replied, "You may defend your honor, sir, so long as you do so only with words."

Hendrick turned to Shulgi. "I am Hendrick, reconstructor of stray signals."

At first Shulgi scoffed, then he regarded Hendrick with interest. "What does that even mean?"

Hendrick scoffed right back at him. "This fleet—and every ship in it—is a massive recorder of every signal that goes out from it, or comes into it. Signals that are not organized in some expected way are not analyzed—but they *are* recorded. Now that I know what type of device you were using to communicate with Anzû, and the approximate period in which you were using the device, I need only identify your communications among the stray signals recorded by these vessels. From there, it's a relatively small matter to decrypt the signals and reconstruct them."

Shulgi's face dropped and he observed Hendrick with suspicion. "You lie, African."

"Do I?" said Hendrick haughtily. "I know already that you have spoken with Anzû on your device. All I need do is analyze the frequencies that Anzû is accustomed to using, find those signals among the fleet's vast record of unidentified signals, and decrypt and reconstruct them. From there, I can pinpoint the precise location of your radio at any time in the past. With any luck, I can tell whether you were eating while you spoke, or perhaps whether you had a head cold while speaking, and—of course—what you and Anzû said to one another."

Shulgi seemed to credit what Hendrick was saying. "But what difference would it make? Anzû already knows all that information. What of it?"

Hendrick shook his head at this man's stupidity. "But as yet Anzû is unaware that you shared all those conversations with the Anunnaki so that they might use the information to oppose his attempted conquest of Earth."

"But I did *not* do that!" protested Shulgi, a little less confident now.

"Of course you did," said Hendrick with a wicked smile, "at least, Anzû will be persuaded of it. And for your reward you'll receive the back of his hand. Oh, he'll grant you immortality all right. But not the kind you hope for, with a jug of wine in one hand and a womanly breast in the other."

Shulgi was beginning to show fear. "What do you mean?"

"You underestimate your new master's penchant for revenge and cruelty," said Hendrick. "History teaches how Anzû punishes treachery. He will confer upon you only the *purest* form of immortality, where you'll need neither food nor water, nor even air to keep you alive, and you'll have no escape from consciousness, as you will never sleep. And then your hateful Anzû will cast you out into interstellar space, where you'll float forever; alone and aimless, with no hope of the relief that only death can provide." He fixed his gaze far away. "Forever," he intoned. After a moment, he shrugged. "Or, at least for a few million years, after which you'll eventually burst into flames from coming too near a star or being drawn into a planetary atmosphere somewhere."

Shulgi was truly horrified now and doing a poor job of concealing it. "But that's despicable." He tried to dismiss the nightmare that Hendrick had imparted. "Lord Enki would never engage in deception such as this you espouse—even against a sworn enemy like Anzû."

"Have no fear on that score," Hendrick assured him. "Lord Enki's honor would in no way be besmirched. The *United States* would plant the seed in Anzû's head without need of Anunnaki assistance. As everyone knows, we humans are masters of deception."

For a time, there was silence in the room. Shulgi, bathed in sweat envisioning the horrors painted by Hendrick's words, looked up at Hendrick and asked imploringly, "What must I do to avoid this endless torture?"

"You must cooperate immediately and fully, with your whole heart and soul, first, by providing the name and contact information of everyone in this fleet—and the royal fleet—who has cooperated with you or Anzû or expressed sympathy for your selfish cause. After that, I leave it to the allied intelligence of the Anunnaki and the Americans to explain what further demands they might have for you."

"And if I do what you ask," said Shulgi, "can you promise that the Anunnaki will not put me to death?"

Hendrick shook his head. "Your fate is for the Council to decide. But, take heart; the Council was persuaded many years ago to spare *Anzû's* miserable life. Perhaps they'll spare yours now. But whatever the Council decides, if you will cooperate fully as I have said, for my part I will ask the Council to spare your life and I will urge the President to add his voice to that chorus."

"Mister President?" Shulgi implored pathetically. "Will the United States join in asking the Council to spare my life?"

The President sighed and cleared his throat. "I'm no king, Shulgi. I cannot bind the United States with my lone voice. Our Constitution requires that such a decision be reached with the advice and consent of the people's representatives. However, if you cooperate fully right now, and if I'm still alive when the question of your fate arises, I'll personally ask the Council to spare your life."

Shulgi wept, and seemed more miserable than the most abject traitor ever to throw himself on the mercy of his nemesis. He began crawling toward Enki's feet, apparently intending to beg forgiveness, but Enki could not bring himself to suffer the indignity. When Shulgi reached out to touch Enki's sandal, Enki shook off his touch and said to the guards, "Get him out of here. Don't abuse him, but show him no deference—or *I shall hear of it.*"

Shulgi was unceremoniously dragged out of the room, and the door snapped shut.

Every eye turned toward Hendrick, who avoided meeting their gaze. He felt more than a bit unclean, it's true. With abandon, he'd conjured up baseless horrors and inflicted them on the prisoner—shamelessly, without scruple or hesitation.

On the other hand, he may have helped save the Earth from conquest or destruction. He shrugged.

Hey, poker's poker.

CHAPTER 19

FOUR THOUSAND YEARS ago, nature had fashioned a hole in the Antarctic ice cap, one of few features of the frozen continent to have changed little since that time. On the ground below the hole, Anzû's acolytes had gradually built a complex consisting of a dozen glass-and-steel buildings large enough to house a complete aviation community, including one tower soaring nearly a hundred meters from its foundation.

Even so, the frigid, wind-blown complex was a lonely outpost. The exteriors of the buildings had always been kept dark, except for a single blue safety beacon situated at the highest point of each roof. The decision to forgo exterior illumination had been strategic, to frustrate a potential invader wishing to estimate the overall size of the installation. But that decision had been made when humankind's artillery was horse-drawn, and its aviation no more than a pipe dream. Now that humans had developed jet and rocket aircraft (and had even begun tinkering with antimatter engines), the bedrock assumptions underlying the original decision had crumbled, which was just as well, for, at the installation's current level of preparedness, there was so much artificial light leaking out through the windows that anyone audacious enough to fly down through the hole could readily approximate the installation's size.

The hole in the "ceiling" upstairs was only one of two means of flying in and out and, for that matter, the smaller of the two. Though the hole was strategically the more important, the enemy had obviously learned of its location and approximate size. (If Anzû ever discovered *how* the enemy made that discovery, he would personally ensure that the heads of those responsible would roll.)

If invaders were to attack the installation, whether with conventional or nuclear weapons, they would no doubt descend through the visible hole, hoping to compromise the escape of a high-value asset, namely, Anzû himself. Escape through the hole would need to be steeply vertical, making the would-be escapee an easy target. In addition, anyone attempting to escape through the hole would have no choice but to run the gauntlet of enemy aircraft darting downward in the opposite direction at top speed.

Fortunately, there was no reason to believe that the enemy had learned of the *other* way out from under the ice. Barely a mile from the landing strip began a winding ice tunnel several miles in length on a twenty- to thirty-degree incline; at its far end was a *second* hole through the ice, this one exiting under a permafrost ledge that concealed it from above. The tunnel's dimensions, contours, twists, and turns had long been mapped by Anzû's forces and, long ago, he occasionally flew out that way. But these past few years, though Anzû's forces had continued to map any changes in the tunnel, it had gone unused ... for fear of discovery.

ANZÛ'S FLAGSHIP CRAFT descended gently through the main hole in the ice and came to rest alongside a short runway painted onto the snow-swept floor several hundred meters below.

Though his flagship required a staff of eighteen for full operation, it could carry as many as forty more at need. An hour ago, he'd summoned aboard thirty of his top progenitors to confer with him, and expected their arrival in the next couple of days.

From his cockpit, Anzû could redirect each of the craft's ten external cameras in any direction he pleased, and watch their feed without moving from his chair. At this sensitive point in the growing hostilities, he kept one camera focused straight up toward the hole.

Anzû leaned forward and pressed a microphone button that connected him with the base's communications room. "Muranu," he said, "what do we hear from our friendlies aboard the enemy fleet?"

There was a brief rustling at the other end of the connection, and Muranu's face appeared on the communications screen. The video went only one way, as Anzû had no desire to advertise his damaged visage to the crew on a regular basis.

"I was just about to call you, my prince," said Muranu. "It has now been at least six hours since we've heard anything from our friendlies."

Anzû found this worrisome. "At least six hours?" he asked. "Why do you say *at least*? Check your records for the latest incoming communication from someone on the fleet and give me a precise answer."

"Yes, my prince," replied Muranu, "I'll do that right now." Anzû watched his communications officer's expression pass through several changes. "It's been *nine* hours now, sir."

"Is that interval unexpected?" demanded Anzû.

Muranu poked a few more keys. "Yes, sir. Historically, at this time of day the lengthiest hiatus in communications from those quarters is four and one-half hours. We're well in excess of that now."

"Have you checked all your equipment?"

"I have, sir," said Muranu. "I've run diagnostics on all our satellites. I've also checked for the Aurora Australis and other ionization phenomena that might have gotten in the way."

"And?" demanded Anzû, letting his irritation show.

"Nothing, sir. We can find no reason for the hiatus other than … that our sources have stopped transmitting."

A chill crept up Anzû's spine, but there were still a few questions to ask before he would reach even a tentative conclusion. "Any large craft in the vicinity?"

"No, sir."

Anzû grunted. "At least until a few days ago, the enemy had been minimizing radio communications, presumably based on their suspicion that they'd been compromised by our agents, correct?"

"That was our working hypothesis, sir."

"Has the level of their ship-to-ship communications resumed since our agents ceased transmission?"

"Communications among enemy craft are all encrypted, sir, so we can't read them. But we *can* tell that they've increased by eighty percent since the latest transmission by our spies on the fleet. And some quite recent communications seem to have been transmitted by non-local targets."

"Meaning?" inquired Anzû.

"Meaning that our friendlies have likely been caught and thwarted. The enemy appears to have resumed normal communications among themselves, and also with distant craft … possibly the royal fleet."

"Where *is* the royal fleet?" demanded Anzû.

"We're still not sure, sir," replied Muranu. "They've concealed themselves efficiently. Our best guess is they're somewhere in the Mars system."

"Alert fighter squadrons at both poles," said Anzû. "Prepare radar and weapons to defend against a possible invasion of mini-drones."

"Are we expecting to be challenged from the Mars system, my prince?"

"No," said Anzû. "But mini-drones are the enemy's only available half-measure. If I'm interpreting the situation correctly, the enemy has re-secured his communications, which places a big premium on him knocking out our comms preemptively. We can't afford that—" Anzû released the Send button and muttered to himself "—unless I can get that bastard ambassador on our side, assuming he's still alive." He pressed the Send button again. "Have they resumed communications with the ambassador's craft, *The Way Forward*?"

"We can't be sure, sir," said Muranu, "but some transmissions seem to be originating from north of the ecliptic plane. Based upon instructions we implanted in the android pilot, that *could* be the ambassador's craft."

Anzû leaned into the mic. "So, the ambassador's craft may be transmitting?"

"That's conjecture only, sir," said Muranu. "But it would be consistent with the craft's suspected location."

"Is it the android pilot who's sending the transmissions?"

"No. Or rather, not if he's still in charge. Whoever's transmitting from *The Way Forward* is not transmitting on the frequency we assigned, sir, so that's quite unlikely. Although we can't dispense with the possibility that the android's been … commandeered, sir, it seems more likely that …" Muranu's face flushed visibly and his voice trailed off.

"It seems more likely," said Anzû, finishing his thought, "that the ambassador has assumed control over the craft."

"Yes, sir," said Muranu.

"But the ambassador's not qualified to pilot it," said Anzû.

"*Completely* unqualified, sir. Records show he's never piloted a craft of any kind."

"What about that inconvenient blonde—the one who's managed to foil my plans so far?"

Muranu shook his head. "Our best research shows her field training to have been limited to submarine warfare."

Anzû nodded contemplatively. "That will be all for now, Muranu," he said, and broke off the comms link.

"So … who's piloting the craft?" Anzû wondered aloud while visions of his ancient nemesis floated around in his head.

IT WAS MORE than a month since David had communicated with anyone on Earth. Seated in the cockpit of *The Way Forward*, he squeezed

Catharine's hand and hesitantly looked to Ninurta.

"You're *sure* it's okay for me to call now?" asked David skeptically.

Ninurta nodded. "The few bastards who'd been covering up Shulgi's misconduct are all out of the loop permanently and ... secured. We're also back on the ecliptic plane, so no one triangulating our signal will have any reason to believe it's us. Besides, the encryption method has been completely reset for the whole expeditionary force."

"What if Anzû's already broken the new code?" asked Catharine.

Ninurta scoffed. "You give him too much credit. He's brazen, not *brilliant*. The only ones having access to the backup encryption method until a couple of hours ago were King Enlil and Lord Enki. And, before you ask, *yes*, there are secondary and tertiary backups that we'll switch to if we lose confidence in the present one."

David was still nervous about calling. "Because ... you know, it's not *essential* for me to speak with them right now."

"To the contrary, it *is* essential," said Ninurta. "I'll remain with you, if it makes you feel better."

For some reason David couldn't guess at, he accepted Ninurta's suggestion. "Okay," he said and prepared to tap the squawkbox on the pilot's table. "I'll put it on speaker. But ... what time is it in Washington, D.C.?"

"Ten-thirty in the morning," Ninurta assured him.

David exhaled loudly and pressed the button for the admiral's encrypted office phone. Before the phone was answered, they could hear the switching system forward the call, presumably to the admiral's mobile phone.

"David, is that you?" asked the admiral incredulously.

David's stomach turned. "Yes, admiral. It's me." He could hear the relief in the old man's voice.

"Is, *um*, everybody in good condition on your craft?"

"Yes, sir," said David with an inner smile, "she's fine."

"Thank God," said the admiral. "And how's your android?"

"Well, admiral, to be honest, he's gonna need a new skull and a shitload of circuit boards."

"You really whaled on 'im, eh?"

"Not I, sir," said David. "That was your adjutant, who's listening in, by the way. She's quite the warrior."

Catharine rolled her eyes as though to ask: *Do you have to tell everyone?*

"I've known that for some time, kid," said the admiral. "Are you calling to chat?"

"No, sir. I—I ..." David's voice trailed off. "I have a ... plan."

There was a moment's silence. "Well," the admiral sighed, "that makes *one* of us. We've kind of run dry here. We've got the analysts looking at every proposal, and any move we make ends up ... with nukes."

"That's what I figured, admiral."

"Does your plan end with nukes?"

"No, admiral, it doesn't. Not if it works."

"I'm all ears."

"If I may suggest, admiral, given how badly our comms were compromised, we should probably do this with everybody on one call. If it gets the thumbs-down, there'll be no need to waste additional discussion on it."

"Okay," said the admiral.

"The logistics are gonna require cooperation from several services. We'll need some flyboys trained on the SF-5—"

"We'll bring in Gary and Buck."

"Yes, sir," said David. "At least one of the flyboys will have to be borderline ... nuts."

"I *said* Buck would be there, didn't I?" asked the admiral so matter-of-factly that David nearly laughed aloud.

"We'll also need communications experts, sir. The best."

"NSA," said the admiral, as though checklisting equipment for a camping trip.

"Sounds good," said David. "We're also going to need Lord Enki's cooperation."

The admiral sounded hesitant. "Well, of course, we'll have to keep him advised."

"That won't be enough, sir. We'll need his cooperation to help execute the plan."

"That means we need the President, too."

"No question, sir," said David. "When you hear my plan, I think you'll agree we can't proceed without his direct involvement. If the plan doesn't work, it'll be too—"

"Too *what*?"

"It'll be too damned dangerous for anyone other than the Commander in Chief to deal with," admitted David. "The USA's gonna need contingency plans ready to go the moment the plan goes south ... *if* it goes south. We should also have Hendrick at the meeting. Where is he, sir?"

"He's back on Enki's pyramidion," replied the admiral. "Why *Hendrick*?"

"We may not need him, but—remember those jammers?"

"Sure," said the admiral. "If we need a bunch of those, I'd expect the Anunnaki can bring 'em to the party. But Hendrick's always an asset. We'll bring him in, too. Anybody else?"

"Just by way of full disclosure," said David, "we already have someone additional listening in here. We picked up a hitchhiker who shall remain silent and nameless."

There was a long silence. "Is it ... *Ajax?*" the admiral ventured in informal code that would probably be understood only by a scholar of ancient Earth history. Ajax was a great warrior, grandson of Zeus or, in the Sumerian Pantheon, *Anu.*

David nearly laughed aloud as Ninurta cocked his head this way and that, as though trying on the admiral's metaphor for size.

"Close enough, admiral," said David.

"Good to hear he's aboard," said the admiral.

David nodded. "You have no idea, sir."

THE AIR WAS salty on David's tongue and felt heavy and wet in his lungs, and he realized that his old familiar dream was resurfacing again just as he'd expected: Inanna and him together in a bed bobbing on a moonlit sea, with two great orbs in the heavens, one white, the other a cloudy maroon. He glanced up at the orbs and confirmed that at this point in the dream the two celestial bodies hadn't yet collided.

Looking down at his hands, which had once looked hopelessly decrepit, he was relieved to find them perfectly smooth and unblemished. He gazed over at Inanna and she smiled at him serenely.

"I'm so glad you're here," she whispered, hugging the pillow snugly as though it were a surrogate for David himself.

He lay down beside her and kissed her on the mouth. *How could I ever prefer another woman to Inanna?* She responded warmly and kissed him back. The illusion was complete, a promise of endless happiness—if only he could live forever.

Though the repeated aspects of the scene had long become familiar to him, he found that the most recent changes had rendered it nearly irresistible. He reminded himself that it was just a dream; a will-o'-the-wisp, a private commercial message urged upon him by his personal demon. But something had changed, and he longed to ignore the wickedness behind it.

Isn't this better, David? asked a soothing voice in David's mind. It was Anzû's, of course. *Isn't this ... isn't she ... what you really want?*

For the first time in a long while, David experienced a moment of weakness and found himself acceding to his demon.

Of course it is, he replied.

David could feel a tremor in Anzû's mind, as though his little acknowledgment had changed *everything*. Anzû asked, *What would it take for you to make her happy, David?*

David considered the question, as he breathed the heavy salt air in and out. *She's no mortal, after all*, he replied, *but a goddess. She knows the rewards of command. In Baalbek, in Babylon. In the Indus Valley. She'll want her ancient lands returned to her.*

Done, said Anzû.

And I will want something, as well, said David.

At first Anzû hesitated. *Given what I have already promised*, he said sharply, *what could you possibly demand for yourself? I'll give you immortality. I'll give you the woman every man desires, as well as the ancient lands to which she makes revanchist claims. What else could you demand of me?*

North America, said David simply.

You overvalue yourself, David. You're not the only man who can serve my ends.

Oh, but I am, said David. *Without me you can be blinded by a single nuclear weapon. You could find yourself unable to communicate with your commanders, and your commanders unable to relay orders to their drones. Unless ... you have me.*

Anzû was thoughtfully silent. If he'd ever harbored hopes that David was unaware of his unique power in this situation, such hopes were now dashed. David clearly knew he had something of great value to bargain with, and he was prepared to play his hand.

Well, at least this might lead to a deal, thought Anzû. And a *quick* one.

North America is my demand, said David. *And it's a small price to pay. Take it or leave it.*

Let me think on this, said Anzû. *In the meantime ... where are you?*

I'm only a few days from Earth, said David. There was silence on Anzû's end. *Where are you, Anzû? Or are you too distrustful to share such information?*

But by then the telepathic link had been broken.

David returned to sleep, confident that this conversation would resume shortly. He only hoped that his outrageous territorial demand would exceed Anzû's patience because, to his great surprise, it was becoming increasingly difficult to fight off Inanna's charms.

CHAPTER 20

"ALL RIGHT, DAVID," said the admiral. "The gang's all here, everyone you requested. Before we get started, on behalf of all of us, let me welcome you and Catharine home."

"I've got you on speaker, admiral," said David, "and your adjutant is participating. We have another participant with us who shall remain silent and nameless."

Catharine leaned toward the speaker phone. "Good morning, Lord Enki, Mister President, admiral, and all the others who've kindly responded to our call. Thank you so much for your show of support. Admiral, you may sometimes hear me addressed by the name *Ketura*, rather than Catharine. Although I'm unaccustomed to allowing others to rechristen me, this particular moniker was conferred by none other than His Majesty King Enlil, a wise gentleman, long may he reign."

"Long may he reign," echoed those on Lord Enki's pyramidion, and the blessing was echoed yet again by those in D.C., albeit in a less organized way.

"So, David," said the President, "what's the plan? What do you hope to gain from it? And what can we do to help?"

David cleared his throat and explained his plan in a few sentences. Evidently, his plainspoken explanation got its point across, as both Enki's pyramidion and the D.C. contingent erupted into the crosstalk of a dozen voices.

The President's voice gradually overcame all the others. "Ladies and gentlemen, from this point on during this call, no one here in D.C. will speak on the phone unless I say so. Is that clear?"

Crickets.

"Okay," continued the President with some annoyance. "Now that that's been settled, let me be the first to ask the obvious question: David, are you planning on destroying yourself and the admiral's adjutant in the course of this mission? Because, if it's been your assumption that such a plan would be approved, you've wasted everyone's time."

David shook his head. "Mister President, I have no intention of placing the admiral's adjutant in the slightest jeopardy."

"And what about yourself?"

"If my plan works, Mister President, I'll return to you undamaged. I assure you that I'll take such measures as are reasonably practicable to ensure my personal safety even if the plan *doesn't* work. But if it doesn't work, my personal welfare will be the least of your concerns." It was time for David to politely assert himself, even if it embarrassed some of the security professionals. "It's my understanding, Mister President, that we are presently in a standoff with the enemy that could be ignited at any time—possibly even *inadvertently*—into a nuclear conflagration of indeterminate size and duration. Do I have that right, sir?"

When the President didn't reply right away, Enki's booming voice did. "That's correct, Mister Ambassador."

"Good morning, Lord Enki," said David. "Thank you. If there is a nuclear conflagration, it's my understanding that tens of millions of people could die in the first few minutes of the conflict, with resultant fallout that's likely to kill hundreds of millions more and could render large swaths of our dear Earth uninhabitable for the foreseeable future."

"That is a likely outcome," said Lord Enki. "Mister President?"

The President sighed loudly. "Yes, but we mustn't forget that our enemy takes the same risks, and he doesn't seem to have anywhere else to go, so he'd perish, as well, as would all his acolytes on this planet."

"I believe that you and our enemy both understand that," said David. "And the side more likely to capitulate, rather than suffer such a conflagration, is the side whose leadership loves its people more." David hesitated. "I have no doubt that *our* side is the more compassionate, which places us in a quandary, as I don't believe we're prepared to cede control of our planet to this interloper."

"Damned *right* we're not," said the President.

"So," said David, "if it's a choice between losing one ambassador or the whole planet, the planet wins that toss. And permit me to remind everyone that the last time there was a deadly air battle with this enemy there was substantial collateral damage, even though only a few nuclear weapons were deployed, the entire population of Earth amounted to no more than a few hundred thousand people, and most of those were far from the site of battle."

There was a long silence.

"Mister President," David resumed, "I'm no stranger to you. You know me well enough to know that I'm no fool and I don't want to die.

But, so far, no one has presented another plan that would give us any shot at eliminating the threat while minimizing collateral damage. In short, at the moment, it's a contest between my plan ... and *no* plan, where *no* plan means waiting for the tinder to be ignited by the enemy at a time deemed most advantageous to him, or by some yahoo on *our* side—with a messianic complex—who decides to ride a nuke to his target of opportunity. As I see it, the less time we take to execute my plan, the less likelihood of such a disaster."

The admiral cleared his throat and jumped in. "David, what would you need from us to proceed with this plan?"

David explained what he would need from Gary and Buck.

There was a bustle at the D.C. meeting, over which the President could barely be heard. "Mister Director, did you have a question for the ambassador?"

"Yes, sir," said a new voice as it approached the phone. "Mister Ambassador, NSA Director here. What if this whole plan is a ruse allowing you to join up with the enemy on terms advantageous to you *personally*?"

The President was evidently offended by the question. "Now, hold on—"

David jumped in. "I *welcome* the question, Mister President. The director would have been remiss not to ask it."

"Go ahead," said the President reluctantly. "You can answer, if you think it's worthwhile."

"To your question, Mister Director, I can only ask what possible benefit you think I could reap out of the plan I've outlined."

The NSA Director said, "Well, what if he offers you immortality ... or a nice chunk of prime real estate?"

"He's already offered me those, Mister Director, and much more," said David.

"So, are you tempted by anything he's offered you?" asked the director.

David paused. He looked up at Catharine and Ninurta, both of whom were obviously jarred by his hesitation, and anxiously awaited his answer—as though there were perhaps a fifty-fifty chance he'd sell them both out.

At least he could *understand* Catharine's reaction. No woman wants to feel that her man can be tempted by another woman, *any* woman— even the Queen of Heaven. The truth was, until this morning, Anzû had been unable to tempt him in the slightest with the promise of Inanna. *So, what was different about today?* he asked himself. Then he realized the truth of it. She'd looked different today. Today, she'd looked exactly like his deceased wife *Sharon*. He silently resolved to make Anzû pay for that dirty trick.

What amazed David more than Catharine's insecurity was *Ninurta's*. Evidently, he regarded David as a genuine rival for Inanna's affection—a former crush of the goddess he loved. Ridiculous. Ninurta was a hero of historic proportions, and, by any measure, an Adonis. (For all David knew, Adonis was a Greek *iteration* of Ninurta.) But, as much as every man has some Narcissus in him, David could only shake his head at any notion that Inanna might set aside the great Ninurta for a half-breed from Canarsie.

David rolled his eyes impatiently at both of them, and turned back to the speaker phone. "Mister Director, one of the things Anzû offers is immortality. Show me a man who proclaims his own death to be such a trifling matter that he wouldn't be tempted by such an offer—and I'll show you a *liar*." David sighed and shook his head resolutely. "But to be tempted is not to betray, Mister Director. I could have accepted Anzû's offer *before* now, or I could accept it *right* now—from the comfort and safety of this antimatter craft. If I were to do so, how could I be *helped* by my plan?"

After a brief pause, the director conceded simply. "I see your point."

"By my way of thinking," said David, "other than arranging the logistics of the plan I've outlined, your toughest job is to plan for what happens if Anzû forces me to kill him. The possible reactions by his forces are almost innumerable, and the task of preparing our forces to respond will be ... bewildering."

The admiral came back on the line. "They could go nuclear, David. And ... lights out."

"That's correct, admiral," said David, "but that's a strong possibility even if we do something else—and it's an *inevitability* if we do nothing."

Lord Enki's voice boomed in. "And what can the Anunnaki do to aid in this plan?" he asked.

"Lord Enki," said David, "the best thing the Anunnaki can do is to act as though you have no idea what's going on. Give our pilots the best jammers you've got. Other than that, don't react at all. Keep away from the whole thing."

"But won't Anzû be suspicious of our inactivity?" asked Enki.

Concerned that Lord Enki might still be stewing over his fighters' earlier failure, David framed his reply carefully. "Not necessarily, my lord. As you're aware, when American fighters engaged with Anzû's in the past … no Anunnaki fighters interceded."

Enki's coldness was palpable. "That was a result of *sabotage* by Anzû's traitors in our midst," he said.

"Yes, my lord," said David. "On the other hand, Anzû doesn't know how the Anunnaki *would* have responded if your fighters had actually received the American distress signal. As far as he knows, Anunnaki policy might be *hands off*."

"We'll do as you've asked, Mister Ambassador," said Enki.

"Thank you, my lord. My advice to my countrymen about Anzû is this," said David. "Use misdirection whenever possible. Confuse him about what you're doing. Make him doubt his understanding of the tactical situation and his own instincts. Keep him on his toes. It'll make it that much easier to knock him on his ass."

⤙∘⟨⟩∘⤚

LESS THAN THIRTY-SIX hours after David's conference call with the heads of state and the U.S. intelligence community, Gary and Buck were already flying their SF-5s south along the Chilean coast.

"Want to point out your future in-laws' winery?" jibed Gary. "Over."

"*What*'re you askin' about?" asked Buck vaguely, returning from a reverie. "Over."

"Muñoz Estates," said Gary. "Over."

"Where's that?" asked Buck. "Over."

Gary shook his head in exasperation as he cycled through camera feeds. "Never mind, boss. You gettin' enough sleep?"

"I s'pose," said Buck. "You know, I think we're just about passin' Sofia's family vineyard. Over."

"Do tell," said Gary with a laugh. "Over."

"Yeah," said Buck glumly, "she's got her own squadron, and today's Game Day. Over."

"She's in the mission?" asked Gary. "Over."

"Yeah," said Buck, "she's second wave. She told me. Over."

"You *know* she's not supposed to tell ya," Gary admonished. "Over."

"Yeah, I know, but—"

"Never mind, Buck," said Gary. "Hey, did they give you a full complement o' dragonflies? Over."

"I think that lady Evelyn said they gave me four hundred and thirty-seven. Your loadout should be on your digital manifest. Over."

"That's what I'm checkin'," said Gary. "It says I only got three hundred twenty-two. Over."

"Probably all they could make in the time allotted," said Buck. "Besides, what difference does it make? Far as I understood orders on this mission, those little bugs're not much more'n chaff. Over."

"They could be more important than that, though," said Gary. "Out."

IN THE SILENCE of space, still far from the battle brewing on Earth, Ninurta's cruiser barreled past the moon behind a long-range antimatter passenger craft.

A few hours earlier, Ninurta had removed himself to the cruiser's communications room. David's face popped up on Ninurta's main screen.

"Hello, commander," said David.

"Hello, David," said Ninurta. "Have you heard from your friend by radio?"

David could only snicker at Ninurta's characterization of Anzû as his friend. "Not yet."

"Perhaps it's time to sleep," suggested Ninurta. "Isn't that when he usually turns up?"

A blue light flashed on David's console. "I may have spoken too soon. I've got an incoming call. I'm breaking this communication. I'll let you know if it's him."

"Go to," said Ninurta.

David terminated his connection with Ninurta and flipped the switch nearest the flashing light. The screen lit up with the words: *Incoming. Request identification?*

"Yes," said David, "request identification." He'd learned from the manuals that he could operate many aspects of the craft with voice commands.

The words that appeared on the screen raised his ire: *It's your new commander, David.*

David stiffened his posture and reluctantly said, "Admit contact."

Anzû's patched-up face filled the main screen, rendered a bit more horrible by its mocking smile.

"To what do I owe the pleasure of this call, Anzû?" said David, concealing his disgust.

"I'd prefer your calling me *commander*," said Anzû. "If that's too much, you can call me *sir*."

"Either will be fine," said David, "but only after I've agreed to join your cohort."

"Oh?" said Anzû, feigning surprise. "I thought that was a done deal."

"You were mistaken ... *commander*." In that context, the deferential word sounded patronizing, which was just what David wanted. "First, I need to speak with you face to face."

"You're dissatisfied with the view from your console?" said Anzû, filled with self-disgust. "You wish to see me live and in-person?"

David nodded. "Yes."

"And how do you plan to arrange the meeting, David? I assume you're not fitted out for a spacewalk. Incidentally, how near are you to Earth?"

"We just passed the moon."

"We?" said Anzû suspiciously.

"The lieutenant commander and I," David specified.

"Oh? She's still with you?"

"Of course. There was no place convenient to drop her off."

Anzû shrugged and winked. "I suppose you could have dropped her off ... *anywhere*. Let me see her, please."

"Later," said David.

"Now!" said Anzû with frightening intensity.

David looked out through the cockpit door. "She's a bit tied up right now," he said with a conspiratorial smile.

"All the better," said Anzû. "Please put on that headset lying on the pilot's table. There's a camera in the visor."

David put on the headset and floated to the dormitory area, where a furious Catharine was bound to a chair with tape and yellow vinyl rope, much as the android had been, but more securely.

"Ah," said Anzû, "the familiar damsel in distress. David, press the Speaker button on your headset. I want to speak with her."

David pressed the button.

Anzû said, "Why are you so angry, my dear?"

Catharine stiffened to hear his voice. "You mean, besides your attempts to have me assassinated?" she asked, glaring at Anzû through the camera. She glanced darkly at David before replying to Anzû. "Because all men are trash," she spat out. "And, by your voice, you're a man."

"I suppose I'd pass for one in the catalog," said Anzû, "though not a lovely one such as you admire."

"Were you not born of a woman, Mister Trash?"

David felt a brief surge of anger emanating from Anzû; not through the electronics, but through their psychic link.

"I was," said Anzû.

"Then why have you no respect for one?"

"Why do you say that?" he asked.

"You've created a whole army of soldiers—" said Catharine "—or should I say a forest of blockheaded trees?—and not one is a woman."

"You're wrong, Ketura," said Anzû gravely. "I respect a woman." He smiled. "I just don't *trust* her. She has her own agenda, such as continuation of the species, but she has no real respect for a *man's* agenda—unless, of course, his agenda happens to coincide with hers. David, press the Mute button." David did so.

Anzû's voice was full of exasperation. "Kill her. Kill her now."

David smiled for Catharine's benefit. "Why?"

"I need you to demonstrate your unquestioning loyalty," said Anzû.

David said in an almost jocular way, "I don't think so." He began walking back toward the cockpit.

"That's an order," said Anzû. "Don't tell me you choose to begin your employment by disobeying a direct order."

Once out of Catharine's hearing, David said, "I'm not in your employ, Anzû. We haven't come to terms, if you'll recall. And I might add that you're not endearing yourself to me."

"Endearing? Why, you—"

Anzû's conversation with David was jarringly overridden by his communications room.

"Commander," said Muranu, "all members of the high command are arrived and seek permission to come aboard."

"Permission granted," replied Anzû, openly irritated by the interruption. "Have them board quietly. Have them all brought to the onboard conference center—and don't interrupt this connection again!"

Anzû pasted a phony smile on his face before hitting the button reestablishing contact with David. "Our conversation will have to resume later, David. I have more important people to speak with at the moment."

"For you," said David smugly, "there *are* no more important people than I."

"Overplaying your hand again. Out," said Anzû, concerned that David was correct in his assessment of his unique value. He wondered how much time he had to persuade David … before it was too late.

"HEY, BUCK," SAID Gary, as they banked over the hole in the ice. "All strapped in and ready to hunt? Over."

"Ready with the bugs," said Buck. "Are we sure the bastard's down there? Over."

"NSA says eighty-eight percent chance," Gary assured him. "Over."

"How did they come up with those odds? Over."

"One o' their guys was explainin' it to me." said Gary. "It's an algorithm, like everything else nowadays. Over."

"Based on what data?" asked Buck skeptically. "Over."

"Based on the frequency of incoming and outgoing communications," said Gary, "figuring in the target value at both ends of the communication. In other words, if high-level enemy officers are frequently communicating by radio with the guy down the hole, it's more likely the guy down the hole is Mister Big. Over."

"Sounds a little shaky to me," said Buck. "And then there's that other thing we talked about. Over."

"You mean the one-way-out problem? Over."

"Yeah," said Buck, "what if you're wrong and his only way out is straight up? Gonna be mutually assured destruction. Over."

"I'm tellin' ya, Buck," said Gary, "he's got another way out. Hey, if *you* had that amount of time to build up your installation, would you leave yourself with only one way out? Over."

"'Course not," said Buck, "but it's not a certainty, so it still comes down to the odds. Over."

"I know the odds," said Gary, "and they're in our favor. Over."

"So, what are they? Over."

"Eighty-eight percent chance there's at least one more way to fly out of there," said Gary, feigning the same level of certainty expressed by the NSA. "Over."

"*Eighty-eight percent?*" said Buck. "Sounds like more of that NSA bullshit. Over."

"It's not their bullshit," Gary assured him. "Over."

"It's not? Over."

"Naw," said Gary, "it's *my* bullshit. Ready to release your bugs? Over."

"Ready," confirmed Buck. "Over."

"Take a deep breath, Buck-o. At the end of this skirmish, we're goin' into orbit. Release the bugs on my count o' three—and good hunting. Over."

"Ready to release on three. And same to you," said Buck. "Over."

"One … two … *THREE!*"

CHAPTER 21

ANZÛ WAS ABOUT to move to the conference center at the rear of the ship to meet with his high command when Muranu's face popped up unexpectedly on the main screen.

"Commander," shouted Muranu with alarm, "radar above the hole reports numerous fresh signals consistent with mini-drones."

Anzû clenched both fists. The timing couldn't have been worse. He'd been just about to parse out instructions for immediate attack because, under present conditions, waiting would be madness; the first to strike with an EMP would doubtless win the upcoming campaign, and there was no telling what unforeseen event could cause first blood to be drawn.

If both sides' command and control were knocked out, Anzû's footing would be as poor as that of his enemy. On the other hand, to have David's telepathic prowess in Anzû's quiver would provide Anzû with a distinct advantage, for then he'd regain command and control, while enemy forces were still groping for each other in the dark.

Anzû expected that his enemy likely knew nothing of David's potential importance, but it might not matter *what* the enemy knew, for David was still plopped before the banquet table like a haughty glutton, ordering an ever-larger piece of pie. *North America* indeed. The man should count himself lucky to be granted so much as his birthplace of Canarsie. *Where the devil is Canarsie, anyway?*

Anzû speculated that he'd soon need to resort to securing David's cooperation by means of false promises. While that wasn't his favored method of dealing, it wasn't as though David had some independent means of enforcing a promise of spoils. And heaven knows it wouldn't be the first time a conqueror reneged on a promise of a piece of his prospective kingdom. Whether this fool David knew it or not, his precious Anunnaki had long been known for such practices.

When did David say he'd be arriving? He dismissed the thought outright for, before he could resume negotiations with David, he'd first need to prevail against the incoming drones. His experts, anticipating a possible drone attack, had assured him that the enemy's initial wave of drones would likely be unarmed, their mission purely one of reconnaissance. From the newest report of conditions above, it appeared the enemy had grown tired of waiting and was now determined to find out what lay beneath the Antarctic hole. While there was considerable firepower down here, Anzû feared it would look unformidable to his enemy's space force, which was so new to the age of compact super-weapons.

He felt boxed in, and the small choice remaining to him commanded his attention: whether to send his high command back to their own craft and risk their destruction on the airstrip, or immediately lift off with all of them aboard.

"Muranu," he commanded, feigning his customary level of self-confidence, "secure all incoming and outgoing lines and prepare to cast us off."

"But commander," said Muranu, "our entire high command is aboard your craft."

"So what?" demanded Anzû.

"Commander," Muranu ventured, "your own standing orders prohibit the gathering of command personnel in a single location when facing the possibility of engagement."

"Do you suppose," asked Anzû in his most sarcastic tone, "that the mini-drones will challenge us all at once? Or one at a time?"

"I, *er*—"

Instead of awaiting an answer, Anzû barked, "Deploy the anti-drone polymer craft. And carry out my orders promptly or I'll toss you in the brig."

"Yes, sir," responded Muranu.

"Once we're untethered, bring the craft steady at an altitude of thirty meters and turn control over to me."

"Yes, sir," responded Muranu. There was a commotion off-camera on Muranu's end. "Sir, if you'll check your vertical camera," he said excitedly, "you'll see that the mini-drones have begun dropping down through the hole into the cavern's main vault."

Anzû stiffened. "See if you can jam their transmissions long enough to give the polymer guns a chance to do their work."

"Yes, sir," said Muranu, "and shall I give the order for buildings to emplace the retractable metal shutters over all windows—just in case the disabled drones begin dropping on us?"

At first Anzû equivocated. "No, don't," he decided.

"But, sir, with enough broken glass, we stand to lose our atmospheric quarantine."

Anzû shook his head, though no one could see. "I know," he conceded quietly, "but the glass is reinforced, and closing the metal shutters would make the installation look even smaller to the enemy. That's not in our interest."

"Yes, commander," said Muranu. "Your craft is now cast off and you're on your way to thirty meters alt—" His voice broke off, and Anzû could hear the men around Muranu beginning to panic.

"*Muranu,*" he shouted, "*what's happening?*"

"*SIR, TWO ENEMY FIGHTERS HAVE DROPPED DOWN THE HOLE, APPROACHING AT SPEED!*"

Anzû gasped and his stomach turned. The enemy had evidently found a commander who was strategically competent—something they'd been sorely lacking until now. He wondered fleetingly who it might be.

"Pull yourself together, Muranu. What type of fighters?"

"They're American SF-5s, sir. Orbital class, equipped with laser cannon. The mini-drones appear to be withdrawing through the hole."

Anzû swore too softly to be heard. "Return control of this craft to me at once, and instruct my esteemed passengers to buckle up. This could get rough quite fast."

"Aye, sir. Please don't forget to shut off your insignia lights."

Anzû smacked his forehead and cursed the enemy for throwing him so far off balance that he'd forgotten to do something as elementary as concealing his rank. He killed the exterior insignia lights hoping that, like most mistakes made in battle, it would come to naught.

⟶◦⟶⟶◦⟵

GARY'S SF-5 CORKSCREWED down the hidey-hole at a seventy-degree angle. He'd assumed that, on such a high-powered descent, his craft would shriek like a Stuka dive bomber. Instead, the only sound reaching him from outside was a cavernous echo of the loud swoosh generated by his craft's aerodynamic frame. And even though Buck's craft was only fifteen seconds behind, it was entirely inaudible.

The hole proved to be a foggy circular gap through a thick ice shelf that went on for several thousand feet. Heading nearly straight down, Gary couldn't immediately see past the hole's bottom, shrouded as it was in a thin, crystalline cloud. But he hadn't long to wait; in a split second, he dropped out of the hole, piercing the cloud, and found himself about a thousand feet off the ground in the main vault of a gigantic cavern. At its base were numerous metal buildings whose interior lights had been left on—a stupid choice in defending against an aerial attack, where defenses are few and darkness the most reliable among them. At the high point of each building flashed an intermittent blue beacon.

Sprawled out on the floor was an airstrip that seemed surprisingly compact to Gary, accustomed as he was to jet aircraft requiring a lot of runway. The airstrip was home to a wing of about a hundred craft of various types. Perhaps thirty were fighters. As Gary surveyed the small force, a couple of the fighters switched on their running lights, telegraphing an intention to pursue.

But the craft that had already drawn Gary's earnest attention had all its running lights on, and it sat stationary fifty meters above the runway. Its roof bore a luminescent digital display like a small version of a billboard in Times Square. On the display appeared a single, unchanging insignia. Gary grabbed the mic. "Buck, you see that craft with the billboard roof? Over."

"Wait," said Buck sarcastically, "lemme put on my sunglasses. Of *course* I can see it," said Buck. "Over."

"Is that the insignia from hell?" asked Gary. "Over."

"Affirmative," replied Buck. "Gotta be the flagship. Over."

As though on cue, the flagship switched off its roof display and its insignia lights went black.

Gary snickered. "Too late, asshole."

The flagship made a sharp right turn and zoomed off at high speed and very low altitude. Gary pressed the mic button. "Bucko, he's exitin' pronto stage right and keepin' low. Can I call 'em or what? Over."

Buck replied, "What a dodo! He's about to take the back door outta here with two American fighters on his tail. Is it time for jammers? Over."

"Let's flip 'em on, Buck." Gary turned on his jammer. "Over."

"Mine's on," said Buck. "How 'bout yours? Over."

"Mine's on," replied Gary. "You got a solid link to the bugs? Over."

"Five by five, man," said Buck. "Clear signal, clear echo. I sent 'em up a few thousand feet so they can see where we exit the ice. I'll start a locator beacon as soon as you tell me there's daylight ahead. Any bogey that tries to follow us out'll be met by a nifty surprise at the tunnel exit. Over."

Almost too good to be true, thought Gary. "Thank God they brought back the tail gun," he said. "Keep a little distance between you and me and throw your tailgun on automatic. I'll keep my rear vids running, but I'm shuttin' down my tailgun just to be safe. I'll take care of whatever's ahead. Over."

"That's the way to do it, boss," said Buck. "Don't let 'im breathe … and don't let 'im turn. He's got a rendezvous in orbit and we're escortin' his ass up there, like it or not. Over."

"I'm matchin' his altitude now, Buck," said Gary. "Follow me. Get ready for some flack, and watch for bogeys. Over."

As Gary matched his altitude to Anzû's flagship, he somehow lost sight of his quarry in the gloom of the cavern. In a moment of desperation, he flipped on his forward landing lights, which lit up the flagship like a moth in a laser beam. Unfortunately, however, his lights also offered the bogey's rear guns a clear target, forcing Gary to decide whether to kill his lights and risk losing sight of his quarry in the dark tunnel ahead or begin a deliberate pitch-and-roll that would make him a harder target but also increase his risk of striking the walls of the unfamiliar tunnel, which would surely be … terminal. He opted for the pitch-and-roll or, more precisely, the pitch-roll-and-pray. He checked his rear view and saw that Buck had already done the same.

"Buck, I see a long tunnel comin' up," said Gary. "It's unfamiliar to me, but I'll bet the bastard knows it pretty well. So, I'm gonna climb up his ass. He'll probably jink at the end, lookin' for a quick kill, so watch out for any tricks. And remember, if we shoot at him first we'll end up in the brig. Over."

"And we'll also face *startin' World War III* charges, right?" offered Buck. "Over."

"Yeah," said Gary, "that, too. Over."

The enemy flagship picked up speed to the point where any collision with the tunnel walls would surely be catastrophic. Not that Gary had much choice in the matter, but he accelerated in tandem.

Suddenly, the icy walls of the cavern narrowed until the open passage ahead barely exceeded the size of the flagship. Gary could hear the flagship's hull begin shattering tiny icicles hanging from the tunnel roof like stalactites.

He prayed there were none of sufficient mass to knock his quarry off course. Though the SF-5 was a bit smaller than its quarry (theoretically giving Gary the better chance of avoiding collision with the tunnel walls), if the flagship in front of him were to strike the wall or get knocked off course by ice, Gary calculated his own chances of surviving the resultant chaos at approximately *don't-think-about-it*.

With so little distance between Gary's hull and the tunnel walls, for the first time things got *loud*. Joining the swishing of the hull came a continuous high-pitched shriek, as though the craft itself was telling him he was crazy to try to pilot a fighter through a soda straw.

He wondered momentarily why the flagship hadn't already turned its rear cannon on him, but soon realized that *any* kickback from the flagship's cannon would send that ship right into a wall—and probably even Buck's—and *adios* for both craft. While they remained in the ice tunnel, Gary surmised, there would be no exchange of fire. Unless, that is, some cowboy tried to ride up Buck's ass. Then all bets were off. There was no way of being sure *what* Buck would do. There never was.

Gary grudgingly admired the skill and patience of the flagship's pilot. He had no idea that it was Anzû himself at the helm.

⟳•⟐•⟲

BUCK SPLIT THE screen on his main viewer, giving himself side-by-side views out his front and rear. He flipped on the frontal proximity-alert system, which allowed him to take his eyes off Gary's craft ahead long enough to see if he was being followed. While he didn't get a visual on anyone behind him in the tunnel, his rear-facing radar detector reported that he'd picked up a tail, an orbital fighter that was still a mile or so behind. As straight as the tunnel seemed to Buck, the bogey was around a bend.

Buck wondered if the bogey would be stupid enough to deploy its fire-system radar in such a confined area. It didn't take long to find out. Buck's radar detector signaled that he was being painted from behind, the only possible source being the bogey.

He took but a moment to decide whether to have his tailgun lay down laser or standard cannon fire. Though laser would emit virtually no mass (reducing the likelihood that its kick would slam Buck's craft into a tunnel wall), it could hit a target only in direct line of sight, which would accomplish nothing, as the bogey was still around a bend.

Although gunfire was more likely to throw Buck off his narrow course, physical bullets would remain aloft in the bogey's path for some small but measurable time and might just be there to greet the bogey as it rounded the turn preparing to bring Buck's craft into *its* line of sight.

Buck opted for standard cannon fire, which seemed tactically better and also more likely to create a fireball to his rear. Not only would fire be more likely to destroy the nearest bogey, but it would also be more likely to dissuade the *next* bastard in line from coming too close—*and wasn't there always another bastard in line?*

He assumed manual control over the automated tailgun long enough to pull the trigger on three widely spaced medium bursts. He even dropped a little chaff into the mix, because—*What the hell? Let's see how the bastard reacts to all that.*

Fortunately, the bogey didn't react well at all. Before it could even bring Buck into its line of sight, it ran into his cannon fire and exploded like a comet full of napalm.

Buck watched with his mouth agape as the fireball appeared behind him in the distance and began gaining on him. He couldn't maneuver in the tunnel, and he couldn't accelerate without running into Gary, so he had no choice but to maintain course and speed while orange flames and thick black smoke surged up the tunnel behind him, determined to swallow him up.

An angry voice came in on Frequency Two, one of the only two unjammed radio frequencies. It was Gary, of course. *"You West Texas frickin' cowboy!"* shouted Gary. "I can't leave you alone for a second, can I? Why are you firin' in such cramped quarters?"

Buck waited a few seconds to respond, during which the flames and smoke slowly receded behind him. He took a deep breath and answered as calmly as he could. "No worries, chief," he said, mopping his brow. "Had it all figured out. Over."

"My ass you did!" said a furious Gary. "You nearly knocked me into a frickin' wall. And if you'da scorched the Führer here, you'd have started a war that could end humanity. Don't do that again unless you're actually fired upon, Buck. And, even then, call me first. Gad, you are *hazardous material!"*

"Copy that, boss," replied Buck contritely. "Sorry. Over."

"Well," said Gary, "at least they won't be so quick to send somebody up the tunnel after that crash. Over."

"And if we're not followed out of the tunnel," Buck offered with chagrin, "we can save the bugs to assist us in the escort, at least until we approach orbital altitude."

"Daylight ahead!" announced Gary. "Stay frosty."

The flagship spat out the end of the tunnel like a watermelon seed.

Gary exited a second later into painfully bright sunlight and realized he'd emerged from a hole near the top of a sheer ice cliff. He was about to pull the joystick and send himself skyward until he realized that the flagship ahead of him remained level. Evidently, they were flying under an overhang of solid ice. He pressed the radio button.

"Stay level when you exit the tunnel, Buck. There's an overhang outside the hole. Repeat, remain level until you get a clear visual of the sky. Over."

"Copy that. Over," said Buck as he exited the tunnel, and was careful to remain level, though he veered left to avoid any possibility of collision or running into backward-facing fire.

Buck's rear view showed that the hole he'd just exited had begun spewing copious black smoke, and he surmised that nothing could negotiate such a hazard. But, to his surprise, a blackened, scored enemy fighter emerged from the hole at low speed and tumbled down the icy cliff, striking the cliff twice *en route* to its fiery death on the fjord below. Buck found himself hoping the pilot was already dead before meeting that ghastly end.

No way was that the guy who was hit by fire from Buck's tailgun. That was the guy *behind* him, who must have fatally decided to brook no obstacle in his headlong pursuit—and paid the price. Unsurprisingly, nothing followed the doomed fighter out of the hole. *Well*, Buck figured, *there's no point in sending the dragonflies to run interference in what's now a vacant tunnel.*

From his forward view, Buck could see that Gary was still riding the tail of the enemy flagship. Gary's voice came over the radio on one of the only two unjammed frequencies. "Anzû flagship, this is American Fighter One on Frequency One. On this frequency, please acknowledge your intention to cooperate with our escort. Over."

Buck hit a button on his panel summoning the dragonflies to his own coordinates. They'd arrive in a matter of seconds. Meanwhile, he used the time to catch up with Gary. The enemy flagship was climbing toward orbit at a surprisingly moderate speed, probably wishing to assay the purpose of the proposed escort before attempting escape.

Gary's voice came to Buck over Frequency Two; it was heavily encrypted and reserved for them alone. "This guy's been dialin' like mad for help from his own forces. Over."

"Is he having any success?" asked Buck. "Over." Meanwhile, the first dozen or so dragonflies appeared on Buck's lateral scopes.

"He's had no success getting a single signal out so far," replied Gary. "And he's unlikely to. You can thank the Anunnaki and the NSA for that. At this point, don't you think he'd be damned curious to find out what we want? I mean, we haven't taken a shot at him, so he knows we're not out here to destroy him. I see your bugs are startin' to show up.

Over."

More dragonflies appeared to Buck's right and left. "Yeah, they are. I'd think this guy would want to know why nobody's firing on 'im. Over."

The enemy flagship acknowledged. "American Fighter One, this is Anzû Flagship. Please identify your pilot and the object of your proposed escort. Over."

Gary replied. "This is Lieutenant Gary Sullivan, United States … Space Force—" Out of habit, he'd nearly said United States *Navy* "—we are escorting you to Earth orbit for purposes of parley with our high command. If you cooperate, we will not fire on you. Please identify yourself. Over."

"I was wondering why you didn't fire on us," said the flagship pilot. "Over."

"It's not the object of our mission to commence hostilities," said Gary. "Quite the contrary. Over."

"I doubt the dead pilots in the two fighters you destroyed will be much comforted by your assurances. This is Anzû speaking, Commander of Resistance Forces. I am piloting this craft."

This admission came as a complete surprise. Gary and Buck had thought Anzû would be more wily than to admit he was the pilot. Apparently, his ego had gotten the better of him.

Gary punched an inquiry into his onboard computer: *Voiceprint analysis: Identify hostile radio contact.*

In less than a second, the computer responded. *Identity of hostile radio contact confirmed with ninety-six percent probability: Anzû of Nibiru.*

"It's him," said Gary on Frequency Two. "Over."

"Son of a *bitch*!" said Buck. "Over."

Anzû came back on. "Are you threatening to surveil us to death with your little … bugs?" asked Anzû contemptuously.

"If you remain on current course," said Gary, "we're not threatening you with anything. Incidentally, those *bugs*, as you call them, are equipped with shaped charges which can be emplaced and detonated on contact. Over."

"Oh," said Anzû, "so you *are* threatening me. Over."

"Negative, commander," said Gary, "so long as you stay on course, neither these fighters nor the bugs are any threat to you. Over."

"Will you please withdraw your Anunnaki jammers so I can contact my own forces?" asked Anzû.

"*Negative*, commander," said Gary.

"Did you know," asked Anzû, "that there are several dogfights already going on in Earth's atmosphere? You can see them from here."

Gary glanced down at his scopes, which confirmed what Anzû had just said. "We're aware, commander," said Gary, "but that does not alter our mission. Will the commander allow his ship to be escorted as we have proposed? Over."

"Are you taking me to Enki?" demanded Anzû. "Or some other Anunnaki?"

"Negative, commander," Gary assured him. "If you check your scopes, you can confirm that we are escorting you to the antipodes of Lord Enki's pyramidion. He'd have to see through Earth to get a look at you—or us. Over."

"Is your President in orbit—" asked Anzû "—that you take *me* into orbit? Over."

"We don't know, commander," said Gary. "The person wishing to speak with you on behalf of the United States is Admiral Simmons. Over."

Buck glanced at his video feed and could see he was nearing Earth orbit. In the distance below and behind, he could see two small backup squadrons of SF-5s approaching. By prearrangement, they would remain several miles back. He felt good knowing that his own Sofia was leading at least one squadron, perhaps both.

"An *admiral*?" said Anzû, "To parley with the Commander of All Resistance Forces? I don't think so. I'll speak with no one but your President."

"Commander," said Gary, letting his exasperation show, "our orders—"

"Exactly!" said Anzû. "*Your* orders—not mine. I will parley with no one less than the President of the United States," he said. "I'm due *at least* the courtesy that your people have extended to Enki."

"Meaning no disrespect," said Gary, "but it could take us a great deal of time just to *locate* the President—"

"I've got time," said Anzû haughtily.

There was a crackling on Frequency One, and a man's voice broke in. Buck recognized it as belonging to Dave Schubert. "Perhaps there'll be no need for the commander to parley with the President—"

Gary interrupted, sounding furious. "This mission and this radio frequency are under the military jurisdiction of the United States Space Force. The intruder will identify himself at once or suffer the consequences. Over.”

“Lieutenant Sullivan,” said David airily, “don’t you recognize my voice? This is U.S. Ambassador David Schubert. Over.”

Gary’s voice softened slightly. “Welcome home, Mister Ambassador, but I’d appreciate your begging off this frequency. As I said, it’s under military jurisdiction. Over.”

“Ah,” said David, “but *I’m* not under military jurisdiction, am I? Over.”

There was a long moment of silence, while Gary considered how to respond. At last, his voice returned with greater authority. “Mister Ambassador, as military commander on site, I can commandeer your craft and take you into custody if you push me to it. I suggest you tread lightly. Now kindly get off this frequency. Over.”

“What did I interrupt?” asked David breezily. “Over.”

Anzû interceded. “Mister Ambassador,” he said, “the lieutenant was about to search for the President to engage in a parley. I think we can yield this frequency to the lieutenant while he conducts his search. Don’t you? Over.”

There was another delay after which David said, “Far be it from me to interfere with a military operation. I propose we dispense with any need for this radio frequency, Commander Anzû. Let’s leave the lieutenant to do the necessary. Over.”

“By all means,” said Anzû, as he and David reestablished their telepathic link.

⸻ ❧ ⸻

WHERE ARE YOU, commander? asked David.

While Anzû was prepared to expend some effort to appear cordial, he was feeling the weight of the moment and needed David’s help without delay.

I’m in Earth orbit, replied Anzû, *wh—*

Ah, I see you on my scope. What the devil are you doing in orbit? asked David, as though there was no particular rush. *I expected to find you underground somewhere.*

I was surprised in my underground lair and escorted here with some rough handling, as you can see.

By those two fighters? asked David. *Were they your only escort? They don’t look particularly imposing.*

Never mind that, said Anzû with the impatience of hurt pride, *where are you?*

Where am I? echoed David. *I think you could probably wave to me if you knew which way to look. I'm five minutes away from you.*

Have you thought about what we discussed? asked Anzû.

Yes, said David, *and the more I think of it, the more persuaded I am that my territorial request was appropriate. Have you considered it?*

Well, said Anzû, *I've been a little preoccupied, as you can see, but, yes, I've given it some thought.*

And? asked David, sounding hopeful.

Let's review, said Anzû. *I freely give you Inanna with all her lands and the immortality needed to enjoy her indefinitely, and instead of being happy with the fulfillment of everyman's dream, you demand a major quadrant of Earth in the bargain. Is that correct?*

That's about the size of it, replied David.

Anzû found David's combination of brazenness and disrespect infuriating, but he tamped down his feelings ... for now. *You do realize—do you not?—that, if you were granted what you now ask, you would probably be living better than I?*

Oh, I doubt it, said David. *Have you seen New York lately? It's no picnic, I can assure you.*

Oh? replied Anzû. *Worse than the Israeli-Palestinian problem? Or the Indian-Pakistani issues? How about the Falun Gong? Or the fanatical Communist regimes in China and North Korea? What about Russia's absurd arms race? Or the various warring factions of Africa?*

What can I say? said David in his infuriatingly smug tone. *When you steal a world that has problems, you end up with a world of problems. Look,* said David, in his first concession ever, *having control of North America won't mean I can desert you in every other corner of the globe. If I can help you elsewhere, I will.*

Do you swear? asked Anzû.

Of course, replied David.

Then we have a deal?

No, said David, *but it's beginning to look as though we might.*

That's magnanimous of you, David, Anzû said sarcastically, *but your time's up. It's now or never.*

David hesitated to reply. *I told you that I have to look you in the eye before I'll believe you.*

Anzû was fully confident in his own ability to deceive, but he still needed to consider what David might discover if he were to be brought aboard the flagship. The entire high command would have to be hidden from view. Otherwise, if Anzû's offer were declined, the enemy could learn from David that his general officers had been removed from the field.

Anzû considered the airlock leading directly to his cockpit. If David were to dock there, he would have no need to tour the remainder of the craft; in fact, even apart from the high command, it would be best if David didn't see the rest of the craft.

And if David were to dock at the cockpit airlock, Anzû could dispose of the woman, seize control of *The Way Forward* and, more importantly, of David himself. If David were thereafter to refuse to do as he was told, he could be detained, punished … even tortured until he toed Anzû's line.

But what dirty tricks might *David* play if he were allowed aboard? There seemed no mischief available to David for which he wouldn't pay an immediate price. If he were to draw a sidearm (besides Anzû likely being the faster and better marksman), David would expect to pay for the attempt with a prompt and painful death.

Anzû made up his mind. David must be coaxed into docking, and he must be detained. If David agreed to cooperate, so much the better. If not, Anzû would have at least a short time to bring him to heel.

Come now and we'll talk, said Anzû. *I think you'll be satisfied.*

Very well, observed David. *I see from here that you have more than one hatch. At which should I dock this craft?*

Dock at the cockpit. We can speak most privately there. Just you and I.

⎯⎯⎯⎯⎯⎯⎯⎯⎯⎯⎯⎯⎯⎯⎯⎯⎯⎯⎯⎯

GARY'S VOICE CAME on Frequency Two.

"Buck-o, you're not gonna believe this. Over."

"What's up?" said Buck. "Over."

"NSA says, as far as they can tell, Anzû's got every one of his generals on his flagship. Over."

"*Which* ship?" asked Buck. "Over."

"The one you're lookin' at, dummy!" said Gary. "The bean-counters are countin' enemy command messages. They're down to a trickle, and they're comin' from oddball places—like the second bananas have suddenly found themselves in charge. Over."

Buck couldn't believe they could be lucky enough to have pounced on Anzû at precisely the right time.

"How does this affect our mission orders?" asked Buck.

"Not at all," said Gary, "but it looks like this little parley could be the endgame."

CHAPTER 22

GARY'S VOICE CAME in on Frequency One. "Commander Anzû," he said, "we've been unable to contact the President yet, for which we apologize. The ambassador, however, has asked us to open an encrypted audiovisual channel for you to communicate with him privately while you wait. Is that acceptable to you?"

"You mean you'll be unable to eavesdrop on that frequency?" asked Anzû.

"That's correct," replied Gary.

"Then, certainly," said Anzû. "It will help pass the time."

In a moment, David's face appeared on Anzû's main screen.

"Hello, Mister Ambassador," said Anzû. "I see you're in the pilot's seat. Are your newfound skills up to docking with my craft?"

David nodded. "Commander, you'd be amazed—or perhaps you wouldn't—at how much one can learn when the consequence of ignorance is death. As it turns out, the docking procedure of this craft couldn't be more automated. All I need do is direct it toward the target and give it the instruction."

"Tell me, David," said Anzû, "is your pilot android still with you?"

David sighed. "It was necessary to disable him in order to take control of the craft."

"But he's with you?" asked Anzû.

"In a sense, he is," said David. "His central processing unit is online and performing certain calculations for the craft, but his personality (or what passes for one in an android) is, alas, damaged beyond immediate repair, though we have high hopes for his recovery once we reach Earth."

"Very well," said Anzû. "Shall we proceed with docking?"

"Certainly," said David, keying in the necessary instruction. "Fortunately, there's no need to break this connection while we do so."

ILLUMINATED BY EARTHLIGHT, the antimatter craft moved gracefully into position alongside the airlock nearest Anzû's cockpit. The craft's door connected firmly to the airlock, the clasps locked into position, and the airlock began to pressurize.

Before releasing the door lock, David looked at Anzû on the screen. "Do I have your word that, if we're unable to come to terms, you'll do nothing to interfere with my departure?"

Anzû looked hurt. "Why, of course, David. Why would you even ask me that? Open the door."

David regarded him skeptically. "I'm still uncertain that you're being straight with me. I mean, North America is a big place. Perhaps you think it's too much for me to handle."

Anzû couldn't help himself. He snickered. "It's *far* too much for you to handle, but we haven't come to terms on that score yet."

David's brow furrowed. "Well, if you're unprepared to concede that much, perhaps I should just go now."

"Go?" Anzû said jeeringly. "Where would you go? Who would trust you? You'd be rejected anywhere you go—a stateless person. By now they know you've been trying to cut a separate deal with me for your own benefit. And if they don't, I could do them the service of telling them."

"Where is Inanna?" demanded David. "Or am I to accept your IOU on a matter of such importance?"

"She'll be yours," Anzû assured him with a smarmy smile. "She already loves you."

"And what of immortality?" said David nervously. "What if you change your mind, and I no longer suit your purposes? Would you grant immortality to someone you intend to cheat? Someone who could readily turn adversary?"

Anzû flipped a switch on his control panel, his false smile dropping away, replaced by a hardness exacerbated by the taut, enseamed skin of his face. "David," he said, "I'm through playing with you. Come aboard now or I'll destroy you."

Panic appeared on David's face. He shouted an order at his console. "Release docking mechanism." Nothing happened. "Separate!" Again, nothing happened.

Anzû laughed derisively. "I'm controlling your vessel from here, David. You have no choice now but to come aboard. The chamber is pressurized. Stand back. I'm about to open your door. Oh, and you can forget about North America. Except you can *reside* there, if there's anything left there when I'm done with it."

From where Anzû sat, he could see through the plexiglass of his pressurization chamber. Through that he could see the door of David's craft, which was lazily sliding open, then closed, then open again—but the light was too dim for him to see in.

Anzû glanced at the image on his main screen, which still showed David's cockpit, but now there was no one there.

Anzû rose from his place and opened the interior door to his pressurization chamber. Crossing the chamber, he stood before the door to David's craft and put his arm up to stop the door's incessant alternation.

The docked craft had a derelict quality. In the dim light inside, Anzû could see a lone, seated human figure. As his eyes adjusted to the darkness, it became clear that the figure was that of a severely damaged android taped to a seat, its eyes open but unseeing.

Anzû tried to dismiss the notion that he'd been *had*, but it kept invading his unbelieving mind. *Where's David?* he asked, but then realized the docked craft was not *The Way Forward*.

Could it be a duplicate craft? Where could David have found an exact duplicate of an Anunnaki antimatter craft? A chill ran up Anzû's spine as he began to detect the hand of his ancient Anunnaki foe behind all this. Overcome with horror, he ran back through his own craft's pressurization chamber and returned to his cockpit. There, onscreen, sat David with that woman sitting beside him, looking perfectly comfortable, showing not the least sign of fear or restraint. When she saw Anzû, she smiled smugly and silently gave him the same Canarsie greeting that David had given to Shulgi, the *big* finger that the Italian guys in David's old neighborhood used to give, with two crossed arms and two extended middle fingers.

Anzû collapsed into the pilot's seat. "So, David … what now?"

"Now," said David, "you surrender yourself and control of your flagship to me. Rest assured I'll be far more solicitous of your well-being than you would have been of mine."

"Or mine!" said Catharine.

Anzû sighed. "Oh, but David, you know I can't do that."

"Oh, but you *will*," said David confidently. "You have sixty seconds to do so, or I'll blow you to kingdom come." He pointed to a switch on his console. "If I throw this switch, you're a goner. The engine of that antimatter craft docked at your flagship is wired to self-destruct *big time*."

"I'll just jettison that pile of junk," said Anzû breezily as he reached for the switch.

David shook his head disapprovingly. "That would be pointless, Anzû."

"Why?" asked Anzû.

"Because the craft will still be close enough to blow you out of the sky. Touch that switch and it will be the last thing you see."

Anzû rose and pounded the pilot's table. "Do you think you can destroy a whole freedom movement by killing one person?"

"In this instance? Probably, yes. But don't think me ignorant. I know that every general officer you have is on your flagship with you right now. A flick of this switch, and they're all dead, too. There'll be no reorganizing after that."

Catharine smiled and mimed throwing a switch.

Anzû was crestfallen at last. "Well … if it's the end of my movement, I might as *well* die now."

David shrugged nonchalantly. "Suit yourself. Just seems like a waste of several millennia of effort … *your* effort, I might add." He checked his clock. "Forty seconds and the question will be decided for you."

Anzû leaned forward and said, "You wouldn't dare. You haven't got it in you."

Now it was David's turn to lean forward intently. "*Try me*, you son of a bitch. I have no sympathy for you. I don't come from the same planet as you. I don't have any lengthy history with you. In fact, I don't give a rat's ass if you live or die. One thing I do know, though: If you're dead, you can't keep trying to kill me or Catharine here." He sat back. "And that would suit me just fine. Twenty-five seconds."

Anzû pouted. "Are you saying that, if I survive this, there may be a future for me and my movement?"

David shrugged. "For some reason, the Anunnaki didn't scotch you like a snake the first chance they got. Though I doubt that's a mistake *I* would have made, your fate will be in their hands again, not mine. *Who knows?* They might even hear you out before putting you down like a rabid dog. I guarantee you're better off with them than with me." He looked up at his timer. "In just a few seconds, it'll be my privilege to put an end to you and your stupidity forever."

Anzû brought his hand up to the Control switch and threw it to *External*. "It's done," snarled Anzû. Before he could even move his hand away from the switch, he could feel control of his craft being *seized* by a strong external force. When he looked back at David and his woman, they were all smiles.

"Where *are* you?" demanded Anzû with exasperation. "When did an antimatter touring craft gain the capacity to control a complex vessel such as this?"

"I'm on *The Way Forward*," said David, "which is presently aboard a battle cruiser. It's the battle cruiser that's controlling your ship. Incidentally, I have an old friend here you might recognize." He beckoned to someone offscreen and, to Anzû's fury, his ancient foe Ninurta traipsed into the frame.

"Hello, Anzû," said Ninurta impassively.

"So … it *was* you," said Anzû, almost to himself.

"Take heart, you beast," said Ninurta. "You will be fortunate enough to receive the judgment of King Enlil, which will be far kinder than you deserve."

Anzû silently buried his face in his hands and rested it on the pilot's table in utter defeat.

CHAPTER 23

For the following week, the denizens of Earth were treated to more dazzling pomp and circumstance than they'd ever seen.

In a worldwide broadcast of an event attended live by more than a million people, Ninurta's titanic battle cruiser appeared above the platform at Baalbek, slowly descended, and hovered there enigmatically. A platform descended from its base, bearing Inanna and Ninurta side by side in full ceremonial dress.

Holding Catharine by the hand, David approached the lectern to introduce the celestial couple. "Good evening," he said, which proved enough to set the crowd to chanting. *Kid from Canarsie ... Kid from Canarsie.* David smiled and let them go on briefly, then raised his hands to quiet them down. This event was not about him, after all. Besides, knowledge of his central role in the capture of Anzû had been suppressed to this point. He couldn't help but wonder how he'd be treated once his full role became widely known.

"It is my distinct honor as U.S. Ambassador to the Anunnaki," he said, his voice echoing off the surrounding hillsides, "to reintroduce to you—" The crowd reached a frenzied pitch as Inanna deigned to curtsey to them "—Inanna, Queen of Heaven and men's hearts. At Her Majesty's side stands His Royal Highness Prince Ninurta, eldest living son of His Majesty, King Enlil, whom—I can barely believe I'm saying this— whom you will have the honor to see in person next week on the Temple Mount in Jerusalem." A hush fell over the crowd as the momentousness of the upcoming theophany was universally acknowledged; it was almost as though God Himself would appear.

Inanna and Ninurta embraced passionately and the crowd erupted in approval. David gave full vent to the revelry for several minutes before reining it in. "You cheer, having not yet heard Prince Ninurta's feats of military prowess in overcoming Anzû for the second time in the brief history of Earth's civilization. Let us praise—" Barely had he got those few words out than the rest of his sentence (indeed, the rest of his *speech*) was drowned out by the crowd.

Ninurta humbly approached the lectern and regaled the crowd with tales of his ancient battle with Anzû, providing a few hints that David himself had played a significant role in his more recent victory.

As Ninurta spoke on, David breathed a sigh, rather from relief than exhaustion. It seemed stressful enough that he was expected to be in attendance next week to hear the king in Jerusalem. But more immediately, his participation had been arranged in judicial proceedings to take place in two days' time.

THE U.S. SECRETARY of State had declined U.S. jurisdiction in the prosecution of Anzû on grounds that U.S. criminal practice was ill-equipped to resolve cases where the offenses had been largely (though not wholly) committed outside the territorial United States and, in some cases, off-world. In so doing, the secretary had overruled David's strenuous argument that the civilized world (including the United States) had managed to do a creditable job in prosecuting and adjudicating the international Nazi war crimes at Nuremberg. Once more, David had proved little more than a thorn in the secretary's side.

Once an interplanetary forum had been established to decide the matter of *Rex versus Anzû* and the secretary had committed Anzû to the custody of the Anunnaki for prosecution, the secretary urged David to accept a position on the panel of judges. But David had gently declined on grounds that he'd been an eyewitness to many of Anzû's crimes and, in a few cases, an intended victim. Consequently, David would doubtless be required to offer eyewitness testimony, and could not allow himself to be placed in a position to assess his own credibility. Though no additional grounds had been necessary, this was sufficient to keep David in the secretary's doghouse.

The Anunnaki, as custodians of Anzû, had in turn brought the matter to the Dagon, a species they evidently regarded as a kind of trusted ancient protector. The Dagon had then established a multi-tiered procedure bringing their own experts in criminal procedure together with those from Planet Nibiru and the United States.

At the Dagon's specific request, David had allowed himself to be conscripted as a 'friend of the court' in the field of American criminal procedure. As a condition of his participation, he'd insisted that he be permitted to have both Catharine and Shawn sit silently at his side; after some very Talmudic-looking consideration, the judges granted his request.

David began to suspect that one of the Dagons' principal objects in ensuring his participation in the case was to better judge—not Anzû, whom they seemed to regard as something of a lost cause, nor even the Anunnaki—but *humanity itself.* While David was disturbed by the concept that humanity was being judged by a powerful alien civilization at all, he was most distressed by the implicit notion that all human conduct could be reliably generalized from his own personal conduct, which seemed to him an unfairly small and unrepresentative sample.

THE TRIALS OF those Anunnaki accused of conspiring with Anzû had been left to Anunnaki courts, which could readily be convened on craft of the royal fleet or Enki's contingent orbiting Earth. David was relieved to learn he would not be asked to assist in those proceedings, unless his testimony proved necessary.

David's attendance *was* required, however, at the interplanetary court preparing for Anzû's trial that soon convened on Lord Enki's pyramidion. It consisted of a panel of five judges: three Dagon, one Anunnaki, and one earthling. The first day of court was taken up entirely by conferences among the judges striving to agree upon substantive and procedural rules that would satisfy the requirements of all three legal traditions.

Court had convened for its second day by the time the tribunal was ready for Anzû's arraignment. The sole prisoner, Anzû was humiliated by being forced to show his damaged face publicly as he was brought forth in shackles to hear the charges against him and enter his plea. Among the many and varied charges recited were a few for which David listened most closely, namely, those arising out of the prisoner's attempts on the lives of one David Schubert and one U.S. Navy Lieutenant Commander Weldon (first name Catharine, also known as Ketura).

Anzû sat stoically between his lawyers, turning toward David a few times to glower at him. When the time came for the prisoner to enter his plea, the prisoner and his counsel rose, and his counsel addressed the panel of judges.

"May it please the Court, it is the prisoner's intention to enter a plea of guilty to all charges this morning," said defense counsel, "but the prisoner respectfully requests an opportunity beforehand to explain his actions."

The chief judge, a hoary old Dagon named Brogo, conferred with the other judges inaudibly (except for the occasional *glick* that seemed an unavoidable part of every Dagon conversation). Satisfied with the unanimity of judicial views on the subject of arraignment, Brogo addressed defense counsel. "The prisoner has no right at this time to address the Court concerning any justification for his actions. *Glick.* He will, however, be granted such an opportunity prior to sentencing."

Counsel nodded and stepped back from the bar only a bit disappointed, having received the adverse ruling he expected.

David rose from his chair (as he hadn't yet done) and waited to be recognized by Chief Judge Brogo.

Before recognizing David, the chief judge looked to his fellow panel members, all of whom shrugged in turn.

"Mister Ambassador," said the chief judge at last, "have you something to say?"

"Yes, your honor," said David hesitantly. "May it please the Court ... while the Court is no doubt correct that the prisoner has no right to explain his actions at this point, in the interests of justice—and to further the manifest *appearance* of justice—I would respectfully ask the Court to allow the prisoner to offer his explanation for the crimes to which he is today entering a plea of guilty. I expect that the security measures taken for the safety of court personnel and spectators are sufficient to guarantee our safety—and I trust that the prisoner will not, by his present speech, attempt to foment rebellion or disrespect for this tribunal or its proceedings. However," he continued, "as billions of sentient beings are watching these proceedings remotely, and as the prisoner's statement will much resemble a closing argument, I make my request contingent on the prisoner's consent that, upon completion of his statement, the prosecution or I will be given an equal opportunity to rebut his explanation."

The judges had begun to confer with each other when Anzû's lawyer rose to protest. "Your honor, even the prosecution has no right to make a statement at this time, let alone a friend of the Court."

David said laconically, "Neither has the prisoner."

Defense counsel wagged his finger at David. "And *you*, Mister Ambassador, have no right to be heard."

David shrugged and said, "Neither have you."

The chief judge seemed non-plussed by the colloquy between lawyers but ultimately put the question to defense counsel. "Does the prisoner consent to the rebuttal requested by the ambassador?"

Red-faced, defense counsel dropped his pen contemptuously on his notes. "He has no right."

The chief judge waited a respectful time for defense counsel to answer the pending question directly, then shrugged. "I will take your failure to respond to mean that, much as the prosecution declines to consent to the prisoner's making a statement, the prisoner likewise declines to consent to rebuttal of his statement. *Glick.* There being no mutual consent to alteration of the time-honored sequence of criminal procedure, the Court will move on to the next order of business. *Glick.*"

Anzû regarded David with several widely differing expressions, in sequence. At first, he seemed perplexed that one of his formerly intended victims would seek Court leave to let him speak in his own defense before having a right to do so. In a moment, however, Anzû's expression changed to one of suspicion, as though he suspected that David had cynically decided to encourage the Court to give Anzû all the rope he'd need to hang himself. But finally, in yet a second rethinking, Anzû's expression softened into one of grudging respect. He beckoned his counsel to confer with him privately.

The conference between Anzû and his counsel began in heated disagreement. In another moment, a chastened defense counsel addressed the Court. "Your honor, the prisoner consents to the requested rebuttal."

Surprised and a little put out, the chief judge glanced over at David as though to say, *You never stop playing for advantages, do you?* He said sternly, "The prisoner will rise."

Anzû calmly rose.

The chief judge looked at him askance. "Prisoner Anzû, do you understand that you are under no compulsion to allow a rebuttal of your statement, but that if you do give a statement, upon its completion the prosecutor or the ambassador will have a right to provide a rebuttal? *Glick.*"

"I am aware, your honor. Thank you."

"And you understand that, if you say anything in open court, your statement may be used against you in sentencing or in the event you attempt to change your plea?"

"I understand."

"And you have taken the opportunity to discuss this with your counsel. Is that correct? *Glick.*"

"Yes."

"And you still wish to proceed with your statement and allow the requested rebuttal?"

"I do," said Anzû.

"Then," said the chief judge, "with the prisoner's informed consent and his having availed himself of advice of counsel, at the urging of the ambassador in his capacity as a friend of the Court, the Court grants the prisoner ten minutes to present his justification for his actions in respect of the crimes to which he is pleading guilty today. *Glick.* Such time will not be deducted from the time to be allotted for any explanation the prisoner may choose to make at a later time prior to sentencing. Both the prisoner and his counsel are hereby cautioned that any willful attempt by the prisoner to foment rebellion or disrespect for this tribunal or its proceedings will result in forfeiture of the prisoner's remaining time today and the imposition of penalties for contempt of court. Proceed."

Anzû began slowly. "I am Anzû," he said, surveying the courtroom to see just how badly he was despised by those present. *Quite* badly, judging by the sneers. "Everything I've done for the past six thousand years has been for a single purpose, namely, to preserve what little freedom remains to the people of Nibiru, a people with a proud and bloody history of risking all to throw off oppression in all its forms, no matter how handsome the oppressor's face, and no matter how rational or beneficent the oppressor believes his exercise of authority to be.

"A Nibirune's life is owned by no one other than himself. If he or she wishes to spend a life in poverty, declining all the seductive 'opportunities' by which the oppressor tries to ensnare him, he has that right and needs no one's leave to exercise it. That's because such right is conferred *not* by the king, nor by the state, nor even by a majority of society. Even were society *unanimous* against him, the choice would still belong to the *individual*.

"Though imposing limitations upon the powers of the state may be a good start, such limitations are doomed to fail if society once loses its will to enforce them or, worse, actively cheers on the state's expanding tyranny.

"A Nibirune's right to choose his own life arises out of the very operation of nature. He is born free. If one prefers to think theologically, his freedom is conferred by God—not by false gods such as Anu's heirs, but by the God whose works resulted in the natural condition of the individual's freedom.

"Under the heirs of Anu, freedom has all but disappeared from my native planet of Nibiru, and conditions there are suffocating. They're anything but free. As it is the meddlesome state itself that decides how far it may intrude into the life of each citizen, unsurprisingly it seems never to recognize *any* limits on itself. This must change; if not peaceably, then by other means. I, Anzû, am not the sole proponent of this view, nor will this view perish with Anzû. My supporters are representative of all Niburunes from all walks of life and demographic groups, and their views are always welcome."

A woman's voice came from the gallery. "Then, where are the women in your organization?" she demanded.

Chief Judge Brogo nodded to the bailiff, who removed the woman from her seat and escorted her out into the hall. "Proceed," he said. "*Glick.*"

Anzû ignored the heckler's question as though to answer it would be beneath him. "We came to Earth many years ago to build a few paltry pockets of freedom where we could be left to our own choices. Instead, after all this time the Anunnaki return in force—offering no good reason for their reappearance, I might add. I submit to the Court that the real threat to the freedom of earthlings is posed not by a few thousand liberty-seekers such as we, but by those who have returned here *uninvited* for the purpose of imposing upon everyone within reach their own self-serving conception of the good life."

Anzû looked up at the chief judge as humbly as he knew how. Although the chief judge was obviously displeased by the prisoner's lack of contrition, he didn't appear to think that Anzû had violated his instructions. "I thank the Court for this early opportunity to be heard," said Anzû, resuming his seat.

David conferred briefly with the chief prosecutor. Evidently, they decided it would be David who would speak, as the chief prosecutor could be overheard ending their discussion with, "I hope you know what you're doing, Mister Ambassador."

David nodded humbly. "So do I," he said, and turned to the Court. "Your honor, I will address the prisoner's statement."

"Tread carefully, Mister Ambassador," said the chief judge dolefully. "This procedure is already highly irregular."

David took a deep breath and looked straight at Anzû.

"Far be it from an American such as I to condemn the desire to breathe the air of freedom, or even to oppose the right to take up arms against genuine tyranny. Nor am I well-poised to defend the Anunnaki monarchy, were it in need of defending.

"Suffice it for me to observe that many of the happiest nations on Earth are constitutional monarchies. And the Anunnaki monarchy, whatever its flaws, has approved the rules governing the conduct of this manifestly fair and public trial, and has made no objection to the prisoner having an opportunity to try to explain away his heinous conduct in respect of the numerous felonies to which he is today pleading guilty.

"And may I remind the Court that such felonies include the making of unprovoked war on the United States, attempting to murder the President of the United States and the maker of mankind, namely, Lord Enki, while they were engaged in the laudable endeavor of making peace between our worlds. Do we need reminding that the additional felonies to which the prisoner is pleading guilty include the attempted murder of additional American citizens without benefit of trial, or even of lawful arrest?

"The private justice meted out by this prisoner before being apprehended wasn't based upon evidence presented to impartial judges, and the sentences he handed down were anything but measured (as this Court's will be) to fit the crime; they were instead rather *summary*: A bullet to the brain. I ask everyone in the courtroom today to imagine the kind of trial *you* would have received if the shoe were on the other foot, that is, if *you* were a prisoner in Anzû's court and on the bench sat—not these impartial jurists bound by the venerable legal traditions of three different planets—but instead by Anzû's cronies.

"Ladies and gentlemen, you cannot afford to purchase the self-portrait that this snake oil salesman is selling. He poses as a freedom fighter whose values are as universal as freedom of conscience and the freedom to refrain from the commonly accepted responsibilities of life in civil society. But, if those are his values, what need had he of a standing army of drones, part plant and part animal, lacking any capacity or desire to think for themselves? For what valid purpose does he need artillery? Why automatic weapons? Why an air and space force? What does a man of the people need with an arsenal of nuclear and antimatter weapons, which he had aplenty?

"If the prisoner were what he holds himself out to be, he would need none of those things. But the prisoner is *not* what he pretends to be: a mere countercultural rejectionist. He's not a hippy; he's an *authoritarian*, a man whose sole object in life is to be *the all-powerful boss*. If you think Anunnaki society is authoritarian, just wait for the establishment of *his* society. We earthlings spent our entire twentieth century *horrified*, watching authoritarianism up close, and we can tell you that the price of admission is always assessed in lives—*tens of millions* of them—and they are so often the lives of complete *innocents*.

"Authoritarianism never dares to appear publicly as itself; it's too harsh. Instead, it cloaks itself in a fairy tale—perhaps a fairy tale where the all-powerful boss ensures that only people *who look like us* are allowed to live; that's the *Nazi* fairy tale. Sometimes the fairy tale is one where the all-powerful boss ensures that everyone has perfectly equal rights, receives perfectly equal pay for his labor, and never wants for material goods; that's the *Communist* fairy tale. And there are many other fairy tales, limited only by the mountebank's capacity to fabricate lies. But whichever authoritarian fairy tale you *think* you're buying, you may rest assured that it will never come to pass at the hands of the all-powerful boss, and its ending will closely resemble the most horrific of Grimms' fairy tales—with *real* children being thrown into *real* ovens. We must learn from history for, with today's superweapons at hand, we can no longer afford the price of admission to such fairy tales—they are Utopian *lies* and they are *never* implemented as promised.

"Don't be deceived. The enemy *is* the all-powerful boss."

The courtroom was absolutely still. Before a reaction could develop, to avoid any accusation of grandstanding David bowed to the Court. "I thank the Court for this opportunity to be heard."

A FEW EVENINGS later, amidst the largest crowd ever to assemble on the planet, protected by a blanket of security measures never before imagined, King Enlil's personal escort craft landed on the Temple Mount, carefully avoiding the venerated space formerly occupied by the Al-Aqsa Mosque (and, long before that, by the Temple of Solomon).

When King Enlil emerged aglow from his escort craft and assumed his full height of nearly thirty feet, a unified gasp emerged from the crowd. There was no cheering tonight, just silent awe and respect.

On this occasion, the king was briefly introduced by his half-brother Enki. King Enlil chose to address the assemblage calmly and quietly, which lent gravity to his words. He told them of his blessed father's visit to this spot thousands of years earlier, and of his family's deep respect for the God of Abraham and his issue—of Moses, Jesus, and Muhammad. He pledged to do all in his power during his reign to bring the great religions together in mutual respect and peace.

After a speech of what seemed like a few minutes (but in fact lasted well over an hour), the king resumed his seat in the shuttlecraft and was flown from the Temple Mount back to his crystal palace in the sky, barely visible on the edge of space.

EPILOGUE

A YEAR LATER, after a long vacation in the Bahamas spent incognito, David and Catharine (now a married couple) found themselves once again aboard Enki's pyramidion, this time in a banquet hall full of hundreds of dignitaries and their spouses, each resplendent in their own species' version of formal eveningwear. The long-awaited wedding ceremony of Ninurta and Inanna had just finished, and guests had begun to mill about and mix cheerfully.

Ten or so Dagon congregated near the altar. Among this number were Brosa and Brogo, who'd served as chief judge in *Rex versus Anzû*. Whenever David glanced in Brogo's direction, he found himself the subject of the Dagon's perplexed scrutiny. David could only shake his head as, despite his openness at their many conferences, Brogo evidently still found him inscrutable, and no doubt found the human race to be characterized by gamesmanship, deceit, and violence.

In a row of chairs immediately behind the Dagon attendees sat several Anunnaki, a few of whom were aged beyond human comprehension, their longevity having given way to the usual infirmities of old age: poor eyesight, poor hearing, limited mobility, and a certain mental vagueness that made them objects of fondness while at the same time giving rise to a sense of relief that they no longer wielded the power of command.

Amidst all the well-wishing and bonhomie, the diminutive Brogo excused himself from the group he'd been speaking with, shuffled his lonely way to the dais, and approached the lectern, where he silently raised his hands in a vain attempt to call for attention.

David checked his copy of the engraved program and pointed out to Catharine that, indeed, Brogo was scheduled to address the crowd with a brief announcement before any of the guests could retreat to their private rooms. As many in the crowd seemed more interested in a hearty bout of eating and drinking than going to sleep, David thought Brogo's appearance on the dais a bit premature.

Being slight of stature, Brogo found himself unable to gain the crowd's attention. He leaned in toward the microphone and, instead of beginning with his voice raised, he rubbed his chin anxiously and emitted a quiet *glick*.

Seeing that no one was paying attention to such an august personage, David (and, to their credit, a few young Anunnaki males) began whistling and shouting to get the crowd to quiet down. Eventually it worked, and all eyes lighted on Brogo, who seemed quite pleased to be at the center of attention at last.

"Queen Inanna, Beloved of Anu," he said, "and Lord Ninurta (who, if you have failed to notice until now, are our bride and groom)—" Cheers and chants arose from the young people present "—have asked me to inform (or remind) you of the ancient Anunnaki tradition pursuant to which the bride and groom, on the night of their nuptials, sometimes send small, but (hopefully) meaningful gifts to their guests. *Glick.* As you will all be spending the night aboard this pyramidion, by prior arrangement the bride and groom have sent such gifts to your respective rooms, which already await you there. The bride and groom extend to you their sincere hope that you will accept these gifts in the loving spirit in which they are given. Now, some cynics in the past—and I will forbear from mentioning any names—have suggested that this announcement is simply a polite technique of dispersing you all to your rooms—"

This suggestion gave rise to good-natured derisive laughter.

"*It won't work!*" shouted one inebriated young Anunnaki.

Brogo smiled in his strange Dagon way and emitted an audible *glick*.

"But the bride and groom in this instance have disclaimed any such intention, and they intend to remain available to speak with one and all for the next few hours." He surveyed the crowd. "And, with that, the scheduled ceremonies have come to their end. Thank you all for coming. You are on your own. *Glick.*" The crowd applauded enthusiastically, which raised the old Dagon's mood. He stepped mincingly off the dais and resumed his mingling.

Catharine tapped David on the shoulder. When he turned, she introduced to him a very young Anunnaki male. Though he was nearly David's height, he came as close as David had ever seen to a preadolescent Anunnaki male.

"This is Namkuzu, of the line of King Enlil," said Catharine. "He wishes to tell you something."

David extended his hand, which was a little awkward, as handshaking was not an Anunnaki custom. But Namkuzu did his best to accept the proffered hand amiably, and shook it lightly.

"What did you wish to say?" asked David with a smile.

The youth seemed a bit embarrassed and his face reddened. "I wanted to tell you, Mister Ambassador, that I heard your condemnation of Anzû at his … arraignment. Is that the right word?"

David was a bit chagrined. "*Arraignment* is the right word. I might take issue with the other word *condemnation*, as that was not my intention—although I can see how you might have understood it that way."

Namkuzu braced himself and said, "I want you to know that you are a hero of mine."

As any man would be at a time like that, David was veritably bursting with pride, but he thought it prudent not to let on. "Be careful with the word *hero*, dear Namkuzu. Are you familiar with Moses of the Bible?"

Namkuzu nodded enthusiastically. "He who led the Israelites out of Egypt?"

David nodded.

Namkuzu said, "Yes, he also is one of my heroes."

"Do you recall what happened when Moses reached the border of the Promised Land?" asked David.

The boy nodded. "He couldn't go in."

David nodded. "That's correct, but why not?"

"Because he'd slain an Egyptian long before."

"I see you are already a learned young fellow, Namkuzu," said David. "Tell me. Do you know of King David?"

"Yes," said Namkuzu. "Yet another hero! He conquered the lands about, united the Israelites into a single kingdom, and, at God's instruction, purchased the platform for construction of the Temple."

"Excellent!" said David. "But what happened when David proposed to commence building the Temple?"

"Yahweh forbade him to do so, and instructed him to leave that task to his son Solomon."

"Why did God forbid David from having any hand in building the Temple?" asked David.

"Because David had been a man of war and had blood on his hands," said Namkuzu, who now realized that he was being led to a conclusion by the Socratic method. "Are you saying that you, too, are unworthy because you have blood on your hands?" he asked.

David smiled at the young fellow's quickness and patted him fondly on the back. "I'm just suggesting that you need a better class of hero."

Namkuzu nodded thoughtfully, shook David's hand, and disappeared into the crowd.

Catharine, who'd heard the whole conversation, said sardonically, "You have such a knack for alienating your fans."

David shrugged. "That young man may someday be king. He can't afford to have stars in his eyes."

IN ANOTHER HALF-HOUR, David and Catharine stole away to their room. Consistently with a habit of long standing, upon entering David went straight to the bathroom to wash his face. He quickly patted his face dry, and emerged to see Catharine seated on the edge of the bed, her shoulders drooping. At her feet lay a formal-looking envelope, its golden seal broken and its contents removed.

In Catharine's hand was a calligraphed letter with a gold seal at its base. Though when David had first opened the door to their suite, he hadn't checked to see whether anything had been slipped under it, what she was reading was very likely the promised gift from the bride and groom—except that Catharine was weeping uncontrollably, and these were obviously tears of misery; not of joy or relief.

Only one thing he could think of would put her in such a state. Her father had been undergoing testing on his heart. Perhaps this was bad news about that. On second thought, he realized that such news would not have arrived in a calligraphic letter under royal seal. He was at a loss. His new bride was suffering. When he could bear it no longer, he spoke up.

"What is it, Catharine?" he asked with trepidation. "Is it about your father?"

She looked up at him as though he were quite mad, mascara running down her cheeks. "What? No! He's fine."

"Then what's the matter?" he asked. "Why are you so upset?"

"It's our gift from Inanna and Ninurta," she replied, thrusting the letter toward him and turning her face away.

As he took the letter from her, his mind went in a dozen directions. Hoping she was just overreacting to some extravagant sign of affection from the bride and groom, he began to read silently. The letter was indeed formal.

To Our Dearest Friends Ambassador David Schubert and His Lovely

Wife, Lieutenant Commander Catharine Schubert, née Weldon, USN: Words cannot express our gratitude to you both for your loyalty, companionship, and wisdom in helping us through the troubled events of the past few years and, at last, bringing the two of us together forever. There is only one thing of equivalent value that we can confer upon you, a gift granted to only a handful of your kind, namely, immortality, or as near thereto as we can grant. It is our sincerest hope that you will accept this gift in the spirit in which it is offered and that you will use it to remain together until parted by the God of All Things. Although we can conceive of nothing as valuable as this, if you decline, rest assured that we will think of something else that you will treasure.

The signatures at the foot of the letter had been manually applied by the bride and groom themselves: The signature of *Inanna, Beloved of Anu, Queen of Heaven* was so beautifully inscribed that it bespoke the signatory's breeding. Immediately below that was the signature of *Ninurta, Prince, and Heir Apparent of Enlil, King of Nibiru*; though the groom had taken care to stay *within the lines*, as they say, his penmanship lacked the dignity of the Queen's.

Catharine regarded him dolefully, though her sobbing had let up. "You probably think that's no big deal," she said, "the prospect of immortality."

"Why would you think that?" he said.

"Because that bastard Anzû kept tantalizing you with it all the while he wanted me dead."

"And you can see how I chose," said David. "He's in prison forever, and you're alive and well, thank God. I can understand why having your life threatened would cause you horror, but why would the prospect of long life shake you so badly?"

"We're born to bear up under only *limited* hard times," she said, wiping the mascara off her cheeks with a tissue. "Good things happen to us—some bad things, too—and then we're off, and the world is someone else's problem."

David nodded. "It's like I've often said: Death is easy, it's *life* that's scary. But why should a longer life be scarier than one of customary duration?"

She crumpled the tissue in her hand and said, "For such a smart guy, you can be awfully dumb."

"So I've been told countless times," he said, taking a seat next to her on the bed. "Tell me what I'm missing, Catharine." He stroked her hand. "I don't want anything *you* don't want."

"Are we going to have children?" she asked.

"I certainly hope so," he replied (to what seemed to him a blatant *non sequitur*). "As many as you can stand."

"Well," she said, "what role do we expect to play in our children's lives when we get older?"

"You mean after they're educated and move out?" he asked.

"Yes."

"Well," he said, "then we go and play with our grandchildren, and give our children moral support … and money."

"Who dies first?" asked Catharine.

"What?" he asked as though she'd radically changed the subject again.

"Who dies *first*?"

This was getting difficult. He shrugged. "I don't know. The eldest?"

"No," she said. "I mean between us and our kids?"

He shrugged. "Usually, it would be us."

"Why not them?" she demanded.

"Look, Catharine, in some instances a child might die before its parent, but it's more likely the parent who goes first."

"Why?" she asked.

"Because the parent is older—"

Catharine interrupted him. "And parents have roughly the same lifespan as their children. But what if the parent lives *forever*?"

"Ah," said David. It finally made sense. "Then it's the child who dies first."

"Am I being asked to watch my children die?" she asked. "What sort of gift is that? And, if *you* die first, do I want to spend forever grieving you?"

"Look," he said off-handedly, "if that's how you feel, then we'll just decline. *Thanks but no thanks.*"

"Do you think the Anunnaki have something to gain from our accepting the gift of immortality?" she asked.

David shook his head. "Look, Catharine. I think they're terrific people and I'm not going to question their motives. They're offering us something that just about every human being has wanted for millennia. Gilgamesh nearly killed himself striving to obtain it. If we're going to decline, let's do so gracefully."

"Let's go and talk to Doctor Zia," she said and went off to fix her makeup.

THE DOOR TO Zia's anteroom was opened by an android who looked exactly like the pilot who forgot how to bring David and Catharine home from the Mars system and declined to relinquish control of *The Way Forward*.

Catharine and David both gasped and instinctively took a step backward.

"Good evening, Catharine and David," said the android. Observing their warlike stance, he said gravely, "I must warn you that I'm no match for you physically. I'm the *real* Enkidu—the one who piloted you across Africa. If you wish to get the better of me in a physical altercation, you can readily do so. I'll offer no resistance. But, knowing the two of you as I do, if you do me harm, you'll feel just *awful* afterwards."

"Enkidu?" said David hesitantly.

"Yes, sir," came the reply. "My identity and memory have been fully restored. That other … *creature*—or what was left of him—has been thoroughly disassembled for spare parts."

David tested the android's memory. "Do you remember Queen Inanna's reaction to being jilted by Gilgamesh?'

Enkidu gasped and pulled them both into the room by the hand. He shut the door behind them. "David, you're not thinking clearly. That same lady was just remarried tonight. You can't *really* ask me to discuss such dreadful things on this joyous occasion. Heaven forbid!"

David almost laughed. "Okay, Enkidu," he said, "I believe it's you."

But Enkidu remained quite serious. "I see that Catharine has been weeping. Is there anything I can do to help?"

"Is it that obvious?" asked Catharine, peering at her reflection in the nearest mirror. She waved the gift letter at Enkidu. "Queen Inanna and Lord Ninurta have gifted us immortality," she told him sadly.

Enkidu's jaw dropped open and he looked to David, then back to Catharine. "I thought … I thought that's … what all humans *want*."

David shrugged. "Not *all*, evidently."

Catharine was impatient with David's response. "Enkidu," she said, "would *you* accept a gift of immortality?"

"I'm afraid I'd be a poor choice to receive such a gift, madam," replied Enkidu, "as I'm already afflicted with that condition—I mean immortality."

Catharine said, "Suppose I were to explain to you that, if you were to accept immortality (or *that condition*, as you'd call it), any children you brought into the world would die before you?"

A single glance at David let Enkidu know that the best he could manage was to help calm the lady down. "I think, madam," he said apologetically, "that such a question would best be posed to someone capable of bringing forth children. Would it not?"

The door to Zia's chamber popped open and Zia emerged, still looking dapper in his formal clothing. "David, Catharine," he said expansively, "two of my favorite people in the solar system." He glanced at Catharine's moist eyes and Enkidu's chagrined expression. "Has my valet said something to displease you, Catharine?"

Instead of answering, Catharine handed Zia the letter and waited for him to read it. At first, Zia seemed quite pleased by the nature of the proffered gift, but, having once been mortal, he could readily imagine the storm of feelings it had aroused in Catharine. "I must tell you, Catharine … and David, that I've seen Lord Ninurta and Queen Inanna bestow many gifts upon their friends, but never a gift of this kind … of this *magnanimity*." He refolded the letter carefully and handed it back to Catharine. "Whatever apprehensions this offer may arouse in you, it should likewise arouse great warmth and pride. The bride and groom obviously regard you as close family." His eyebrow rose. "Very close indeed."

"But, Doctor Zia—" said Catharine with dismay. "Oh … I barely know how to ask the question I have in mind."

"Permit me to pose it on your behalf," said Zia reassuringly, "if I may. You'd like to know how it felt to have my sons predecease me. Is that it?"

Catharine nodded, a bit shamefaced.

"Well, as you know," said Zia, "I had three sons, and each was granted primacy in a different part of the ancient world. I watched with pride as they grew from childhood to maturity. When each of them grew old, it became quite clear that life held little remaining promise for them, other than the unavoidable pain and indignities of old age. By the time each of them passed, he was wizened; he'd lost his accustomed ironclad grip on reality, and he'd also lost sight of life's promise. They were ready to go when they went, and I couldn't have been more proud of them."

"Did it hurt you to see them … pass?" asked Catharine.

"Like a knife through the heart," admitted Zia gravely.

"And do you mourn them still?"

"Catharine," said Zia, "mourning never ceases, but it lessens over time—at least to a point where the pain inflicted by memory is exceeded by the love and pride that remain—and will ever remain. I still think of them, usually one at a time—because they were very different from one another, you see—but I'm glad I had such time with them as the good Lord gave me, and I'm grateful to have watched them flourish, along with their families."

"Do you still miss them?" asked Catharine.

"Every day," said Zia with a sincere smile. "But, remember, every new person I meet is descended from them, just as you are. *You* are my family, descended from one or more of my beloved sons."

This gave Catharine pause. "And what of the loss of your wife so long ago?" asked Catharine. "That must be an unendurable pain."

Zia gave thought to her words. "*Enduring*," he said, "but not unendurable. Life is as valuable to me now as it ever was." He sighed philosophically. "We work towards our goals, expecting to achieve less than all of them, knowing full well that we'll lose loved ones along the way, yet we welcome new friendships and take pleasure as we find it."

Catharine perched on an upholstered chair and took a deep breath.

Zia said, "But I think there's someone you should talk with whose testimony on that subject will be more valuable than my own."

BEFORE NINURTA COULD begin the ritual bath preparatory to his wedding night with Inanna, there was a knock at the door to his suite. His valet answered it and, a moment later, knocked on the door to Ninurta's private chamber.

The valet leaned through the door discreetly. "It's the Dagon, my lord."

"Brogo?" asked Ninurta.

The valet shrugged. "They all look so much alike, my lord. This one is old. I think he was the one who spoke briefly after the reception."

Ninurta put on a robe and said, "Let him in."

It *was* Brogo, looking as though he regretted bothering the groom on his wedding night. But, he'd evidently felt impelled. Ninurta let him in and closed the door.

"To what do I owe the pleasure, Brogo?"

Brogo seemed to be engaging in an inner discussion and needed to arrive at a point of agreement with himself before answering. At last he said, "My lord, the Dagon have … misgivings about the earthlings …

David, in particular."

"What sort of misgivings?"

"He has a certain … intensity," said Brogo. "He never seems completely at ease. *Glick.*"

Ninurta snickered at this. "I should think that would be more of a problem for his new wife than for either the Anunnaki or the Dagon."

Brogo nodded emphatically. "Yes, of course. It's probably in my imagination, but in my long experience, someone who habitually keeps such tight control over his feelings is often capable of doing … terrible things. *Glick.*"

"Well, Brogo," said Ninurta, "I can tell you without hesitation that David is capable of doing things that are—wise, courageous, bold, and dedicated, but in my experience, he's never done anything one might call *terrible*." He strained to recall David's actions. "I understand that, before he and I met, he'd put an end to one of Anzû's drones and one of the progenitors. But I don't see how that can be held against him, since, in both instances, his actions were necessary to protect the life and safety of Ketura, the woman now his wife. In fact, he would have been remiss not to have taken the actions he did."

"But then, my lord," ventured Brogo, "you yourself have been called the Destroyer for many Sars."

"There you go, then," Ninurta said reassuringly. "You've never known me to resort to violence unnecessarily, have you?"

Brogo nodded thoughtfully. "No, my lord. But getting back to David, did he do no violence to Anzû himself?"

"None," replied Ninurta, "although he did *threaten* to do so."

"Yes," said Brogo, "I heard that he was instrumental in subduing Anzû and that, in doing so, he threatened to blow up his spacecraft, which would have resulted in the immediate deaths of Anzû and his entire high command. Is it true?"

Ninurta nodded.

"Can you provide me with greater detail?" asked Brogo.

Ninurta took a seat and proffered one to Brogo. "There was an antimatter craft aboard my battle cruiser which was a virtual duplicate of David's craft, *The Way Forward.* We took David's craft onboard my battle cruiser. Then, we … modified the antimatter engine on the duplicate so that it would detonate if David were to throw a switch on *The Way Forward*, which all the while remained aboard my cruiser. We then sent the duplicate craft to dock with Anzû's flagship, and David pretended that he was aboard the duplicate. Thank heaven Anzû bought into the ruse."

Brogo nodded. "And making Anzû believe he would be destroyed if he didn't surrender: Was that also a ruse? Or would David's switch actually have destroyed Anzû and his high command?"

"Oh, it would have destroyed Anzû and everyone aboard. As you can imagine, the ruse was David's idea. He came up with the plan to keep himself and Ketura safe aboard my cruiser while tricking Anzû into believing they were aboard the craft that would dock with Anzû's flagship."

Brogo regarded Ninurta with less than complete approval. "Yes," he said, "humans are quite natural at games of bluff. That's their reputation. *Glick.* If Anzû had not surrendered, was it David's plan to detonate the craft?"

The conversation was interrupted by another knock at the outer door.

Ninurta's valet knocked softly on Ninurta's inner door.

"Come," said Ninurta.

The door opened a crack. "My lord, it's Doctor Zia with two more humans."

Ninurta waited a moment and, when his valet failed to take the point, he asked impatiently, "Do the other humans have names?"

The valet took the point, bowed apologetically, and said, "David and Ketura."

Ninurta looked to Brogo inquiringly. "Would you wish to leave privately before they come in?"

Brogo thought for a moment. "No, my lord. I'd care to stay, if I may. *Glick.*"

Ninurta turned to his valet. "Please inform them that Brogo is here and show them in."

Zia marched in confidently, bowed to Ninurta, and nodded respectfully to Brogo. "My lord, Master Brogo, I bring you David and Ketura."

David and Catharine entered sheepishly. David bowed and Catharine curtsied.

"What can we do for you, my dear friends?" asked Ninurta.

David took it upon himself to reply. "We wish to thank you, my lord, and Her Majesty from the bottom of our hearts for the wonderful gift, but we wonder ... how the immortal grieve the loss of those closest to them, such as a child or a spouse."

Ninurta studied each of David and Catharine separately, as though to ascertain which was prime mover of the question. He decided it was Catharine, and that David was acting as her voice and protector.

"Concerning children," said Ninurta, "I would refer you to Ziusudra here, who has experience in this. As for me, well, you know the children of the Anunnaki are not only immortal themselves, but they pass that trait on to their children. Not so for humans, such as Ziusudra and yourselves. In any event, both he and his late wife grieved their losses as well as nature would allow, I expect."

Ninurta waited a moment to see if perhaps Brogo had something to add, but he remained mute.

"As for the loss of a wife … or a husband," continued Ninurta, "it is as difficult to grieve as you might imagine. My new bride still mourns the loss of her former husband of old, my good friend Dumuzi, bless his memory. But I think his memory is of some comfort to her yet."

At last, Catharine spoke softly for herself. "And *you*, my lord, who suffered the loss of your beloved wife so many millennia ago?"

Ninurta sighed. "I have wondered for many years," he began, "whether my enduring pain of that loss is the same as would have been endured by any other Anunnaki who's lost a wife."

"And?" asked Catharine.

"I've come to believe that, as far as grieving the loss of one so *close* is concerned, no two beings and no two losses are alike. I'll add this, Ketura. I believe that my grief was far deeper and longer because I'd been instrumental in bringing about her death. If I'd learned—as I *should* have—the awesome power of those weapons, I'd have removed her from the area where the deadly cloud might travel. But," he sighed, "being still young, it was not in my nature to think so deeply before acting, and so I did … what I did. And the blessed Bau, whom some have called Gula, died by my ignorance. It's difficult enough to forgive oneself for *unavoidable* errors, but one so avoidable and costly as that, well …" His voice trailed off.

"Thank you, my lord," said Catharine. "I'm sorry to have recalled such grief to your lordship's mind on such a happy occasion as this, but my mind is uneasy."

Ninurta smiled wanly. "I'll assure you of this, Ketura: Your immortality would not bring about the premature demise of your children. Far from it, immortality would afford you every imaginable opportunity to guide and protect your children throughout their lives. And, as any grandparent will tell you, if you're fortunate, your children will themselves give you grandchildren and further descendants in whose countenances you will continue to see your children till the end of your days."

"Thank you, my lord," said David. "We thank you again and will leave you to your private discussion."

Brogo nodded to Ninurta, as though encouraging him to ask David something. It took a moment for Ninurta to catch on but, when he did, he said, "David, permit me to put one question to you before you go."

David bowed expectantly.

"If Anzû had declined to surrender," said Ninurta, "would you have thrown the switch and destroyed his craft with Anzû and all his high command aboard?"

David studied the faces of Ninurta and Brogo and determined that, in all likelihood, it was *Brogo's* question, and—never mind that David had been under existential duress during the confrontation and that his choices had been quite limited—his answer would be unfairly used to support adverse inferences about all of humanity.

He bowed and prepared to address his answer to Ninurta (who had, of course, posed the question). Opening the door behind him and taking Catharine by the hand in preparation for a prompt exit, he smiled broadly and said, "As a great man once said, my lord, 'That's not for you to know.'"

Though Brogo was manifestly perplexed, Ninurta couldn't help but smile to hear his own words thrown back at him.

And David and Catharine left without further discussion.

Brogo sighed. "I can't help but think we may have a *new* Destroyer in this solar system." He observed Ninurta intently. "*Glick.*"

WHEN DAVID AND Catharine returned to their sumptuous room, David held out his hand, palm up, and said, "All right, lady fair. Give it here."

At first she thought him presumptuous but, realizing the grief that the letter had caused her, she handed it to him. "What are you going to do with it?"

"I'm going to remove it from m'lady's sight," said David. "And, without settling anything substantive, I'm going to put it aside for the night." He folded the letter, put it back in its envelope, and feigning clandestine activity, shoved it in the top drawer of his nightstand and slid it quietly shut. When he'd finished, he winked at Catharine and held his finger up to his lips.

She laughed, as she always did when he did something foolish for her sake. "Then, what are we going to talk about?"

"Well," he said, removing his shoes, "what do we hear from our old friend the admiral?" He kicked his shoes aside.

"He and his wife are both well," she said, removing her earrings, "although he insists they're going to take it easier from now on."

"Why?"

"He won't admit it," she said, "but he thinks he's beginning to lose his memory for detail." She put her earrings in their case and put it in her nightstand. "He told me Gary is back in the smuggler's trade with his old friend Hendrick by his side. Meanwhile, he says, neither of them needs the money; it's just their chosen career."

David snickered. "To each his own. And Buck?"

"Gary reported that the last time they met was at Sofia's family place in Chile. Buck was wearing a pancho he called a … a *chamanto*, I think, and his hands were stained red with grape juice."

"I thought he said they can't grow red grapes down there," said David, donning his pajamas.

"Hey," she said, putting on her nightgown and letting her hair down, "give the guy a break. He's new there. He's experimenting." She sighed and looked at the bed. "Do you really think we're going to sleep soundly with this … this decision hanging over our heads?"

He snapped his fingers as though he'd remembered something, zipped open one of his bags, and removed Elijah's mantle. He opened it and spread it out smoothly over both their pillows.

"I think this will help," he said with a smile as he got into bed and patted her side of the bed invitingly.

"What does this mantle do, exactly?"

"I'm not sure," he said. "Didn't come with a manual. But it seems to make things … better—*easier* somehow."

She still seemed skeptical.

"It comes with quite a pedigree," he assured her.

Still only partly convinced, she got into bed, and David turned out the light.

THE END

Thank you for reading *Destroyer from the Lost Planet*. If you enjoyed the book, please consider leaving a review on your favorite retailer. Reviews greatly help authors both with reaching new readers and improving our stories. I would love to read your thoughts.

Here's a special preview of the first book of my historical mystery series, In the Den of the English Lion. In *A Second Daniel*, you'll follow Noah Ames in this gripping tale as he seeks to uncover a plot against the Queen in 1500's London.

A SECOND DANIEL
PROLOGUE

UNCLE AVRAM HAS hinted that his special customer's house across the Thames can be seen from this hillock in the market square, but the only thing young Menachem can make out on the opposite bank is a scary-looking castle looming in the distance. Wherever the customer's house may be, Uncle Avram has promised to take him there to deliver groceries as soon as the sun goes down. Menachem is eager for even this small adventure outside the Southwark food market.

It's nearly dusk, and red clouds streak the sky. Church bells clang in Southwark Priory on the near side of London Bridge, and north across the river in the walled City of London. The rain of the previous evening still dampens the packed dirt under the market, and a few small pools of muddy water dot the ground.

By this time in the evening, business has dwindled. Around the market, each family closes its booth at its own pace, the day's receipts by now fixed in amount, whether good or bad, with nothing to be done about it at this late hour. A cloth is dropped over the entrance to each booth, telling the casual shopper that food can no longer be purchased here.

Uncle Avram, known locally as "Avram the Jew," selects the perfect produce for his special customer. The best specimens have been withheld from general sale all day, stored in special wooden crates covered by a tarpaulin. As he still needs to supplement their quantity, he traipses about the booth scowling, intently studying each potato, each parsnip, each carrot, to ensure it's clean of rot and dirt, and can pass for the most desirable of its kind. He dusts his wares thoroughly, crates the items he's just selected, and loads everything onto his oxcart. The evening air grows chill as he sets about hitching his cart to the ox.

Menachem spies his pretty cousin Rachel peeking and smiling at him around the edge of one of the carts. Though he's lived with Avram and his family for little more than a week, already he seems to have captured her heart. She has a visitor this evening, her stout cousin Beth. As the children have been taught to keep silent whenever Avram fusses about his special customer's order, what ensues is a little dumb show, such as those seen nearby at The Theater and The Rose before the real play begins.

Having apparently noticed how taken Rachel is with Menachem, Beth prances into Menachem's full view with an exaggerated feminine strut, one shoulder jerking forward with each step, and a preening air about her upturned nose. Rachel makes no attempt to conceal her jealousy, and shoves Beth arse first into a puddle, which makes a little *splush* that Menachem finds even funnier for its quietness. Silently, Rachel points derisively at Beth, who lurches to her feet and drags Rachel out of view. A brief scuffle ensues, the only sign of which is an occasional soft slap or rustling sound. The girls reappear, slightly muddier than when the show began.

Uncle Avram finishes hitching together ox and cart. "Ready," he says, winking at Menachem and grabbing the reins. Menachem clambers up and settles in beside his uncle. Aunt Sarah waves goodbye, and the girls follow suit, still eyeing each other warily.

The ox jerks the cart out of a small rut, and Avram and Menachem begin their trip in comfortable silence. As the market diminishes in the distance, London Bridge looms ever larger.

Uncle Avram hands him a long wooden switch. "You keep those people away from the cart," he says, pointing at a painted woman, "and away from the food. Half of them have more money than we do. They are not so poor as they look."

Menachem accepts the switch and assumes a forbidding countenance for their trip across London Bridge, which he soon realizes is not used merely to cross the river. For much of its length, it's occupied by activities beyond the range of his experience. The furtive glances of those involved remove any doubt that such activities are improper, perhaps even unlawful.

A brazen woman, the tops of her breasts exposed, begins to approach the cart but, seeing Menachem's innocent face and Avram's threatening glare, she stops and recedes into the gloaming. Another woman raises her skirts to flash her legs, but then reverses course, realizing there is no business to be had from this cart. Halfway across the bridge's span, a few beggars huddle around a small fire to ward off the coming chill. From the corner of his eye, Menachem spies what appears to be two men grunting and humping beneath an outsized coat so large it must have been made especially for concealment.

He is not as shocked as another child his age might be. Having heard Bible tales of illicit practices, he is strangely reassured to see that they weren't conjured up merely to frighten little children into behaving themselves. He glances at his uncle's face and takes comfort from his sober eye and his steady hand on the reins.

At the far end of London Bridge, it's rumored, one can often see severed heads on pikes. Now, with a new queen about to be crowned, all the heads have been cleared away. Rumor has circulated that the new queen regards such displays as detestable signs of barbarity and that she'll replace them with new heads only under the most pressing of circumstances.

As they leave the bridge, Uncle Avram points to his left and breaks the silence. "Over there is Chancery Lane, where there's a whole building for the conversion of Jews to Christianity." He smiles, shakes his head, and laughs. "Goyim." He jerks the reins, and the cart turns right.

On their left soon appears the walled castle Menachem spotted from the hillock in the market square. Over its long stone wall peer several stone buildings and one tall white tower.

"What place is this?" he asks, his eyes wide.

Avram snickers. "This is the customer's house. We're bringing them groceries."

Menachem whistles softly. "They must be very rich, and happy!"

Uncle Avram shrugs. "Rich, yes." He pauses. "Happy?" He shrugs again, but says nothing.

"There must be a lot of people living here," says Menachem. "Surely, we can't be bringing food enough for them all."

The cart approaches a gate guarded by four burly men wearing colorful uniforms and holding long pointed pikes. As the cart draws close enough for Menachem to read their expressions in the fading light, they seem in no mood for a chat.

Avram slows the cart to a crawl, his posture stiffening. A few cautious words pass between him and the foremost guard. Avram draws a paper from his pocket and hands it to the guard, who examines it though there is barely enough daylight left for reading.

"That's the royal warrant, all right!" says the guard, returning the paper.

Avram pockets the paper and discreetly palms a coin into the guard's hand. The guard takes a step back, at first raising his hand to wave them through. But as his eyes light on Menachem, he shouts "halt!" and smiles sheepishly, evidently embarrassed by his hesitation.

"If you don't mind my asking, Goodman Jew, who's the English boy?" He nods toward Menachem. "I mean … who is he to *you*?"

Avram's head jerks around toward the boy, as though he's completely forgotten that his nephew's been seated beside him the whole time.

"Oh, he's not English," Avram says cautiously. "He's a distant cousin, an orphan, who just came to us from Poland." He leans toward the guard, and whispers something inaudible.

The guard nods gravely, and regards Menachem with pity. Drawing his great head so close that Menachem can smell the whiskey on his breath, he smiles discreetly, winks, and says hoarsely:

"Welcome to the Tower o' London, boy."

Menachem isn't sure what it is about the way the guard has spoken those words, but there is something threatening inside them, as though the Tower of London is not at all a place to feel welcome. The guard takes a step back, and waves them on.

A few manly shouts are heard calling and answering, some from above the wall, some from inside what now appears to be a giant compound of stately stone buildings.

The cart creeps up the cobblestone path to a giant gate of latticed iron. There the ox stops unprompted and waits, as though it has done this before. Chains clank, and wood creaks against metal. Slowly, the gate begins its rise, revealing sharp spikes along its base. Menachem shudders to imagine what such spikes would do to someone unfortunate enough to be caught under them when they drop.

They pass into a tunnel-like enclosure with a latticework iron gate exactly like the first at the opposite end. The gate behind them clanks shut, trapping them in the tunnel.

No longer able to contain himself, Menachem asks quietly, "What are these gates called?"

With a hushed awe that matches Menachem's own, Avram replies, "They're called a 'portcullis.'"

Menachem mouths the word, and whispers, "Are they to keep the Jews out?"

Avram suppresses a laugh, his face reddening. He composes himself, and replies, "No. They're to keep out the goyim who don't bring groceries." He tousles the boy's hair. The gate ahead of them creaks up, and the cart advances into an open cobblestone courtyard.

It is now full dark. No light shines from any building except for a modest stone cottage, also dark but for the glow of coals still smoldering in a tall fireplace beneath a carved wooden hearth, such as one might see in a great kitchen. The cart turns toward the cottage, and a cold breeze runs through Menachem's cloak and up his spine like icy fingers, as though he has passed into some ancient fairy tale where anything might happen.

The second gate thunders closed behind them.

A low fence surrounding the dark cottage blocks the cart's way to the rear door, which means that the crates will have to be carried in one by one. Avram and Menachem climb down from the cart, careful not to stumble in the dark. Avram pulls a torch from the rear of the cart, lights it, and lodges it in a sconce on the fence. He takes a sack of potatoes from the cart, hands it to Menachem, and points to the rear door of the cottage. "I'm giving you one small sack, so you'll have a hand free to open the door."

Just then, a muffled shout escapes a building across the courtyard. A man's voice. Though it sounds distressed, there seems to be no fear in it. Avram turns first in the direction of the shout, then back to his nephew and nods toward the cottage's rear door. "Go ahead. I'll be in soon." He takes a few hesitant steps toward the source of the shout, which has died away in the night.

Menachem turns toward the cottage door, carrying the sack in the crook of his left arm. Apparently the door has been left unlocked by design, as the key has been left jutting out of the lock. He turns the iron knob and goes inside.

He finds himself in a kitchen that must have been left dark and vacant no more than a few hours ago. There is still a stuffy heat inside, along with unfamiliar scents of finely prepared foods. A few droplets of water cling to the base of a pan hanging from a hook above the fresh-water basin. The stone walls have kept the chill wind out, except for the breeze now entering through the open door behind him.

Across a work area the size of his uncle's booth, an archway leads out of the kitchen into an unlit hallway. He closes the door behind him, half expecting his uncle to barge in before it can fully close. The breeze dissipates, but his uncle does not appear. He comforts himself in this strange new place by softly singing a tune he heard Rachel sing just yesterday. Although the lyrics are unknown to him, his wordless and soft young singing voice overcomes the gloom of the small cottage. He places the bag of potatoes on the marble base jutting out of the fireplace.

Sensing a presence behind him, he is too frightened to turn. He gasps, and his eyes go wide.

A cultured young woman's voice emanates from the archway across the kitchen, with a lilt of humor. "If you leave the potatoes so near to the flame, they shall be roasted long before anyone will care to eat them."

Menachem turns, and there, directly beneath the arch, stands a graceful young woman in a rich gossamer dressing gown. The deep red glow of the firelight illuminates her as something in a dream. He wonders fleetingly whether she might not be some beautiful wraith rather than a real woman, but he quickly dismisses the thought, as the bemused stare that holds him motionless is humanly warm and benevolent. Her most striking feature is her long red hair. Not the brassy red that he has sometimes seen affected by fine older ladies, but a rich auburn that reminds him of warm sunshine, newly tilled earth, and roan horses.

She appears to have been interrupted in preparing for bed, as she wears no makeup. Her face is a healthy pink. Though her eyelashes are nearly invisible but for the flimsy shadows they cast on her lids, her dark red eyebrows betray a sharp intelligence and afford her an air of confidence and authority. Perceiving his adulation, she casts him a broad smile with the slightest suggestion of impishness. "Put the potatoes on the wooden board, and bring one to me."

Menachem lifts the bag off the pediment. It is already hot to the touch and, left where it was, would soon have been scorched from the heat of the dying fire. He places it on the board, where he realizes he should have laid it in the first instance, and opens it to remove a potato for the lady.

"What tune were you humming when I came in?" she asks.

Menachem strains to recall whether he was indeed humming before she made herself known. For an instant he cannot recall any part of his life that took place before she spoke to him. Then he remembers Rachel, and the song. "I think it's called 'Greensleeves.'"

"That's what I thought. My father wrote that song," she says wistfully. She steps forward, lifts her skirts off the floor, and perches delicately on a bench facing the fire, only a few feet before him. Although he can feel the fire's heat at his back, all he can think of is the warmth exuding from her.

"Are you a cook?" he ventures.

"No," she replies, "although this is my kitchen. Are you the grocer's boy?"

He bows courteously. "At your service," he pronounces beautifully, just as he was taught by Aunt Sarah.

The Red Lady (which is how he now thinks of her) giggles with delight.

"And what is your name, squire?"

He plays along with her elevated courtliness. "I am known as Menachem, madam."

"And your surname?" she asks. He looks at her, puzzled. She rephrases her question. "Your *family* name?"

"I have no surname," he replies humbly.

"Well," she says, "I can see you are a quick learner, anyhow."

"And what, may I ask, is *your* name?"

She muses for a moment before answering. "You *may* ask, squire. I think that I shall not tell you my first name, for you may not call me by it. But my *surname* is 'Tudor.'" She stresses the word "surname," as though to caress him for attentiveness to his lessons.

Menachem's mind races. He has heard that name before. "Is that not the name of the royal house of England?"

She smiles. "Why, yes, Menachem, it is!" When she says his name, it sounds like *Manokkem*.

After a moment's thought, he ventures: "Are you a relative of the Queen?"

She regards him forlornly. "Alas, I am not. But where is my potato?"

As Menachem is about to hand it to her, she snatches it away, and her coy expression dares him to snatch it back. She is too quick for him, tossing it from one hand to the other, always too gingerly for him to reach. She giggles, and the music in her voice makes her seem little more than a schoolgirl having him on. She raises the potato over her head, and Menachem, not about to be defeated, places a foot on the bench beside her and steps up. Reaching as high as he can, he tugs the potato from her grasp.

He steps back down and sees that her expression has changed in an instant. Now she seems to be fighting off a sadness. Although he doubts it has anything to do with the potato, he kneels before her and offers it back to her with both hands.

She laughs despite herself, and tries in vain to fight the tears forming at the edges of her eyes. She blows her nose into her handkerchief. "You may keep the potato, Squire Menachem."

"Why are you so sad?" he asks, sorry for any part he has played in her dismay.

She tries to speak several times, but no voice will emerge.

"Have you any children?" he asks.

She shakes her head, and the tears well up again. He has put his finger on it. He assures her calmly, "You are young and beautiful, and shall no doubt have *many* happy children."

She draws herself together, and clears her throat.

"Alas," she says, "I am so lowly a person that I lack the authority to make such decisions for myself."

From the corner of his eye, he sees men with torches emerge from a big stone building far across the courtyard.

She sees him notice them. "They're looking for someone."

"For whom, I wonder?"

She laughs sulkily. "For *me*."

The door behind him bursts open, nearly stopping his heart, and lets in a blast of cold air. It's Avram, and he's alone.

"Uncle!"

But Avram's expression is frozen in amazement. His eyes, wide as saucers, are riveted on the Red Lady's face, and at first he seems unaware that his nephew is in the room. Then he kneels reverently, his eyes downcast, and pulls Menachem beside him by the back of his shirt, pressing him down onto bended knee.

"Forgive him, madam, please. He is just a boy who knows nothing."

She smirks. "He has done nothing requiring an apology, Goodman Grocer. But you do him wrong to say he knows nothing." She casts Menachem an appraising eye. "He speaks English beautifully." Her glance darts skeptically from the small, swarthy grocer to the tall young boy whose hair is very nearly the color of her own. "Is he of your family?"

Avram fixes his stare on a place just before the lady's feet. "He is distantly related, madam. His parents lived in Poland, but ... passed away in a fire."

"How dreadful!" she replies. "His English has nothing of the Pole about it. He is *not* Polish, is he?"

"Indeed, he is not, madam. His people went to Poland from Flanders many years ago, but they continued to speak English in their home."

She nods knowingly. "That is because they *are* English, having been deported to Flanders by my illustrious ancestor Edward the First. Is that not right?"

Beads of sweat begin to form on Avram's forehead and glisten in the red light of the coals. "You are correct, madam."

"An achievement of which my family can be right proud," she says sardonically. "How long has he been with you in England?"

"Less than a fortnight, madam."

To Menachem's young eyes, an idea seems to be forming in the lady's mind.

She cocks her head. "In such a brief time, has anyone in your family grown especially fond of him?" Avram evidently has no idea how to respond. "Do not be coy, Goodman Grocer. You know what I mean. Would your wife or children be bereft by his absence?"

Avram is dumbstruck, his eyes now boring a hole in a spot before her feet. Menachem somehow has the strange feeling that his life is being negotiated between the Red Lady and Avram, and that the Red Lady clearly has the upper hand. Avram appears to be drowning.

"Well, madam," Avram shrugs. "We *all* welcome him, but it is the women who seem to be especially fond of him, especially my daughter."

The Red Lady looks askance at Menachem and smiles bitterly, as though she knows him to be the devil himself. "I can understand *that*, Goodman Grocer." She straightens herself and stands up to her full height, a simple motion that nearly causes Avram to swoon.

She regards Menachem, and sighs. "You are beloved of women. You sing well, and speak beautifully. All in all, you seem headed for an easy life, Goodman Menachem." She brings her chin up to a proud height. "I shall ensure that your life is made *less* easy"—Menachem looks up at her imploringly—"but far more meaningful"—she hesitates—"and im-portant. Goodman Grocer, would your family object to my placing this boy under my protection, in the custody of an educator at Merton College, Oxford?"

"But, madam, there is the matter of his Hebrew religion—"

She waves away his concern. "His private religious practice will be fully respected, and he will be permitted to visit with you and your lovelorn daughter on holidays."

Avram's shoulders fall in relief. Through the windows, torches ap-proach, ever closer to the cottage. The shouts of men can now be heard, some guttural, others belonging to cultured nobility.

"Your name is Añes, is that correct?" she asks.

"It is, madam."

"Well, let's make *his* a little more English," she says pensively. "He shall be known as 'Noah Ames.' Now, will that be all, Goodman Añes?"

"Yes, madam. Thank you, madam."

"You are most welcome. I will send for Goodman Ames in a few days."

The torches are now very close. Menachem is sure that, if the kitchen were illuminated by more than glowing embers, the men outside would have discovered the Red Lady well before now. Down the dark corridor behind the lady, there is a loud banging on the heavy front door, through which a man commands sternly, "Open up, in the name of the Queen!"

Now the lady's eyes open wide. "Go!" she says excitedly, waving them out the rear door.

Avram scoops Menachem violently into his arms and rushes out of the door, shutting it quietly behind him. At first he appears to duck down, but Menachem sees that his knees have buckled beneath him. Avram struggles to stand again, and rushes away toward the oxcart, pulling Menachem behind him by the hand. Reaching the bushes, Avram lowers his head and quietly vomits.

While Avram composes himself and feebly struggles to find a water bladder in the cart, Menachem watches through the windows of the cottage as a strange scene unfolds.

A man and a boy enter through the front door. The man is quite stout, and appears to suffer from a crippling foot injury. Discovering the Red Lady, he claps his hands in relief and collapses into a chair, removing one boot and rubbing his foot, while the boy lights candles throughout the kitchen. The lady's hair is just the color Menachem perceived in the firelight. The man dispatches the boy through the front door. Although Menachem cannot hear the instructions given the boy, he assumes he has been sent to assure the other search parties that the Red Lady is found.

The man's voice is too deep to make out, but the words of the lady, though muffled by the windows, can be heard. "Sir Henry," she says, "I have told you that I will not be kept under guard like a common criminal!" She kneels to massage his wounded foot. "Your gout must be so painful! Poor Neville!" She wags an admonishing finger. "How could you allow yourself to be enlisted on a pointless errand such as this?"

Sir Henry places his hands sympathetically on her shoulders, and peers deeply into her eyes. Although she stamps her foot and turns away, from that point the voices die down, and the lady's words can no longer be heard.

"Menachem," whispers Avram, "come over here, out of the light." He places himself and the boy outside the view from the cottage windows. Sounding exhausted, he points to a stump and says, "Sit." He stoops and hugs Menachem as though he loves him more than his own life, and begins to quake, although whether from fear or relief Menachem could not say. "It is true, what they say. God protects children and fools. Blessed art thou, O Lord our God, the Lord is One." He draws his nephew's face from his chest, holds him squarely by the shoulders, and looks him in the eye.

Menachem can no longer bear the silence. "Who was the Red Lady?"

Avram regards him incredulously. "Who did she *say* she was?"

"When I asked her, she would not tell me her first name, and said her family name is 'Tudor.' But she said she is not related to the Queen." Voice full of concern, he asks, "Will they hurt her?"

Avram regards him skeptically. "Think hard, Menachem. Is that *exactly* what she said?"

"I—I asked her if she was a relative of the Queen, and she said"—his eyes roll up in deep recollection—"'alas, I am not.'"

Although Avram is apparently losing patience, he says indulgently, "Menachem, we are Jews. We live by our wits, or we do not live long. If a lady at the Tower tells you she is named 'Tudor,' but she is not a relative of the Queen, then who is she? You know this. *Who is she?*"

Menachem's furrowed brow slowly relaxes. Much of what he has heard and seen begins to fall into place. Tears stream from his eyes.

"She is the Queen."

Can't wait to see what happens next? Get your copy of *A Second Daniel* here.

https://books2read.com/a-second-daniel

ABOUT THE AUTHOR

Neal Roberts and his wife live happily on Long Island, New York. They have two grown children and a handful of grandchildren. Neal is a practicing attorney and adjunct law professor, and spends as much time as possible researching his next novel while enhancing his lawyer's pallor. When he's not writing contemporary sci-fi novels or practicing law, he can generally be found teaching in the field of intellectual property law. Connect with Neal at his website (authornealroberts.com) or on Facebook (Facebook.com/authornealroberts) and join his mailing list (bitly.com/FreeHistorical) to know when upcoming books release and to grab your free short.

ALSO BY NEAL ROBERTS

In the Den of the English Lion

A Second Daniel, In the Den of the English Lion, Book 1 (Historical Mystery): London 1558. An orphan from a far-off land is renamed "Noah Ames," and given every advantage the English Crown can bestow.

London 1592. Now an experienced barrister, Noah witnesses what appears to be a botched robbery outside the Rose Theater, a crime he soon suspects to be part of a plot against Queen Elizabeth herself. Steadfast in his loyalty to the Queen, Noah must use every bit of his knowledge and skill to lure her most disloyal subject onto the only battlefield where Noah has the advantage ... a court of law – though in doing so he risks public exposure of his darkest secret, a secret so shocking that its revelation could cost him everything: the love of the only woman who can offer him happiness, his livelihood ... even his life.

The Impress of Heaven, In the Den of the English Lion, Book 2 (Historical Mystery): LONDON 1600. When the Earl of Essex is removed from command and placed under arrest for reaching a forbidden truce with the Irish rebels, Serjeant Noah Ames reluctantly accepts a commission to investigate the earl's fitness for command, and the two are pitted against each other once again. Meanwhile, Noah's beautiful daughter, Lady Jessica, has sought to remarry into the nobility, but events have thus far frustrated her plans. One day, Noah attends a briefing where the Queen's new commander displays maps of English military positions in Ireland. Noah's suspicions are aroused when he sees that one map is missing a watermark appearing on all the others. When he informs his young barrister friend Jonathan of his concern, he inadvertently sets in motion events that throw Jonathan and Lady Jessica together on a journey across England into ever greater peril.

A Dragon in the Ashes, In the Den of the English Lion, Book 3 (Historical Mystery): LONDON 1600. When an attempt is made on Queen

Elizabeth's life, Serjeant Noah Ames races to her rescue, then sets out to identify the culprit among a band of foreigners who've newly arrived from the Continent to join with the seditious Lord Essex. In the course of his investigation, Noah uncloaks an unmitigated reign of evil that has resulted in the murders of kings, queens, and religious minorities ... and which now threatens Noah's life for reasons no one would ever suspect. Will Noah pay the ultimate price for forgetting that the past is never past?

All the Men as Mad as He, In the Den of the English Lion, Book 4 (Historical Mystery): LONDON 1600. Though Queen Elizabeth has ordered the Earl of Essex's release from confinement, she's thwarted his return to social and military grace by barring him from court for an indefinite term. Unsatisfied with this humiliation, the Queen considers whether to cut off his sole remaining income, as well. Noah Ames strongly advises against it on grounds that the Queen will thereby lose any remaining influence over Essex's conduct and also place him in desperate financial straits. When several seemingly unrelated men are found murdered, Noah begins to suspect that such murders reveal Essex's treasonous intention to return to court in bloody defiance of the Queen's order.

Shakespeare's Treason, In the Den of the English Lion, Book 5 (Historical Mystery): LONDON 1600. The Earls of Essex and Southampton, imprisoned in the Tower of London pending their trial for high treason, incriminate Noah Ames's dear friend Sir Henry Neville. When the one man whose testimony can save Sir Henry suddenly vanishes, Noah must solve the mystery of his abduction and bring him back in time to save Sir Henry from a traitor's death.

From Heaven to Earth They Came

Goddess from the Lost Planet, From Heaven to Earth They Came, Book 1

Maker from the Lost Planet, From Heaven to Earth They Came, Book 2

Destroyer from the Lost Planet, From Heaven to Earth They Came, Book 3